MY ONLY LOVE

Cheryl Holt

Zebra Books
Kensington Publishing Corp.
http://www.zebrabooks.com

ZEBRA BOOKS are published by

Kensington Publishing Corp.
850 Third Avenue
New York, NY 10022

First Printing: April, 2000
10 9 8 7 6 5 4 3 2

Printed in the United States of America

Chapter One

Maggie Brown searched the crowded teahouse, looking for George. From her small table in the corner, she wasn't able to see the front door of the establishment, so she couldn't be completely sure if he'd entered or not. Knowing the man as she did, she was quite sure he'd give a cursory glance to the throng of people, and if he didn't notice her right away, he'd leave, using her absence as the perfect excuse to call on her later in the day.

She still shivered every time she thought of the last time he'd visited. Two weeks ago, he'd stopped by late at night as she and Anne were preparing to retire. Drunk and abusive, he'd demanded the right to join her in her bed, saying it was high time he was repaid for allowing Maggie and Anne the privilege of living rent-free in the small home he owned. Only Anne's presence, stern and insistent that he depart immediately, had saved Maggie that night. Another time, she might not be so lucky.

It was hoping too much to think he might have requested this meeting because he'd finally found the courage to apologize for his abominable behavior. She could live to a ripe old age before any apology ever sprang from his pursed lips. His kind never answered for their behavior, no matter how despicable. No, he wanted to talk to her about something else entirely, and whatever it was, it wouldn't be good.

Ever since that horrid evening, they'd been waiting for the payback they were sure was coming. George was nothing if not predictable, and the stab at his ego, as well as his manhood, would not easily be forgiven or forgotten. George wasn't likely to overlook the fact that he'd offered her a chance to pay the rent while flat on her back and she'd had the audacity to refuse.

Certainly, he viewed his offer of a sexual liaison as a boon for Maggie. After all, she was merely the daughter of a recently deceased courtesan. Why wouldn't she grab at the chance to be his paramour just as her mother, Rose, had done? Maggie shuddered at the thought. Never in her life would she attach herself to such a man as George Wilburton. If it took every bit of her savvy and resources, she'd find a way to live a different life from Rose's.

Rose Brown, Lord rest her soul, had been a mistress for several gentlemen in her short life, as had their dear friend, Anne Porter. Both women had been cast into the role of kept women at an early age due to family misfortunes.

As young beauties, they'd had few attributes besides their looks and bodies to carry them through life. A combination of breeding, education, and pure luck set them above common prostitutes. Instead of daily customers, they'd consorted in a more respectable way through long-term affairs with various gentlemen who saw to their financial needs in return for regular and monogamous sexual favors. It was a precarious existence, one fraught with uncertainties and fluctuating fortunes, and consequently, they'd spent day after day of each year wondering what would happen if the men in their lives tired of them and sent them packing.

Maggie had grown up in the small house she thought of as her mother's, watching various men come and go through

Rose's life as she'd been passed from one nobleman to the next like a prized steer. Her beauty and charm had been legendary, but it had begun to fade as she approached forty without ever finding what she'd so desperately wanted: a lifelong stipend from one of her lovers that would carry her into her old age. Instead, she'd found herself reduced to accepting the likes of George as her keeper.

George was a penny-pinching, rude boor who reviewed and complained about every farthing Rose spent. A man who was so lacking at his bedroom skills that Maggie had often heard Rose and Anne whispering and laughing whenever he left the house. Still, he'd served his purpose the past few years.

His attentions had allowed them to continue living in the house where Maggie had grown up. They'd had a roof over their heads and food in their bellies during the three years Rose had serviced George. Anne had been able to stay with them, as well, so she hadn't had to search for a new gentleman when her last was killed in an accident. When Rose became ill, George could have tossed them into the street, but hadn't. They'd had a place all through the dreadful months until she eventually passed away.

But now, what was coming their way? Maggie was afraid to know.

Just then, she saw George across the room. She rose slightly and waved to catch his attention. He was a thin, gaunt man, painfully plain, and Maggie couldn't help wondering once again what her mother had ever seen in him.

George made his way through the packed restaurant, muttering apologies occasionally as he knocked into a table here and there. He'd grown his sideburns longer, she noticed, since the last time she'd seen him, letting them bush farther out across his cheeks. Probably to distract from his quickly thinning hair. Unfortunately, the added facial hair had just the opposite effect. He looked balder than ever.

George's clothing and jewelry, as well as the carriage he'd rudely parked in front of the establishment, gave testament to the fact that he was a gentleman of some means. The owner, himself, ran to the table and held out a chair, clapping his hands and ordering the serving girls to bring extra tea, extra biscuits. Whatever George wanted he would receive.

"Hello, George," Maggie said, welcoming him. They'd long since given up any attempts at formality. It was hard to maintain proper courtesies when he'd spent three years coming and going from Rose's bedroom whenever he wanted.

"Magdalina, thank you for being prompt."

Maggie felt him undressing her with his eyes. He had a way of doing that, of running his gaze from the top of her head to her breasts and back up again. Since it happened every time they were together, she was long past worrying about the insult of it. Her resemblance to her beautiful mother was uncanny in nearly every way, and male heads often turned in her direction, lingering much longer than was proper. She was used to such bold assessment, and always held her own when they looked.

Neither tall nor short, just right in height to hold a man's gaze, her body was slender and rounded in all the right places. Her breasts and hips were soft and full, accented by her tiny waist. Light brown hair fell in long, glorious waves highlighted with streaks of gold and auburn. The locks curled delicately around a heart-shaped face, accenting the creamy-smooth, rosy cheeks, the pouting lips. Her eyes were an exotic shade of blue, causing people—but especially men—to look twice, hoping to see something in the fathomless depths. The hue changed with the color of her clothing, and looked violet today, set off by the purple tint of her black mourning outfit.

When he kept looking, she colored slightly, angry that he would treat her with such disrespect in a public place. Refusing to make it easier on him by looking away, she returned stare for stare until she realized that there was more to his look this time than mere sexual regard. Fearing that Anne had been right, that he was about to get even with them both, she felt a tiny frisson of fear creep up her spine.

She tried for a smile, her mind racing with the possibilities of what was coming, as she said, "I was surprised to receive your message. I hope I've not displeased you with the household expenditures. I've tried to be frugal."

"I've not called you about the accounts. They matter not to me any longer."

Maggie reached for her napkin and tried to keep from anxiously kneading the edge between her fingers. If George wasn't worried about money, something dreadful was going to happen. "What is it, then? If I may be so bold as to ask?"

"I've decided to remarry."

Maggie held her breath, waited while he devoured a plate of biscuits, then held it out to the server for more. The girl quickly scurried away, and Maggie could no longer stand the suspense. "And?"

"I'm going to sell the house."

Maggie gasped. Although Rose had never owned the house, it had first been purchased by Maggie's father, the Duke of Roswell, when Rose was his mistress twenty years earlier. Rose had become pregnant with Maggie, and the Duke had broken her heart by dumping her on a friend because of it. The house had changed owners, but her mother had continued living there.

Six different times during the nineteen years of Maggie's childhood, Rose had managed to use her beauty and sexual prowess to lure a new keeper. As one gentleman gave her up, he'd merely sell the property to the next man Rose managed to find as a protector. Maggie had never lived anywhere else, and couldn't imagine anyone being so heartless as to take it away from her. "You're going to sell my home?"

"I'm afraid so. My fiancée is quite an astute woman, you see, and I've no doubt she'd be greatly displeased if she learned I was keeping you."

"But we're not ... you're not ..." She blushed terribly. Since she'd grown up in a house with two courtesans, she was used to frank sexual talk, but she hadn't had the experience of speaking of such things with a man before.

"I doubt my fiancée would see the distinction."

She laughed, hoping to make light of the situation, but failing miserably. The fear in her voice was too evident. "Do you plan to put me out on the street?"

"We will need to find you an accommodation."

She breathed easier. If he was willing to find her another place, perhaps this wouldn't have to end so badly. More than anything, she wanted to be able to keep Anne from having to go back to servicing another gentleman. "I don't need much," she said. "I'm sure the price of such a small place would hardly be noticeable to you."

George looked at her hard, at first not understanding what she meant, then realizing that she'd completely misread what he intended. "I'm sorry. I didn't say that very well. *You* will need to make other arrangements for yourself. I would certainly be glad to assist you. As a favor to your mother, of course."

"Of course," Maggie murmured, wondering what type of *assistance* he had in mind. *There must be more to it than that,* she knew. It had to be part of another ploy to get her into his bed, something she had sworn would never happen. "What must I do to get you to change your mind?"

"Nothing will change my mind."

For the first time, she noticed the firm resolve. He fully intended to put her out. Tears welled into her eyes. "You promised my mother—on her deathbed, I might add—that you would let me remain. She's only been dead six weeks. You swore to her, and she's hardly cold in the ground."

"I did not want to add to her distress at the time, and"— he shrugged—"when I made the promise, I meant it. I truly had no intention of putting you out. But the situation has changed. I'm marrying, and I can't think it would be very sporting of me to use my wife's funds to support my mistress's daughter." He looked away, fiddled with the food on his plate, then looked back, obviously embarrassed. "Plus, I've had a rather small run of bad luck. Until I'm wed, I can use the extra cash from the sale of the property."

"That *property*, as you so blithely refer to it, is the only home I've ever known."

Maggie wanted to be furious, but she couldn't be. After all, George had let them stay long after Rose's illness prevented her from functioning as his paramour.

"How long do I have?" she managed to ask.

"I'll give you three months."

"But I have no money. No skills. I've never been employed. What do you expect me to do?"

"You could marry, I suppose."

"In three months?" They both knew there were no prospects on her horizon, and it was highly unlikely that she could meet a man who would wish to marry her in such a short time.

"What would you have me do, Maggie?"

"Let me stay in my home. Give me a chance to land on my feet. I'm still suffering so from the shock of Mother's death that I've not been able to begin moving forward again."

"I realize you're still grieving, but I've explained why I can't be more of a help." George shifted uncomfortably, then said, "I had thought of one idea. I doubt if you'll find it acceptable."

"Tell me."

"I thought I could introduce you to some of my friends. I'm not without connections, you know. Perhaps we could . . . we could . . ." He swallowed, his Adam's apple bouncing visibly as he laid the suggestion on the table. "We could find someone who would purchase the house under the same arrangement I made with your mother."

At first, Maggie didn't understand his meaning. Once it dawned, she went red with fury. "Are you suggesting I sell myself as my mother did? You wretched bounder!" It was nearly a shout, and heads turned in their direction. She lowered her voice and leaned across the small table. "After all the promises you made to her about how you'd look after me!"

"What other choices do you have? You said yourself that you've no skills. No options. You must think about what you have that's marketable. As far as I can see, there's only one thing." He eyed her casually, obviously thinking about how quickly one of his friends would snatch her up and regretting the fact that he would not be the one to enjoy the secrets she had to offer.

With a sinking heart, Maggie lowered her eyes. While she'd spent years telling herself that she'd not fall into the trap that had captured her mother, she was perilously close to the edge at the moment. If she didn't find a protector, a keeper, what would become of her and Anne? Hating the words she knew she had to speak, she continued staring at the table, playing with the tablecloth. "If I agree—and I'm not saying I do, mind you—how would we go about it?"

"It's quite simple really. I would tell a few gentlemen that you are available. I'd make introductions. If any of them were interested, the two of you would come to a personal agreement. I'd negotiate terms on the house. The fact that you're so pretty and still a virgin would make you highly sought after."

Maggie grimaced at the term. She sounded like a cow being led to slaughter. "I don't know. I need to think about this."

"Certainly. But don't take too long."

She stood up, looking about absentmindedly. "I'm sorry, but I'm not feeling too well. I've got to go."

"Three months, Maggie. Three months is all the time you have."

His voice faded as she walked off in a distracted state through the crowd. Outside, she looked for a cab, then decided against it. With doom lurking around the corner, the last thing she needed was to waste a few coins on a hired coach for the short ride home. She walked along, wondering how someone who had just turned nineteen could feel so old.

The past two years of her life should have been spent in celebration of her approaching adulthood. Her mother had seen her educated, had envisioned a trip to the Continent, parties and socializing, introductions to young men. A good, solid marriage to someone who was kind and dependable. None of those things had happened. Instead, she'd spent the time watching over Rose as her health increasingly failed.

Now, with a snap of his fingers, George expected her to change her focus. To magically be ready to resume her prior life. Just how was this grand reversion to be accomplished?

"Men . . ." she muttered as she reached her stoop and climbed the three steps to the door. "Worthless, the lot of them."

Pulling open the door, she stepped into the small front room. The place had seven rooms altogether, scattered across three floors. It was small and simple, but it was home.

"Maggie, is that you?" Anne called from the top of the stairs.

"Yes, Anne." Maggie glanced up to see Anne descending as regally as a queen. The round, lush curves of her glorious body were only accentuated by the plain black dress she wore. The auburn of her hair, the green of her eyes were striking as a bit of afternoon sunlight caught her with its rays. At thirty years of age, she was more beautiful than ever.

"Well, what did he want?" she asked.

Never one to bandy words, Anne always got right to the heart of the matter. In a world where people rarely came right out and said what they meant, she could be frighteningly blunt. She started down the stairs as Maggie took her time hanging up her cloak and hat. How could she tell beautiful, wonderful Anne, who had been their good friend and companion for so many years, what was going to happen? "Let's go sit down."

"That bad, is it?"

"It's very bad."

"Let's have it, then," Anne insisted as they sat together on the small couch. "What?"

"He's getting married."

"Someone's actually marrying the pitiable clod? The poor woman obviously never gave him a roll under the covers before making her decision. I hope she knows what she's in for."

Maggie managed to chuckle. "And he's selling the house. We have three months to decide what to do."

"Well, I suppose that's fair warning. What did he advise for us?"

"He suggested I let him send my name round to his friends. He thought he could find me a gentleman with little trouble."

"That rat!" Anne rubbed a weary hand across her brow. Somehow, she'd known it would come to this. She should have taken action as soon as they realized Rose was ill. By now, she could have been set up with a gentleman of her own, and they'd have somewhere to go. She didn't mind taking on another man if it meant keeping Maggie from having to do such a thing. Unfortunately, finding a protector wasn't easy. A woman needed referrals from other gentlemen or female friends to spread the word, and she'd lost so many contacts over the past few years. It would simply be too hard to find a suitable man in such a short time.

Her mind in a whirl, she asked Maggie, "Have you thought of contacting your father again?"

Rose had written to him when her illness had taken hold, and it became clear that she'd not recover, but the Duke hadn't even bothered to answer. "If he didn't respond to Mother's dying request, I can't imagine I'd fare any better. At least he knew her and supposedly loved her once. I've never even met the man."

"But you're his daughter. Perhaps if you tried again."

"You know it's a wishful fantasy, Anne," Maggie said quietly.

"Yes, I suppose it is." She sighed as she stood and moved to the fireplace, staring into the empty hearth and not turning back around until she'd managed to force a brilliant smile onto her face. "We must make the most of our time, then. What would you like to do?"

"I don't know. I need some time to think."

"Well, I think we should go on our holiday—just as we planned."

"You can't mean it. With all this trouble looming over our heads?"

"It's the best plan I can think of. Besides, we've already paid the fares and the rent for our room at the inn. I doubt if we could get our money back. The peace and quiet out of the city might help bring things into clearer focus. You know as well as I do that your mother would want us to go. It was her favorite place in the world."

"Perhaps you're right."

"Of course I'm right." Anne moved to stand behind the sofa and massaged her fingers into Maggie's tense shoulders. "We'll only be gone for a few days."

"If only . . ." But she didn't finish the thought. *If only* things in her life had gone differently. She'd traveled down that road so many times the past few months, and the trip had never ended up anywhere worthwhile.

"If only what?"

"Nothing."

Anne walked around to the front of the sofa and gave Maggie a tight hug. "We'll see this through, you and I. We'll go on our holiday, and we'll throw away these awful black clothes. We'll eat and sleep and breathe the sea air, and we'll come home rested and ready to take on the whole bloody world."

It was impossible to resist Anne's enthusiasm, so Maggie agreed with her, trying to look confident. "I'm ready if you are."

Anne smiled in return. "It will be all right, Maggie. I just know it will. We'll make it all right."

Chapter Two

Adam St. Clair snagged a glass of wine off the tray of a passing waiter and tried to look inconspicuous, which was hard to do under the circumstances. He was the unmarried Marquis of Belmont, and every woman in the place was trying to catch his eye. Young and old, tall and short, fat and thin, plain and beautiful, each female hoped his gaze would come to rest on her and her alone.

It didn't help that he'd been graced with his father's tall physique, broad shoulders, and dark hair and eyes. Throughout his twenty-nine years, he'd heard how handsome he was, how virile, how exquisitely endowed, and his good looks made the women want him all the more. He didn't delude himself, though. If he'd been short and squat with a face like a toad, they would still flock to his side, hoping that some of his attention would fall in their direction.

They all wanted him, and they all had ulterior motives. Some wanted to share his title, some wanted the trinkets all his money could buy, some wanted the benefits an alliance with his family would bring.

Unfortunately, he didn't want any of them in return. What he wanted was to find himself a willing, experienced lass who freely offered her kindness and friendship, who liked him for the man he was with no strings attached, but the chances of such a thing happening were next to none. Instead, he was standing in the midst of another stupid ball, wearing uncomfortable clothing, partaking of bland food and watered-down wine, while smiling and nodding until his face and neck ached.

The gossip about his approaching nuptials was incredible. Would this be the year he would select someone out of the Season's crop of debutantes? Bets were placed and lost as various deadlines came and went and he made no move to announce his choice. The past Christmas, the New Year, his February birthday, the Ides of March, Easter, now May Day. On each date, the gaming halls were ripe with wagers as various friends and acquaintances tried to read his mind. Gad, even the *Times* had gotten in on the act, running a wretched caricature of a gentleman who looked like himself frantically running through a maze entitled "The Marriage Market."

The pressure was unbearable, not because of what any of them thought or said, but because of the deadline he'd placed on himself. He intended to select a wife by the end of the year so that by his thirtieth birthday the following February, he'd be well on his way to being married. Glancing around the room, he was reminded again of how dismal were his prospects of finding someone suitable.

He understood his duty to his title, his family, and his role as one of the wealthiest aristocrats in England to marry and marry well, but he simply could not make up his mind. For the past few years, as his mother harangued and members of society held their collective breath, he'd watched one crop of girls after another make their debut, hoping one young woman would catch his eye and ease the painful process of selection.

None of them did.

The summer Season was upon them once again, and the three months of parties and balls stretched endlessly ahead.

He'd somehow convinced himself that this was the year he'd find a suitable bride, but as he looked around, he couldn't see why he'd led himself to believe such a thing. In reality, theirs was a small world. He knew all the families and all their daughters, and the sad fact was that the young ladies bored him to tears.

Most were certainly pretty enough, but they were bred and raised to keep nothing between their ears but air. They could barely read and write, let alone carry on an intelligent conversation. No poignant thoughts, no lengthy philosophical discussions, no heated debates. And heaven forbid, no displays of emotion. Just endless smiling and polite dialogue until sometimes he felt he just might scream. To saddle himself with one of the young ninnies was unthinkable, yet he had no choice.

Everyone knew it. He couldn't even turn around without some mother, aunt, father, or friend thrusting a girl under his nose. What he wouldn't give just to chuck it all and run off to live his life as an anonymous person. Surely, there had to be a place, a tropical island perhaps, where he could just be himself.

His younger brother, James, pulled him out of his depressing reverie. Facetiously, James commented, "Look, Adam, it's your lucky day. The Duke of Roswell, the great Harold Westmoreland himself, has arrived, with his pretty daughter Penelope by his side." He laughed as Adam winced. "Looks like they found you."

Adam groaned. He couldn't go anywhere without their arriving a few minutes later. "Do you think they have someone following me to learn my every move?"

James, at age twenty-seven, two years younger than his brother, was perhaps the only person in the world who understood the incredible pressures placed on Adam. While some men chafed at being younger brothers, James remembered to thank the good Lord at least once a day for sparing him the burdens of a title. "Look at it this way. At least you'll get the meeting out of the way early. Then, we can enjoy the rest of the night."

"Easy for you to say, since you're not the one upon whom Penelope has set her sights," Adam grumbled.

"You lucky, lucky man." James chuckled, not meaning it in the least.

The Duke and his entourage made their way down the ballroom steps, and eighteen-year-old Penelope surreptitiously glanced across the crowd, trying to catch a glimpse of Adam. Almost without realizing he was doing it, he took a step back, gaining some shelter and time from the leaves of a tall potted fern.

James whispered out of the side of his mouth, "Coward."

"With good reason," he whispered back. "Could you imagine being shackled to that little virago for the rest of your days?"

"I shudder just thinking about it." James glanced casually across the crowd. "Look, there's the Arnold chit." She was a pretty little thing. And sweet, too, which was a refreshing change of pace from most of the women he met at these High Society affairs. James had spoken to her numerous times, but as with most of the females to whom he was attracted, her mother always ran him off before he could say more than a few words of welcome. No one wanted a lowly second son turning their daughters' heads as long as the older son was available.

"It looks as though she's temporarily lost her mother," Adam said. "Perhaps you should go sweep her off her feet while you have the chance."

"Good thing I brought my broom. I'm in the mood to do a little sweeping." James laughed, then deftly made his way through the throng to the girl's side.

James flirted outrageously as Adam watched, thinking how James was a leaner, trimmer version of himself. He had the same St. Clair good looks, although his hair was a redder shade of brown. When seeing the two brothers together, people had often been heard to comment that they'd inherited all facets of their father's personality. Adam had gotten his hard, ruthless, unemotional side while James had been graced with the casual, generous, fun-loving nature.

As a result, James had a definite way with the ladies; nary a one could resist him. Adam envied him his easy charm, and not for the first time, cursed the Fates, which had made him the firstborn. How nice it would be to be able to meet a girl, ask her to dance, enjoy a lunch, or take her for a drive in the park without the whole of London speculating on the meaning.

He sighed as the girl's mother appeared like a thunderstorm and hustled her away from James's attentions. Unfortunately, as James rejoined Adam along the line of potted plants, mother and daughter were only a few feet away on the other side, oblivious to the presence of the St. Clair brothers, who couldn't help but hear their every word.

"You'll not talk with him again," the mother scolded.

"Mother, he's very sweet."

"But he's not the Marquis."

"I know that."

"Then you'll not encourage him. You must focus your energies on the elder of the two."

"For pity's sake, Mother, the Marquis is not interested in me and never will be. Will you get that through your head?"

"He will be if we play our cards right. Now"—the brothers could hear the shifting of feet and the rustle of gowns as the pair moved away—"I've heard that St. Clair will go to the buffet table shortly. Let's find a strategic spot so we can enter the line right behind him . . ."

Adam regarded James out of the corner of his eye, wondering how many times this had happened. Too many to count, certainly. The only bright spot Adam could see in marrying was that James would finally be able to find a wife on his own without being overshadowed by his older brother.

There was a red splotch of color on each of James's cheeks, which Adam knew meant he was furious. Other than that, he appeared outwardly calm as he sipped his wine.

"I'm sorry," Adam said.

"For what?"

"For . . . for . . . I don't know. I'm just sorry." He downed his own glass, grabbed another from a passing waiter. "I hate this! I hate her and her bloody mother!" he muttered vehemently. "I hope she ends up married to a sailor."

"A blacksmith!" James offered.

"A farmer!"

"God, yes. With ten squalling brats!"

"All of them cross-eyed and dim-witted!"

"And only her mother available to act as nanny."

"Touché." Adam smiled and touched his glass to the rim of James's in a toast, glad to see that their mockery had restored his good humor.

Across the room, Adam saw his cousin, Charles Billington, talking to an unknown dark-haired man. Even from a distance, it was clear they were exchanging heated words.

Although their mothers were sisters, Charles barely resembled his two St. Clair cousins. He'd inherited the Billington looks, so he was several inches shorter than the two brothers, a thin, good-looking man with blond hair and blue eyes. Now twenty-eight, he'd grown up to be a best friend, and was considered nearly a third brother.

Adam motioned with his glass. "Look, there's Charlie."

James followed his gaze. "Perhaps we should follow in his footsteps, and let ourselves move outside the rules of Polite Society. Maybe then, we wouldn't have to suffer all these female troubles."

"It's certainly worth a thought."

Charles was a popular portrait artist who managed to make a fair living by painting renditions of Society's lovelies. He occasionally supplemented it with questionable transactions about which they chose to remain ignorant. As an artist, he was allowed many eccentricities, and as the seventh child of eight—four older ones were boys—he wasn't concerned about appearances, and the freedom he enjoyed always seemed to land him smack in the middle of some type of commotion.

His short tour as a soldier, which had ended early due to a serious wounding and extended recovery, might have dimmed his appetite for nefarious adventure, but it hadn't. He couldn't seem to resist the lure of any type of dubious person or enterprise.

They watched in silence until the argument ended, and the other man stomped away in a huff. Charles strolled to meet his cousins as though he hadn't a care in the world. Adam couldn't help but admire his aplomb amidst the stares he received as he passed.

"Trouble in paradise?" James asked with a grin.

"Just a small disagreement over a few pounds." Charles sighed wearily. "Perhaps I should expend more of my energies in chasing women. It would have to be less exhausting."

"I don't think Adam would agree with you," James said with a laugh.

"I suppose not," Charles agreed, as he glanced around the immediate area and saw all the young maids who were pretending not to notice that Adam was in proximity. "So what has the two of you hiding in the ferns, toasting and chuckling?"

"We're discussing how *lucky* we are with the ladies," Adam retorted.

"Right," Charles snorted. "You two should convert to Catholicism just so you could enter one of the religious orders and put yourselves out of your misery. I hear there's a nice monastery outside Bath."

"I should be so fortunate," Adam quipped as he saw the Duke's white hair gleaming through a break in the crowd. Penelope couldn't be far behind.

James gave him a brotherly nudge. "Might as well go face the music. If you keep hiding in here, they'll think you're trying to avoid them."

"I *am* trying to avoid them," Adam responded.

Charles chided, "Now, now, we can't have you upsetting the Westmorelands, can we? Poor Penelope's feelings might be hurt."

"I doubt that," James teased. "She doesn't have any."

"Ooh, a vicious cut." As the Duke's party moved closer, obviously heading straight for Adam, Charles turned to leave.

"Are you abandoning us?" James asked.

"Sorry, but I don't seem to have the stomach for fawning tonight." Charles was swallowed up, leaving the two brothers alone once again.

They waited in silence for several minutes until the Duke was only a few steps away. Penelope was hanging on his arm, accepting, with a regal nod of her head, the bows and curtsies that she felt were her due.

James took a deep swallow of wine. "Brace yourself."

"I'm braced," Adam responded with a resounding lack of enthusiasm.

The group surrounding the Duke enveloped them like a fog. James smiled and chatted easily, while Adam stood at his side, silent and watchful. They made the expected bows over Penelope's hand. She was a pretty thing, with her father's white blond hair curled perfectly round her heart-shaped face. Her cheeks and lips were a rosy hue and her eyes a startling blue, set off well by the blue piping on her virginal-white gown. Much too plump for Adam's taste, but the extra weight filled out her arms, bosom, and face, making her look like a beautiful porcelain doll.

"How lovely to see you tonight, Adam," she said in a breathless voice as she gave him her most perfect smile. She'd known him since she was a babe, and their fathers had been good friends, so she'd always felt free to call him by his given name, something she loved to do since it put her ahead of the game with so many of the others vying for his hand. It irked the competing girls no end that Penelope and the Marquis were on a first-name basis.

"As it is to see you again. How are you enjoying the ball?" he asked, wanting her to think he hadn't paid enough attention to her to notice that she'd just made a grand entrance.

"Why, we've only just arrived. I've not even begun to fill

my dance card yet.'' She held it out, knowing he couldn't refuse.

"Then, by all means, allow me to be the first to sign." He had to give the girl credit; she'd cornered him well. He couldn't get out of dancing with her now.

"I shall expect a quadrille, sir, and nothing less." She and her father had argued vehemently over whether she should waltz with St. Clair. Penelope thought that if she forced closer physical proximity, she might have more success in capturing his attentions, but in the end, they'd decided against it. The quadrille was a good second choice, though. While she wouldn't be held in his arms, the dance would continue nearly half an hour, and she'd be able to stand beside him the entire time as they stepped out the intricate moves.

"It will be my pleasure," Adam said, biting back the urge to grind his teeth at the amount of time he'd have to spend chatting with the girl during the lengthy dance she'd requested.

The Duke moved his group away but not before whispering in Adam's ear, "Meet me in the library in fifteen minutes." He eyed James curtly. "I've something to discuss with you in private."

Since Adam made it a point to ignore the Duke's directives, he arrived ten minutes late, knowing how greatly the slight would irritate. It was a rare occasion when he bowed to anyone's will, even a man as exalted as the Duke of Roswell. Although Harold Westmoreland outranked him, their fortunes and properties were similar in size, and Adam could trace his lineage back three generations farther. Plus, the man was only in his mid-forties, so he could hardly use his great age to press his advantage. Much to the Duke's continued dismay, Adam simply wouldn't come to heel the way everyone else did when he ordered them about.

As Adam entered the book-lined room, he wanted to laugh at how Harold had staged the meeting. He'd moved a large wing-back chair to the end and centered himself between two carved statues. He sipped on a glass of cognac, and the effect made him look decidedly royal.

Refusing to play the game by the Duke's rules, Adam moved to a side chair and sat out of the man's line of vision, causing him to have to swivel his chair slightly if he wanted to make eye contact.

"Yes, Harold?" Adam asked, when he had things arranged more to his own liking. "What is it?"

"I thought you might like to know that I've received another marriage offer for Penelope."

"Congratulations. When is the happy occasion?"

Harold's face reddened. He was at his wit's end, trying to figure out how to snare Adam St. Clair. Short of marrying Penelope off to a foreigner—something he refused to do—he couldn't find her a husband of sufficient rank. Adam was the only Englishman currently searching for a wife who he could stand personally and who had the necessary title and funds to join with the Westmoreland family.

Penelope was demanding the union and she was more furious every day that Adam refused to ask for her hand. She'd tried everything she could think of—short of compromising herself. Harold refused to insist she stoop that low.

"Listen, you," he said, trying to contain his irritation but failing. "I'll have you know that I've had just about enough of your posturing."

"What posturing is that?" Adam asked, loving the way he could cause such a rise.

"You know very well what I mean. I've half a mind to accept the offer. It would certainly serve you right to lose your chance at her."

"Then accept it, Harold. It matters not to me."

"What the hell is the matter with you?"

"I've told you before, and I'm telling you again: I haven't made up my mind. Penelope is a darling girl"—he gritted his teeth past the lie—"and if you find her a suitable match, you should take it. There's no sense waiting for me."

"What is taking you so bloody long?"

Adam shrugged. He wasn't about to discuss the situation with Harold Westmoreland. James and Charles were the only two who'd been taken into his confidence about the situation. They were the only two he trusted. If he told the Duke anything, the man would find a way to use it as leverage. "I've not made a decision. It's as simple as that."

"No, it is not, because you are toying with my daughter's affections." Actually, Harold could have cared less about what Penelope wanted. It was what he, himself, wanted that mattered.

"Harold, you and I both know that I've never done one thing to encourage her. If she has designs on me, and you've let her think they're progressing, then I'd say the fault lies with you. Not myself."

"What is it about her that is keeping you from making up your mind? I know she's terribly young, and no one knows better than I how dreadfully demanding she can be at times, but she'll grow into marriage. They all do, so I don't see how you could think to make a better match. I simply don't understand what it is you want."

"It's nothing to do with Penelope." How he hated this. The fine line Harold forced him to walk was unbearable. He couldn't insult the girl outright, nor did he want to sound like a bungling romantic fool looking for compatibility and desirability, but he had to give some excuse. "I plan to be married for several decades, and I'm simply trying to be certain that I'll be able to tolerate whomever I select."

"Good God, Adam, they're all the same in the dark."

"It's not the dark I'm worried about. It's the next morning across the breakfast table."

Harold barked sharp laughter. "Then get yourself a mistress, for pity's sake. Spend your mornings with her. Your father did it for years. I don't see why it's such a problem."

Of course, Harold didn't see the problem. He'd been linked to one beautiful woman after the next for nearly three decades. At that very moment, his current *leman* was in the ballroom, eyeing him from a discreet distance. He would return to join her later after seeing his family home. As with all the men of their station, he thought nothing of his actions.

But he'd not been in the St. Clair household and watched what wretched despair his father's mistress had caused. Aston St. Clair had fallen madly in love in his mid-twenties and kept the woman all the years of his life. He'd sired three bastard children with her and had had the audacity to provide for all of them after his death, giving them a lovely home, trust funds, and most importantly, recognition. While James insisted he didn't mind, Adam and his mother could barely stand the humiliation of it.

Every day of their lives, Adam's mother, Lucretia, had been forced to live with the shame of knowing that her husband found her lacking in every respect. The rift Aston's mistress brought to their marriage caused her to harden until she was now a bitter, lonely old woman. Never had a day passed without Lucretia warning Adam of the heartbreak he would force on his future family if he ever did such a thing to his own wife.

No, there'd be no mistress for Adam St. Clair. He'd marry and be faithful to his vows, no matter how much it cost him. That's what was making his choice so difficult, but he'd never admit such a thing to Harold Westmoreland.

Appearing as bored as possible, he stood. "Is there anything else?"

"I'll give you one more month to ask for her hand."

"Then you will be waiting in vain," Adam retorted. With a brusque nod of his head, he left the room, returning quickly to the crowd before the Duke could follow and accost him again. Relieved, he could see James waiting where he'd left him.

James gave a wry smile. "I'd ask how it went, but I can see by the murderous look in your eye that I shouldn't't."

"Bastard," Adam muttered, "grilling me as though he was Father."

"That bad, was it?"

Adam looked around at the glittering crowd. "Did you ever wish you could just vanish? Just get away from here? Where no one knew you or expected anything from you?"

Across the room, James spied the Arnold girl flirtatiously smiling toward Adam. "Yes, I wish it all the time."

"Let's go, then. Just the two of us. We'll travel somewhere anonymously. Pretend we're farmhands or such. We'll drink and play and bed women and enjoy ourselves."

"What a positively scandalous idea," James said, "but the Season's just begun, Adam. Mother would have an apoplectic fit if you suddenly popped off."

"I care not what Mother would think about it."

He eyed Adam with new interest. "You really are serious, aren't you?"

"Absolutely. I feel I shall go mad if I don't escape all this—just for a time."

James smiled, liking this impetuous train of thought. Adam never did anything on the spur of the moment. His entire life had been spent studying and working and the weight of his responsibilities never lessened.

Loving the opportunity to tease him for a second, James said, "I feel duty-bound to mention the heartbreak all the girls and their mothers will endure if they can't find you to torment."

"I'm sure they'll be able to survive my absence for a few days."

"Well, then, let's do it. Where would you like to go? Any ideas?"

Adam closed his eyes for a moment, pondering all the possible directions they could take. "Let's just head for the country. Maybe we can end up along the coast."

"We haven't gone in ages, have we?"

"No," Adam agreed, "and it's high time we went again."

"An excellent choice. When would you like to leave?"

"How about right now?"

"I'm ready if you are."

Just then, the orchestra struck up a few bars of the next song, and Adam winced. "Oh, no."

"I'd say your quick escape is foiled." James chuckled and patted him on the back. "That definitely sounds like a quadrille."

"How about in thirty minutes?"

Chapter Three

Maggie stared out at the ocean. The waters were bright blue, reflecting the beautiful May sky. Hardly a cloud drifted by to mar the perfection of the lovely day. The winds had not yet begun to blow, so only a gentle breeze rippled, just enough to tease the hair along her cheeks, but enough to cool the warm air. Below, a small, secluded beach shimmered and beckoned to her to sink her toes into the cool sand. Without hesitating, she started down the well-defined trail that led to the shore.

She'd been to the beach a handful of times in her life, when her mother had found herself between lovers and needed a respite from her worries in the city. They'd always come to the Tidewater Inn, the place where Rose had vacationed once with Harold Westmoreland, the Duke of Roswell. Even though her relationship with the Duke had ended horribly, she'd remained fond of the spot. Always, Rose had seemed to find the solace she needed during their too-short visits. They would return to London with her mother full of ideas and plans as to how they would get themselves another income, how she would find herself another paramour.

After Rose died, it had only seemed fitting that Maggie and Anne do the same thing, although now that George was set on turning them out, she couldn't help worrying that the money they'd scrimped so hard to save should have been put to a much more practical use. Like a month's rent on their own flat.

Reaching the bottom of the trail, she shook off the distressing thoughts. The money had been gone in any event, the coach fare and inn reservation prepaid, so they'd not have been able to get a refund. As Anne had said, it did no good to worry about it, and as usual, she was right. Besides, weren't they entitled to a bit of a holiday after what they'd endured the past year? Rose was the only family that Maggie and Anne had in the entire world, and her death had been long and painful. Surely, it was not improper that they take a few days to catch their breath before moving on to the next phase of their lives.

On the beach, she was blissfully alone. Glancing at the trail she'd just descended, she couldn't see anyone following her down. Up the sloping hill, where the Tidewater Inn was hidden by the rocks and trees, there was no one watching from any of the viewing benches. Even if there had been, she'd hardly have cared.

It felt so good to be out of her stifling mourning attire. The lightweight green cotton of her dress felt cool and comfortable. She removed her slippers and set them on top of a large rock; then, hiking up her skirt, she tied a knot in the hem so that her legs were exposed all the way to above her knees. Modesty prevented her from going further, so she left her stockings on.

Running across the sand, she gasped as her toes caught the last bit of a wave as it finished its curl and retreated. The water was a frigid contrast to the balmy air temperature, and she squealed in surprise and delight. The undertow pulled at her feet, and she jumped away, judged when the white sea foam would next rush to meet her, then ran toward it. Over and over again, she played the game of tag as she hurried toward the water, then ran back to safety. Occasionally, the ocean outsmarted her, drenching her legs and the bottom of her skirt.

Heedless of the bright sun and the effect it would have on her pale complexion, she tugged at the strings of her bonnet and tossed it toward the sand, where it floated to the ground. Uncovered, she turned back to the water, loving the feel of the wind as it played through her hair and pushed at her clothing. She closed her eyes and tipped her head back. With her arms outstretched, she whirled in small circles, commanding the burdens of the past few months to float away on the falling tide.

Adam stood on the trail and watched with amusement. When he'd left the inn a few minutes earlier, the beach below had looked deserted, and he'd thought to have a quiet afternoon stroll all by himself. His disappointment at not being alone was short-lived, as he found himself intrigued and delighted by the young woman so artlessly enjoying herself. Obviously, the girl thought she was unobserved, so it was the height of rudeness to stand spying on her in such a fashion, but he couldn't help himself.

There must have been a time in his life when he so easily and thoroughly relished such a simple moment as the girl before him was doing, but for the life of him, he couldn't remember when it might have occurred. As a boy, he'd had no joyful summer holidays. Certainly, he'd traveled with his mother to their various country estates, but the trips were never for pleasure. Only work. Studies were unending. His mother never thought it proper for the servants to see him wrestling or playing, so he'd endured a lifetime of sitting in the schoolroom, listening to tutors, practicing his lessons, learning about the management of his family's vast estates.

James, unburdened by title or worries about his reputation, had spent his youthful days frolicking and causing trouble. When Adam thought back to how jealous he'd been as a lad of his younger brother's freedoms, it was a wonder they'd been able to mature as friends.

How he wished he knew how to join the young woman on the beach. To hold her hand as they splashed into the waves. James would know how; he would not hesitate, but Adam could not imagine doing anything so frivolous.

Instead, he watched, finding joy in the obvious delight of the woman running below. She was a beautiful sight. The wind had kicked up, loosening her hair from its pins. It fell in a glorious light brown cascade down her back. The steady breeze played with the fabric of her simple dress, pushing the thin cloth against her torso, leaving little to the imagination as it outlined her full breasts, the nipples just barely discernible, the flat plane of her stomach, the mound of her sex, a length of thigh. She'd daringly bared her calves, and the display gave her a seductive air, making her look as though she'd just enjoyed a romp with her lover or, perhaps, was waiting for him to appear.

Adam couldn't believe that the thought actually made him aroused. No doubt James had been right. He'd definitely gone too long without a woman.

Shaking his head at his foolishness, he decided to return another time so as not to interrupt the woman's moment of playful solitude. Turning to go, he saw her out of the corner of his eye as she stumbled and fell. He halted as she crossed her foot over her knee and looked at the ball of her foot. Even from a distance, he could see the blood beginning to flow through her torn stocking and drip onto the sand. She must have stepped on a shell or some other spiked object.

Without hesitating, he hurried the remaining steps down the trail and jumped onto the sand. "Hello," he called out, waving, then paused so as not to frighten her.

"Hello," she said, returning his greeting warily.

Knowing she'd be worried about her vulnerability at the moment, he wanted to reassure her, so he stayed where he was. "It looks as though you've injured yourself."

"Yes, I stepped on something quite sharp."

"May I offer assistance?" She hesitated. "I'm staying at

the inn up the hill. Perhaps I could help.'' The mention of the inn seemed to calm any fears she might be harboring about his intentions. She smiled, and the effect was dazzling.

"I'm staying there, too." She stared at him, trying to make a quick decision about his character. He was casually dressed in breeches and boots, although his clothes were of the finest quality, and she couldn't help wondering who he was. Perhaps a gentleman's assistant or the like, not a threatening stranger at all, but just as he seemed—someone who could help with her present dilemma. "And, yes, I believe I might need some assistance."

He took a step closer, then another, easing his way across the sand. Once he was next to her, he dropped to his knees, resting his hands on his thighs. She was even prettier up close, her hair a myriad of highlights set off by the bright sun, and there were two small dimples, one on each cheek, when she smiled. A smattering of freckles across her nose. Her skin smooth and pale, her nose slightly upturned, her lips rosy red. She worried the bottom lip between her teeth.

Although she looked as though she hadn't yet reached twenty years, she was a far cry from the young women with whom he sipped tea in fancy drawing rooms. There was an air about her—a calm, a peaceful nature that seemed to emanate from deep within, as though she'd seen and endured many hard things in her short life and was a stronger person because of it.

It was the damnedest thing, but he felt better just by being in her presence.

"So . . . how bad is it?" he asked.

"I just took a quick glance." She blushed prettily. "I feel like such a ninny, but I can't stand the sight of blood."

"May I look?" he asked, pointing toward her injury.

She wrinkled her nose, then looked away, holding her foot in his direction while she thought about how shocking the moment had quickly become. She was alone on a deserted beach with an unknown man who was, far and away, the most handsome creature she'd ever seen. He was tall and broad, his shoulders wide, his hips narrow, his legs impossibly long. His hair was dark brown, nearly black, a tad bit longer than was proper, and curled round his collar in the back.

A shock of it fell over his forehead, dangling between two heavy brows, accentuating the stark lines of his face. His eyes were deep brown, looking as black as his hair in the bright light of day, and as she gazed into them for the first time, she realized they were the eyes of a lonely man. There were worry lines round his mouth, an air of weary sadness about his person. Somehow, she knew he rarely smiled, and couldn't help wondering why, or thinking how devastatingly beautiful he would appear if he did.

The hands that reached for her foot were large and strong, his fingers long and slender, and he wrapped them around her ankle and gently lifted her foot so that her heel rested against his thigh. Never before had a man seen her feet, let alone touched her in such an intimate way. With her skirts lifted, her legs covered only by stockings, as she rested back on her elbows, she felt the complete wanton.

If Anne could only see her now!

He slid his palm across her stocking-covered skin, and she was overcome with the strangest wish that he would kiss her foot. Right there on the arch.

The very thought was so scandalous that it sent a previously unknown and unexperienced flash of desire up both her legs to the very core of her womanhood. The feel of his skin was warm and pleasant, and it set her to blushing again. She was glad that she was looking away so he wouldn't notice.

Adam rested her heel against his leg and tried hard to ignore the intimate position that had arisen between them. Her legs were as beautiful as the rest of her, long and slender, and he had the strangest flash of what it would feel like to have them wrapped around his waist. He looked down at the tiny foot he held in his hand, nestled only inches from his groin, and couldn't fight the flight of fancy that had her pressing it where he most wanted to be touched. The image made him rock hard.

Luckily, the girl was oblivious, staring off toward the water, although even if she'd been looking directly at him, surely such an innocent young thing would never realize the signs of desire she stirred in him.

Forcing himself back to business, he looked at the bottom of her foot, which was a mess. The cut was deep and severe, the stocking slashed and embedded in the wound, the entire area crusted with sand, shells, and drying blood. It had to hurt like hell and was only going to get worse, because she probably would need to have it sewn.

"How does it look?" she asked in a husky voice that brought an image of silk sheets and breakfast in bed.

He shook his head to clear it. What was it about this girl that had such an effect on him? "It looks quite bad."

"Really?"

"Yes. I'm afraid you may need some stitches." He regretted the words the moment they left his mouth.

She gasped, thoroughly overwhelmed by the prospect. She'd never had stitches before; they sounded dreadful. "Are you certain?"

"Well, no," he lied, not wanting to alarm her any more than he already had, "but we should wrap it to stem some of the bleeding, then get you up the hill. There's bound to be someone about at the inn or in the village who could look at it and make a better assessment."

She pulled her gaze back from the water, looking at him instead of her foot. Their gazes met and held, and Maggie had the strongest urge to rest a palm against his cheek, to tell him everything would be all right, although she had no idea why such a thought popped into her mind. Something about the way he carried himself made him look like a man with the weight of the world on his shoulders.

She said, "I've nothing with which to wrap it."

"Nor do I, I'm afraid. Perhaps we could tear a bit of petticoat."

She glanced back to the water, then whispered, "I'm not wearing one."

The knowledge that there was so little between them sent a new wave of desire surging through his loins. He looked up toward the sky.

"Lord help me," he groaned softly.

"What did you say?" Her head came swinging around to find him sitting there calmly, but looking at her the way a cat looks at his favorite bird just before pouncing.

"I said, perhaps you could help me by giving me one of your stockings."

"Are you suggesting I disrobe?"

"No, no." Adam actually flushed at her words, feeling as though she'd read his mind. He'd like nothing better than to see the little beauty completely naked, but he was willing to settle for a bit of bare leg. "Actually, the stocking on your injured foot is embedded in the cut, and as the blood dries, some of it is sticking to the wound, which will make it painful to remove the longer we wait. I thought perhaps we could remove it now, then use it to bind the cut."

Maggie paused, deciding the idea had merit. "I suppose you're right. We should do that. Turn your head." Adam shifted slightly. "More. And no peeking!" He turned a bit further, too far to be able to see anything interesting, but close enough to sense what she was doing. His thoughts were pure agony.

Almost as if it was his hand instead of her own sliding up her leg to untie the garter, he could feel the skirt falling back, exposing a silky expanse of inner thigh. It would be soft and warm. He'd catch a hint of her musk. He'd lean closer, place a kiss on the delicate skin, kiss her again, higher and higher still, until . . .

"Ow!" Maggie broke him out of the lusty reverie he'd been enjoying. She had the stocking down around her ankle and was trying to work it away from the cut.

"Let me do that," he ordered. He leaned forward, tenderly and carefully freeing the slinky bit of fabric. Eventually, it came loose, and he slipped it over her toes, taking much more time than necessary as he savored the bit of exposed leg. Her calf was smooth and slender, covered with a soft down of blond hair. Her feet were delicate and tiny.

With the lace stocking lying in his hand, he couldn't resist running it through his fingers. The sheer material was still warm from resting against her skin. An essence of her smell clung to it, and he had to physically resist the urge to press the thing against his face. He shifted her foot between his thighs to hold it steady. The position was more comfortable for her but more painful for him as her toes hovered only inches away from where he truly wanted them to rest. "This will hurt."

"All right."

"I'll try to be gentle." Adam couldn't believe how the innocent exchange of words conjured up a much different, definitely carnal, moment.

Slowly, he began wrapping her foot, unable to keep from noticing the fine quality of her lace stocking. The girl must have some money to own an undergarment so fine. Not for the first time, he wondered who she was. A twinge of excitement worked its way to the surface as he decided it was possible that she was a noble's daughter who'd been stashed in the country—a girl he'd never met before. Although knowing his luck with women, it was certainly more likely that she was the child of a wealthy merchant.

Maggie couldn't help but notice how he regarded her lace stocking. Her mother, never one to scrimp on the essentials, always wore the finest unmentionables, insisting that a woman in her position never knew when she'd be required to undress at a moment's notice. Since seduction was her business, she'd always spent a good share of her small income on the finest Italian silks and Belgian laces.

Upon Rose's death, Maggie had begun wearing some of the

exotic items, loving the way they felt against her skin. Surely the Queen didn't wear such fine intimate apparel.

"What a waste of beautiful lace," Adam murmured regretfully, looking at the bloodstain and the tear on the bottom.

Maggie could think of no tactful way to converse about her underwear. Instead, she managed, "Are you finished?"

"Just about." Using both ends of the stocking, he tied a secure knot on the top of her foot. "Is that too tight?"

"No. It feels fine." She wiggled her foot slightly, then winced with the pain. "Well, maybe not fine. But the bandage is excellent. Thank you."

Unable to resist, he rested his hand on the back of her ankle and stroked up the back of her calf as far as he dared. To his surprise, she didn't protest his incredible breach of manners, and he let his fingers rise nearly to her knee, loving the sleek feel of her skin, the warm pulse radiating from her.

Maggie couldn't raise her eyes from where he massaged in small circles just below and behind her knee. The action sent a wave of pleasure cascading up the backs of her thighs, continuing up her spine until even the hair on her head seemed to tingle. She forced herself to meet his gaze. He had leaned over her, his face only inches away, and he was staring so intently that butterflies started dancing in her stomach. Suddenly, she was overcome with the thought that he wanted to kiss her, which had to be ludicrous.

Although maybe it wasn't so far-fetched. Anne swore she had fallen in love with Stephen the moment they met. She insisted such things were possible. Maggie shook off her wayward thoughts, wondering what her gallant gentleman would think if he knew how erotically her mind was working. Kissing her was probably the farthest thing from his mind.

"Violet," he said softly.

"What?"

"Your eyes. They're violet. I was wondering."

Maggie's heart did a flip-flop. Her mother had protected her from wayward advances, so she'd had very little actual experience with men. Especially someone as dashing as the stranger kneeling in front of her. Completely at a loss as to how to respond, she swallowed, then said, "I don't know if I can stand."

"Let me help you get your balance." He reached out with one hand, then settled the other on her waist, loving the excuse it gave him to touch her far too intimately. He leaned back on his haunches, then rose, pulling her up with him. For the briefest second, she swayed and he caught her, her body stretched out the length of his. He could feel every inch of her. The pert breasts, the flat stomach, the soft mound. With every fiber of his being, he had to resist dropping his hand from her waist to her buttocks and pressing her up against his swollen loins.

He broke the contact between them, not wanting her to suspect his aroused state. "Don't step down on it," he said.

"I won't."

Maggie looked up into his beautiful eyes—eyes fringed with dark, long lashes that were longer than her own. What was the connection she was feeling to him? She knew he was feeling it, too. Although inexperienced, she wasn't uneducated in the arts of loving. In their brief moment of bodily contact, he'd been aroused; she was sure of it. She couldn't wait to get back to the inn to talk with Anne.

Gingerly, she touched her foot to the ground, realizing she couldn't step on it if she wanted to. Looking up the beach cliff, she turned to him and sighed. "How shall I ever manage to get up the hill?"

If the question had been posed by one of the women who flirted with him in London drawing rooms, he might have shook his head at the obvious ploy. This young woman was so lacking in guile, so concerned, that he couldn't help jumping at the chance to play knight-in-shining-armor. "Why, my beautiful damsel, I shall simply have to help you." With that, he swept her up in his arms.

"What are you doing?" she gasped as one arm balanced behind her knees, the other secure behind her back.

"I'll carry you up."

"What about my hat? And my shoes?"

"I'll send someone back down for them." As she looked ready to protest, he whispered, "Wrap your arms round my neck." When she hesitated, he coaxed, "It's all right. I promise I won't drop you."

The possibility that he might *drop* her was the last thing on her mind. The look he was flashing her made him appear to be the Devil's own. The rascal was too handsome for his own good.

Doing as he asked, she shifted slightly and draped her arms across his shoulders. The shift pushed one of her breasts against his chest and, as he began to walk toward the beach trail, each flex of his muscles caused a most sensational rubbing against her nipple. It was like nothing she'd ever felt before, and set off a tingle low in her stomach. She had to fight every reflex of her body, which begged her to arch against him like a stretching cat.

Adam carried her with ease; she was a tiny little thing. He held her tighter and closer than necessary, loving the feel of her breast against his own, of her hip wedged against his stomach. As they silently climbed to the top of the short hill, he let his imagination wander to what she'd look like unclothed. Beautiful. Slender, with rosy-tipped breasts, a slim waist, curvaceous hips. And all that beautiful light brown hair cascading about her shoulders and down her back.

With great regret, he reached the top of the cliff and the manicured lawns of the small inn, not knowing if he'd have an excuse to see the girl again once he handed her over to others. A gardener saw them immediately and, after receiving quick instructions, ran into the inn's main room. By the time Adam stepped inside with the girl in his arms, the proprietor was waiting beside a chair. Adam sat her down, holding her in his lap.

"The young woman's cut her foot," he told the proprietor. "Have you a surgeon in the area?"

"No, sir, but my wife does some healing. She's quite good at it if I do say so myself."

Before Adam could send for the man's wife, she stepped into the room. She was a short, stout woman who came to kneel in front of them. She looked up at the girl. "Miss Brown, what have ye done to yourself?"

"I stepped on a shell or something down at the beach. This kind gentleman . . ." She looked into his eyes. "I'm sorry, but I don't even know your name."

"Aston Carrington," Adam lied easily, using the false name under which he had registered with James.

"How do you do, Mr. Carrington. I'm Magdalina Brown."

"I am charmed to make your acquaintance, Miss Brown."

Maggie smiled at him, then looked back at the proprietress. "Mr. Carrington was kind enough to wrap my injury and help me up the trail."

"Let's have a look, then." The woman carefully undid the bandage, clucking her tongue as she looked at the cut. "Oh, ye've done yourself good with this one."

"Will it need to be sewn?" Adam asked.

"Just a few nips." She patted Maggie's knee. "Hold on there, sweeting. We'll have ye cleaned and stitched in no time."

Maggie groaned at the woman's words, and Adam hugged her tighter. The woman left and quickly returned with a small bag of doctoring equipment, towels, water, basin, and bandages. She handed a glass to Maggie. "Drink this, dearie."

"What is it?" Maggie asked, wrinkling her nose at the smell, although she knew very well what it was. She couldn't have spent the last year next to a deathbed and not have known.

"Just a bit of laudanum."

Maggie hesitated, and Adam took the glass into his own hand and tipped it to her lips. "It's for the best, Miss Brown."

Unable to refuse when he was looking at her that way, she drank it down quickly. "Ooh, that was terrible," she gasped, then shuddered.

For some unfathomable reason, he had an overwhelming

urge to offer her comfort. Deciding not to resist it, he whispered, "You're being very brave."

"I hardly feel brave. I'm scared witless."

"Just keep looking at me. We'll get through this together." He slipped his hand into hers and squeezed.

The proprietress, washcloth in hand, knelt in front of Maggie, cleaned the wound, then prepared her needle and thread. Looking up at Adam, she gave a nod, indicating she was ready. "I'll need you to hold her tight so she doesn't jump."

"Don't look," he told Maggie. Gently, he pressed her face into the crook of his neck, where he could feel her warm breath pulsing over his skin. "I'll be right here with you."

"Thank you." As the proprietress inserted the needle and closed the first stitch, Maggie took a deep breath and held it. "That hurts," she said softly so only he could hear.

"I know, little one, but it will be over soon." Surprised and overwhelmed by the emotion he was feeling for the girl, he placed a light kiss on her hair, then wrapped her tightly in his arms, holding her as though he could absorb some of the pain. Never in his long life could he remember wanting to comfort another in such a fashion. It was a new and wonderful experience.

The doctoring woman was efficient, and had the six stitches and covering bandage in place before either of them knew what had happened.

"Let's get you up to your bed." He smiled at Maggie. "Which room?"

"Five. Left at the top of the stairs."

The proprietor led the way and gave a quick knock. Anne opened the door to a surprising sight as the owner stepped away and Maggie entered, carried in the arms of one of the most handsome men Anne had ever seen.

"Oh, my, what's happened?" she exclaimed as she noticed the bandage on Maggie's foot.

"It's the silliest thing." Maggie tried to wave away her concern.

Adam placed her on the bed while Anne fussed with the pillows. "She stepped on something jagged down on the beach," he said.

"Aston rescued me." Maggie smiled, using his first name. Already feeling the effects of the laudanum, she'd forgotten her manners.

"Aston Carrington," he lied again as he introduced himself to Anne. "I just happened along after she'd cut herself."

"Anne Porter." Anne returned his smile, looking at him carefully. He seemed very familiar, and she was trying to place him in her mind, but was careful not to seem as if she was doing such a thing. "Thank you, sir. Maggie is my dearest friend. I can't tell you how much I appreciate you helping her."

"It was my pleasure," he said. Maggie was drifting, and he gestured to Anne to step away from the bed. His curiosity had gotten the best of him. "Are her parents here?"

"No, sir, she has no parents. I'm all she has in the world in the way of family."

"I see." He didn't really. The response only served to pique his curiosity further. "The owner's wife gave her six stitches and a dose of laudanum. She's to rest and stay off her feet for a few days."

"How disappointing," Anne said with a sigh. "We're only here for a short holiday. This will ruin much of her fun, I'm afraid."

"If you need anything, my brother and I are staying in room number ten."

"I'll remember, and thank you, again. I appreciate all you've done."

With that, and no longer able to think of a reason to linger—after all, he and Maggie Brown were strangers—he stepped to the bed, telling her softly, "I'll check on you in the morning."

"I'd like that," she responded with a contented smile on her face.

Unable to help himself, he leaned forward and placed a light kiss on her forehead. "Rest well, little one."

Embarrassed and confused by the tender feelings welling around the vicinity of his heart, he made his good-byes to Anne and took his leave.

Anne closed the door behind him, her brows raised in surprise as she went through the motions of making Maggie comfortable, even though the young woman was already sleeping. "So, my girl," she queried softly, "what have you gone and found for yourself?"

Chapter Four

Maggie sat in a chair by the window, waiting for the knock on the door that would come at any moment. Her foot sported a new bandage and was gracefully balanced on a small stool. Although it throbbed like the dickens, it didn't hurt nearly as much today as she'd imagined it might.

Aston Carrington had sent a note earlier, asking if it would be all right to visit, and of course, they'd accepted without hesitating. As Anne had pointed out, there was nothing wrong with attentions from a dashing male, and a little flattery and flirting could only lift Maggie's spirits before they went back to the difficult choices facing them in London.

Maggie ran a hand across her hair, hoping she looked all right. Anne could usually work wonders, but when they'd packed for the brief holiday, they'd not imagined that they would be receiving a handsome guest. They hadn't brought much in the way of finery, no fancy ribbons or hairpins. They'd not even brought nice gowns, thinking the highlight of the sojourn would be the dining room downstairs.

They'd done the best with what they had available, and

Maggie, remembering how Aston seemed to enjoy the color of her eyes, had dressed in a simple lavender day dress. The hue of the fabric lightened her hair so it looked nearly blond, and darkened her eyes so they looked nearly purple. Before hobbling over to the chair, she'd glanced in the mirror and had had to admit that she looked quite pretty. She'd gotten all of her mother's best features, and for the first time in her life, she wished she actually had the clothing and accoutrements necessary to further highlight her good looks.

Anne sat in the chair next to her. "This is your first gentleman caller."

"I wouldn't label him a *caller*. He's just coming to check on my welfare."

"That's close enough for me. Are you nervous?"

"No. Just excited. Wouldn't it be fun if he asked me to go for a ride or to dine with him?"

"That would be splendid. Nothing in the world is better at raising low spirits than the attentions of a handsome man."

"Do you suppose he's a rogue and a scoundrel?"

"We can only hope. They're much more fun."

Maggie chuckled as a brisk knock sounded, cutting off further comment. Anne went to the door, smiling to find Maggie's new friend standing there with a bouquet of flowers in one hand and a stick of driftwood, perfectly shaped like the finest walking stick, in the other. "Good morning, Mr. Carrington."

"Good morning, Miss Porter. How is our patient?"

"Recovering nicely. Do come in and see for yourself." Anne stepped back so he could enter.

Adam hovered in the doorway and took a deep breath. Maggie was lovely, prettier than he remembered, if that was possible. Sunlight was coming through the window from behind her shoulder and it accented the highlights in her hair. The simple gown she'd chosen perfectly matched her eyes. Even her injured foot was lovely. Somewhere, she'd found a bit of purple ribbon to tie around her bandage, and he wanted to laugh at the cute gesture made on his behalf.

The night had been a restless one, passed tossing and turning in his bed, thinking about her. It had been a very, very long time since he'd worried about anyone. Oh, he worried plenty, of course, about the estates, about his business holdings, investments, and the like. But not about another person. The feelings of concern were both odd and welcome.

He wasn't sure why he felt so attached to the girl, or so protective of her, but he did. The sentiment was there, like a tangible thing that had reached out and grabbed hold, and for the time being, he decided to give in to his desire to take care of her. If nothing else, spending a few days in her company would be like receiving a cherished gift.

Wasn't this the reason he'd run away from London in the first place? To meet a woman like Maggie? To relax and play and enjoy a few days' rest without all the pressures people were always putting on him? Sweet, beautiful Magdalina Brown was like a bright ray of sunshine on a cloudy day. He intended to bask in her happy glow for as many days as he had the chance.

"Hello, Miss Brown." He stepped forward and bowed over her hand. "You're looking lovely today. And much better than the last time I saw you." Propriety required that he drop her hand, but he didn't. The strange connection he'd felt to her from the very first was there again, drawing him closer. He couldn't let go. Instead, he laced his fingers through hers and squeezed. She smiled up at him with that look in her eye that he'd seen the previous day, and all of a sudden, he felt so much better.

"I'm doing quite well. Thank you again for helping me. I'm glad you arrived when you did."

Maggie squeezed his hand in return, loving the warm play of his skin against hers. She felt connected to him as she never had to another, as though she'd been looking for him without being aware of it. It was the strangest thing, but she felt as if she'd always known him, and that was why she could sense the great air of sadness and loneliness that pervaded the room when he was in it. Being in his presence made her want to wrap her arms around him and protect him from the burdens of his world that seemed to be weighing him down.

Adam reluctantly lowered her hand to her lap, and sat in the chair next to her. In a quick glance across the room, he saw that Anne was sitting in the far corner, seeming to be engrossed in a book and leaving them alone as much as was possible in the small space. They were a strange pair of ladies, and he couldn't help wondering about them both.

"I thought these might brighten your day." He handed Maggie the flowers he'd picked in the gardens behind the inn. With the most genuine smile he'd ever witnessed, she held the small bouquet to her face and inhaled deeply as though they were the finest hothouse roses.

"They're lovely, Mr. Carrington. Absolutely lovely." Maggie couldn't believe the tears that welled in her eyes over such a simple gesture. It was the first time a man had ever given her a gift, and she was simply overwhelmed by the thought of it.

"Call me Aston, please," Adam requested, hating now to ask her to use his false name. He'd give anything to hear the true one on her lips, but it was too late to tell her the truth. The ruse would have to continue.

"And please call me Maggie."

"Thank you, Maggie." He said her name just because he wanted to hear how it played on his tongue, and he liked the sound of it. He reached beside his chair and handed her the other gift. "I thought this might help you get about for the next few days."

"What a wonderful idea."

"It's not much." He'd found the stick while taking an early stroll. Perfectly shaped, and short enough for her to lean on. He'd snatched it up and had one of the stable boys sand off the rough bark. It had seemed like a good idea at the time, but now, as she held it in her beautiful hands, it seemed a pitiful gift for one he considered so extraordinary.

"It's exactly what I need, and I hadn't even realized it," she said.

"I found it on the beach this morning." He was embarrassed to admit it, thinking now that she might take offense.

"It's a fascinating piece of wood, isn't it? Look at all the knots and how the various grains run through it." She ran her hands across it as though it was the finest gift any woman had ever received. "I wonder what kinds of adventures it's had, floating in the ocean. Perhaps it was tossed into the waves by a fierce jungle savage, and it's come all the way from some exotic land, just to wash up on shore when I most needed it."

"Let's imagine exactly that."

One corner of his lovely mouth lifted, and Maggie realized it was as close as he'd come in her presence to actually smiling. He was obviously not a man given to moments of spontaneity. Perhaps she could change that. "Shall I try it out?"

"Only if you think you're ready. I don't want you to hurt yourself."

"Pooh . . ." She waved a hand in dismissal. "With this marvelous stick, I'm sure I could walk to London and back if need be." Standing, she took a few cautious steps, then a few more, limping around the small room before returning to her chair. "It's perfect. Thank you for being so thoughtful."

"You're welcome. I only wish I'd had it carved from the finest oak especially for you."

"No, no. This is much too special." Maggie couldn't get over her image of him walking the beach and thinking of her. Finding the stick. Bringing it back simply because she needed it. So few people had ever been kind to her in her life that it was surprising and touching to be on the receiving end of such a considerate act.

Adam couldn't believe that he actually flushed at her praise. With all the wealth at his disposal, he'd always been able to give any type of expensive gift he wished, but he'd never had such heartfelt thanks from any recipient. He cleared his throat past the lump that seemed to have formed. "Miss Porter mentioned last night that your injury will ruin your holiday. I hope you won't let it.''

''Oh, this lovely trip could never be ruined. If nothing else, I can sit by the window and look out at the beautiful countryside. It is so lovely to be away from London that nothing could spoil my adventure.''

What a breath of fresh air she was. ''So you're from London, then?''

''Yes. And you?''

''My brother and I are from Portsmouth. We're here on business for our employer.'' He and James had concocted the lie well in advance of arriving at the Tidewater Inn, but now, as he spoke it aloud, the words left a bad taste. Lying to her was offensive, but it couldn't be helped. Their acquaintance could never last more than a few days anyway. Surprisingly, the fact filled him with a desperate longing. How many times in his life had he had to give up some pleasure in the name of duty and responsibility? Maggie would be just one more regret in a lifetime of them.

Not wanting to delve too far into the lie about his employment, he continued in another vein. ''Is this your first time to the ocean?''

''No, I've been here five times. My mother always enjoyed this place. My father brought her here when she was younger.'' Maggie never told anyone the truth about her father, who he was or what he was, so she wouldn't mention those first heady days when Rose had been so madly in love with Harold West-moreland. ''Her memories of the time were such good ones that she always came back for the quiet and solitude.''

Her voice caught at the mention of her mother. Although it had been over two months since her death, the grief still bubbled to the surface at the most inopportune moments. She pressed a thumb and finger against the bridge of her nose, took a deep breath, and smiled tremulously. ''She only recently passed away. It's still hard to talk about her.''

Adam was at a loss for words. He'd only had rare occasions

to comfort others during their grief, so he had little idea how to go about it. His own mourning for his father, a man to whom he'd never felt close and whom he'd hardly known, had seemed stilted and false. He reached for her hand and held it in his own. "I'm sorry. I didn't realize . . ."

"It's all right. We're not dressed in black, so you couldn't know."

Anne entered the conversation for the first time. "Rosie was terribly ill for a very long time, Mr. Carrington. We felt like we mourned for her every day, and we wanted to celebrate her life by coming here."

"Yes," Maggie agreed. "She was always so very happy here. That's how I like to remember her." Maggie looked at him with eyes so full of hope and anguish. "Do you think it was disrespectful to leave our black at home?"

"No. I think you've the right idea. I'm sure she would have wanted you to find some joy in your memories."

"That's what we were thinking, too."

Adam resolved then and there to make her short holiday an enjoyable one. He'd already inquired at the desk and knew she and Miss Porter had only booked the room for four more days. He intended to make the most of them. "The weather is very beautiful today, and I hate to think of you cooped up here in your room. I was wondering if you'd do me the honor of joining me for lunch? With Miss Porter, of course."

"That sounds lovely. What do you think, Anne?"

Anne wasn't about to intrude on Maggie's first romance. She shook her head. "No, thank you. I was thinking of taking a quick stroll through the village. There's a very old church there that I've been dying to visit." She smiled knowingly at Mr. Carrington. "But you two should certainly enjoy yourselves."

Adam was curious that the older woman seemed to have no desire to chaperone Maggie, nor did she seem to think a chaperone was required. For a moment, his usual panic assailed him.

Were they setting him up for some breach of the girl's reputation, hoping to force a union?

No, no. He nearly gave a visible shake of his head. His paranoia about the designs of the fairer sex was getting out of hand. No one in London knew where they were or where they'd gone. He and James had chosen the Tidewater Inn at random as they rode down the country lane. It had been a spur-of-the-moment decision. They'd only just settled in their rooms when he'd walked to the beach the previous afternoon and stumbled across Maggie. It simply wasn't possible that she would know who he was.

Anne assessed Aston Carrington, wondering again why he seemed so familiar, but she still couldn't place him. He was looking at her strangely, though, and she couldn't help laughing. "Mr. Carrington, please don't look so aghast at my suggestion that you dine alone with Maggie. I should probably say that I'm neither Maggie's relative nor her chaperone. I'm her friend and have been for many years. She is a woman full-grown, with a good head on her shoulders. She's completely capable of deciding if she'd like to take lunch with a gentleman. It's not for me to say yea or nay."

Adam hated that the perceptive woman could see through him so easily. What else did she see? "Actually, Miss Porter, I was planning a picnic down on the beach. If I can find my wayward brother, I'd like to invite him to join us. It would be a great assistance to me if you would accompany us, also. He talks incessantly, and having a fourth person along will provide Maggie and me an occasional respite from having to keep up with his banter."

Anne chuckled, wondering what his brother was like and thinking that it was a grand day to be escorted to a picnic by a handsome gentleman. It had been a long time since such a thing had happened to her. "Well, if I can offer such important assistance, then I gladly accept your invitation."

"Wonderful. How about if I stop by at one to escort you down?" he asked, turning back to Maggie.

"That will be lovely."

The time to take his leave had come so quickly, and much to his surprise, he didn't want to go. Like a lovesick schoolboy with his first crush, he wanted to linger away the day by her side.

"I'll be off, then," he said, and hoped the great reluctance he felt wasn't visible in his words.

Maggie reached out her hand to take his as he stood. She didn't want him to go and wished she could think of some excuse to get him to stay. Chastising herself for her silly eagerness, she reminded herself to be content that they would spend part of the afternoon together—a boon she hadn't imagined when she received his request for a visit to her room.

With a gentle smile, and a squeeze of her fingers against his, she said, "Please don't go to too much trouble on our account."

Surprising himself again, he gazed into her eyes and professed, "I can't imagine that anything I would do on your account would ever be too much trouble." Bowing over her hand, he used the polite gesture as an excuse to intimately kiss the back of her hand. Her skin was soft and warm and smelled of lilacs. Softly, he added, "I'll count the minutes until one o'clock."

"I'll miss you every moment until then," she whispered.

His heart did a little flip-flop. No one had ever said such a thing to him before. He gave her a smile and a wicked wink and left the room, his step much lighter than it had been on arriving.

James sat in the taproom, relaxed in a chair and glanced at a London newspaper that was a few days old. He'd heard all about Adam's adventure with the girl the day before and knew he'd gone for a visit. While he hadn't been surprised that Adam had helped the lass—after all, he could be the complete gentleman when the situation called for it—he was intrigued that Adam felt the need to check on her welfare.

The times were rare when Adam involved himself in the day-to-day workings of others. His own world was so full of heavy responsibility, and his view so focused on the path he walked, that he rarely noticed what was happening to those around him. It wasn't that he was uncaring or unfeeling; it was simply that he had so many important matters on his mind that he'd never get anything done if he stopped to worry about every little thing.

That the girl could so easily poke through his defenses was an interesting development. Adam had mentioned she was a pretty little thing, but there had to be something more to it. This adventure was turning out to be more interesting by the second.

Adam entered just then. James couldn't help but notice the change their days away from London had already wrought in his older brother. With each passing hour, he seemed more relaxed, more at peace. At the moment, he looked downright happy!

James was chuckling as Adam sat down across from him. "Whatever has come over you, brother? You look ready to take on the world."

"I finally had a good night's sleep for a change."

"So did I, but I don't look like you. I think I should take you on holiday more often."

"It does seem to be doing wonders for me."

"I have a feeling it's a little more than that. Perhaps, I should visit your wounded bird myself. She seems to have some amazing restorative properties of which I'm unaware." He raised a brow in question.

"You'll keep away from her, you despicable wretch. I know you too well. The poor thing wouldn't be safe round the likes of you."

"Now, there's the fox warning off the wolf," James said. Adam's tone was teasing, but underneath, James couldn't help but hear the possessive ring of his words. What was going on?

"You sound smitten. Who is this girl who has managed to catch your attention so quickly?"

"As I told you yesterday, just a young woman here on holiday with her friend. I find her quite extraordinary."

"How come?"

"I haven't the faintest idea. She just makes me feel better." He flushed slightly in embarrassment. "I sound absurd. Don't pay any mind to me. I don't know what's come over me today."

If James hadn't known his brother as well as he did, he might have thought he'd gotten a bite from the love bug. Since emotional displays were completely foreign to the man, and always had been, James knew that couldn't be it.

Or could it? James asked himself. Stranger things had happened. What a wonderful experience it would be for Adam to have a spot of innocent romance before returning to the city. As far as James knew, it had never happened to his brother before. "So . . . am I to be allowed an introduction to this woman who has so completely captured your fancy?"

"Yes. We've a luncheon engagement with her. We're going on a picnic. And tomorrow night, there's a dance in the village. You're coming with us to that, too."

"Dining and dancing? Whatever has come over you?"

"I don't know, but I can't seem to control myself, so I've decided not to fight it."

"Why must I accompany you?"

"Because I want you to entertain her friend."

"What's this?" James growled low in his throat. "You're setting me up with a woman? I thought I told you never again to do such a thing to me after the debacle with the Heathrow sisters."

"James, that was ten years ago," Adam snapped in exasperation. "Don't you think my tastes might have improved since then?"

"Hardly. You may have almost reached thirty years, but what you know about women would fit on the head of a pin." He downed the pint of ale he'd been sipping and pushed back his chair. "You know I hate simpering young things. What will I have to say to her while you're wooing your beloved?"

"Actually, she's not young."

"She's old?" he gasped.

"She's your age. Or perhaps mine. And she's not *simpering*. She's quite astute and, I would say, fetching. Yes, I would describe her as fetching."

James could just imagine the sort of woman with whom Adam expected him to pass the afternoon. He grumbled, "You'll owe me for this."

"Ha! After you meet her, you'll be down on your knees thanking me."

"You wish." He stood, and Adam stood with him. "Just so you know the sacrifice I'm making for you, one of the lads in the stable tells me there's a tavern with a despicable reputation just down the road. They employ several delightful young women of dubious character. I had planned to spend the afternoon receiving succor in the arms of a girl named Peggy. She's supposed to be quite limber."

"If you promise to behave yourself and mind your manners during our lunch, I'll go there with you later tonight. I find I could use some *succor* myself."

James shook his head in amazement as they headed for their room. If Adam was ready to picnic with a commoner and roll around with a whore all in the same day, the world must surely have spun off its axis.

Chapter Five

Maggie tapped her uninjured foot to the sound of the music. A trio of musicians played on a makeshift stage at the end of the barn, and while they were certainly far from the best in all of England, they managed to turn out one lively tune after another. The crowd of dancers was wildly enthusiastic for each piece.

She wanted to join in, but most of the dances were so involved that, with her bandaged wound, she couldn't have kept up with the other participants, and would only have frustrated the movements of those around her. All she could do was watch from her place on the bench.

Growing up in the city had definitely limited her life experiences, she decided, for she'd never imagined that such an event was possible. The entire neighborhood surrounding the Tidewater Inn had been invited to a local wedding celebration in the village, and indeed, it seemed as though everyone from the surrounding countryside must be there. Grandmothers, babies, and every age in between were playing, talking, and eating as well as dancing. A long buffet table was set against one wall, filled with foods cooked and baked by the local women.

Previously, Maggie had attended two balls with her mother and George Wilburton. Although they had interested her because of the novelty of going to such affairs, she'd thought them both to be dry, boring events. Conversations were strictly controlled, interaction among the guests overbearing and polite, the women rude and venomous with their gossip and innuendo.

This gathering was very different. Everyone knew everyone else, and there were no fussy manners or societal strictures required as friends and neighbors joked and chatted. Watching it all was so enjoyable, but, oh, how she wished she could jump to her feet to take a place in the line. Just then, Anne and James whirled by, laughing and smiling. Aston came next, coupled with a grandmotherly type who had urged him into the dance line without waiting for a refusal. What she wouldn't give to be able to join them.

Whenever she caught sight of Aston, he always seemed to be looking directly at her and no one else, as though she was the only person in the entire place. Just the thought of it, that Aston Carrington could have developed a *tendre* for her, caused those silly butterflies to begin swirling in her stomach.

Quickly, she took a deep breath, tamping down her sense of elation. Always a realist, she wasn't foolish enough to think that there was any type of future for them. In two and a half days, when the time came to return to London, she'd never see him again. He'd made no mention of *later*. For whatever reason, he could not contemplate a *later* with her. So, she had these precious few days to spend with him, and so far they had been an eye-opener.

Finally, she understood the heat of desire. Without hesitation, she would give herself to Aston if he asked, would bask in the glory of his loving attention without thinking twice about any possible consequences. The urge to be with him in every way was too strong to be denied, and for the first time in her life, she was glad she'd been born a woman—so she could feel this way about a man.

Adam saw her through the horde of people, far and away the prettiest woman in the crowd. Sitting there in her simple pale blue dress, with her hair piled in lovely curls on top of her head, she was the most spectacular woman he'd ever seen. Even in a London ballroom, she'd have turned all the heads.

The previous day had been the best of his life. Sitting with her at the beach, laughing and talking about their lives and pasts, was so comforting. He'd never spent a day like it. Had never known he could enjoy such a deep feeling of friendship with a woman. His only regret was that he couldn't tell her who he was, which meant he couldn't reveal the truth about so many things. How he longed for the freedom to unburden himself completely. Theirs was an emotional connection that defied all logic, and he knew she would understand the pressures and forces that shaped his life, and by understanding, the weight would be lifted.

How hard it would be when they parted in two and a half days. For not only would he miss her terribly, but knowing her had frustrated so many of his plans for the future. He'd always suspected that this type of relationship with a woman was possible. Although he'd never encountered such a thing before, he'd believed that ultimate trust and friendship could combine with desire to establish the base for a lifelong romance.

Now, he understood why he'd been avoiding matrimony and why he'd been unable to select a wife: because he'd secretly been waiting for the feeling of connection he'd found with Maggie but had never found with another. What a twist of fate to find her, to finally comprehend what it was for which he'd been searching so long, and to know that he could not have it.

A connection like theirs was a once-in-a-lifetime event. No matter how many other women he met, he would not find the emotional link he'd found with Maggie. The thought of returning to London to resume his futile search for a bride appeared to be more distasteful than ever.

Marriage to Maggie was out of the question for a man in his position. She was, after all, a shopkeeper's daughter. Since his emotional attachment to her went far beyond a fierce physical yearning, he wished he could make her his paramour. She had no family to appease, and a liaison with the Marquis of Belmont could only work to her benefit. While he'd briefly toyed with the idea, he knew he couldn't do it, because she deserved better than to end up as the concubine of a man like himself.

The music ended, and he escorted his elderly partner back to her seat, fending off several other, more boisterous requests for a dance as he gradually worked his way back to Maggie. He settled himself beside her, and as with every other time their bodies chanced to touch, whether thighs, shoulders, or hands, he felt as if he'd been struck by lightning. Any brief contact always ended up making its way to his groin, causing a painful throb.

"I finally escaped," he said.

Maggie raised the edge of her shawl and fanned his heated face. "I think you neglected to mention something about yourself when we were talking yesterday."

"What's that?" he asked warily.

"You're quite the ladies' man. Every grandmother in the place has her eyes on you."

"I have to admit they've worn me out. I can't keep up with them."

"They're all watching to see the moment you're rested up so they can drag you back out to the floor."

"Well, they can try, but I'm not going again. I'm staying here with you." He slipped his hand into hers, where the clasp of their fingers was hidden under the folds of her skirt. "May I tell you again how pretty you look tonight?"

"Just being with you makes me feel pretty."

"Are you enjoying yourself?"

"Very much. I attended a few balls in London, but they were a far cry from this."

The mention of London had him squirming. What would it be like to attend a ball, only to find her there? What would she think of him if she realized he wasn't some working man from Portsmouth? He shook off the thought, refusing to let memories of London, or his life there, intrude on this brief foray into fantasy. "This does seem to be a better way to hold a celebration, doesn't it?"

"Yes. Everyone looks so happy." Anne and James spun by again, and Maggie sighed. "Oh, I wish I could dance. That's the only thing that could possibly make the evening more wonderful than it already is."

Just then, the musicians struck up a different type of tune, one she hadn't heard before. It was a slower version of the waltz, which was the rage of London dancing rooms. The bride and groom made their way to the center of the floor, where they danced alone for a few minutes amidst clapping and laughter. Then other family members and friends joined them until the floor was full once again.

Adam turned to look at Maggie. "I would do anything to make your night perfect." He held out his hand. "Dance with me."

"How will we accomplish it?"

"Leave that to me." He stood and helped her to her feet.

Maggie didn't hesitate. This was her chance not only to dance, but to hold Aston close as she'd been longing to do all evening.

They were toward the back of the barn, near the double doors, which had been propped open to let in the fresh night air, and the waltz was nothing like it was in fancy London ballrooms, where partners twirled in perfect circles in time to the music. This wasn't a dance of precision, and there were people of all ages and capabilities surrounding them. No one paid them any attention.

He leaned down and whispered in her ear. "Put your arms around my neck."

Maggie reached up and did as he asked, and felt his arms

slide around her waist. He lifted her slightly so that her feet dangled just off the ground. The tips of her toes brushed the tops of his. She tipped her head back and looked up into his eyes, liking the smile she saw lurking there. "What will everyone think?"

"I don't care."

"Then neither do I." She gave him one of her beautiful, dimpled grins. "This is perfect."

"Yes, it is." She was such a tiny thing, light and compact. As he held her closely and stared into her eyes, the rest of the crowd faded away, and it seemed as though they were the only two people in the place. He could feel every inch of her stretched out against his long frame. From her breasts to her thighs, she was pressed tightly against him, and because she was minus many of the fancy petticoats and other undergarments worn by most young ladies, there was little left to the imagination.

Just as it had the afternoon he'd first met her at the beach, his desire for her burned away all rational thought. He wanted her as he'd never wanted another woman. She had to feel his aroused state, and the shameful thing was, he didn't care. What he wanted more than anything was to flex his hips, hoping to ease some of his ache against the V of her thighs.

Maggie had thought the night couldn't possibly get any more marvelous, but it had. The pressure of his broad chest wedged so tightly against her own caused her breasts to swell painfully. They were full and aching, her nipples hard and erect, and even though they poked against his shirt, there was no easing of the heat she was feeling.

Wantonly, she wriggled closer and felt what she knew was his aroused member pushing against her stomach. Knowing she kindled such hot desire increased her excitement to unbearable heights.

For a heady moment, she wondered if she should offer herself to him. To give him a gift of her virginity so she would always remember that he had been the first. Her virtue was not something she cherished or pined away to protect for some future

nameless, faceless husband. As her mother and Anne had told
her many times, sometimes the *right* man might come along,
but he would never be able to marry you. That was simply the
way of their world. Wasn't it best to give herself to someone
like Aston whom she cherished with her whole being?

Adam tried to move slightly to break the intense body contact
between them, but before he could make any change in their
position, Maggie wrapped her arms more tightly around his
shoulders.

She whispered, "Hold me closer."

He groaned low in his throat and complied, whispering in
return, "You don't know what you're doing to me."

"Yes, I do. Don't let go."

"I won't."

Maggie rested her cheek against the center of his chest, her
ear pressed over his heart, where she could hear it beating
steadily. She closed her eyes and held on as Aston slowly
twirled her in small circles in time with the music. The sounds
of the barn lowered and dimmed until there was nothing left
to hear but the night around them. Whether by accident or
design, she didn't know or care, they'd danced their way out
of the barn and across the yard.

The full moon was up in the sky, shining down so brightly
that the farmyard looked to be flooded with daylight. A few
well-placed lanterns glowed down the long drive toward the
main road. Carriages were parked on both sides as far as Maggie
could see, and an occasional couple strolled past as they came
or went from the barn. For the most part, though, they were
alone. Aston carefully shifted her weight so that her uninjured
foot touched solid ground, but she balanced herself against him,
loving the excuse to continue leaning close.

As Maggie raised her face to smile at him, he was certain
he saw a hint of deep emotion in her eyes. Although he agreed
with James that he was not always an astute man when it came
to dealing with women, he could easily read her message.
Perhaps she was in love with him, or thought she was; it would

certainly be typical enough for a young woman like herself to think such a thing about an older man who had showered her with the attention he had the past few days.

The realization that she cared for him pleased him, but frightened him at the same time. He was glad to know that she felt the same bond drawing them together, to know that she was experiencing some of the same incredible sensations of everything being just right. But he was also afraid of how hurt she would be when they parted in a few days. He'd certainly been careful in the time he'd spent with her not to give her the impression that this was more than a holiday encounter, but she was quite young. Chances were good that she wouldn't understand.

The very last thing in the world he wanted to do was hurt someone for whom he felt such deep regard.

Unable to resist, he ran a hand across her hair, which appeared to be white-blond in the moonlight. "Would you sit with me for a few minutes?" he asked.

"I'd like that very much."

Adam looked around and saw a bench in front of the nearby farmhouse. While much of the yard was brightly lit, it was in deep shadows. They could enjoy a private moment without anyone seeing them. "How about there?"

Together, they walked to the bench, although Adam had his arm around her waist and nearly carried her. Her hip and leg were braced against his, and he couldn't get over the feeling of how well she seemed to fit next to him. The bench was a small one, and there wasn't any place for him to sit except right next to her with their thighs and knees touching. He rested his arm across the back and turned to her. "I thought we should talk for a moment."

"I don't want to talk." Maggie enjoyed seeing the look of surprise he flashed her. She'd thought about it long and hard, and she wasn't about to let the entire evening pass without something wonderful happening. "I know this sounds terribly forward of me, but I've never been kissed before and I was wondering if . . .'' Whatever courage she possessed deserted her. It was easy to think about flirting with a man, but the reality was that she'd never done it and wasn't sure how to accomplish her goal.

"If what?"

She bit her bottom lip, staring up into his beautiful brown eyes. He was so close now that she could see the twinkle of the lamp lights reflecting in them. His breath brushed across her face. She said, "I was wondering if you would kiss me."

All thought he'd had of a serious talk vanished. What could it hurt to give her one little kiss? That was what he'd been dying to do since the moment he'd first set eyes on her. He shifted, moved his arm from the back of the bench, and laid it across her shoulders. "Close your eyes."

Sitting perfectly still, she did as he asked. With every fiber of her being she wanted to reach forward and wrap her arms around him, but she'd already flagrantly asked for a kiss, so she forced herself to patiently wait for it. "Like this?"

"Yes. Just like that." Adam leaned forward, touching his mouth to hers. Her lips were soft and warm and tasted of the berry punch they'd been drinking. The simple, intimate touch was as enchanting as he'd imagined. He pulled away slightly, hovering near so her sweet breath could move over his face. At the break of contact, her eyes fluttered open, her long lashes slowly rising to frame her exquisite violet eyes.

Maggie thought her heart might burst. Touching the tips of her fingers to her lips, as though she could keep the taste of him there forever, she then reached out and laid the same fingers against his heart. His was thundering as briskly as her own. "There's something between us, isn't there?" she said. "You feel it, too."

He wanted to deny it, but with her looking at him with such open affection, he couldn't lie. "It's something I've never felt before."

"It's quite wonderful."

"Very wonderful, but Maggie . . ." His conscience was getting the better of him. No matter how he tried to disguise his behavior, he was playing with her, and it was time to put an end to the game.

Whatever he was going to say, she couldn't bear to hear. She raised her fingers from his heart to his lips, stopping his next utterance. "I don't want to hear any words of caution or regret from you."

"We need to talk."

"About what?"

"About this . . ." He gestured between them, unable to find the words to adequately describe the emotion that seemed to flare whenever they were together. "*Whatever* this is between us, nothing can come of it. I've already taken incredible liberties with you, and I feel like a cad. You've no parents around to offer guidance, and it's allowed me to take complete advantage."

"You've not done anything I didn't want you to do."

"But I'm afraid I've given you the wrong idea."

"In what way?"

"I can tell that you're hoping for more. But there can't be."

"Have I asked you for more?"

"No." Surprisingly, he was upset to realize that she hadn't. When was the last time a woman hadn't asked anything of him?

"Then why are you worried?"

"Because you're young and inexperienced, and I'm afraid I'll end up hurting you."

"I may be young and inexperienced, but I'm not stupid." Maggie sighed. "I knew from the moment I met you that there could never be anything between us. Men like you simply don't fall into the lives of women like me. I'm well aware that this is real life, and not some fairy tale, but simply because we can't ride off into the sunset together doesn't mean that I should deny what I feel for you. We're so very, very lucky that we met. I'll remember you fondly every day of my life."

"Oh, Maggie, you sweet girl." He shifted away, moving his arm from around her shoulder and leaning forward with both elbows braced on his thighs. His face resting on his hands, he stared out across the yard, and through the lights coming out of the barn, he was certain he saw James and Anne slipping off into the woods for a lovers' tryst. That he could do the same with Maggie!

He muttered more to himself than to her, "Dear Lord, how I hate my life!"

She rested a palm between his shoulder blades and rubbed in small, gentle circles. "Are you married?"

He shook his head, not looking at her. "No, but I will be soon."

So that was the way of it. "Is that why you're so unhappy?"

"What makes you think I'm unhappy?"

"I'm not sure why, but it seems as if I know many things about you. Don't you love her?"

Thinking of Penelope Westmoreland, and the others like her, with all their plotting and pretense, he shrugged, then shifted to face Maggie once again. "I always hoped I would find a wife who could make me feel the way you do."

"And how is that?"

"You make me feel strong and kind and good. You make me feel that your world is complete only because I am in it and I'm the very best thing that ever happened to you."

"I believe you're all those things. And more." Maggie reached for both his hands and laced her fingers through his. "You know, my mother always said that some people are destined to love one another. That their hearts and minds move on a similar plane which is shared by no one else. Perhaps that's what has happened between us."

Earlier, as Adam had watched her from across the crowded barn, he'd been thinking very much the same thing, but with the words coming from her own lips, he refused to credit what she'd said. If he did, it would require him to believe in the typical woman's fantasy of romantic love, which he did not. It would mean that she was most likely the one and only acceptable companion he'd find in his life. It would also mean that his search for an acceptable mate was futile, and his future even bleaker than it already appeared. "Your mother must have been quite the romantic," he said.

"In many ways, she was, but she was also a realist. I've inherited a little of both from her. That's why I refuse to feel regret or shame or anything else except impossible gladness that we met." In the most brazen fashion, she raised her hands around his neck and leaned forward so her breasts were fully resting against his chest. "Kiss me again, please. As though it's the only time you'll ever have the chance."

How could he refuse? With her plump breasts rubbing against him, her thighs pressed against his own, her radiant eyes beseeching, what else was there to do? All his firm resolve flew out the window.

This time, when he lowered his mouth to hers, there was no hesitation on her part, no innocent waiting, no passive acceptance. This time, she met his kiss with a ferocity that equaled his own. And he was lost.

His lips covered hers, hot and demanding. Wanting more and never having enough, his tongue begged entrance, and she invited him inside, her own dueling instantly with his. A distant growl rumbled, and he realized the sound was coming from his own throat. He sucked on her tongue, bringing it deeper into his mouth, his own plunging in and out, again and again, imitating the primal rhythm he wanted to employ with his swollen phallus.

Across her hair, her shoulders, her waist, her hips, his hands roamed at will. Somehow, she ended up on his lap, her small round buttocks pressed against his raging manhood, and he was finally able to ease his groin against her. It didn't help. He needed to be buried deep inside.

Busy fingers moved from her hip, back to her neck, his thumb working against the pulse that pounded at the base of her throat. Tangled in her hair, he tipped her back over his arm, as he finally abandoned her mouth to nibble his way under her chin, down her neck to her bosom. He nuzzled against her breasts, through the fabric of her dress. Wanting more and never having enough, he slipped a hand under the bodice where her erect nipple pebbled against the center of his palm.

Maggie was certain she'd died and gone to heaven. Everything he was doing was so overwhelming that any inhibitions she might have harbored were completely gone. When his hand slipped under her bodice to search and find her nipple, she wanted to sob with relief that he'd finally touched her where she wanted to be touched. Her breasts were full and throbbing, and she knew that he could put his mouth there and ease some of her agony.

With a flick of his wrist, he bared a breast to his view. It was as beautiful as he'd known it would be. Her pouty nipple, round and full, begging for his attention, he paused long enough to raise his eyes to hers.

"My God, Maggie, but you're so lovely." Lowering his mouth, he ran a slow hot tongue across her, then pulled her nipple far inside.

Swallowing a cry of pleasure low in her throat, she arched her back, offering up as much of herself as he would take. Her hands sifted through his hair and pulled him close, closer, and he suckled greedily. A desperate pulsing started between her legs. She was wet and hurting and wanting so much more from him than this.

His lips left their mark, and she groaned aloud, but her cry of protest was stifled as he quickly made his way back to claim her mouth. Their tongues sparred until he pulled away, working across her eyes, her forehead, a cheek, an ear, where he inhaled deeply of the lilac scent of her hair. "I want you, little one. I want you so badly."

"Then take me. I am yours. Take me away from here and love me as you would like to do. To the woods, or your room, or the beach. Anywhere. Just say the word and I will go anywhere you ask."

The desire he felt was stronger than anything he'd ever imagined he could feel for a woman, but he was a rational man and, amazingly, the reasoning part of his brain was still working. He simply could not have her. Gripping her tightly, his breath coming hard as though he'd run a long race, he smoothed a hand across her hair while he calmed his surging impulses.

From the first moment he'd laid eyes on her, he'd dabbled with the idea of taking her, thinking he could use her for a few days of pleasure, revel in her sweet and trusting nature, and then cast her aside when it came time to return to London. Now, with the opportunity for physical intimacy staring him in the face, he realized his folly. To have her was to hurt her, and he simply could not do it.

"I can't, little one."

"Yes, you can. It's something I want very, very much."

"You can't know what you're asking. It could never be more than a quick romp in the forest. You deserve so much more than that."

"Let's not talk of what I *deserve*. I only know what I want. I want you to lie with me, to show me how it can be."

"No, Maggie, you only think you want to do this now, but later, when you realize all you gave to me, you'd hate me."

It was on the tip of her tongue to tell him the real truth about herself—that she might have been a maid but was hardly innocent in the ways of men and women—but she'd already fabricated such an intricate lie about Rose and their life that she could hardly change the tale at this moment in their relationship.

Instead, she rested a palm against his cheek. "I could never hate you for anything. No matter what you did, I would always love you. I *do* love you. With all my heart."

He winced at her declaration. What a fool's path he'd trod! She was little more than a girl, and he'd inappropriately courted attention on her. He was ashamed with himself, for he knew better than to behave so, and the time had come to take matters in hand. "That is exactly the reason we can't take this any further. I am older and wiser in these matters, and I can see that your innocent heart has led you to believe that an emotional attachment has developed between us."

"Don't lie, Aston. You may not be able to speak about it aloud, but I know you feel the same things I do. For whatever reason, we share deep feelings for one another. Denying them won't make them any less real."

"I was wrong to let this get started. I'll not let it go on." Holding back his moan of regret, he shifted her bodice until her breast was once again hidden from his view. Not trusting himself to be alone with her any longer, he set her on her feet, then stood beside her, saying, "Let's return to the barn."

Maggie stared up at him, wondering how he could so quickly move from the throes of passion to this brooding, stately gentleman. Her own body still felt as though it was on fire. She slipped her hand in his. "Don't be angry with me."

"I'm not angry."

He gave her the half smile she'd come to expect. "Then pardon me for acting so brazen."

"No pardon is necessary. I've enjoyed every minute with you. It is simply the fact of my life that I cannot have the things I truly, truly desire."

The regret in his voice was so great that she couldn't resist the urge to comfort. She wrapped her arms around his waist and held him as tightly as she could. "It will be all right," she said. "I know it will."

Adam didn't respond. He held her for a time, then shifted away. "We'd better go back inside."

Chapter Six

James pulled Anne into his arms and kissed her thoroughly. His hands roamed across her hair, her shoulders, her arms, her back. Shifting lower, he grabbed her buttocks with both hands and, moving in the same rhythm as his tongue, he stroked her mound back and forth across his pained manhood.

She groaned low in her throat as James pushed her back against a nearby tree. After they had spent the night dancing and holding one another, she could no longer ignore the desire raging between them. Needing the contact as much as he did, she reveled in the sensations as he worked his enlarged member against her.

His hands left her backside and rose to lower the bodice of her gown, and her breasts swung free. They filled his hands, and he rubbed his thumbs over the swollen nipples. Wrenching his lips from hers, he struggled to control his breathing as he applied more pressure, causing her to squirm.

"You like that, do you?" he said with a chuckle.

"It's been a long time for me."

"For me, too." For while he regularly consorted with whores

and other women of dubious character, he couldn't remember when a woman had raised his desire to such frightening heights. As he touched his lips to her bosom, he whispered, "Oh, my beautiful Annie."

The moon gleamed off his brown hair, and she shifted her fingers through it, loving the texture. As he sucked one nipple, then the other into his mouth, she pulled him closer, wanting more and never getting enough.

He kissed his way up the swell of her breast, her neck, her chin, to take small love bites against her bottom lip. "I want you, Anne. But not here. Not like this. Come back with me to the inn. Come to my room when everyone is asleep."

His request wasn't a surprise. After all, she was an experienced consort and had been since the age of fifteen. What he offered would have been so easy to accept, yet she hesitated. "Oh, James, I don't know . . ."

"Say yes," he whispered, continuing the pressure on her nipples. "Say you'll come to me. Let me love you in my bed all night long. I want to hold you in my arms until dawn, and together we'll watch the sun rise through my window."

Anne was torn. She wanted this more than anything, but knew with absolute certainty that nothing good could come from it. She sighed. "I just can't."

"Why, love? You're a widow, I'm a grown man. There's no one to know but us." With a sudden revelation, he laid a hand on her stomach. "If you're worried about a babe, I promise I'll be careful."

Anne smiled, thoroughly enchanted that he would concern himself with such a thing. He reminded her so much of her beloved Stephen, whom she still missed every moment of every day. "It's not that, although it is kind of you to think of such things."

"Then what? I know you want me as badly as I do you."

"Well, I believe I would want to make love more than once."

With a lusty laugh, he reached for her hand and pressed it to his manhood. "I think I can guarantee a stunning performance of numerous enjoyments. Once will definitely not be enough with you.''

''I didn't mean it that way.'' Anne couldn't help but smile, but how to explain without giving herself away? ''I care for you, James. I can't imagine loving you for one night but never being able to enjoy your company again. It would simply hurt me too much.''

At her words, James stopped the sexual movement of his hips, his gaze intense. ''It doesn't have to be for only one night.''

Anne felt certain he was about to say things he didn't mean, perhaps whispered professions of love and commitment, in order to lure her to his room. She placed her fingers against his lips to silence him. ''Please, don't say anything to me that isn't true, James. You see, I know who you really are, so I understand how limited our involvement would have to be.''

''Whatever are you talking about?''

''I know you're not James Carrington. You're James St. Clair, and your brother is Adam St. Clair.''

''But that means . . .'' He gazed across the woods in the direction of the barn, immediately wondering if they were somehow scheming against Adam.

Anne laid a hand against his chest. ''Don't look so worried. I haven't told Maggie who he is.''

''Why not?''

''Because I wanted her to have her first romance. They're so drawn to one another, and I was afraid if she knew Adam's true identity that she'd not give him the time of day.''

Unbelieving, he raised a mocking brow. ''The infamous Marquis of Belmont? Preposterous.''

''Not really. She's received some fairly abominable treatment at the hands of some of your peers.'' She was thinking of Maggie's father, the Duke of Roswell. ''She truly believes Adam to be Aston Carrington, a gentleman's assistant from Portsmouth. If she knew differently, I'm not sure she'd have wanted to get to know him better.''

"Now, that's a switch. Every woman in London is throwing themselves at him. It's really been quite a stressful time."

"Is that why you're here?"

"Yes, we ran away, like two naughty schoolboys. It's turned out to be the best idea. I haven't seen Adam so happy or relaxed in years."

"It's been good for Maggie, also, to learn how it can be with a man. Her mother and I tried to explain it many times, but it's hard to understand until it happens."

Anne shivered slightly in the cool night air, and James leaned forward to enfold her in his arms, running his hands up and down her back. "You're a strange pair, Anne Porter. Aren't you worried that she'll return home with a broken heart?"

"She's tougher than you know, and she understands better than anyone exactly what's happening."

"And what is that?"

Without batting an eye, she said, "He's simply toying with her until he finds something better to do."

James could hardly deny it. "Is that what you think I'm doing with you?"

"It's exactly what you're doing with me." To ease the harsh sting of her words, because she didn't mean them to sound so severe, she rose and kissed him lightly on the lips. "But, please, let's be honest about it. 'Tis the reason I can't join you in your bed. I would want more than you could ever give me; I can feel it in my heart, and I refuse to start something we can't finish."

"But Annie, I am not Adam. I can see any woman I wish. You are a widow. There's no reason I can't call on you when we return to London."

"There's every reason."

"Name one."

Very gently, she removed his arms from around her and tucked her breasts back into her dress. Undoubtedly, he wouldn't want to continue when he knew what type of woman she really was, and she hated having to admit it. She'd hoped he would only have fond memories of her when they parted at the end of their holiday. "Don't you wonder how I know who you are?"

"Yes, as a matter of fact. I can't recall ever meeting you previously."

"You did. On one occasion. It was at a ball hosted by your Aunt Lavinia in honor of your cousin Charles's twenty-fifth birthday. I attended with a good friend of mine, Stephen Frasier . . ."

"I remember!" James declared. "You were wearing a dark green gown, made of velvet. With gold piping, here and here"—he made a slashing motion across her chest and shoulders—"and your hair was longer than it is now, swept up on your head. You were so lovely. I was jealous of him all evening." He played with a lock of her hair. "How did you know Stephen?"

"As I said, he was a good friend." She waited for the realization to sink in, but it didn't seem to, so she said, "A very, very good friend."

"You were his lover?"

"More than that."

"His mistress?" She nodded once, quickly, and he added, "I remember now that I'd heard he was keeping someone. But why do you think this would make a difference to me?"

"Because he was not the only one. I first contracted with a gentleman when I was fifteen. There have been several since then." She looked down at the ground, irritated with herself for being embarrassed about the course of her life. She'd made the only available choices at the time and wasn't about to justify or apologize for them. A man in James's position would never understand.

"I see," he said tightly, incensed that they'd spent almost two glorious days together, and she'd lied about everything. The fact that he'd lied as well was easily overlooked in his hasty attempt to convince himself that she was nothing but a well-paid prostitute. "Is Anne Porter your true name?"

"Yes." Anne could tell from his tone that he was angry, but she refused to be shamed by her past, especially when it had led her to Stephen and the great love they had shared. "But now you understand why I can't lie with you."

"Not really. It seems to be your life's calling, lifting your skirts for whichever man has enough coin to tempt you." Not knowing what had come over him, for it was simply not in his nature to be rude to a woman, he was enraged at the thought of her with other men, even someone he'd known and liked as well as Stephen Frasier. He wanted to lash out, and he did. "Would it make you more agreeable if I paid you for it?"

As though he'd slapped her, Anne stepped back. "Don't play the bastard with me, James St. Clair. I've been mistreated by better than the likes of you, and I'm not about to stand for it." She turned away, straightening her dress and her hair, hiding her furious tears from his assessing gaze. Once she'd gained control of her emotions, she faced him again. "What I had intended to say was that I couldn't join you in your bed because I believed I might fall in love with you after I did. I can see I was mistaken; I could never develop any kind of *tendre* for a horse's ass such as yourself."

Without waiting for a response, she headed toward the farm-yard.

"What are you doing?" Adam asked of his brother as he stepped through the door connecting his room to James's. His portmanteau was packed, and the stable boy had brought their horses round to the side door of the inn. There was no use in delaying their departure a moment longer.

"I'm writing a note to Anne Porter."

"Whatever for?"

"To tell her good-bye."

"I asked you not to." Adam had wanted to leave as discreetly as possible.

"I know, but I owe her an apology. I said something hideous to her last evening."

"I wondered about the tension between the two of you on the ride home. I thought you were getting on nicely."

"We were, but then I managed to make a complete ass of myself."

"Still, James, what's the point? You'll not see her again."

"So? I've always prided myself on being a gentleman. I can't leave without telling her I'm sorry, and I'm embarrassed to admit that I'm too much of a coward to face her." James looked up from his writing table. "What about you? Will you leave without a word to Maggie?"

Adam shrugged, trying to look dispassionate as he ran his fingers over a small figurine on the windowsill. "What could I possibly say?"

"How about something that would make your leave-taking less harsh? That you've been called away? That you're sorry to depart so quickly, but you have to go, and that you cherished meeting her?"

"No. She'd only ask what had called me away, and I'd have to fabricate some story or other. I've already told her too many lies to count."

Staring out the window, he gazed longingly at the blue waves crashing to shore down below. What he wouldn't give to be able to stay through the final days of Maggie's holiday, but he couldn't. Problems had begun the previous night after they'd returned to the barn. He'd left her sitting on a bench while he'd gone to search for James and Anne to see if they were ready to leave.

While walking through the crowd, he'd run into a wedding guest with whom he was acquainted, a wealthy merchant who handled some of the St. Clair family's shipping business. The man happened to have his two unwed daughters with him, and of course, Adam had had to suffer through the introductions. By the time he departed with Maggie on his arm, he could feel the buzz through the crowd as his identity had quickly passed from one person to the next.

That morning, when Adam came downstairs to eat in the inn's dining room, the local squire just happened to be present—with his niece in tow. More introductions followed, plus an invitation to join the squire's party for breakfast, which he could not politely refuse. As a consequence, he'd spent nearly an hour being regaled about the niece's finer points.

His feelings for Maggie were confused and odd, but one thing was certain: He did not want to hurt her. If she was sitting next to him and heard him addressed by his true name or title, what would she think? How would she react if, during the final two days of her stay, they ran into a doting father who wanted to introduce his daughter? How would Adam explain what was happening? What would she say if she was suddenly faced with the cold, hard fact that he had lied about everything?

Surely, it was better to let her return to London and her life there with her memory and feelings intact. A selfish part of him wanted that. To know that Maggie always remembered him fondly. It was the coward's way out, but he couldn't think of a better way to end it.

"She's terribly young, Adam," James pointed out. "Don't you think she'll be hurt if you just disappear without a fare-thee-well?"

"A good-bye will hurt her more."

"But wouldn't you like to see her again? I thought perhaps you could explain the true situation to her, beg her forgiveness. Then, you'd be able to continue seeing her in London."

"To what purpose?"

James shook his head at his brother's obtuseness. "Simply because it would make you happy. Need you a better reason than that?"

"You are such a romantic, James. You know I could not, in good conscience, shower any attention on her. She certainly has the looks and demeanor to fit in to Polite Society, but she's an innocent. If she appeared in public on my arm, she'd be swept up in the hurricane of attention which follows me. The women of our circle would eat her alive, and she'd only be humiliated in the end. I could never offer her any serious emotional engagement, which is what she would want. And what she deserves."

"Have you asked her what she wants? Perhaps she cares about you enough to put up with some of the bad in order to enjoy some of the good."

Adam had thought of it, but he didn't dare ask her. "She's young, James. Too young to know her own mind or to realistically assess the circumstances. She might think we could have an innocent flirtation, but you know it couldn't be done with one such as she. As it stands now, she already fancies herself half in love with me." Adam didn't dare admit, even to himself, that he was also half in love with her. "And I can't do anything to make it worse. I've taken enough advantage of her naivete as it is."

"So, set her up as your mistress. Keep her by your side."

"You know I'd never do such a thing to Mother or my bride-to-be."

"Your loss, I'd say."

The dig was a deep one, and Adam refused to respond. "Let's be off. I want to depart before some other daughter is shoved in my face."

Anne answered the knock on the door of the room she and Maggie shared. One of the proprietor's sons stood there with a sealed piece of paper in his hand. With a polite smile, she accepted the missive and closed the door.

"What is it?" Maggie asked from across the room where she practiced hobbling about with the walking stick Aston had given her as a gift.

Anne's brow wrinkled as she pushed her thumb through the seal and looked at the bold signature scrawled across the bottom.

"It's from James." With that curt explanation, she tossed it, unread, on the small writing table.

Maggie regarded her critically. Anne had been dreadfully silent ever since they'd left the dance, and Maggie had had the decency to let her stew over whatever had happened. It didn't take a genius to know that it involved James. She asked gently, "Aren't you a little curious?"

"No. I've no wish to hear anything the man has to say."

Maggie nodded thoughtfully. "Well, I'm dying to know what he's penned. Do you mind?" Anne didn't respond, silently going to stand by the window while Maggie scanned the contents of the short note. "It says he's terribly sorry. That he behaved abominably." Maggie looked across the room at the stiff set of Anne's shoulders, but no explanation was forthcoming. "He begs your pardon and hopes if he ever runs into you again that you'll be able to say you've forgiven him."

"Not bloody likely," she muttered.

"He seemed so nice, Annie. What did he do?"

"Nothing except show his true colors. He's a contemptible snake in the grass." The thought of his trying to apologize with a pitiful note brought her temper to the flash point. "What else did the bastard write?"

"It says . . . they've gone back to . . . London?"

"Good riddance," Anne snorted. "To the two of them. We've enough troubles without bringing the likes of them into our lives."

"I thought they were from . . ."

"Portsmouth?" Anne glanced over her shoulder at a confused and bewildered Maggie. "No. They're from London."

"But why would they lie about something like that?"

"Because they consider us so far below their lofty station," she responded bitterly, "that they didn't want us to know who they are."

"I thought they were Aston and James Carrington."

Anne sighed and sat down on the bed. She'd meant to break the news to Maggie gently, not have her learn it like this.

Perhaps after the holiday had ended and her first love had long departed. The last thing Anne wanted to do was take out her anger on Maggie, but she was still so upset by James's behavior that it took extra effort to calm herself.

She motioned her friend to the chair next to the bed, and Maggie sat down. "They are Adam St. Clair and his younger brother, James. Adam is the—"

Maggie cut her off. "The Marquis of Belmont? That Adam St. Clair?"

"Yes, I'm afraid so."

"Are you certain?"

"Yes."

"How long have you known?"

"Well, I was curious the first day when Adam carried you upstairs after you'd cut your foot; he looked so familiar. But it was when I met James. He'd gone to school as a lad with Stephen, and I met him once at a party."

"Why didn't you say anything?"

"Because you and Adam hit it off so quickly and so well. I wanted you to enjoy yourself. I thought if you knew his true background, that you'd not give him the time of day." Anne reached out a hand to Maggie. "I'm sorry. I thought it was important to keep their secret."

Maggie wanted to be angry with Anne, but she couldn't be. Anne always tried to do the right thing, even to the point of jeopardizing her own future by staying to take care of Rose in her final days. Maggie reached forward and took Anne's offered hand, giving it a squeeze of encouragement. "I'm not angry. Not at you, anyway." She scanned the note again, her own temper beginning to flare in conjunction with Anne's. "Those rats! Playing with us, then sneaking off like a pair of thieves in the night! Why would they act in such a way?"

"It's the kind of people they are. There are plenty of men in their class who are true gentlemen, but for each one, there are a dozen more who are cads."

"But they both seemed so sincere."

"Of course they did. They've so much practice at saying one thing and meaning another. Their entire lives are lived that way. Look at your father and what he did to Rose."

Maggie's emotions warred with each other, and she couldn't decide if she was more sad or angry. While she'd known she was destined to suffer a broken heart in two days' time when she and Anne left for London, she'd thought it would be because of how much she'd miss Aston—no, Adam. She'd not expected this . . . this . . . deception and intrigue.

She turned James's letter back and forth in her hand.

"What are you looking for?" Anne asked.

"I thought maybe . . ." She was embarrassed to have Anne realize the state of her own naivete. She'd believed everything Adam had told her. She blushed bright red. "Well, maybe that he'd added a note or something for me. But he didn't."

Everything had been a lie. Innocent though she was, she wanted to tell herself that only his background and name had been fabricated. That the emotional attachment she'd felt with him had been real. But she knew better. All of it was untrue. Every bit. Even his pretending affection. How he must have laughed at her foolish romantic statements!

"I'm sorry, Maggie," Anne said. "I never meant for it to end like this."

"I know. It's just . . . My Lord, to think I nearly slept with the man."

"Truly?"

"Yes. Last night. I practically threw myself at him."

"Why didn't you go through with it?"

Anne had been so upset when they'd arrived home from the dance that Maggie hadn't had the opportunity to discuss the evening's events. She looked up at Anne with sorrowful eyes. "He refused me."

"Perhaps there's a remnant of conscience beating under that thick exterior after all."

"I doubt that. He must have his pick of women. What would he want with the likes of me? The thought of an inexperienced virgin probably bored him silly.'' Tears suddenly flooded to her eyes. Knowing him had meant something to her. The fact that it hadn't meant anything to him was the worst humiliation of all.

"I know you're confused and hurting now"—Anne rose from the bed and stepped to the chair, kneeling down beside her—"but this has been a good lesson for you."

"Yes, it has. I'll hate all men forever."

"No, silly goose." Anne chuckled. "You need to make good choices. The right man will come. You just need to be sure you toss aside all the rogues before you reach him."

"I feel so bad."

"I know, but it will pass. Give it time. In the meantime, we've only two days left of our holiday, and I refuse to let them ruin whatever time remains. What would you like to do today?"

"I hadn't really thought about it. Give me a few minutes?"

"Certainly." Anne patted her knee, then stood. "I just remembered . . . I need to make our reservation for dinner. I'll just run down and be back shortly."

Maggie gave her a weak smile as Anne left the room, appreciating the chance for privacy. She scanned James's letter again, then hobbled to the window and looked out. The sun shone brightly. The waves, blue and inviting, crashed down below, but she hardly noticed any of it. The day appeared gray and dreary.

She kissed her fingertips and waved them toward the road that was at that very moment returning Adam to his real life in London. She vowed, "I'll miss you. Every day and forever."

With that, she turned away and forced a smile to her lips. By the time Anne returned to their room, she was determined to appear happy so her friend would not know how desperately her heart was breaking.

Chapter Seven

Maggie quietly opened the door to her home, hoping Anne was out or otherwise occupied so that they wouldn't have to immediately discuss what a frustrating day it had been. There was always the slight chance that Anne had found a position, but Maggie was beginning to despair. The spark of hope that they'd harbored of finding suitable employment had dwindled.

Her feet swollen and aching, she felt as though she'd walked from one end of London to the other since leaving early that morning, but the lengthy distances couldn't be helped. In less than three weeks, they were supposed to be living elsewhere even though they had no money to make the move a reality. George was prepared to turn them out onto the street if need be; he hadn't changed his mind.

Originally, the three-month time period that he'd given them to find other arrangements had seemed like such a long time, but now, with the deadline staring them in the face, the days had passed lightning fast. Although neither of them had admitted to it yet, they were both secretly starting to panic.

Maggie had begun her search for a job by contacting the

women's shops where Rose had shopped over the years. All of the owners were kind and concerned, but none of them had an opening. One proprietor had offered to put out another girl in order to make room for Maggie. The fact that Maggie had briefly considered agreeing to such a thing only confirmed how desperate her situation had become. Her conscience won out at the last minute, and she'd turned down the woman's suggestion.

After contacting the shopkeepers she knew, she began talking to those she didn't know. While certainly not an expert, she'd always had an eye for color and fashion, and thought she could bluff her way through in a position as a clerk. Her looks and the way she carried herself always got her in the door, but not a single proprietor would take a chance on her without experience. Times were hard, and there were simply too many women needing employment. No one had to hire someone who'd not worked before.

She'd tried to interview for a few positions as governess, but without references, no one would consider her. One gentleman had let her in the door, but from his comments, it was clear he'd expect more than nanny skills if she was hired. She'd fended off his advance that came at the end of the interview and ran from the house with her skirts flying.

With her options quickly dwindling, she'd taken to walking the streets of every respectable neighborhood and even the streets of those that weren't. Starting early and continuing through the day, she went from one shop to the next, not caring so much about what type of wares were sold in a place as much as the possibility that someone might hire her. Maggie's confidence, as well as her pride, had taken a severe beating in the process. For while she received many offers, none of them had to do with gainful employment.

Two months had passed since their disastrous holiday at the beach. Two months in which she and Anne had knocked on doors, begged for help, asked for the return of old favors. All to no avail. Maggie could not find employment anywhere. Neither could Anne. In a matter of days, George would turn

them out on the street with only their clothes and the handful
of coins they'd managed to stash away.

Anne appeared at the top of the stairs and slowly worked
her way down. When she reached the bottom, although it was
painfully clear from Maggie's demeanor that there was no news,
she asked, "Any luck?"

"No. How about you?"

"Madame LeBlanc was extremely polite when she informed
me that I was certainly pretty enough but that I was simply too
old to work in her fine establishment. I'll be thirty years in a
few months. I'd nearly be old enough to be a mother to many
of her customers."

Maggie shook her head in commiseration, but couldn't help
being secretly relieved. The thought of beautiful, sweet Anne
having to go to work in a brothel was just unthinkable. "I
won't say I'm sorry. I can't bear the thought of you in one of
those places."

"The fancier ones aren't so bad," Anne insisted with more
enthusiasm than she felt. She was ready to make the jump to
full-time prostitute. The older and more practical of the two,
Anne saw the deadline approaching much quicker than Maggie
did. She'd accept any offer that kept them off the streets, feeling
that once they lost their home, there'd be no hope for either
of them.

"Oh Anne, what a state our world has come to. I can't
believe we're even having this conversation."

"I know. It does seem a bit like a dream, doesn't it?" Anne
took Maggie's hand. "I've just made tea. Let's have a cup and
see if things don't look brighter after we've finished."

Together, they went and sat on the two worn chairs in the
parlor. Maggie rested her head against the back and closed her
eyes, listening to the noise from the street drift through the
windows. The sounds and rhythms were soothing, and by the
time she'd emptied her cup, she felt better.

Opening her eyes, she watched Anne staring serenely out at
the hustle and bustle. The sunlight of the late afternoon glowed

in her face, making her look young and vibrant, and Maggie couldn't help thinking again how lucky she was that Anne was part of her life. How much more frightening the situation would be if she was all alone!

Maggie broke the companionable silence. "I have an idea. I've been thinking about it for a few days now, and I was wondering what you would think."

"What is it?"

Swallowing hard, she forged ahead before her courage failed. "Perhaps I should let George introduce me to some of his friends . . . as he offered to do in the beginning." Anne sat quietly, not offering any comment, which caused Maggie to feel a desperate need to fill the silent void. "It would certainly solve all our troubles. And if I met someone like Adam St. Clair, I know I could tolerate what I would have to do to pull it off."

Anne smiled at Maggie's bit of naivete. There were few men like the St. Clair brothers around. Not with their wealth, looks, and charm. But still, the idea had merit. She laughed softly. "I have a confession to make," Anne said.

"What's that?"

"I asked George to do that very thing. Only for me. I thought perhaps I could find a position with a gentleman for myself."

"What did he say?"

"He and Madame LeBlanc have something in common. They both think I'm too old."

"You're eight years younger than Mother. He certainly took up with her quickly enough."

"I know, but I didn't think I was in any position to point out such a thing."

"I suppose not."

They both laughed at the ludicrousness of their situation, until their mirth gave way to another long silence. Finally, Maggie said, "So . . . what do you think? Would you hate me if I did such a thing? I know you and Mother wanted so much

more for me, but I can't think of what's to become of us if I
don't try."

"Maggie, how could I hate you for doing what I spent most
of my life doing? It's the state of our world that we have to
find a way to get by. The very fact that we're women narrows
our choices. I can't be angry with anything you choose to do
if it will help get us out of this mess."

"Is it so awful?"

"It can be or not. It depends on the gentleman. I'm older
now, and much more experienced. If you received an offer, I
could help you decide if you should accept it."

Maggie closed her eyes and whispered a short prayer. Who
would ever have thought her life would come to this? Resigned,
she sighed. "Let's do it. How do I begin?"

Anne reached across and gave her hand a supportive pat.
"First, we'll send a message to George that we want him to
start talking to his friends. Then, you and I need to start working
on your wardrobe."

"You make it sound simple enough."

Anne chuckled, for it was really going to be amazingly
effortless. Maggie's lack of conceit kept her from realizing
what a beauty she was. Anne had no doubt that many gentlemen
would consider snatching her up—even those who hadn't
known they were looking for a mistress—once they had the
good fortune to set eyes on her. "Trust me, it will be incredibly
easy."

Adam followed the crowd up the walk and into the mansion.
A servant stood ready to relieve him of his hat and cloak. He
handed them over silently and turned to the stairs, ready to
make the climb to the grand ballroom. Feeling like a condemned
man, he took the steps slowly as though the gallows awaited
him at the top.

Each time he attended one of these affairs, he hated them
more. The shallow conversations, the insipid women, the boast-

ful parents. Since his journey to the beach in May, it had only gotten worse. He'd taken the trip as a lark, hoping a few days of frolic and play would relieve some of the tension and drudgery of his days. The attempt hadn't worked. Instead of easing his anxiety and stress, the holiday had only served to crystallize how deeply he despised everything about his life.

Meeting Maggie Brown was the worst thing that ever happened to him! He thought of her constantly, how she smiled and laughed. Her frank talk and healthy opinions. Her absolute—but absurd—assertion that they were meant to be lifetime lovers and soulmates. How could one slip of a girl so fully occupy a man's thoughts?

Often, he drifted back to that night outside the barn and how openly and honestly she'd offered him her innocence. How stupid he'd been to refuse her! While she had been ready to settle for whatever small amount of happiness they could find together, he could not do the same. In reality, he was a coward. He'd been given the chance to grab something wonderful, and he'd been too afraid.

As a result, he found his mind wandering at meetings, his attention completely distracted with memories of her. While driving through the streets of London, he was constantly on the lookout for her, thinking and hoping that he might see her in the crowd. He was going around like some lovesick, besotted swain.

He'd never asked where she lived, but supposed he could hire someone to find her.

And then what?

The question inevitably presented itself. What would he do if he located her? Nothing about their situations had changed, except that she would learn the truth: He was a liar and a scoundrel. He didn't want her to ever harbor those opinions, although the chances were good that she already felt that way, considering the manner in which he'd left her at the inn without so much as a wave of the hand.

Finding her wasn't an option.

Instead, he'd immersed himself in the task of selecting a wife. Spending more time out. Escorting more women to various events. Taking more introductions. Attending more parties, as he was doing this evening.

Through it all, he'd developed an interesting and unexplainable attachment to Penelope Westmoreland. Something about the girl reminded him of Maggie. It wasn't that they looked so much alike, with Penny blond and plump while Maggie was brown-haired and thin. The resemblance was more subtle than that. Oddly, they shared many of the same facial features, hand gestures, and body movements. On numerous occasions, he'd found himself staring at Penelope, watching for the occasional glimpses of Maggie to poke to the surface.

Sometimes, he wondered if he was going mad.

After being announced, he descended into the room, avoiding eye contact with others as much as possible while looking for James or his cousin Charles and not finding the safety of either man's company. He managed to make it to a back wall and hovered in the corner, sipping champagne.

A voice to the left caught his attention and he turned, groaning inwardly when he saw George Wilberton standing there. He'd known the pompous man forever and couldn't abide him. Pasting a congenial look on his face, he acknowledged the old acquaintance.

"Wilburton, what brings you out? I thought you were in the country, preparing for your nuptials."

"I've a few matters to attend to before leaving the city. You wouldn't be in the market for a small town house, would you?"

"I can't say that I am."

George eyed St. Clair carefully. He hadn't planned on approaching the man, but what could it hurt? He liked a pretty face as much as anyone. "Actually, the property comes with an addition which might intrigue you very much."

"What's that?" Adam asked out of a need to keep the conversation going more than any genuine interest.

George leaned closer, whispering conspiratorially, "A woman."

"A woman?" It was the last thing Adam would have expected from a dullard like Wilburton. He couldn't help the bit of surprise that escaped with his question. "You keep a mistress?"

"I've had one for years." It had been on the tip of George's tongue to tell the truth about his relationship with Maggie, but even as a boy, he'd always desperately wanted to impress St. Clair. He couldn't prevent the small lie or the massive implication it carried.

"Hmm . . ." Adam mused. You really could learn something new every day. "Has she been worth it?"

"Absolutely."

"Really?" In Adam's experience, his acquaintances who kept women generally ended up finding them a nuisance. All except his blasted father, who'd had the audacity to fall in love.

"She's exquisite, but I've been keeping her for some time now, and I can't continue." George tried his best to sound bored about the entire affair. "She needs to find a new arrangement, so I graciously told her that I'd make a few introductions."

"Of course." Adam kept a straight face at the man's condescending attitude. "I'm sure she's extremely grateful."

"Oh, she is. And she has been." He wiggled his eyebrows suggestively. "Would you like to meet her. She's quite exceptional."

"If she's so *exceptional*"—Adam couldn't help the sarcasm—"why are you parting with her?"

"My fiancée," he said with a sigh. "You know how particular some ladies can be about this sort of thing."

"Yes, I do," Adam agreed, thinking of his mother and the hatred she harbored toward his father because of the whore who'd colored all their lives.

"Still, she's a lovely woman," George said. "I'm committed to doing what I can to see to her welfare while I still have the opportunity. She's with me this evening. Are you sure you wouldn't like to meet her?"

Adam was humored. The thought of a man like Wilburton

keeping a mistress was so absurd, it would have been laughable if it wasn't so pathetic. His interest was piqued. There was nothing he'd like more than to meet the woman who was desperate enough to provide regular sexual services to a man like George Wilburton. The image would probably be good for several days' worth of chuckling.

Trying to sound casual, he shrugged and took a long draw of champagne. "Why not? I'm sure I'll find her charming."

George scanned the crowd. "Ah . . . here she comes now."

Maggie peered at her reflection in the mirror. There were few times in her life when she'd looked better. Anne had done her usual excellent job with Maggie's hair, and it was piled in glorious display on the top of her head. A few delicate curls framed her face. They'd used various paints to rosy her cheeks and deepen the violet of her eyes, but the colors were so lightly applied that they seemed natural.

Her gown, the palest lavender trimmed with deep purple, was worn off the shoulder so that most of her bosom was exposed, and the expanse of creamy skin was broken only by a single strand of pearls borrowed from George. The high waist of the dress perfectly accented her rounded breasts and slender figure. The cut and flow of the fabric made her appear taller, lithe and willowy.

"What am I doing here?" she asked her reflection.

When she'd initially broached the idea of becoming a mistress to Anne, it had seemed like a good one. But now, closeted alone in the women's retiring room with the ball in full swing below, she was having desperate second thoughts. As Anne had said, she might meet the love of her life, or more likely, a cad and a bounder—which in Anne's eyes was not necessarily bad as long as the man was not cruel.

Rose was probably turning in her grave.

The door to the outer room opened, and she could hear the noise of the crowd downstairs filtering in behind whoever had joined her. Not wishing to speak to anyone, she turned to go, but stopped at the sound of two women's voices in the outer room.

"Lord Belmont should be arriving any minute, Penelope."

Maggie nearly groaned aloud at the possibility of running into Adam. In the two months since his abrupt departure from the Tidewater Inn, she'd certainly thought about him often enough. For even though she was angered and humiliated by his lies and actions, she couldn't put him out of her mind. How many times would such a dashing, handsome, educated man appear in her life? Very likely never again.

What dastardly luck to have him show up on a night when she was intent on selling herself to the highest bidder! She had to get out of there. Reaching for the door, she paused again as the woman named Penelope answered her friend.

"I can't wait to see the look on his face when he sees my dress. Here, pull my bodice down a little lower." A rustle of expensive fabric. "Yes, that's it. Just a little more. How's my cleavage?"

"Lean over a little," the other woman replied. "Ummm . . . Perfect."

"He'll certainly get an eyeful . . . if I can only get him to stand close enough." Penelope giggled; then the other joined her.

"Proximity shouldn't be a problem, considering how attentive he's been to you lately."

"Too true," Penelope agreed. There was another rustle of fabric. "Look at this."

"What is it?"

"That French perfume I was telling you about. It's supposed to have a secret ingredient which will make a man fall madly in love with the woman who's wearing it. Adam won't be able to resist me another second. Let's go into the other room. I've decided I want to dab some on my nipples."

"Oh, you horrid girl," the friend gasped in delight. "What if your father notices?"

"I doubt the Duke will get close enough to my bosom," she said sarcastically. "Besides, what could Father possibly say about it in a room full of people?"

Maggie took a quick inhale of breath as the door opened. Before she could move, think, or react, there she stood face-to-face with her younger half sister. She knew all about Penelope—born to the Duke's lawful wife nearly a year after Rose gave birth to Maggie—but had never set eyes on her.

Until now.

Close to the same height, they stood nearly eye to eye, each taking the other's measure. Maggie could see so many similarities, and she actually felt a pang of sympathy for Penelope as her eyes scanned Maggie's face for recognition but didn't find it. Somehow, Maggie doubted the girl knew she had a sister.

Maggie spoke first, wanting only to leave and never again set eyes on the cherubic beauty who had grown up with everything that could have been Maggie's if the world was a just and fair place. She wasn't by nature a petty or jealous person, but it was hard to think of a civil thing to say when Penelope was here perfuming her breasts to entice Adam St. Clair while Maggie, the *other* daughter of the Duke of Roswell, was here to sell herself so she could keep a roof over her head. Resentment and envy tasted bitter.

"Excuse me." She stepped aside to let Penelope and her friend enter.

Penelope didn't move. The woman across from her seemed so familiar, but she couldn't place her. Penelope was sure she knew everyone in their circle who was close to her own age. From head to toe, the woman was perfectly attired and quite stunning. Penny hated meeting rivals about whom she knew nothing, and it quickly occurred to her that there were those at the ball who might find this woman lovelier than Penelope herself. A horrifying thought!

"Pardon me for asking"—she forced herself to smile—" but I feel as though I should know you. Have we met?"

"No."

"I am Lady Penelope Westmoreland." She waited for the usual flash of fawning recognition; everyone either knew who she was or straightened to attention when they found out. Not seeing the reaction she expected, she felt forced to add, "My father is Harold Westmoreland, Duke of Roswell."

"Yes, I know." Maggie had no intention of introducing herself or chatting, so it was extremely rude when she didn't respond with her name after Penelope had given her own. She slipped past the two women, no easy task with Penelope so carefully blocking the exit. "Have a pleasant evening."

"Well . . . !" was Penelope's insulted comment as Maggie stepped into the hall.

"Who was that?" Maggie heard the exasperated voice of Penelope's friend ask, but the rest of their comments were shut off by the door closing.

There were probably five hundred people in attendance at this particular ball. What were the chances of her being trapped in a small room with only a nipple-dabbing Penelope Westmoreland for company? Or of finding out that her half sister had set her cap for Adam? If Maggie remained, she was certain to be accosted by Penelope again, a confrontation she wanted to avoid at all costs.

With the way the evening was going, she'd probably meet up with her father, who would, no doubt, recognize her since she looked exactly as her mother had looked during the years they were lovers. The thought of being snubbed by him in public was more than she could abide.

Then, there was Adam to consider. Running into him was out of the question, especially if there was the slightest chance that Penelope might be hanging on his arm when it happened.

Her face was a furious red, and she wished she knew where there was another retiring room so she could bathe her face with a cool cloth before returning to the ballroom. Unfortunately, she didn't, and she was ready to plead a headache and leave the ball before it became any more disastrous.

Making her way down the stairs, she circled through the crowd to the back of the ballroom, hoping George had waited for her where he said he would. Through the throng, she caught sight of him, drinking champagne and blustering to whoever stood next to him. She stepped around a group of people and moved to his side.

George looked up and saw her coming. "Ah . . . here she is now," he said to his companion. "Maggie, I'm glad you've returned. There's someone I want you to meet."

Chapter Eight

"Adam St. Clair, Marquis of Belmont, may I present . . ." George never finished the sentence, because he happened to glance at St. Clair. Never before had he seen such uncontrolled rage sparking from a man. He'd known St. Clair since they were schoolboys, and the man had always had a reputation as a cool head who never showed his emotions. At the current moment, he looked as though he was about to strike something . . . or someone.

"I'll take it," Adam said between clenched teeth.

"Ah . . . what was that?" George asked, confused.

Enunciating each word clearly, Adam repeated himself. "I said: I'll take it. The house and the woman."

George glanced to Maggie, who was shaking like a leaf and looked as though she was about to flee into the crowd. Before she could, St. Clair reached out and took her arm just above the elbow. The move looked casual, but George could see his fingers digging into her arm. "But . . . we've not discussed the terms or the price or—"

Adam cut him off. "Whatever price you're asking is acceptable. Present a contract to my solicitor first thing in the morning. You'll have a bank draft by noon.''

''But wouldn't you like to know . . . I mean . . .'' He shook his head, completely at a loss. ''May I at least introduce you?''

''There's no need for introductions. Miss Brown and I are old friends.'' With a painful squeeze on her arm, he asked, ''Isn't that right, dear?''

''Oh, yes,'' she managed to choke out, ''the *best* of old friends.''

''There you have it.'' Adam nodded to Wilburton. ''The house is sold, as is the woman. Neither is any longer your concern.'' In a swift, proprietary gesture, he brought Maggie closer to his side. ''Now, if you'll excuse me, I'd like to go and begin enjoying the *benefits* of my recent purchase.''

No doubt about it, Maggie thought to herself, this was the very worst night of her entire life. Seeing Adam standing next to George was so shocking, so surprising, that the moment didn't seem real. She felt paralyzed. Vaguely, she heard Adam say he was purchasing the town house and purchasing her, but the words came to her ears as though she was hearing them through water.

If he meant it, her home was saved. Her life secure—at least for the time being. Anne was taken care of. This was what she'd been hoping for, wasn't it?

Yes, but not in this fashion. There was no escaping the anger in his tone or his eyes. In fact, she'd never seen anyone so furious in her entire life. The pain of his fingers digging into her arm was like a knife prick jolting her back to reality.

''It's very nice to see you again, *Lord Belmont*.'' She deliberately emphasized the fact that she knew his true identity. Meeting his irate gaze with one of her own, she said, ''But I think there's been some mistake. I've already promised George I would meet with a friend of his. I couldn't possibly leave.''

''There will be no need to meet with anyone else. Everything's arranged.'' He glared at Wilburton, daring him to disagree. ''Isn't that right?''

"Well . . . yes . . . I suppose . . . " George had absolutely no idea what to do. Maggie was looking at him with equal parts terror and fury, but St. Clair was giving him pure fury and nothing else. The last thing in life he wanted to do was cross swords with the Marquis.

Maggie could do worse, he thought suddenly. Didn't the stupid girl realize the stroke of luck she'd just had? Besides, the girl and the house were a ball and chain around his neck, and he'd never believed he'd rid himself of them so easily. Resolved that supporting St. Clair was the proper thing to do, he pulled himself up to his full height and cleared his throat.

"Yes," he said, full of assurance, "everything's arranged. May I be the first to congratulate you, Maggie. You've snagged yourself quite a prize." The corners of his mouth lifted in an attempt at a smile, but it wasn't returned by either party. "I'll see your solicitor first thing in the morning, St. Clair."

"You do that," Adam said, and turned to go without a word of good-bye. He had an arm around Maggie's waist and another on her wrist so she couldn't escape. They started through the crowd toward the stairs.

"Let go of me." She tried to twist away but to no avail.

"Stop it. We're leaving."

"I'm am not going anywhere with you," she hissed. She'd braced her heels against the floor, trying to stop his forward movement, but it didn't do any good.

Adam was more incensed than he'd ever been in his life. He understood, just now, how and why a man might come to beat a woman. At the moment, he wanted nothing more than to take a strap to her. When he thought of all the innocent blathering, romantic talk, and silly lies! How she'd begged him to give her her first kiss, to be her first lover, and how he'd denied himself by trying to act noble and restrained.

All the while, she'd been whoring for Wilburton. Briefly, he wondered if Georgie-boy knew how well she'd cuckolded him when she was off playing by herself. How many men had she taken to her bed while on her little holiday?

With a hard yank, she was tucked against his side. The brief struggle turned a few heads, but he was holding her so carefully and with such a lack of emotion on his face that no one seemed to notice they were fighting in the middle of the dance floor.

"Cease!" he whispered harshly in her ear. "The very first thing you will come to understand about me is that you will never ... I repeat: never! ... make a scene while we are in public." He wrenched her around so they stood eye to eye. "Do you understand me?"

Maggie took in the trembling fury that shook him slightly, the rage in his gaze. The last thing she wanted, as well, was to make a scene. She relaxed her stance, took a slow, deep breath, and let it out. Quietly, she said, "Yes, I understand you."

"Good. Let's leave, then, shall we? I'd say we have a few matters to discuss, and a few preliminaries to get out of the way. And, then, I have every intention of *exploring* my new property for the remainder of the evening."

There was no doubting what he intended, but Maggie would deal with it when they got outside. Masking her face with a look of pleasant boredom, she hurried to keep up with his long strides.

As they walked through the ballroom doors and started toward the stairs, she came face-to-face with her father. In the brief encounter, she had the quickest moment of surprised realization that they looked very much alike. There was also the unexpected pleasure of hearing his sharp intake of breath and seeing the rise of his brow as he got a good look at her before Adam hustled her past without so much as a nod of the head.

In spite of the din of noise from the people and the orchestra, she couldn't help but hear Penelope's voice coming from behind her where the girl stood next to the Duke. "Father, who is that woman with Adam?"

"I don't know," he answered distractedly, "but I intend to find out."

The statement reverberated through her head as Adam whisked her out into the cool night air.

His coach was magnificent, befitting a man of his wealth and station, with a driver and four liveried footmen. The inside smelled of leather, and the brass fittings were polished to an outrageous shine. Trying to still the wild beating of her heart, she glanced at him out of the corner of her eye. It seemed impossible that this imposing stranger, more handsome than ever in his black formal attire, was the same man who had laughed and loved with her two months earlier.

Quietly, she offered, "I don't understand why you're so angry with me."

"Then you're either stupid, which I know you're not, or incredibly naive, which I used to believe but which I now seriously doubt."

"This isn't how it looks."

"Really? I could swear I just purchased your favors. In my book that makes you a first-class whore. Considering that fact, you have the audacity to sit there and ask me why I'm angry? You're incredible."

"We were just so desperate."

"Who is 'we?' "

"Anne and I."

"Ah, yes, the indomitable Miss Porter," he said rudely. "Is she a whore as well?"

Maggie could put up with just about anything, and had for much of her life, but she wasn't about to sit and listen to insults about her loyal friend. "I don't have to take this from you. I'm leaving." She moved to the door, ready to leap from the moving carriage if that was what it would take to get away from him. He was much quicker, grabbing her arm and tossing her back on the seat.

"Sit down! Now!" he shouted.

With a furious jerk, she wrenched her arm away from him and flung herself back to the farthest corner of the coach, sitting as far away as she possibly could, which could never be far enough. "What do you know about it? What do you know about anything? You have no right to sit in judgment of me."

"You couldn't have told me what was happening?"

"Told you what? That we are being tossed out of our home? That we have nowhere to go? Pray tell, just what would you have done about it?" She was pleased to see that her words shut him up. The silence lengthened, became uncomfortable, and she added, "You have no idea what life is like for people like us, so spare me your righteous attitudes. You were quick enough to lay your money on the table to buy me."

Adam heard nary a word of her protestations as he chose instead to amuse himself by slowly undressing her with his eyes. She was a beauty, all right. More perfect than he remembered, the jewel he imagined she would be in a ballroom full of his peers. A pretty package wrapped around a black heart. Well, he could use her as well as the next man and ease his loins in the process. Just the thought of what was coming, of taking her hard and fast, set his manhood to rising.

Although he appeared completely calm, leaning back, an arm resting casually on the seat, inside he was churning at the thought of her spreading her legs for George Wilburton. "So what was the point?" he asked.

Her head came swinging up. "The point of what?"

"Playing the innocent with me on your holiday. Did you think it would be easier to lure me to your bed that way? Or did you think I would be more greatly aroused at the thought that I was to have a virgin?"

"Of all the nerve . . ." It was pointless to argue. Instead, she turned and made a point of looking out the window. "I'm not even going to dignify that with a response."

"What's the matter? Can't decide which answer would serve you best? I wouldn't think an accomplished liar such as yourself would need much time to get her story straight."

"A liar like myself? Now that's the pot calling the kettle black, isn't it, *Aston*? I know that Aston was your father's name, but how did you come up with *Carrington*?"

"You're good. Answer my questions with questions. Take the offensive." He settled himself back further, pushing his hands against the leather lest he use them to grab her and shake her. "I must say I'm greatly looking forward to having a piece of you. Ever since we left the shore, I have regretted not taking you that night. Now, I'll get to see if the reality is anything close to the fantasy."

"If you think I'm going to bed you when you sit there insulting me, my best friend, and my life, you can think again. It is not going to happen."

Adam reached into his pocket, checked his timepiece. It was hardly past midnight. He'd be able to pass several hours with her. "Protest all you want," he said, "but remember this: I now own your home. When we arrive, you will service me, or you will pack your bags and head for the streets. The choice is completely up to you. It matters not to me what you decide to do."

He tried to act as nonchalant as possible, but his insides were churning, not certain what he would do if she refused. He wouldn't turn a dog out in the middle of the night, let alone a woman, but he felt the threat was necessary. She needed to understand from the very beginning that he, not she, would set the boundaries of their relationship.

"What if I fight you?"

"It will only serve to arouse me further." His anger had reached a slow burn, and it was fueling the pulse throbbing between his legs. He tried to convince himself that he would have her before the night was through. Whether or not the threat was one on which he could follow through was another matter entirely.

Maggie inhaled sharply. "You'd take me against my will?"

"I doubt you would resist for long. After all, you've wanted me in your bed for some time now. Your curiosity is about to be assuaged."

Once again staring out the window, she recognized the passing buildings. It was only a matter of minutes before they pulled up in front of her house. Only a matter of minutes to make her life-altering decision. Give herself to Adam or walk off into the night. No doubt he'd make her do such a thing. In his current state, he was probably capable of anything.

She took a slow, tremulous breath, then turned to look at him. "I'm not the woman you think I am."

"Were you, or were you not, just peddling yourself at the ball, trying to find the best situation for yourself? Well, dear, trust me. You've managed to skim the cream off the top of the bucket. There is no greater catch than me. So tell me"—he picked at a speck of dust on his trousers—"how many men have you serviced? Am I to enjoy the fruits of only Wilburton's labors, or have there been several to teach you your loving skills?"

"You think I've lain with George?" She would have laughed if the situation hadn't been so absurd.

"He says you are quite exceptional."

She squinted, as though trying to bring him into clearer focus, for it was difficult to believe that this was the same man who she thought had been her first love. "I still don't understand why you're so angry with me. I don't mean anything to you. Why do you care what I've done with my life?"

Adam clenched his teeth, refusing to look too closely at the reasons why he was upset. The logical part of his brain understood that he could only feel this well of emotion if he had deep feelings for the girl. He could not face that fact, so he covered his confusion with more hostility. "There is nothing I despise more than a deceitful woman. And no one plays me for the fool and gets away with it. You might do well to remember that during the course of our relationship. By the way, you still haven't answered my question. How many others have there been?"

"You want to know how many lovers I've had?"

"Yes. Is it one, a few, or many?"

If she'd been closer, she'd have slapped him. As it was, there was simply no reasoning with the man. Rolling her eyes, a gesture that Adam missed in the dim light, she said sarcastically, "Oh, there have been absolutely dozens. I can barely control myself where men are concerned."

An innocent at love games, she didn't understand how severely her statement would upset him. The muscle twitching in his cheek was the only sign of his outrage.

He held out a hand. "Come here."

"No."

"Come." It wasn't a shout, but close enough in the small confines of the carriage. He grabbed her wrist and pulled her across the short distance separating them so that she was between his legs and balanced on one of his thighs. Placing her hand on his swollen manhood, he used his palm to pressure hers to stroke him back and forth. "I'm sure I will find that you have been worth the wait."

Just then, the carriage rumbled to a stop. Maggie would have fallen to the floor if Adam hadn't held her pinned against his body. He set her back on the opposite seat, then stepped out first when the coachman opened the door. After whispering something to the man, he reached in and offered his hand to Maggie. "Well, what is your decision?"

Home or the streets? She stepped out, glancing up and down the dark avenue. In her neighborhood, there were none of the fancy street lamps that dotted more expensive lanes. The shadows looked dark and foreboding. There seemed to be no choice, really. She swallowed, then said softly, "Promise me one thing."

"You are in no position to ask for anything." Her knees buckled, and she nearly fell to the ground, causing him to grab her around the waist. The glow from the lantern on the carriage haloed her, making her look smaller and so very pale. Her eyes were shiny with tears. His wrath ebbed somewhat. She was so lovely and so young. And she was shaking. He pushed the thoughts away, needing his anger to fuel the next step of their encounter.

"Please . . . All I ask is that you promise not to hurt me. I'll do whatever you want. It's just that ... that you seem so enraged, and it's making me afraid. Please just say you won't hurt me.''

He winced. His driver and all four of his coachmen must have heard what she said. What in the hell was she thinking? Beating a woman wasn't his style, no matter how much he was provoked. ''Contrary to what you seem to believe, I am not an animal.''

''You swear you won't hurt me?''

Good God, but she sounded like a begging child. He was glad the night shielded his red cheeks as he vowed, ''You have my word.''

''All right, then,'' she answered hesitantly. ''Let's go in.''

Maggie unlocked the door. Anne had put out all the lamps. Walking the familiar path in the dark, she slipped her hand into Adam's and led him up the stairs. At the top, they crossed to her doorway just as Anne stepped into the hall with a candle lighting her way.

''Maggie, are you all right?''

Adam moved from the shadows, answering before Maggie could. ''Everything is fine,'' he said.

''What are you doing here?''

''It seems, madam, that I have purchased myself a house and a whore.'' He took Maggie's arm. ''I intend to enjoy the pleasures of the latter.''

''Wait.'' Anne blocked the doorway to Maggie's room, eyeing them both suspiciously. She put a finger on Maggie's chin and lifted her face, forcing the girl to give her a direct look. ''Tell me that you're all right.''

She smiled tremulously. ''I'm just a little nervous.''

''Are you sure this is what you want to do?''

''Yes.'' Maggie's eyes pleaded for understanding. ''I'll explain everything tomorrow.''

''Explain it now,'' she insisted.

Adam reached out and physically moved Anne from the doorway. ''I hardly think this is any of your business.''

"It is my business. Maggie is my friend, and this is our home."

"No. This house now belongs to me, and I have no desire to support you as well as Maggie. You'll go in the morning."

Maggie gasped. "No, Adam. Please. I need her to stay with me. There's nowhere for her to go."

Anne's eyes blazed with fury. "Don't beg on my behalf, Maggie. Especially not the likes of him." She glared at Adam. "Don't you dare hurt her."

"I have no intention of hurting her."

"Look at you! You're too angry to be contemplating joining with her. There will be no way to do it without causing her some injury." She looked at Maggie, her gaze beseeching. "Don't do this, Maggie. Come to my room. We'll talk about it like we planned, and you can go through with it tomorrow if it's still your wish." She held out her hand, waited an eternity as Maggie stared at it but didn't reach for it.

"No. I don't want to wait," Maggie finally said. "It will be all right, Anne. You'll see."

"Oh, Maggie . . ." Anne sighed.

Adam stepped between them. "Good night, Miss Porter." He pushed Maggie into the room and followed her, closing the door and turning the lock with a loud click. "Light a candle," he said. "I want to be able to see everything."

Chapter Nine

With shaking hands, Maggie somehow managed to light the candle next to her bed. Searching for and finding her retreating courage, she turned to face him, resolved to get through the night with her dignity intact. She could do this!

"I am doing this for Anne more than for myself," she told him. "I could not bear the thought of her left alone on the streets. Please tell me that you'll not make her leave."

Adam shrugged. "Then convince me to let her stay."

"Very well." Maggie probably knew more about loving than any virgin in the kingdom. Rose and Anne never held with the theory that a young woman should be naive about what happened in the bedchamber. As a consequence, Maggie had grown up listening to candid discussions, and she'd had the various sex acts explained to her in any number of ways. Still, while she knew what a woman did with her hands, mouth, and body, and what a man did with his, it was all theory. She wasn't exactly certain how to put it into practice, but was fairly sure she could pull off this first encounter with some degree of skill.

He had to enjoy the event. He just had to!

By morning, if she played her cards right, she would have her home secure and her finances arranged. Chances were good that Adam would provide for her later, after the affair had ended. Especially if there were children. In her young mind, she couldn't imagine that he would abandon her if they created a child together. She refused to give any credit to the notion that he might act as her father had acted toward her mother.

Resolved, she decided to give him every bit of her heart and her passion, to do everything he asked, to be everything he wanted. In the end, she had no doubt he would realize that, no matter the reason he had originally entered into their bargain, it was a good and beneficial arrangement. By morning, he would be calm, sated, and happy. And her world would be safe.

Across the small room, he stood silently watching. She took the few steps separating them, coming to rest her palms against his chest. His heart was pulsing steady and strong as she smoothed her hands upward under the lapels of his coat, urged it off his shoulders, down his arms, and tossed it on the chair. His fingers moved to his cravat, but she stopped him.

"Let me do that." Slowly, she began undressing him. An inch at a time, his chest was bared. She rested her palms against his flat stomach, then worked her way up to his chest. It was covered with a thick mat of dark hair, which was soft and springy, and she massaged through it over and over again.

As his shirt fell to the floor, she realized that this was the first time she'd ever viewed a man's chest, and she was quite sure she was looking at a magnificent one. His shoulders were broad, his waist narrow. The hair that was scattered across the top narrowed to a vee, then disappeared in a line into his trousers. Her eyes couldn't help but follow. His state of arousal was readily apparent. Unable to resist the lure of his body, she leaned forward and nuzzled her face against his chest, inhaling deeply the smell of his warm skin. She worked her face back and forth while her hands busied themselves below, stroking the hard bulge between his legs as he'd shown her in the carriage.

So far, he hadn't moved or spoken, and she wasn't sure at all if she was pleasuring him. She couldn't resist flicking her tongue against his small, hard nipple. Her reward was a groan deep in his throat. Encouraged, she nipped it gently, then closed her lips and sucked it into her mouth.

Adam had tried to remain silent and stoic. He'd meant to have a detached, unemotional sexual joining, with the only purpose welcome release. He'd thought he wanted a coupling that would set the tone at the beginning of their relationship to let her know that they would join physically but in no other way. But as her lips found his nipple, and her long, slender fingers worked between his legs, he could no longer hold himself in reserve.

The anger that had burned for the past hour hit the flash point and turned to pure desire. Suddenly, he was swept away, and there was nothing else he wanted in the entire world more than this woman. The slow, careful initiative with which she'd begun the encounter would never do. Very much like a charging wild animal, he pounced on her, taking control.

He covered her mouth in a bruising, demanding kiss that left no time for thinking or planning. Only reacting. He simply took from her, then took some more. His tongue thrust far inside, claiming her and requiring her response. She gave it, answering with savage abandon as his hands plunged into her hair, scattering pins with a few ferocious jerks. Her locks fell past her shoulders to her waist, causing him to moan as he ran his fingers through the silky strands. Using the hair for leverage, he wrapped a handful around his fist and tipped her head further back, allowing himself greater access.

Her neck exposed, he worked his way down, across her bosom, seeking her breasts. There was nothing gentle about his probing as he wrenched at the fabric. Not able to feel her closely enough, he dropped one hand to her buttocks to work her mound against his manhood while the other searched under the neckline of her dress, finding her nipple hard and ready.

He yanked against the bodice and a breast sprang free. Giving no tame licks or tender sucks, he assaulted it viciously, tugging the firm tip into his mouth, nipping it with his teeth. Maggie squirmed against him, trying to shift closer to the pleasure but move away at the same time. Her struggles only aroused him further, and he kissed his way back to her mouth.

"I need to feel you against me."

"Yes, whatever you want." They had played at the edge of this fire during their short tryst at the beach, but now, he was offering so much more, and she was ready. Her nineteen-year-old body was primed for whatever was coming.

Spinning her around, he started at the buttons and hooks covering her back, but his fingers were shaking so badly he couldn't manage. In growing frustration, he grabbed the silk with two hands and ripped it down the middle. The gown fell off her shoulders and slid to the floor.

"My dress ... " she whispered in dismay, but he cut her off, turning her back to face him.

"I'll buy you a thousand more." His mouth covered hers again, leaving no opportunity for discussion or complaint.

With expert hands, he worked at stays and straps, until she stood before him in a circle of bone, lace, silk, and satin. Only a thin chemise covered her, and he pulled his lips away from hers long enough to admire the erotic shape of the body hiding beneath it. The chemise was something he'd never seen the likes of, made completely of lace. It was transparent in all the right spots. He could see the pink of her nipples, the shadow of her navel, the mound of her woman's hair.

The undergarment covered the body of an angel. Breasts just the right size to fill a man's hands, neither too large nor too small. A tiny waist, curved hips, and long, long legs that, shortly, would be wrapped around his waist. With her lips swollen from his kisses, her cheeks flushed from her pounding heart, she was desire incarnate. Every man's dream. Every man's fantasy. And she was his to do with as he pleased.

He fisted a hand in her hair again, tipping her head back so she had to look up. "Undo my breeches."

Trying to control her shaking fingers, she carefully worked at the front. He waited impatiently until the flap was open, and they were loose around his hips. Taking her hand, he guided it inside, placing it exactly where he wanted it—clutched around his swollen manhood. Tentatively, she stroked him, and was surprised to find him firm and soft at the same time, like velvet over steel.

"Harder," he said, and when she still didn't get it right, he wrapped his fingers over hers, showing her how he wanted it. "Like this."

Quickly, she adjusted to the rhythm he desired, and for her manipulations, she was rewarded with another moan of pleasure, which caused her to grow more bold. While her hand continued its erotic dance, she rubbed her cheek against the pile of springy hair on his chest. Purring like a cat, she inhaled deeply, loving his smell of sweat and musk, which tantalized and aroused her senses.

"Pleasure me," Adam ordered, forcing her to her knees with gentle pressure on her shoulders. She hesitated, so he became more explicit. "Take me in your mouth. I want to feel you this way."

Maggie wasn't about to protest. Whatever pleased him she was determined to do. Closing her eyes and hoping for the best, she reached for him, ran her tongue across the tip, and was rewarded by him clenching his stomach muscles. She sucked him inside, and the reality was like nothing she'd imagined. He tasted wonderful, all hot and salty.

His manhood reacted like a living being, sensitive and reactive to whatever she did, but almost before it began, it ended as Adam suddenly jerked away, pressing her face against his stomach. His breath was coming in spurts, his legs and buttocks tensed like granite. She reached to guide him back inside, and he slapped at her hand.

He couldn't believe how quickly she brought him to the point of release. Using every ounce of self-restraint to keep from spilling himself then and there, he hissed, "Stop!"

"What is it?" she asked, not understanding how close she'd lured him to the edge.

Instead of answering her question, he lifted her off the floor and flung her on the bed, grabbing the hem of her chemise and tugging it up and over her head, baring her thighs, hips, stomach, breasts.

Taking one moment to enjoy the view, he scanned her from the top of her head to the tips of her toes. His eyes were dark with passion, his face flushed, his breath coming fast and hard, his manhood heavy and pulsing.

"I am well pleased with you." He managed to force out the words, then bent his head to her breast and suckled.

As he shifted across her, Maggie was fascinated at how it felt to have a man pressing her against a bed for the first time. He didn't feel heavy, and the touch of his body down the length of hers was arousing and exotic. The hair on his chest brushed her stomach; the rough fabric of his breeches scraped her bare skin. His strong arms wrapped tightly around her back, allowing him greater access to her breasts, and he enjoyed them both, sucking and squeezing her nipples, alternating from one to the other. The tugging of his lips and fingers started a spark of painful sensation in the pit of her belly.

The ache was the same as that at her breasts. Pleasant but terrible. She fought against it just as fiercely as she struggled toward it. Adam wedged his knee between her thighs. A hand left her breast, slid down her stomach, then cupped her mound. With two fingers, he worked his way inside. She had never before been touched in such a way, and the stretching felt odd but welcome.

At the same time his fingers stroked her, his thumb found the small nub at the very center of her womanhood. She knew about this spot, and she also knew that many men did not know of it. Or if they did, they would not use it to bring a woman pleasure. He flicked across it. Once. Then again. And she shattered like a million pieces of glass scattered across the heavens.

From far off, she heard a voice crying out, and eventually recognized it as her own. Her next earthly sensation was the low rumble of a pleased chuckle coming from the man whose hands had so exquisitely tormented her.

"You're so ready for me," Adam said, lifting his head to look her in the eye. "Watch me as I fill you for the first time."

With no more preparation than that, he nestled himself between her thighs, palmed her knees to the side. Lifted her buttocks. Nudged against her cleft once. Again. Then, plunged to the hilt.

She'd known there would be pain. Had expected it. Had been ready for it, but nothing had prepared her sufficiently. Crying out in agony, she arched up off the bed.

Adam's eyes widened in shock. A virgin! "What the hell . . ."

"It hurts," she managed, trying to catch a deep breath.

"Jesus Bloody Christ," he cursed. At the pained look in her eye, he wanted to ease some of her distress. "Try to relax," he coaxed, knowing such a thing would be impossible.

Overcome with a sudden tenderness for her that he didn't want to feel, he meant to pull out but couldn't. Never before had he been so aroused. Never before had he taken a virgin. The knowledge that he'd been her first, coupled with the slick feel of her virgin's blood and the tight squeeze of her muscles contracted around him, was his undoing. Some primal urge swept over him, and he could not have stopped if a platoon of soldiers had entered the room with drawn sabers and ordered him to halt.

His entire body tensed as he thrust his hips once. Again. And again. On the fourth penetration, his seed flooded her, and he collapsed in exhaustion by her side.

* * *

Maggie woke with a small groan. She felt sore everywhere. Especially between her legs. Which brought back with stunning clarity what had happened between her and Adam the night before. Cautiously, she opened one eye, then the other, hoping to find him gone but wishing him to still be there at the same time. Shifting to her side, she came full awake when she saw him relaxed in a chair next to the bed. Fully dressed, he appeared ready to depart, which was frightening to consider.

Had he been displeased? Was he still angry? Had last night all been for naught?

A lone cart clattered by below, and with a quick glance at the window, she could see the first hint of daylight coming through.

The ache between her legs was excruciating, and she sat up carefully, taking special pains not to wince. Realizing the bedcovers were at her waist, she reached for them and pulled them to cover her breasts, missing the smirk he gave to her attempt at modesty.

"I'm glad you've awakened, for I must be on my way."

"A-all right," she said as calmly as possible. Her lips were chapped and dry from his kisses, and she had to run her tongue across them before she could speak. His voice seemed overly loud in the small room, and he looked so dispassionate, so stern. She wasn't sure how they were supposed to act toward one another after what had happened a few hours earlier, but she didn't think this was quite the way it was supposed to go. Fear clutched her heart.

He started with, "I want to discuss the terms of our arrangement with you before I leave, so you'll have some idea of what will be happening. I'll also send you a copy in writing. That way, there won't be any surprises or disagreements over what I expect."

"That would be helpful," she said, trying her best to appear unruffled, all the while wondering how he could sit there so unmoved while her senses were reeling, her emotions churning, and every bone in her body aching.

"You will provide sexual favors to me and no one else. In return, I will provide for all your needs. I shall expect you to service me three nights per week. The number of nights may increase or decrease in the future; I will have to see how events progress." He was determined to keep her at arm's length, but the thought of having her every night was certainly worth considering. "For now, three nights should be sufficient. One of those nights, we shall enjoy an evening out before we begin our intimate relations."

"What do you mean?"

"I mean that I shall escort you to the theater. Dining. Or other entertainment I deem suitable for the two of us to attend. I shall provide for your clothing and personal expenses. By next Friday, I would like you to make a list of the shops you intend to frequent, and I shall set up accounts for you. I will expect you to consult with a particular modiste whose style I admire. She will help to ensure that you are adequately attired."

"You're very kind." She dropped her eyes, hurt that this was turning into such a business proposition. For even though that was what it was, her young heart had convinced her it would be something more.

"I've had a look about while waiting for you to awaken. If you are to be my companion, you will need adequate accommodations. This house is not suitable. Neither is the neighborhood. I will set my assistant to finding something better. I'll let you know as soon as it's ready."

"But . . . but I've always lived here."

"It's not acceptable."

"I don't need anything else. I don't want anything else."

"It is not acceptable," he said again, considering the matter closed.

Maggie gazed at him in the pale morning light. His cheeks were deeply shadowed with his morning's beard, his hair tousled from sleep. He looked grumpy and adorable except for the dead calm in his eyes. Whatever human part of him lurked in there seemed to be very much in hiding. Not wanting to antagonize him, she lied, "Whatever you wish will be fine."

"Two more items." He motioned with his index finger. "First, our relationship will last only until I am married, which will occur sometime in the next year. So, our liaison will continue for twelve months at the outside. Probably shorter than that. You need to be looking to the future about what you will do next."

She gave him a weak smile. "So you've selected someone, have you?"

"No, but I'm about to."

"I see." Maggie's heart ached. She'd been thoroughly schooled on the mechanics of loving, but completely unprepared for the emotional upheaval it would cause. There was simply no way anyone could explain how personal the sexual act was. Something about having Adam inside her was more intimate, more invasive, than anything should be. She couldn't imagine him doing it with someone else, or his finding it such a casual event that he could do it with one woman and then talk about marrying another in nearly the same breath. Her entire world had shifted off its axis during the night, and he seemed hardly affected at all.

"What will happen to me when you marry?"

"You'll simply have to find yourself another situation, which shouldn't be a problem. After I'm through with you, there will be any number of men who will be willing to take my place."

The man was unbelievable! Cold as stone and heartless as a lump of coal. She meant nothing to him. She was nothing to him. What she'd done the previous night had had no impact whatsoever. "And what is the second thing?"

"You will not become pregnant. If you do, I will cast you out the very day I learn of it. I will not claim the child, I will not support you or it, and most importantly, I will not have you shaming my wife or my mother with your bastard."

"It would be your child, too," she responded testily.

"No. My children will be born to my wife."

Never had she heard such cruel words spoken. They were a slur against herself, her mother, and any child she might accidentally conceive. Over the lump in her throat, she managed to ask, "What if it already happened last night?"

"I apologize for my lack of control. I had anticipated being more careful. However, do not concern yourself. It is rare for a babe to be created from one coupling."

Without much confidence in his assertion, she said, "I hope you're right."

"In the meantime, I will not be denied my pleasure, so there is a woman with whom I wish you to meet. She will instruct you on various methods of prevention."

"As you wish," she agreed rather than mention that she'd been raised by a professional courtesan and was currently living with one. They had taught her well, but the fact remained that no method was entirely successful. Maggie's heart was broken, and all she wanted was for him to leave. "Anything else?"

"Not for the time being. I am busy this evening, but I shall stop by tomorrow night around eight so that we may continue becoming acquainted." He leaned down, kissed her on the forehead, and said in a husky whisper, "I am very much looking forward to it." Silently, he left the room, closing the door behind.

Maggie slid down under the covers and began to cry.

Chapter Ten

Anne looked up at the sound of Adam's footsteps on the stairs. The man was nearly skipping with joy. Maggie must have played her part well, for he certainly walked as though he'd been well pleased.

"Good for you, girl," she whispered, hoping more than anything that St. Clair would treat Maggie with kindness and not overly damage her heart when it was over.

Adam saw her as he reached the bottom stair. They eyed each other silently and suspiciously for a few seconds; then Adam tipped his head in acknowledgment. "Good morning, Miss Porter."

"St. Clair," was all she returned by way of greeting.

He took in her cloak, the packed bag that rested by her feet. She appeared ready to follow through on his command that she move. In his haste to depart, he'd forgotten the events of the previous night. She was such a lovely thing who had, at one time, so thoroughly enchanted James. What had come over him to treat her so harshly?

Greatly embarrassed by his behavior, he swallowed, cleared his throat, swallowed again. "I see you're packed to go."

"I thought it best to leave right away. I'd just like to say good-bye to Maggie if that's acceptable to you." She paused. "Actually, I'm going to say good-bye to her whether it's acceptable to you or not."

"Miss Porter . . . Anne." He took a few steps into the small parlor. "I was angry last night. I'm sorry for what I said. Maggie wants you here, and I'd prefer it if you'd remain."

"I have no desire to stay." She refused to have her life so precariously balanced on the whims of a man with a temper like his. Every time he became angry, he'd lash out, and she'd spend a good share of her time packing and unpacking.

"But Maggie said you have nowhere to go."

She shrugged. "I've had nowhere to go before in my life, and I always managed to land on my feet. I'll find something this time as well."

At a loss, he nodded. "Well . . . if you change your mind, you may return."

"Thank you, but I won't be back."

"Good day, then, and good luck." His words sounded so lame, and he felt an absolute bastard. She nodded in response, and it was such a gesture of dismissal that he felt completely put in his place. "Maggie needs her maid. Could you send the woman up to her?"

"I'll have to see to her. We don't have any servants."

"Why not?"

"Who would pay for them?"

"But I thought . . ." He glanced toward the stairs, thinking of Maggie's virginal state, of Wilburton's snide remarks.

"Thought what? That Wilburton was keeping her?"

"Well, yes." Anne seemed to be reading his thoughts, and he hated it. "He as much as said he was."

"I'll just bet he did." Anne stood, brimming with anger. "For good bloody sakes, didn't you even take the time to notice she was a virgin?"

Not until it was too late to be more gentle. His cheeks flushed red. "Yes."

"Then how could you think Wilburton had been sleeping with her?"

"I didn't know what to think."

"He was keeping her mother, you fool," Anne said with a disgusted shake of her head. "Rose. He was keeping Rose."

"She died some time ago."

"Yes, and he let us keep living here, but he hasn't sent any money in months. We've barely enough left for food, let alone servants. So, pardon our lack of manners, but if you want a morning cup of tea, you'll have to get it yourself."

"Wilburton has been starving you?"

Anne immediately backed down, reining in her temper. It didn't do any good to rail about life's injustices to a nobleman like St. Clair. It was a waste of time and breath. "I'll not say anything bad about the man. He let us stay long after Rose was in any condition to service him, and he let us keep her here so she could die in her own bed upstairs. And he only made me earn the rent a handful of times." Anne hadn't meant to admit such a thing to anyone, and now it was her turn to blush bright red.

"You had to service him so you and Maggie could stay?" Adam could barely ask the question.

"Please don't tell Maggie," she insisted, horror-struck that her confession had slipped out. "She doesn't know, and I don't want her to."

"No," he agreed, feeling half sick. "I won't tell her."

Anne moved past him, too upset now to remain in the room, but she paused in the doorway with her back to him. "I'd best see to Maggie. Then I'll be on my way."

"Tell her I'll send some servants over today. A maid or two, an abigail, a cook. If there's anything I can do to help you . . ."

"There is one thing." She didn't turn around, but continued to stare straight ahead. "Just promise me you'll have a care with her. That you'll never hurt her or be cruel to her, and that you'll toss her over gently when you're through. Promise me that if you can.''

Silence became his answer as Anne waited for a response but didn't get one. She walked out of the room and up the stairs.

Adam watched her go. 'Twas obvious she thought he harbored reprehensible intentions toward Maggie, and he nearly called her back to explain himself, but didn't. The fact was that his mind was reeling from the drastic turn of events taken during the night, and he could barely think clearly, let alone predict the future. Quietly, he slipped out the front door and walked around the corner to where his carriage had been waiting through the night.

Anne tapped lightly on the door to Maggie's bedchamber, then stepped inside to find the young woman snuggled under the covers and weeping copiously. Anne walked across the room and sat down on the edge of the bed, stroking a hand across Maggie's hair.

"Is he gone?" Maggie asked once she'd calmed down enough to ask.

"Yes."

"Good." Maggie sat up and turned around to face her friend. Her hair was a tangled mess, her cheeks red and tear-streaked. "Bastard."

"Bastard," Anne agreed. "Was it so terrible, then?"

"It hurt, but it wasn't so bad. We only did it once."

"Was that all he was good for? He seems more virile than that."

"No, we fell asleep after."

"Did he give you any pleasure?"

"Yes."

"Well, at least he knows how. That's something positive, I guess."

"I guess," Maggie agreed dishearteningly, then wailed, "Oh, what am I going to do?"

"Well, first, how about if we get you cleaned up?"

"Yes. God, yes." In agreement, she leaped off the bed as though it was filled with snakes. There was a bloodstain on the middle of the sheet. Embarrassed, she said, "He didn't know I was a virgin."

"I gathered that. Why didn't you tell him?"

"He was so smug about everything."

"Bastard," Anne muttered again, examining Maggie from head to toe, touching a few bite marks and bruises. "It won't hurt the next time."

"I know." A shudder passed through her entire body. "I can't imagine doing it again, though. Not with him or anyone."

"It gets easier. You just close your eyes and get through it. Once you're more experienced, you can learn ways to get them to finish faster. It just seems overwhelming now because it was your first time."

Maggie slipped her arms into her robe. Finding her knees weak and legs shaky, she perched on the edge of the mattress, shifting slightly to one side in deference to her sore bottom. She looked up at Anne, her eyes weary, her soul heartsick. "I can't stay here, Anne. I can't do this for him. I thought I could, but I can't."

"Are you sure it would be so terrible?"

"He's not offering me anything, really. A liaison until he marries, which will be in the next year. No future support. In fact, if I find myself with child, he said flat out that he'd put me out on the street."

"I don't understand men," Anne said, shaking her head.

"Neither do I." She reached out and took Anne's hands in her own. "I'm sure this probably sounds foolish, but I expected more."

"In what way?"

"More from him, I guess. He was so angry when he saw me at the ball, and heaven only knows what George said to him before I came along. But he can be considerate and funny and gentle, and I thought . . . I thought if I gave myself to him that he'd . . .''—her voice dropped to a whisper—"he'd care about me.''

Anne felt sick. Maggie's heart was already broken, and it would only get worse. That was simply the way of it. For a kindhearted, loving girl like Maggie, a relationship with the likes of Adam St. Clair was the very worst thing that could happen. Gently, she said, "That's what we all wish for, Maggie. Unfortunately, it rarely happens. Men want only one thing from women like us, and when they get it, they're off to their next challenge.''

"Isn't that the truth! I poured my heart and soul into making love with him, and when I opened my eyes this morning, all he could talk about was how he was in such a hurry, and that he'd decided I could bed him three nights a week, and if I was a really good girl, he'd take me out to the theater on occasion.'' Tears welled into her eyes again, which surprised her; she thought she'd cried them all out. "I feel like such a fool.''

"Don't.''

"But I wanted so much for this to work out so you'd be safe, but I didn't even accomplish that much.''

"Don't worry about me.'' Anne patted her hand. "He had an attack of conscience on the way out and told me I could stay if I wanted.''

"How gallant.''

"Wasn't it, though? I told him to stuff it.''

"But you won't really leave me, will you?''

Anne pulled up a chair to face her and sat wearily. The message had come the night before, after Maggie had already left for the ball. "I need to tell you something.''

"What is it?''

"I received an offer yesterday from an old friend of mine. She's starting a new business, and she wants some women with experience to help her get going.''

"What kind of business is it?''

"It's a brothel, Maggie." She hurried on before Maggie could voice a protest. "It's a nice enough place. I'll have my own room, and I won't have to service a man unless I want to. She's willing to give me a chance, so I'm going to do it." She smiled, trying to lighten the moment. "I'm sure it will work out for the best."

"Oh, Anne, please say you're not going to."

"I have to. You said yourself that this situation with St. Clair is only temporary. If we don't do something, in a few months' time we'll be right back in the same fix. This way, at least I can start working toward a new life." She'd been trying to find just such a position for the past year, and now that it was available, she wasn't about to pass it up. "By the time he's finished with you, I hope I'll have a way to help you."

"But I can't bear the thought of you leaving me. And I can't bear the thought of staying here and doing this with him night after night. Now that I've had intimate relations with him, I can't imagine it continuing. I truly believe it's something that should only happen when there's love between the two parties."

So young. So innocent. So incredibly, stupidly naive. Anne shook her head. "Spoken like a true romantic. Unfortunately, love and romance won't put food on the table or a roof over your head. At least, they never did for me. I've got to make my way, Maggie. For both of us."

"Well, I can't stay here either. What Adam wants from me should be so beautiful and should make me so happy. Instead, I feel cheap and dirty. I'm afraid of the kind of person I'll become if I remain."

Anne sighed. "Would you like to come with me? I asked my friend about you, and she said she'd give you work."

"I could never work as a whore!" Maggie gasped.

"I told her that. That you'd need something else. In the tavern or in the kitchens. As a maid. She said if you worked hard, she would let you stay. You'd have to share a room in the attic with some of the other serving girls."

"That settles it easily enough for me." Maggie stood carefully. "Help me wash. I want to pack and go before he has a chance to return."

Adam sat at the desk in his library, reviewing the last of a stack of correspondence. The only task left for the day was a long, tedious supper with his mother. After, it would finally be time to head to Maggie's. He'd been quite proud of himself for the last thirty-six hours. After leaving her bed the previous morning, he'd completed a full day of work, appointments, and commitments. In the evening, he'd escorted a young lady to the theater, and had even managed to act as though he enjoyed carrying on a conversation with her.

He'd slept through most of the night, with only a minimum of sexual frustration causing him to toss and turn, then spent another day handling family business and other personal affairs. All without dropping everything and rushing to see her earlier than he'd told her he would arrive. As her protector, he was entitled to drop in whenever he wanted, and he'd certainly desired to visit, but he'd managed to restrain himself. He felt it necessary to set the right tone for their affair. If the woman believed he was smitten, she'd become assertive and demanding, and Adam couldn't let that happen. He intended to control the rhythm of their relationship.

Still, he was worried. Something about their parting hadn't seemed right, although he couldn't quite put his finger on the problem. Maggie had been so unusually timid and quiet that memories of those last few moments together continued to plague him. Their coupling had been incredible—on his end of things. He'd ridden her rough and hard, too hard for a virgin, and he couldn't help but fret over how she was feeling. She was probably sore, wondering if it would always be like that.

Very likely, on the morning after, he should have spent some time praising and reassuring instead of concentrating on the business end of the relationship, but he had been too overwhelmed to be thinking clearly. By the light of day, his actions had seemed so shocking. That he'd taken a mistress, something he'd vowed never to do, was a bit frightening and onerous. Needing time and distance to arrange his thoughts about the matter into some semblance of order, he'd left her side as quickly as possible.

But, oh, how he'd wanted to stay. She was so lovely in the early dawn. Her hair mussed and tangled, her lips still rosy and swollen from his kisses. What a sight!

Closing his eyes, he rubbed a finger and thumb along the bridge of his nose, trying to work away the stress he'd endured during the last two days, but all he saw behind his closed lids was the view of her breasts first thing that morning when she'd sat up and the covers had fallen to her waist. Her lovely nipples had been the color of ripe peaches.

"Oooh," he groaned to himself, and pressed his palm across his crotch, trying to ease some of the pressure. Only a few more hours. He smiled, but it and his erection quickly evaporated as his mother's footsteps sounded in the hall outside. Instantly, he was swamped by guilt, pondering what had possessed him to have purchased Maggie's favors while knowing how badly his mother would be hurt if she knew.

Following quickly on the heels of the guilt was irritation at the fact that he was a Marquis, one of the wealthiest, most powerful men in the kingdom, nearly thirty years old, but still scampering around at his mother's heel, dancing to her tune because he was afraid to offend her. Whether he took a mistress or not was really none of her business.

Lucretia St. Clair entered the room without bothering to knock. She was a short, stout woman who'd not aged well. In her late fifties, her hair was a dull gray, her face lined with wrinkles of unhappiness, her hands purpled with spots. Adam had never understood her, but he cared for her out of a sense of duty and respect—the same duty and respect she'd drilled into him every day of his life. Her family traced its lines back centuries further than most others and was one of the oldest in England. He'd been raised as she'd been raised—with an eye toward what was best for country and title, not necessarily what was best for the people involved.

If she'd ever had a cheerful moment, Adam had not seen it. For all the wealth and position into which she'd been born and married, she'd remained a bitterly unhappy woman. Her arranged marriage to Adam's father, Aston, had been a disaster from the first day. Lucretia claimed it was because he had a mistress at the time of their wedding, one Grace Stuart, who he had kept all through the years of his life. Aston had never voiced his opinion on the matter—letting his actions speak for themselves.

The man had sired three children with Grace Stuart, lavished her and them with love, attention, and affection, and for the last two decades of his life, lived openly with her, having the unmitigated gall to die in her bed while in the middle of the carnal act. Through all those years, he was rarely home. Adam and James hardly knew him, and Lucretia never saw him. They communicated through a solicitor if she needed anything. The humiliation had been so great that Lucretia never recovered from it.

His Aunt Lavinia insisted that Lucretia had been born harsh and disillusioned. That her spiteful ways and hateful attitude had driven Aston from their home and life. That whatever had come her way over the passing years had simply been what she deserved and no more. Adam didn't know.

All he knew was that she was his mother, and he had the duty to take care of her. And the responsibility to put up with her. He sighed as she entered the room.

"Good evening, Mother."

"Adam, I'm glad you're here. I've prepared the invitations for the house party. I wanted you to look them over before the final engraving is done."

The Season was ending soon, and their gathering would be one of the fine country affairs held after people left London. Scheduled for the end of September, it would also be something more than a simple house party, because they were inviting a dozen or more marriageable young ladies. "I'm sure whatever you've selected is fine," he said.

"Nevertheless, I insist you look." She placed them on the desk.

"They look excellent, Mother. Truly," he said as he gave a cursory glance. His eye caught the dates. Two weeks! Gad, he'd forgotten that he'd agreed to spend that much time eyeing the candidates. The length made it sound like some form of medieval torture. More surprising was his reaction to the realization that he'd not be able to see Maggie the entire time. The girl was already taking over his thoughts and life, and he'd only bedded her once. What would happen to him after a dozen times? After a hundred? He shuddered to think.

"Perhaps, one week, though. I'm not sure I can abide two."

"It will be two. We can't expect the ladies to make the trip for any less of a stay."

"Mother, they'd come to spend time with me if it was going to last only an hour."

"Two weeks. No less."

"All right, Mother. Whatever you feel is best is fine with me." He gave her a placating look, which sent her on her way. Years ago, he'd learned that it was best simply to agree with whatever she wanted, which he did on a regular basis. Then he would go ahead and do what *he* wanted despite her wishes. It usually worked out well, although in this instance, it would be hard to accomplish. Leaving his own house party a week early would be the height of rudeness, and all the guests would feel slighted.

The headache brought on by his mother's visit vanished instantly with the appearance of his brother. Adam had been so busy that they'd not seen each other in over a week. The room filled with James's energy as he burst in laughing and full of good humor. Pouring them both a stout whiskey, he pulled up a chair across the desk.

"What have you done now?" James asked with a twinkle in his eye.

"What do you mean?"

"I mean that I was just at the club, where I was accosted by no less than the grand Duke of Roswell, himself, demanding to know the identity of the woman you escorted out of the ball Thursday night."

"Could you imagine having that man as a father-in-law?" Adam's headache was suddenly back.

"Better you than me." James chuckled, and continued. "Now, I must admit that from his description, I could only guess that the woman was the lovely and incredible Maggie Brown."

Adam's head came swinging up. "You didn't tell him her name, did you?"

"Of course not. So . . . it was her. Wherever did you find each other?"

"Better fill your glass. You will not believe this."

James sipped quietly as Adam related the events of the night. He tactfully omitted the steamier details of what happened in the bedroom, but James got the general drift that Adam was ecstatic at his run of circumstance and couldn't wait to join her later in the evening.

"You always did have the Devil's own luck. I'm jealous," James said. Trying to sound as casual as possible, he asked, "What about her friend, Miss Porter. Any word on what's become of her?"

"Actually, I saw her for a moment." Adam was too embarrassed to mention that he'd nearly tossed her out on the street.

"How was she?"

"She seemed the same. Pretty. Astute."

"Astute is a good word for her." James chuckled. "Any idea where she's living these days?"

"No," he truthfully replied, "but Maggie would probably know how to get in touch with her." Just then, the butler knocked and entered, and Adam asked, "Yes, what is it?"

"One of the footmen you sent over to the house on Mulberry has returned. He says he needs to speak with you."

"Send him in."

A few moments later, a young man, part of the small cadre of servants he'd sent to Maggie's house the day before, stood in the doorway. Visibly nervous, the man stood wringing his hat in his hands, waiting to be recognized.

"Hello, John," Adam said, motioning him to enter. "What is it?"

"Lord Belmont, I went to the house as you asked. With the ladies you sent, and, well, they asked me to come and talk with you, you see."

"About what?"

"Well, we've spent the better part of two days there now, and there's no one there, and the ladies thought it was somewhat odd, and that maybe we ought to let you know, seeing as you were planning on visiting this evening."

"There's no one there?"

"No, sir. We've cleaned, stocked up the food, started receiving the new furniture and whatnot that's been arriving, but there's nobody about."

"Not even last night?"

"No, sir. And the abigail tells me the ladies' chests and such are partly empty. Like they took some of their clothes."

Adam looked over at James, trying to make sense of what he was hearing. In a matter of hours, he was to join Maggie in her bed. It was unthinkable that she wasn't there. For the past two days, all he'd thought about was her and what their next encounter would be like. She couldn't be gone! He managed to ask, "Anything else?"

"There was a note. Left in one of the bedchambers. Mrs. Perkins said I ought to bring it to you."

Adam reached out his hand and took the sealed missive. "Thank you."

The footman cleared his throat. "The ladies and I were wondering . . . ah . . . should we stay there or leave or what?"

"Tell everyone to stay, until I know more of what's going on."

"Very good, milord. Thank you. I'll be getting back then . . ." He hesitated, then slipped away once it became clear that the Marquis was distracted.

Adam hardly noticed the servant's departure as he scanned the brief words penned by Maggie.

Thank you for your generous offer, but I find I cannot accept what you have so graciously proposed. Good luck in your future marriage. I wish you much happiness.

He turned the note over and over, thinking there must be something more. A further explanation or a better good-bye. Some hint to what she was thinking or where she'd gone. His brow creased, he looked up at James. "I can't believe it."

"What's that?"

"It's a note from Maggie, declining my offer."

James had the audacity to laugh aloud at the news. He raised a glass in toast. "Bravo for you, Maggie-girl."

"You find this amusing?" Adam managed to sputter.

"Very. I've lived to see the great Marquis of Belmont put in his place." He laughed again, downed his drink, then asked, "What is it about those two women? Do they simply bring out the worst in us, or do we always act the bastard and they're the only two with enough courage to tell us so?"

"I fail to see how I have acted the bastard toward Magdalina Brown."

"Let me guess. You angrily dragged her out of a ballroom full of curious spectators, threatened and chastised her all the way home, wooed her by painfully ending her maidenhood, then spent the rest of the night telling her what a great catch she'd made for herself."

Too embarrassed to admit that was pretty much how it had gone, Adam blustered, "What makes you think that's what happened?"

"Because, brother, you are so bloody predictable."

Adam was stunned, shocked, and completely at a loss. No

woman had ever refused him anything. Every female he'd ever known practically threw herself at his feet. Women he'd never even met lay in their beds at night, planning and scheming on how to lure him into their lives. Finally, he'd reached out to have more than a passing acquaintance with one of them, and she'd thrown his offer back in his face.

He looked at James. "I will never understand women as long as I live."

"What don't you understand?"

"I offered that girl everything a woman could want. A new home. All the beautiful clothes she could wear. Food on her table. Trips to the theater. If she'd continued to please me, she could have had any number of jewels and trinkets."

"And let's not forget the privilege of being allied with one such as yourself." James was being facetious, but Adam didn't catch it.

"Exactly. And it wasn't enough. What more could she possibly have wanted?"

Seeing the look of consternation on his brother's face, James decided to take pity on him. "You really don't know?"

"Do I look like I know?"

"Adam, sometimes I really and truly worry about you."

"Why?"

"Because I don't understand how you could have lived to be twenty-nine years of age and still be so obtuse when it comes to women."

"I admit it without hesitation. I am ignorant where females are concerned, but if you're so wise, tell me what she wanted."

"She wanted what you could never give her."

"I am one of the wealthiest men in the land. What could she possibly desire that I could not provide?" he asked, his exasperation at a limit.

"Part of yourself."

"Which part?"

"Your heart, you bloody fool. She wanted the only thing you would never give."

"She wanted"—he paused, the idea being so preposterous—"love?"

"It would seem so, and it appears that if she couldn't have your heart, she didn't want anything from you at all."

"But it was a business arrangement," Adam growled in frustration.

"To you. Obviously, it meant something more to her."

"I say it again: I will never understand women as long as I live."

Chapter Eleven

Charles Billington pressed back into the soft leather of his seat and glanced casually around the darkly paneled room of his club. Thank goodness, his oldest brother, the Earl, was kind enough to continue paying his dues. Charles could never have afforded them on his own, and his brother was only too happy to spring for the coin that enabled him to continue frequenting the place.

Membership was a financial necessity—for the base of Charles's income was generated through contacts with the other members. Many of his portraiture contracts came from the men he met, and he worked hard for his money, diligently painting their wives and daughters.

As the seventh of eight children, and the fifth son, Charles had had to do something to be able to afford his own living arrangements, his style of life and preferences hardly being conducive to continuing habitation in his mother's home. While his brother wasn't overly keen on the fact that Charles worked for a living, he was glad that Charles rarely needed any support.

As for Charles, he made a good living at his art. Not a grand one but a good one, and he enjoyed painting and the freedom his income brought. His mother, Lavinia, who marveled at the eccentricities of artists and was therefore a great patron of the arts, was so pleased to have one in the family that everyone else was forced to be glad as well.

There were other benefits to club membership, as well, for Charles never seemed to have quite enough money, and he refused to go hat in hand to his brother, so he always had his eye out for inventive ways to make a few extra pounds. Other members of the club had, on occasion, been interested in his various schemes and enterprises, and there was so much money floating around among them that Charles was always happy to help them part with it. On those occasions when the business dealings went sour, the men were discreet, too proud and embarrassed to talk about financial losses with others.

At least, that was what he'd believed in the past. Unfortunately, he'd made the wrong choice this time. Robert, his current companion, sat next to him in another snit, and Charles had well and truly had enough of his tantrum. He wanted only to carry out his business affairs with the utmost discretion and decorum, and his patience with the lad was at an end.

"What would you have me do?" he asked Robert with a pleasant enough smile on his face. It was one he'd perfected years ago. He could talk about nearly anything without giving a hint to others about his true feelings concerning the current topic of discussion.

"I'm weary of your patronizing me!" Robert said. "I need my money back, and I need it now." The second son of a minor baron, he was a pretty young man, with dark hair and indigo eyes. His cheeks always had a healthy blush, but they grew downright rosy when he was in the middle of an upset. As he was now.

"How am I patronizing you? I've told you what happened. I lost money, too, and I'm quite stressed about it." Robert wanted Charles to return the money he'd invested, but Charles simply didn't have it. Never again would he make the mistake of taking money from such an impressionable young man. He knew better.

"I won't be ignored by you," Robert responded, his temper growing by the moment. "I won't stand for it."

"I'm not ignoring you, Robert. I simply don't know how else to explain it to you so you'll understand. Now, listen: The investment didn't succeed. The money is gone, and we can't get it back. I clarified all the risks to you before we started, so I don't know what else you expect from me."

"I absolutely must have the money back! I must!"

Just then, relief swept Charles's features as he saw his cousin James enter the room. The perfect excuse for escape. "There's James. I'm sorry, but we'll have to continue this another time."

"See . . . this is exactly the sort of thing . . ." Robert started to whine.

"Get hold of yourself this minute." Charles silenced him with a vicious glare. "I will not be embarrassed by you in here, especially not in front of a member of my family. Excuse me." Without giving the boy a chance to argue, he stood and walked across the room to the bar, where James had already swallowed the amber contents of his glass.

"Pretty, that one," James whispered, with an imperceptible glance toward Robert.

"Trust me, cousin, looks can be deceiving." Holding out his own glass to have it refilled, he tipped it back as well.

"Do I detect a note of displeasure?"

"You detect an entire symphony of displeasure."

"Then, I'd say I arrived just in the nick of time."

"Just in time for what?" Charles asked.

"Actually, I'm on a desperate mission of mercy, and you're just the person to assist me."

Charles chuckled, wondering what kind of scheme James had in mind. There had certainly been hundreds of them they'd enjoyed together. He was game for anything that would remove him from Robert's presence. "I'm all ears."

"We're going to kidnap Adam." They'd nabbed him numerous times over the years when they felt he needed rescue from the burdens of his responsibilities.

"From where?"

"The soiree at the Duke's. He looked like a man on his way to the gallows when he left."

"Penelope hasn't managed to snag him this week, has she?"

"Not yet."

"Thank God," Charles muttered.

"He's spending entirely too much time with her, though, if you want my opinion. I thought we should stir things up a bit."

"It will certainly set her into a fine fit of pique if we make off with him."

"We can hope, at least."

"May I ask where we're taking him?"

"A brothel." The two men left the bar and started toward the stairs to retrieve their cloaks on the way to James's carriage. "It's a new place. Just opening tonight."

"Yes, I'd heard something about it. They're offering numerous interesting diversions. Or so I heard."

"Just what Adam needs."

"He's jammed up, is he?"

"Brokenhearted is more like."

"What?" Charles asked, not sure he'd heard right. It was hard to imagine Adam letting himself be upset by anything— or anyone. "You're joking."

"No, I'm not. Remember the girl I told you about?"

"The one you met on holiday?"

"Yes. Well, he ran into her again and went to the trouble of setting her up as his mistress."

Charles's eyes were as wide as saucers at the thought of Adam doing something so out of his character. "This woman I definitely want to meet."

"Well, you won't get to. She threw his offer back in his face."

"No!"

"It's true. Then she disappeared without a trace." And so

did Anne, he nearly added, but bit his tongue. No use starting across that bridge. "He's been absolutely unbearable ever since."

"And you're hoping to ease his . . . stress . . . shall we say?"

"That's the least of it. I can hardly tolerate the man these days."

"A brothel it is, then."

"What do you think?" James asked, looking around the finely decorated private room of the brothel. The madam, an actress in her younger days, was a woman with whom James had consorted through the years, and when she'd decided to open her business, he'd received an invitation.

At James's question, Adam's assessing gaze followed his brother's. Considering some of the places to which James and Charles had dragged him over the years, it was certainly nice enough. He'd been angry when they'd originally told him where they were headed, but the private welcome and comfortable decor had helped to slacken his irritation. Maggie had disappeared precisely a month earlier, and he'd had no sexual release since the brief night of passion he'd spent in her arms. A few hours of sexual activity would be a welcomed diversion.

Still, he refused to let his two abductors know he was too approving. "I guess it will do."

"Madam Barbara says we can go through as many of the girls as we want."

"Certainly obliging of her."

"She's sending in her prettiest and most experienced girl first, so we'll get off to a good start. She wants us to tell our friends how much we enjoyed ourselves."

"Good God," Adam snorted, "next thing I know our visit will be the talk of the town."

"I can just hear it now," Charles chimed in, adding in a bad imitation of a feminine voice, "'The Marquis of Belmont is one of our most satisfied customers.'"

"Bloody hell." Adam shook his head. "I'm leaving."

"No, you're not." James forced him to remain with an angry look. "You're going to go through as many girls as it takes to drum Maggie Brown out of your system—for good. I'm tired of the way you've been acting."

"What way is that?"

"You've been a total ass. I know I speak for everyone who's come in contact with you for the past month when I say we're all sick of you." It was the truth. Adam had been short-tempered, rude, surly and downright mean since the evening he'd learned that Maggie had disappeared.

Adam's behavior had gotten so bad that even their mother had noticed, and she was so self-absorbed that if it had finally come to her attention, that was proof that the matter had gotten completely out of hand. "If a few tumbles with some pretty girls won't loosen you up, I don't know what will."

Just then, the door from the hall opened. A lone woman entered. Charles was the only person facing the door, and in the shadows, he couldn't see her face, but he could make out from the sway of her sheer dressing gown that she wasn't a serving maid.

"I believe refreshments have arrived," he joked.

At hearing the comment, a throaty laugh escaped from the woman. "I heard you gentleman had worked up an appetite." James and Adam were sharing a deep-cushioned sofa. Moving closer, she walked behind them, trailing a finger across their shoulders as she passed. She stepped round the edge of the bulky couch and into the light.

If someone had been watching, it would have been hard to guess which person was more surprised. Charles, Adam, and James all knew her. And she knew them.

"Anne?" Charles and James asked at the same time.

"Miss Porter?" Adam demanded, incredulous.

Anne pressed the tips of her fingers to her lips. "Oh, my God . . ."

James broke the tense moment, jumping to his feet. "Anne, is it really you?"

"Yes, it is I," she admitted, her shoulders drooping.

"Whatever are you doing here?"

"Working." She shrugged, as though that should explain it all.

"Here?"

"Why not?" she asked back, trying to sound certain.

The room grew unbearably silent, making Anne painfully aware that she was nearly nude, and the three men were looking at her with varying degrees of shock and outrage. She was wearing only stockings and mules with a sheer robe over all, and her entire front was on view for their inspection, from the valley of her breasts to the dark mound between her legs. She tugged frantically at the lapels of the robe, but considering that the fabric was fairly transparent, the move did little to alleviate the situation.

For James, who had been initially mesmerized by seeing her, it took a moment to realize she was naked. Then he shrugged out of his coat and jammed her arms into the sleeves. "Here. Cover yourself."

"Thank you," she murmured weakly, looking to the floor. Too embarrassed to look him in the eye, she glanced over to Charles, who was assessing her with a kind, but knowing, gaze. Tears welled into her eyes. "I'm sorry, but I don't think I can do this. I'll have Barbara send someone else."

She turned to leave, but James's arm wound round her waist and gripped her tightly before she could make her escape. He pressed her cheek against his chest and nuzzled his face in her hair, while running a hand up and down her back as though quieting a skittish horse.

"*Cher*, I won't let you stay here," he said softly. "I want you to leave with us." He looked to Charles for confirmation of his decision.

"He's right, Anne." Charles nodded in agreement. He'd met her years earlier when she was mistress to their friend Stephen

Frasier. After Stephen's death, he'd never learned what happened to her. To think that this had been her end! "We can't let you remain."

"It's all right. Really." She tried to sound more positive than she was. "It's a good situation for me." Which she hoped would prove true. But this was her first night and these her first customers, so who could know if all Barbara's promises would come to pass?

"You can't mean that," Charles said, comforting her. "What would Stephen say if he knew you were working in such a place as this?"

The mention of Stephen's name in association with what she'd been prepared to do was too much, and she started to cry silent tears. Looking at the floor, she whispered, "I don't have anywhere else to go."

James, crushed by her heart-wrenching confession, leaned down and kissed her cheek. "We'll find you a place."

Up to this point, Adam had been silent, watching the exchange. Finally, he stood, joining the other three and asking tersely, "Where is Maggie?"

"Calm down, Adam," James warned.

"Where is she?" Adam ignored him, his attention completely focused on Anne. Anne met his gaze with tear-filled eyes, but before she could respond, he put up a hand to stop her. "Before you answer, let me caution you that if you tell me she is servicing someone in one of these rooms, I cannot guarantee that I shall be responsible for my actions."

"It's not what you think."

"Miss Porter, we're standing in a brothel. I believe it's exactly what I think."

"She's here, but working as a maid. Nothing more."

"Where?"

"Probably on the floor above. Or she may be down by the laundry. You may have to ask someone."

Adam wrenched his furious focus from Anne to James.

"Take Miss Porter down to the carriage. I will find Maggie and meet you there."

Anne shook her head, wondering why the man was always so bloody angry where Maggie was concerned. "I doubt if she will leave with you."

"We shall see."

Maggie knocked on Monique's door. Once. Then again. And a third time as she'd been taught. No response. She briskly entered the whore's private room, loaded down with fresh water and towels. With newly learned efficiency, she began tidying, preparing for Monique's next guest. The woman hadn't made much of a mess with her last customer, so there wasn't much to do. The bedcovers hadn't even been mussed, which caused her to wonder just what the gentleman had required.

On occasion, she found herself pondering what would be happening in the lavishly decorated rooms, but she tried not to think about it too often. Nothing good ever came of it, because whatever Monique ended up doing was certainly close enough to what Anne would have to do in her own room down below on the next floor. Maggie had specifically asked to work in a different area of the brothel just so she would not have to run into Anne on such occasions.

They saw each other often during the busy days preceding the grand opening, but Maggie knew that would change once business commenced. The brothel had a definite hierarchy, and Maggie, being little more than a scullery maid, was definitely on the bottom rung. Their hours would be quite a bit different, too. Maggie would work round the clock, doing laundry during the day, servicing the rooms at night. The prostitutes, who were considered by all to be the upper echelon of employees, would work all night and rest during the day, rising in late afternoon only to work on their hair, skin, and lingerie for the coming evening of customers.

With a final look around Monique's room, Maggie decided

everything was readied. She wanted to start off on the right foot by being extremely meticulous about seeing to the needs of each woman, for she knew better than anyone how difficult it was to find a job and she wanted to keep this one, no matter that she was already worn down from her laboring. What she would feel like in a few weeks or months after keeping up the grueling pace, she could only imagine.

The pay was minimal, so she'd never be able to save any money, but at least, her meals and bed were included, although her shared room in the attic left much to be desired. The small space had started out clean and tidy, but with a dozen young women packed inside, it was impossible to keep it that way. There was no privacy.

She'd already had a few of her meager possessions stolen, which put a quick damper on any illusions she might have harbored about becoming friends with the others. So far, nothing was as she'd imagined it might be, and any optimism she'd harbored about the future was long gone.

Two sets of footsteps sounded down the hall. Neither set sounded like those of a woman, and Maggie had been warned enough times by the other girls never to be caught above-stairs by an unaccompanied male. In this case, it sounded like two unaccompanied males. Before she had time to wonder what they were doing, for male guests were not supposed to be allowed to roam past the downstairs salons without an escort, one of the men stepped into Monique's room.

He gave a quick look about as Maggie huddled silent and still along the back wall, hoping that she'd be invisible in the dim light. Even from across the room, she could smell the strong odor of alcohol. The men were foxed.

"Is she in there?" the man in the hall asked.

"No, that bitch. When I find her . . ." He stopped, his eyes coming to linger on Maggie. "Well, well, what have we here?"

Trying to act like nothing was amiss, she bowed her head, looking contrite. "Excuse me, sir. I didn't realize Monique had a guest waiting. I'll tell her you're here." She moved toward the door, hoping to make a quick escape.

The man grabbed her arm. "I don't think we need to wait for Monique." He stepped into the room, pulling her backside against his front and pinning her arms behind her back. "What say you, Harry?"

"I say we can always enjoy Monique another time." Harry reached out and ran a hand down her cheek, then her throat, to cup her breast. Behind her, she heard the click of the lock.

Maggie tried to flinch back from the unwelcomed touch, but Harry's friend was holding her too tightly. His painful grip forced her bosom to full display for Harry, who was standing in front of her. They both laughed, and from the look exchanged by the two, Maggie knew something terrible was about to happen. She was frightened, more frightened than she'd ever been, but she knew better than to let them see it.

"Please, sir," she begged, "if I don't get back to my duties, I'll be losing my job."

"Think of this as a promotion." Harry's hands settled on her waist, and she started to struggle.

"I'm just a girl, a virgin," she lied, seeing instantly that it had been the wrong thing to say. The admission only fueled their state of arousal.

"Hear that, Gregory?" Harry laughed viciously. "A damned virgin. Must be our lucky night."

"A virgin? In a brothel? Imagine that."

The madam had warned her not to fight if something like this ever happened. At the time, Maggie had barely paid attention, never imagining that such a horrible event could actually occur. While the woman was probably well meaning in her advice, Maggie quickly realized that there was no way she would let the two men do this to her without a fight.

Yanking her arm free, she swung a fist as hard as she could, managing to connect with the side of Harry's head just hard enough to get his attention. His eyes blazed with fury. "Well, my little wildcat, you like it rough, do you? So do I.'' His eyes met Gregory's. ''Hold her tighter.''

''I want to do her first.''

''No, no. This privilege is all mine.'' His fingers went to his breeches, and she started kicking with her feet, just missing his vital parts. Seeming annoyed more than anything, he grabbed for her ankles, catching one and using it as a lever to pull her legs apart.

Gregory kept her arms wrenched behind her back while Harry moved between her legs, balancing them around his waist. Maggie screamed at the top of her lungs, and he slapped her hard across the face, hard enough to make her see stars, and she wanted nothing more than to sink to the floor and curl up in a ball, but there was no time.

The feel of a hand working its way up the inside of her thigh brought her back to full consciousness. The hem of her skirt was pushed up to her waist, and a groping hand struggled to slip into her drawers, trying to touch her where only Adam had ever touched her before. She squeezed her eyes tight, hoping to shut out what was coming.

At first, so caught up was she in the moment, she didn't realize what was happening. There was pounding on the door, a loud crash, then thuds and kicks. Someone let out a horrible *ooopf* sound when a blow landed, and she was free and falling to the floor. Disoriented and confused, she tried to crawl away, but two strong arms encircled her before she could escape. She started struggling again, hitting and crying out.

''Stop it! Maggie, stop it!'' the voice said over and over.

''No,'' she screamed, trying to break free from the grip holding her.

''Maggie, it's me. It's Adam. You're all right.''

Adam's name, spoken so forcefully and calmly, was the one thing that pierced through her panic and brought her back to reality. Instantly, she stopped struggling and collapsed against him. She trembled fiercely. Behind him, she could see her two attackers lying on the floor. Both were moaning. Gregory's face was a mass of blood and gore, and he looked as though his nose was broken.

"Oh, my God . . ." With fingers to her lips, she looked up into Adam's dark eyes—eyes once so known and so loved. "The other girls told me not to fight, but I had to. I couldn't let them . . ."

"Ssh . . . It's all right. Don't try to talk."

"I think I'm going to be sick." With that bit of warning, Adam shifted her weight, and she vomited over and over onto the rug as she heard steps rushing down the hall.

"Lord Belmont?" The madam's voice. "What's happened?"

Adam's words were muffled in her ringing ears. Something about *attack* and *bastards*. Maggie glanced around and saw two burly men hauling Harry and Gregory out of the room. Once they were gone, Adam pulled her to her feet, sitting her down on the bed, where she perched precariously on the edge. Only his arm firm against her elbow kept her from sliding to the floor.

"This woman is a friend of mine," he told the madam in no uncertain terms. "She's leaving with me."

The madam glanced back and forth at the two of them, and although she momentarily looked as though she might raise a protest or complaint, her features straightened as she realized that it was useless to question any action the Marquis might wish to take. "Certainly."

"Get her a cloak. Have her belongings packed. I'll send for them."

The woman departed, and he stared down at Maggie with an unreadable expression on his face.

"I'm sorry," she offered. It was inadequate and feeble, but she was still shaking too hard to think of anything better.

"It would serve you right if I left you here," he said through clenched teeth, his fingers digging into her shoulders. "Of all the stupid, idiotic, dangerous ideas . . ." He found himself gulping for air, his fear, anger, and outrage spent and replaced by a wave of thanks that he'd arrived in time to help her.

Needing to feel her safe and close, he stood her on her feet and held her in the circle of his arms. Gently, he rocked her as he kissed her hair, whispering, "It will be all right—everything will be all right now," over and over until her trembling slowed. "Let me take care of you. Let me take care of everything."

Chapter Twelve

Maggie looked around at the familiar sights of the bedroom in her childhood home. Many things were different, but much remained the same, as though Adam, in his renovations, knew exactly what she would have wanted him to keep and what to throw away.

Home.

Nothing ever felt better.

Before leaving the brothel, Adam had sent a messenger on ahead, with instructions for the small covey of servants. By the time his carriage pulled up at her door, the lamps were lit, the fires blazing, and a hot bath awaited her in front of the small hearth in her room.

A young woman not much older than herself, who introduced herself as Gail, was her personal maid, and she'd efficiently stripped Maggie and helped her into the steaming water, which was a good thing. Maggie's arms and legs seemed to have quit functioning.

Gail washed her body, then her hair, sudsing and rinsing, then combing out the long ends and fanning them over the rim of the tub so they lay drying in front of the fire. Only when the maid felt all traces of the ordeal had been sufficiently washed away was Maggie allowed to soak contentedly alone.

Sighing with relief, she sunk low into the steaming tub and closed her eyes to better absorb the pleasure. Every muscle in her body ached, her head pounded fiercely, her face throbbed where the man named Harry had slapped her. The bath was just what she'd needed, but the bliss it provided was temporary, for Adam appeared a few minutes after Gail's departure.

They'd not spoken since leaving the brothel. The ride in the carriage had been a tense one, the silence broken only by James and Charles whispering occasionally to Anne. Neither woman had looked at the other during the trip home to Mulberry Street, as though they were two naughty children caught in some sort of awful predicament.

It was hard to know what Adam was thinking as he stood there silently, sipping the brandy from his glass. She supposed she should be wondering about the future. He would certainly be within his rights to toss them out on the streets in the morning and good riddance, but she was too exhausted to worry about what would happen next.

Dear Lord, but she was tired. Tired of hard work. Tired of long hours. Tired of her lot in life. Tired of being alone, of having no one to turn to when she needed help. Tired of everything, and it felt so good to be back home where she felt safe and secure. She didn't want to ever leave again.

Adam emptied his glass and noticed that his hands were still shaking. From the moment he'd heard her cry of alarm as he'd walked down the hall in the brothel, he'd known it was her. Without so much as a second to ponder the consequences, he'd kicked in the door. Seeing her in the arms of those two bastards had been the most horrible thing he'd ever witnessed.

He knew the pair: a couple of low-life second sons, living off the charity of distant relatives, always in trouble with gambling and drink. It had felt so good to hear flesh connecting and feel bone crunching. He hadn't been in a good brawl since he was twenty-two and fighting his way out of a dockside tavern with James and Charles by his side.

Maggie was shaking as well, her face was bruised where one of them had struck her, and Lord only knows how many other injuries she had hidden below the water. Pale and fragile, she looked like a beautiful doll about to shatter into a thousand pieces.

He wasn't sure how to ask, but needed to know.

"Did they . . . ?" His voice sounded overly loud in the quiet room. She was already flushed from the hot water; his question only reddened her further.

"No," she answered, lowering her eyes in embarrassment. "No, they didn't have enough time."

Walking to the tub, he stared down at her. Her breasts were fully visible, the water lapping against her rosy nipples. Below, he could make out the shadow of her mound, and his manhood stirred as he took in the sight. Hell and be damned, she'd been assaulted, nearly raped, tormented, was far past fatigue, but he wanted her. That would always be the way of things where she was concerned.

"Why did you leave?" The question had burned inside him for days and weeks, wreaking havoc with his concentration and his temper.

"I had to." She was so exhausted that she couldn't imagine discussing anything of consequence, but she supposed he wouldn't stop until he had his answers. Then, just maybe, she'd be able to close her eyes and shut out the world for a few hours.

"Was the thought of sharing my bed so horrible that you would rather work in a brothel?"

"Is that what you think?"

"What else should I think?"

"You don't understand anything."

"No, I don't. Look at your hands." He reached into the water and pulled one out, dripping and soaking. Rubbing a thumb across her palm, he turned it up to look at the reddened skin. Before, they'd been soft and fragrant. Now, they were rough and callused, the nails chipped and broken. "What possessed you to do something so rash? You'd rather work yourself like a slave? Or endanger yourself on the streets? I offered you everything you could ever want or need, so you're right: I don't understand."

"What did you offer me?" Her bottom lip started to tremble, but she caught it under her teeth. Taking a deep breath, she forged ahead. "A few quick tumbles? Some dresses and trinkets?"

"Don't forget a roof over your head and food on your table."

"Oh, yes, let's not forget that. And for how long? A month? Two? Six? What were your plans for me after that? Would you pawn me off to one of your friends? Maybe marry me to one of your servants?"

Adam had no answer. When he'd taken her from the ball that night, he'd certainly not had time to consider such things about their future. In the past month, he'd told himself that for those very reasons he was well rid of her.

"You treated me like a whore," she continued, needing to speak her heartbreak aloud, "in my own home where I lived all my life with my mother. And you said . . . you said"—she choked back a sob—"if I bore you children, it would shame you. Your very own children would be a shame to you."

His face flamed bright red. With humiliation and regret. He knew she spoke the truth regarding his words, but he had redrafted his memories of that night in order to pretend it hadn't happened that way. It had, and his harsh words had sent her to the streets, looking for sustenance and shelter.

"I don't know what else to say except that I'm sorry." He reached out and laid a hand on the top of her head. "I know there is no excuse for speaking such things in anger, but I was furious and confused that night, and it is the only explanation I can give for my words. I hope that you will forgive me."

His apology was heartrending and gracious and, she was certain, it wasn't something he'd done many times in his life, but beneath the layers of fatigue and shame, she could feel a deep anger burning. At Adam. At her father. At George Wilburton. At her mother for dying. At her half sister, Penelope, who had so much when she, herself, had so little.

She lowered her eyes to the water and whispered, "I deserve better than you."

One corner of Adam's mouth lifted in a smile. He'd never been so thoroughly insulted or put in his place in his life, but it was hard to be enraged when he deserved every word. "You're right," he agreed. "You deserve much better than me. But, for now, I am all you have. Will you let me take care of you?"

"I don't know. I'm so tired."

"Just promise me you'll remain here. That you'll stay where I know you're safe." He sank to his knees beside the tub, fished one of her hands out of the water again, and squeezed it with his own. "We'll work this out, Maggie. I swear it to you."

She was too tired to think, or argue, or leave. Too tired to do anything but simply remain. With a nod of acquiescence, her composure finally shattered. A tear fell, then another. Before she could stop the blasted things, they were flowing in a torrent down her cheeks and dripping into the water.

"Oh, little one . . . don't do that . . . don't cry," he urged gently. His request only made her cry harder. Not knowing what else to do, he reached an arm around her shoulder. With a tug, he pulled her toward him. She resisted for a moment, then, needing the comfort, turned to him, and his arms were filled with wet, hot, naked woman. He ran a hand up and down her smooth back, whispering in her ear, "It will be all right, I promise. Just rest, and let me take care of everything."

Eventually, her tears ended. He found a cloth in the water, wrung it out, and dabbed it against her face. They didn't speak; there seemed to be no need for words. Maggie was too worn out for conversation anyway.

Gail poked her head in the door, raising a brow at the Marquis in silent question. He motioned to her, and she entered, coming over to the tub, holding out a large, soft towel.

"Let's get you to bed, little one," Adam coaxed gently. Maggie was hardly in any condition to argue, and he took both her hands in his and helped her stand.

Gail dried her quickly and efficiently before her skin had a chance to cool, then slipped a white cotton nightgown over her shoulders and straightened it down. It was a simple thing, soft and welcoming, with little butterflies embroidered across the bodice. A pink ribbon tied in a perfect bow at the neck. In it, she looked pretty, and young, and fresh-scrubbed. Very much like a virginal bride on her wedding night. Gail turned back the coverings on the bed, and Adam helped Maggie sit. Then the two of them tucked her in. She was asleep the instant her head hit the pillow.

Adam turned to Gail. "That will be all tonight. I'll let you know when we're ready for breakfast in the morning. It may be late. Tell the cook."

"I will, milord," she answered quietly. Although she was young, she'd worked in his household most of her life. If she thought anything about what she'd witnessed throughout the evening, or about the fact that he was about to pass the night in Maggie's room, she had the good sense not to let even a hint of it show on her face. "The tub, milord? Shall I have it removed?"

"Don't worry about it. Someone can get it in the morning. I don't want to wake her."

With a final proprietary smile toward her new charge, she curtsied quickly and left.

Adam undressed slowly, lingering over each bit of clothing, postponing the moment when he'd slip between the covers. Probably, he should be a gentleman about the whole thing. He should leave the room, leave the house, go to his own. But the simple fact of the matter was that he couldn't bear to depart. For once in his life, he wanted to hold, soothe, and care for another. Things he'd never done for a woman before.

He lay down next to her, slipping an arm under her head and draping the other across her waist. As if she'd been waiting for him, she shifted slightly, pressing her buttocks against his groin, curling her legs, and he spooned himself along her backside. Nuzzling in her hair, he enjoyed the scent and feel of her, and let sleep take him while he wondered and reveled in the sensations stirred by the simple act of holding her.

Anne sat on the stool in front of her vanity in her old room. Although it was full summer, the night was a cool one, and normally, she would have been chilled by now. What a nice change to have plenty of coal for the small stove. The fire burned hotly on the grate, lit by the servants before she'd arrived, and she sat nearly nude, dressed only in a sheer dressing gown and nothing more, her skin still warm from the steamy bath she'd just taken. The heat was an incredible luxury.

Certainly, she was ready for the respite that would be enjoyed by having someone else care for her for a while. But how long would it last?

"What now?" she whispered to herself. James had said she could stay, but she didn't put any stock in his promises. The English gentlemen with whom she'd consorted over the years spent all their time waxing about their honor and the value of their word, which, as far as she was concerned, wasn't worth much when the stakes were high. She'd had vows made and broken by his kind more times than she could count.

A knock sounded on her door, and she figured it was one of the servants meticulously checking on her before she turned in for the night. It was odd to have people hovering around again after going without them for such a long time, but it was nice, too. Nice to be looked after. The maid who'd attended her had helped her bathe, brushed her hair, laid out nightclothes, and Anne had blissfully let her do all of it, wanting nothing more than to rest and think.

"Come in," she said softly.

The door opened and closed, and Anne looked over her shoulder, her eyes widening in surprise to see James standing there. She'd thought him long gone with Charles, who'd left shortly after she and Maggie had returned home.

"I thought you left with your cousin."

"No. I wanted to say good night first." He seemed suddenly shy. "May I come in for a moment?"

She nodded and gestured toward the bed. It was a small room, and there wasn't really anyplace else for him to sit. He perched himself on the edge, and she turned to face him. Their knees were only a few inches apart. She thought about letting him sit there forever until he worked up the courage to say whatever he'd come to say, but he looked so uncomfortable, she decided to have mercy on him. "What is it?"

"I was just wondering . . . Have you forgiven me? For what happened between us during your holiday, I mean?"

"It's water under the bridge, James," she said, making a dismissive gesture with her hand. "Besides, it's hard to be angry when everything you said about me is true. I'm a whore. It's all I've ever been since my parents died when I was fifteen. Sometimes, I've made more money at it than other times, but I'm still a whore."

"I don't think that about you."

"You're kind to say so, but the facts speak for themselves."

James reached for her hand and took it in his. "Charles mentioned that Stephen had left you some money. What happened to it?"

"Well, he always told me he'd made arrangements for me, so after he died, I went to see his brother, and he told me that Stephen had done no such thing. And that if I tried to say different, he'd say some of his wife's jewelry was missing and that I'd taken it."

"God, I know Frasier. I can't believe he'd do such a thing."

Anne jerked her hand away from his. "That's what happened. I don't care if you believe it or not."

"I didn't mean it that way, Anne. I meant that I can't believe he'd do something so despicable to you, especially when it was so obvious that Stephen cared about you a great deal."

"I cared for him, too." Anne swallowed, unwilling and unable to discuss Stephen further. Tears welled into her eyes, and she fought them back as she admitted, "It's been hard. Since then. If Rose and Maggie hadn't taken me in, I don't know what would have happened to me."

"Or maybe you do know," he said gently, and she raised her eyes to look at him, both of them thinking how far she'd had to stoop to try to get by.

"Yes," she said wearily, "maybe I do. It's a hard world out there. For people like me."

"I realize that. Much more than you'd probably guess. My father's mistress is a friend of mine. I've heard some terrifying stories from her. About women. Her friends mostly, and the things that have happened to them."

It was an interesting admission from one such as himself. Usually, the gentlemen of his class hardly realized there was anyone else alive except themselves. "I'm glad to hear you don't judge me too harshly," she said.

"I don't judge you at all, my dear. In fact, I've missed you." He shrugged unabashedly.

"No, you haven't."

"I have," he insisted. "I felt like a royal ass when we parted previously, and I've thought about you constantly since I returned. I kept wondering if I could find you if I set about it hard enough, but I was too much of a coward to do it. I thought I might knock on your door only to have you box my ears and send me on my way."

"I'd probably have thought about it. I find I don't have much patience for nonsense as I grow older."

"That's one of the things I like about you so much. Your inability to tolerate nonsense. Actually, since that last time I saw you, I've had plenty of time to think, and I discovered that there are many things about you which thoroughly captivate me. That's why I wanted to talk to you."

"What about?"

"I have a proposition for you."

Anne rolled her eyes. "Let's hear it."

"Well, I thought . . . ah . . . perhaps . . . ah . . ." He cleared his throat. "Perhaps I could convince you to become my mistress."

"Come again?"

"My mistress." He grinned from ear to ear. "I've never had one before, but if I'm going to do such a thing, I'd certainly like it to be with you."

Anne realized her mouth was hanging open, and she snapped it closed. She'd thought he was going to request a quick tumble as his reward for bringing her home. Not in her wildest dreams had she expected anything like this. "If you're joking with me, please don't."

"I've never been more serious. I don't have my brother's wealth by any means, but I do have a fair income of my own if you're worried about whether I could manage."

"No, that wasn't it. I'm just surprised. After tonight, I can't imagine why you'd want to have me."

He was so thrilled to have found her again that he could barely contain his excitement. He took her hand again and said very quietly, "I said I don't judge you, Anne. I mean it."

Good Lord, but he looked so sincere! As though he meant every word! Her heart started to pound at the possible implications; however, she was no longer a frightened, inexperienced girl. If it was to happen, she'd have to know everything beforehand before agreeing. Cautiously, she asked, "What would be the terms?"

"There's another one of the things I like about you." He chuckled. "Your directness."

"I imagine it will wear on you the longer you know me."

"I doubt it. I find it most refreshing." He tapped a finger against his lips. "Well, let's see . . . I'd provide for all your needs."

"Define 'needs.' "

"Your own apartment, or you can stay here with Maggie if you'd be more comfortable. Money, clothing, incidentals. Whatever you need, I would provide."

"For how long?"

"For as long as we can stand each other?" Anne snorted at this, so he continued. "I know! I'll set up a trust fund for you, so you can provide for yourself when we part."

She'd heard that line before, and as a younger, more naive woman, had believed it. Not now. Not when so much was depending on what he would really do. "How do I know you'll carry through?" she asked.

"That's the question in these kinds of arrangements, isn't it?" His brow creased as he thought for a moment. "I've got it. I'll set it up with a trustee who'll manage it until such time as you decide you need it. I'll have my solicitor start drawing up the paperwork tomorrow. *You* pick the trustee. I'll arrange it so that once the transaction is completed, I'll no longer have control over the money. Your trustee will invest it and watch over it until the day you need it." He took a deep breath and let it out, feeling as though he'd just run a long race. "How does that sound?"

Still skeptical, Anne asked, "What would I have to do in return to earn my keep?"

"That's the easy part. You'll be my friend and my companion. You'll care for me and shower me with devotion and let me do the same for you. And whenever you join me in my bed, you will do so with all the affection and joy you can muster." He held his breath, thinking that perhaps he'd just proposed the most important agreement of his life and wondering what he'd do if she rejected him.

Sounding as stern as possible, she said, "Let me get this straight. You'll give me everything I've ever desired, and in return, I must give you passion, friendship, and happiness."

"That pretty much sums it up."

"You drive a hard bargain, St. Clair, but I think you've worn me down."

"You accept?" he asked tentatively.

"Yes, I accept, you bloody fool." She smiled, thinking he was so perfectly lovely when he looked at her like that, with his own smile full of desire and mischief. "Would you like to sample the merchandise?"

"Well, I was rather hoping you'd suggest it."

In one fluid move, Anne dropped her robe and leaped onto his lap, her legs wrapped around his waist as she covered his mouth with a hard, desperate kiss. "You'll never regret this a single day of your life."

"I never imagined I would." James flipped her onto her back and took over from there.

Chapter Thirteen

When Maggie woke, it was barely morning. Pale pink light shimmered in the window. She was fully conscious of everything about her. There was no lingering fuzziness about what had happened the previous night or about where she was and who was lying behind her, so big and warm against her back. She was home where she was meant to be, and Adam was there, too, perhaps where he was meant to be—at least for now.

She stretched her legs and winced silently as every muscle cried out in agony. More slowly, she lengthened her legs and shifted around. From Adam's heavy breathing, she could tell he was still asleep, and she wanted the advantage of watching him for a time before he awakened and required attention and answers.

With the cares of the world pushed aside, he looked young in his sleep. Very much as he must have looked as a boy. A shock of dark hair fell across his forehead. His eyelids twitched as he moved through the stages of a dream, and she couldn't help wondering what he was dreaming about and if, by chance, she might be part of it.

A month earlier, they'd awakened in this same room. Adam had been angry and pompous; Maggie had been frightened and heartbroken. She'd left that day, thinking to never return. Adam had brought her home again—where she belonged. With very little thought required, she'd come to the conclusion that she'd stay. She'd remain in her home as Adam's mistress. The decision was an easy one.

From the time they'd first met on their holiday, she'd been overcome by the strong feeling that they were meant to be together. After the events of the past month, it was certainly hard to argue that their destinies were not linked in some way. As though some invisible force was directing their paths, they continually came back to one another. What were the chances that he'd have been the one to stumble onto her at the ball when she was standing with George, looking for a protector? Even more thought-provoking, what were the chances that he'd have been the one to rescue her the previous night at the brothel?

Some things were meant to be.

Almost as if her mother were standing in the room, she could hear her say the words. Rose had been a great believer in fate, that there were some things destined to happen that you could not change no matter how hard you tried. This appeared to be one of them.

When Maggie had left a month earlier, she'd not known if she could take care of herself and make her own way, but she'd learned that she could. The small adventure had been a good one, because it had shown her that she was stronger than she knew and that she could survive through adversity. For now, though, she'd take advantage of what Adam was offering.

During the months he searched for a wife, she would be all things to him. Lover, friend, companion, confidant. Her mother had schooled her well, and she knew what would be expected. Whatever he required, she would do to the best of her ability and without hesitation. She would steel her heart against the feelings she had for him and go about carrying out their business arrangement.

In the end, by the time he'd chosen his bride, perhaps he would change his mind. He'd relent and give her money, a home, perhaps a parting gift of valuable jewelry. Perhaps he would give her character references or letters of introduction to help her on her way.

In case none of those things occurred, she would scrimp and save. Whatever pin money or household funds he provided, a part would always go to her future fund. If he encouraged her to buy something, she would settle for the lesser quality and pocket the difference. Whatever she could sell, she would. If he decided in the end to put her out on the streets, at least she would have coin in her pocket when it happened.

Resolved, she took a deep breath. She wasn't certain how the morning was supposed to go between two lovers, but she had a good idea. Best to start things off on the right foot, by making him glad he'd brought her home. She laid her cheek against the center of his chest, where she could feel his heart pounding strong and steady.

He was warm and smelled like sweat and tobacco and that special musk she would always associate just with him and no one else. She worked her face across the mat of hair, and her tongue found his nipple and flicked against it, bringing it to life. Closing her lips around it, she sucked gently, relishing the salty taste of his skin.

"Mmmm," Adam growled deep in his throat as she moved from one nipple to the other. "I like that."

He still hadn't opened his eyes, but he stretched his legs out and shifted farther onto his side, his weight causing hers to shift with him so that their bodies touched all the way down from breasts to toes. Maggie reached a hand around his waist and settled it low on his back, pressing his hips forward slightly. Still half asleep, he was terribly aroused, his hard staff pushing against her stomach like a thing alive and wanting its morning meal.

Tentatively, she trailed her fingers across his hip and slipped her hand round it, running her thumb along the sensitive tip, causing a hiss of pleasure to escape from his lips. His buttocks tightened, and he rocked his hips forward, letting her hand stroke him. She nuzzled under his neck, then gave him a brief, virginal kiss on the lips, saying, "Good morning."

One corner of his mouth lifted in a smile. "If I open my eyes, I think I'll learn that I've died and gone to heaven." At that, he opened one eye and looked at her. "Ah, I was right. There's an angel in my bed."

Maggie laughed, her voice still husky with sleep. She squeezed her hand around him a little tighter. "I think if you pay attention, you'll see that there's a devil here instead."

"Ooh, perhaps . . ." he murmured as she stroked him again. He pulled her into a tight embrace, squeezing her as though he might never let her go. Eventually, he loosened his grip and looked down into her eyes. "Good morning, yourself. How are you feeling?"

"Better. All right." She laid a palm against his cheek. "I wanted to thank you for last night. For everything."

"Ssh, you don't need to thank me. I'm just glad I was there." He kissed the bruise on her cheek. "Does it hurt?" he asked, running the tip of his finger across it.

"A little."

He kissed the spot again, then brushed her lips with a gentle kiss. Asking permission. Asking again. Maggie gave him her answer by rolling onto her back. Their move on the mattress brought him over her. With a knee tossed across her thighs, he balanced his weight on an elbow. His manhood was a heavy, insatiable thing, pressing against her leg.

"I want to make love to you, little one," he said as his kisses drifted across her brow, her eyes, her cheeks. As though he thought she might protest, he added, "I want to do it slowly and carefully, as if it's your very first time."

"You don't have to be gentle with me, Adam. You can do whatever you want. I didn't mind how you did it before. Truly."

"Well, I did," he said, placing a light kiss against her lips as though she were his chaste bride. "I hurt you with my body and my words. I don't want it to be that way between us ever again."

In response, she raised a shaky hand to the lace at her throat and pulled at the pink ribbon, but he stopped her. "Let me do all the work. You just close your eyes and try to relax."

No request could have been more difficult to heed with a naked, virile, aroused man in her bed and it being only her second time, but she was determined to please him in all ways. Taking a deep breath, she let it out slowly, closing her eyes as he worked the ribbon down the bodice of the gown. The cool air on her nipples told her he'd bared her chest, but she kept her eyes tightly closed, knowing he was looking his fill, and tried to imagine what he would do next. She didn't have long to wait.

"You're so beautiful," he said, as he lowered his head and sucked one of the rosy tips into his mouth. *And I am so glad you're mine.* The thought came unbidden into his mind. *Mine.* Always a frightening word in the past, but now, the idea of it gave him a little thrill, low in the pit of his stomach. Maggie was his, and his alone.

He'd never wanted to possess a woman, had never wanted to be close to one before. Until now. In all the years of his life, he'd never spent the night in a woman's bed, whether she be whore or highborn. Maggie was the first and only. He intended to fully enjoy the benefits of such an incredible moment if it meant he kept her on her back all through the day.

Her nipple was pebble-hard, nubby and sleek against his tongue. Starting with care, he sucked and pulled against it, with greater pressure as he felt her become accustomed to his ministrations. He pulled away, loving the way the thing peaked at him, all wet and rosy from his attention. The tip was moist, and he blew against it, causing her to stir and moan in the back of her throat. Shifting to her other breast, he took the nipple between his teeth, giving it his undivided attention until he felt her hips begin to move back and forth slightly.

After a lengthy enjoyment, he left her breasts, rolling on top of her so she could feel his weight pressing her down. The hair on his thighs and chest created a friction against the cotton of her gown. Matching the slow rhythm of her hips, he worked himself back and forth, the thin layer of fabric separating him from the place he truly wanted to be. The pleasure was painful.

Kissing up her chest and neck, he found her lips, taking them in one slow, mind-numbing kiss after another, and all the while his fingers were twirling her nipples until she was writhing and squirming beneath him. As if by instinct, she raised her legs, wrapping them around him. The hem of the nightgown shifted back, and her silky thighs rubbed against his rough ones.

"Please," she whispered in a voice that sounded nothing like her own. "I need more of you."

"Not yet, little one," he said with a chuckle, dipping his head to take a nipple again.

She arched her back. "I can't stand much more of this."

"Yes, but the wait will make the end so much better." He pulled back, braced one palm against the bed, and worked the other hand down her stomach to slip under the edge of her gown. With one finger, he dipped into her secret space. Another finger joined the first. He pressed in deep and firm, pulling back, easing her open. She was dripping with want.

"I need you," she said, meeting his eyes with a stormy gaze, no hint of shyness or embarrassment from one so young.

He had intended to torture them both further before giving her body what it craved, but he made the mistake of positioning himself between her legs. As he moved across her cleft, the hairs of her mound tickling his length, all his plans vanished.

Through clenched teeth, he said, "It won't hurt this time."

"I know."

She arched up, her hair in full disarray across the pillows, her breasts begging for attention, her lips swollen from his kisses, her nightgown fallen off her shoulders and worked nearly to her waist from top and bottom. He felt like a pirate claiming his prize, an ancient Viking plundering his spoils. His hands reached under her backside and grabbed both buttocks, raising her hips up off the mattress. With a fierce thrust, he plunged inside to demand his due.

As he sheathed himself to the hilt, Maggie rose up off the bed, her arms coming around to hold on to him as her universe immediately shattered. The pressure had been building and building as he'd stroked and fondled her. This time, there was no pain, only joy and pleasure. The black void of it seemed to go on and on.

Her return to reality was a slow one, as feeling and sensation gradually returned. Adam was with her, big and warm and solid. She could smell him and taste him against her lips. His arms were wrapped around her, holding her tightly through each rocking spasm. Her body finally went limp, and he eased her back onto the pillows.

"Oh, what a passionate thing you are, my little wildcat." He took her lips in a stormy kiss, then braced his hands on either side of her head. His eyes gleamed, as he used all his concentration to restrain himself. "Let me take you to that place again, and I will join you this time."

Like a man possessed, he worked his hips, until every muscle in his body tensed. His heart thundered under his ribs, and sweat dribbled down his chest and dripped from his brow. He lifted her, shifting her so her woman's spot was stroked each time he passed in and out. The new sensation caused her to moan deep in her throat. She groped blindly for him, trying to find a center.

"Now, little one. Come with me now."

"Yes. Now." She grabbed for him and pulled him close.

Together, they cried out as Adam pushed into her again and again, spilling his seed until his body shook with the strain, and he collapsed on top of her.

Slowly he came back to his senses and rolled to the side, taking her with him. They lay that way for a long time, letting the slight breeze from the window cool their skin. Maggie's cheek rested against the center of his chest, her hand making lazy circles on his abdomen. After a time, her hand stopped, and he thought perhaps she'd fallen asleep, so slow and steady was her breathing, but her voice surprised him.

"You're very quiet," she said. "You're not displeased, are you?" He had emptied himself so fiercely that she thought he must have enjoyed the act immensely, but she was greatly worried about her inexperience. He'd been silent for so long, and she didn't know if that was a good sign or a bad one.

"Displeased? If I'd been any more *pleased,* I might have died from the passion of it." Absently, he ran a hand across her hair. "I was just thinking that I'd told you I would be gentle. I was a little past thinking, and I'm afraid I got a bit carried away again."

Maggie chuckled. "I noticed."

"I didn't hurt you, did I?"

"Not for a moment." He looked so distressed by the thought, that she couldn't resist rising up and giving him a light kiss. "I rather like it that way. Everything is so overwhelming that I get completely swept away in the heat of it. It's really different from what I'd ever imagined it would be like."

"We do seem to have a certain fever for each other, don't we?"

"Yes. Do you think it will always be this way when we're together?"

"I think there's a good chance." She looked rumpled and well loved and was staring at him with such open affection that his heart ached. Rather than rub his hand across it, he pulled her close so she rested her cheek against the center of his chest again. Instantly, he was overcome by the sense of calm and peace that always descended on him when she was near. He kissed the top of her head. "Thank you."

"For what?" She wanted to tip her head back so she could look him in the eye, but he was holding her too tightly.

"For . . . just for being here with me. For giving me this

part of yourself." He'd bedded scores of women in his life, and thought he knew all there was to know about the sexual act, but nothing had prepared him for the way he felt when he was with her. Powerful, and wise, and strong, generous, and kind. He wanted to protect and shelter her, to guide and teach, to cherish. That was it most of all. He wanted the opportunity to show her how much he cherished her above all others.

Where the feelings came from, or why they sprang so fervently where she was concerned, was a complete mystery and had been from the moment he'd met her, but he knew one thing: What he felt with her was so different, so rare, that he was not about to deny it to her or himself. "I'm glad you came home."

Maggie couldn't see his face, but could feel the emotion in his words. She hugged him about the waist. "So am I. I want to make you happy, Adam. So happy."

"You already do, little one."

They were quiet for another long time, each lost in thought, until Maggie spoke again. "Adam, what were you doing at the brothel last night?"

He swallowed a choked sound. "We shouldn't discuss such things, I don't think."

"Why not?"

"Well, it's not . . . ." He was about to say *proper,* but quickly realized that *proper* wasn't the correct word. Keeping a mistress, lying with a woman not his wife, was hardly *proper.* "I don't know what it is, but I don't think we should discuss such things."

"Could I ask you something, though?"

"All right." He knew agreeing was a mistake, but couldn't think of a better response.

"Do you like going to those places?"

"Maggie . . . you're embarrassing me." Her cheek remained pressed to his chest, and he stared at the ceiling, glad he wasn't looking her in the eye.

"I don't mean to. I just wonder why you would."

"Well, it's different for a man."

"I realize that."

"And it's difficult for a man in my position to . . . ah . . . to . . ."

"Yes, I imagine it would be." She shifted up on her elbow so she was looking down at him. "Please don't go to one again. While we're together, I mean."

"That's an odd request to make of me."

"I know, and perhaps you feel I have no right to ask such a thing, but now that we've been . . . well, intimate with one another, I can't imagine you with someone else. I do believe it would quite break my heart if I found out."

He'd promised he wouldn't hurt her again. He eyed her carefully. "Is it so important to you, then?"

"Very. I want to be the one you come to. Every time. I'll do whatever you ask, and I'll give you everything you need. I swear it. I just want to know that I am the only one."

Fidelity. That's what she was asking for. A word he'd never thought about much because he'd never had to. The idea that she didn't want to share him was curiously pleasing and comforting. To lie with no other but her was not anything he'd considered in his quick and rash journey to becoming a man with a kept paramour. Could he promise her faithfulness?

A quick glance down her body made the answer an easy one. She lay beside him in beautiful naked display. He thought of her crying out in passion the moment he'd entered her, of her exploding again such a short time later, her cries meeting his own as they found pleasure at the same moment.

She would always be more than enough. Much more than he imagined he would ever find, so the vow was easy. "As long as we are together, you will be the only one."

The smile she gave him in return was worth every word he'd spoken. "In that case," she said, "I think I better practice so I get better at it."

She reached down and took him in her hand, and he hardened instantly, ready for more.

Chapter Fourteen

"So, Father, where did he go?" Penelope asked petulantly.

"I'm due to have a report shortly." Harold Westmoreland, Duke of Roswell, looked across his desk at his daughter. She was quite a pretty little thing, but too fat for his liking. He'd always liked his women thin and lithe. Other men didn't seem to mind her weight, though. With her dowry, and his family name, she was an incredible catch. And an incredible bargaining chip for which he would receive money, lands, new alliances. The possibilities for enrichment from her marriage contract were too numerous to fathom. Too bad the only man they both wanted her to marry seemed to have no regard for her at all.

"How could he run off like that in the middle of my party? I didn't even get to dance with him!" She stood and paced. "It was his brother, wasn't it, who convinced him to leave?"

"I believe so."

"That wretch! And that dreadful cousin of his?"

"I saw the three of them walking out together, yes."

"How did those two get in anyway?"

"They were invited, Penny."

"Oh," she responded halfheartedly, flopping back down in her chair in a most unladylike fashion. That was the problem with inviting several hundred guests. Too many unwanted people received invitations. "Just wait till Adam and I are married. I'll make them sorry a thousand times over."

"Well," he muttered, "that's the crux of the problem, isn't it? Getting him to marry you? Don't plan your vengeance too carefully. At this rate, you're never going to get it."

She tried to stare him down with icy blue eyes that were a mirror of his own. As usual, though, he won. Her temper was simply no match for his and never had been. Not in the mood for a tongue-lashing, she smoothed her face into a placid smile. "I don't know what else to do, Father. We dine with him, he sits next to me in our box at the theater, I dance with him, we go riding, and as far as I can tell, I'm held in no different esteem than any of the other women of his acquaintance."

"Why do you suppose that is?" he asked sarcastically. While he wasn't about to lecture his daughter on feminine wiles, he wished somebody would. His wife had a limited number of her own to share or he'd set her to the task. His current mistress had plenty. Pity that he couldn't introduce her to his daughter. Penelope could obviously benefit from a few wise words.

"You're blaming me?" she asked, her shock clearly evident.

He shrugged. "I didn't say that."

"Well, you might as well have. I don't know what you expect me to do. I went riding with him on Tuesday afternoon. We chatted, we laughed, we teased. I thought I'd thoroughly infatuated him." When she'd returned home, she'd had a dreadful backache from all the shifting she'd done to try to get him to notice her bosom. It hadn't worked. He hadn't lowered his eyes to her chest a single time.

"And?"

"He took Jane Cummings riding on Wednesday, Barbara Ferguson on Thursday, and Sarah Walters on Friday."

Harold sighed. Penny was the perfectly bred and raised English girl awaiting a husband, just as were dozens of others who hoped to marry that year. Obviously, in Adam's opinion, nothing about her personality varied from any of the others. Plus, he had no need of increased wealth, and he felt no need of a family alliance, which made catching him seem like an impossible task. How could you sway a man who didn't appear to want anything?

He asked, "What are your plans to alter the situation?"

"I haven't the vaguest idea. The Season is ended, so I'm going to have few opportunities from here on out. Short of compromising myself, which you absolutely refuse to allow, I don't see how to get him to change his attitude toward me."

This was a topic they'd discussed numerous times, always heatedly. He wasn't in the mood to go through it again. "I've told you a dozen times, Penelope, that I doubt Adam could be snared in such a fashion. I also think he might refuse to offer for you if he thought we'd set him up."

"He's a gentleman. He wouldn't dare!"

"Wouldn't he?" Harold sighed. It was odd to think his own daughter, his own flesh and blood, could be so stupidly naive. For just a moment, he felt a twinge of sympathy for Adam, knowing well himself what it was like to be saddled for life with such a ride. Penny was a near-duplicate of her mother. "Trust me, Penny, I know men. I know Adam. If you did something reckless, he'd laugh in our faces. Then, where would you be?"

"Oooh, I hate him! I truly do." A knock sounded on the door of the library, and she stood, knowing from experience that the time allotted for their discussion was over. "I don't know how long you plan to let him treat me this way, Father. He's making fools of both of us." She swung around, well satisfied with her parting remark. The Duke hated looking like a fool more than anything.

"Penelope." His voice brought her up short, and she turned to face him once again. He handed out an envelope. "Take this with you."

"What is it?"

"It's an invitation from the St. Clairs. To a house party in September."

She tore the flap aside and quickly scanned the words. "It's lasting two weeks. Do you know how many others were invited?"

"I'm told it will be a dozen."

"Twelve?! I'm to be one in a field of twelve? How did I receive such an honor?"

"I believe his mother made the list."

"How dare that old bat lump me into a crowd!" In a fit of pique, she ripped the invitation in half and threw it on his desk, then turned her dainty little nose in the air. "Well, I'll show her! I'm not going."

"You will go. And you will be your usual charming self. I suggest you get yourself to the dressmaker's to start planning your wardrobe." He had the satisfaction of seeing her cheeks redden. For all she ranted and raved, she wouldn't go against his wishes. No one dared defy him when he gave an order, especially his headstrong, spoiled daughter. If Adam St. Clair wanted her to jump through a few hoops, then jump she would. "Now if you'll excuse me, I have another appointment."

With a wave of his hand, he dismissed her and watched her leave in a swirl of skirts. The soft soles of her slippers kept him from hearing her furious stomps as she headed down the hall. Just as well that she was angry. Let her stew on the situation for a time. Perhaps she'd come up with some new ideas to use at the St. Clairs' party.

With her gone, one of his assistants came in. "What did you learn?" he asked, hardly waiting for the man to settle in his chair.

"They went to a brothel. A new one, just opened last night over by the . . ."

"Yes, I know the one." He'd received an invitation but hadn't been able to attend the opening because of Penny's blasted ball. "Why did they go there?"

"Well, Your Grace"—the man looked as though the Duke

had just asked the stupidest question he'd ever heard—"I'm not sure, but it being a brothel, my guess would be that they went to enjoy the ladies."

"I know that, you idiot. Why that one instead of another? What did they do while they were there? For how long and with whom?" He tried to know everything about Adam, hoping to find some bit of information that would force the man into a decision. "How long did they stay? Give me the details. That's what I pay you for."

"Yes, Your Grace." He looked through a small notebook, scanning the pages, then met the Duke's assessing gaze. "Well, they booked a private room and were to stay the night, but there was some sort of altercation."

"Altercation? Among themselves?"

"No, with two other guests. The details were hushed up, but it sounds like the other men were forcing themselves on one of the whores when the Marquis decided to offer her assistance."

"Then what?"

"The St. Clair brothers, assisted by their cousin, Charles Billington, took two whores out of the place and left with them."

"The madam allowed them to enjoy the girls off the premises?"

"I'm not sure why they took them away, but the two brothers stayed with the women all night. At a small house outside Mayfair. In fact, the younger one, James, was still there when I left to come make my report to you."

"And the Marquis?"

"Left this morning. But not till nearly the noon hour."

"They must definitely have been worth the trouble," the Duke murmured to himself, and the assistant merely shrugged, having no opinion one way or the other. "What were their names?"

"Who?"

"The two women!"

"Ah . . . one Anne Porter," the assistant said, reviewing his notes. The Duke shook his head; he'd never heard of the woman and motioned for the man to continue. ''And a Maggie Brown.''

Harold sat up straight in his chair. Good God, it was her! He'd thought as much when he'd seen her with Adam at the ball the previous month, but try as he might, he'd been unable to verify her identity. All he'd heard were whispers that Adam had taken the unknown beauty as his mistress. She was Harold's daughter, though; he'd known without being told. No one else in the world could have looked so much like Rose.

''Where did you say the house was located?''

''Took them over to a location on Mulberry. It's some little apartment.''

Well, that confirmed it. Maggie was his daughter and still living in the home he'd bought for Rose twenty years earlier, although he'd heard it had fallen into some disrepair since then.

''I guess the Marquis purchased it recently,'' the secretary continued, ''but the two women have been living there for a long time. From the way the neighbors talk, they don't sound like whores at all, just a couple of pleasant, quiet gentlewomen. So, I don't know what they were doing at the brothel.''

''Would you wait outside?''

''Certainly, Your Grace.''

''I'm going to write a quick message. I'd like you to deliver it for me and wait for a reply.'' The man left without further prompting, and the Duke sat back in his chair, assessing the situation while he decided what to write.

Even after twenty years, he had vivid memories of Rose Brown. He'd enjoyed many beautiful women in his life, but never one who came close to her in looks and style. With her smooth skin, her full breasts, her husky voice and sexual ways. And those violet eyes. She'd had a way of walking and talking that made a man want to throw her down and bed her just upon seeing her.

Apparently, his bastard daughter had turned whore, just like her mother. Surprising as it was to hear that the self-righteous Adam St. Clair had taken a mistress, Harold could just imagine how it had happened. If Maggie was anything like her mother, poor Adam hadn't stood a chance at avoiding her charms.

Since Adam had never kept a woman before, he must have had some special reason for choosing Maggie. Perhaps his attachment to the girl went beyond the ordinary one of man and paramour. It was certainly worth finding out. If so, there had to be a way to use the information to advantage. Quickly, his mind heaving with possibilities and the ways to turn them to good fortune, Harold penned the invitation.

Maggie came down the stairs smiling. Adam had bedded her for hours before departing. Slow and gentle, hard and rough. On her stomach, on her back, with his mouth, his hands, his manhood. She had participated fully, learning and sharing and reveling in the wonderful things they could do together.

Her lips were chapped, her skin rough and abraded, her thighs bruised, and the area between her legs felt tender and raw. All in all, she'd been thoroughly loved and had never felt better. Curious bursts of energy were coursing through her veins. The very air around her felt different and charged, as though she could point toward an object and sparks would fly off her fingertips.

So intriguing were these new feelings of power and excitement that she made it nearly to the bottom step before she realized she wasn't alone. James was on his way out the door, but not quite. Anne was wrapped in his arms, and he was kissing her so thoroughly that the moment should have been embarrassing for everyone, except that the two of them seemed so joyful. One of the female servants stood there with his evening cloak laid over her arm, trying not to watch.

James chose that moment to pause. He gazed lovingly into Anne's eyes, holding her cheek in his palm as he stroked his thumb across her moist lips. "I don't want to go. I miss you already."

"You have to go. If you don't get out of here, you'll never finish your errands."

"I suppose you're right."

"The sooner you go, the sooner you can return," Anne pointed out.

"Oh, God, yes," he agreed, pulling her into another embrace, which took her off her feet. He turned her in small circles, not even stopping his play when he saw Maggie. "Good afternoon," he said to her.

"Hello, James." She smiled as she walked closer. James finally returned Anne's feet to solid ground. Apparently not wanting to lose physical contact with her until the very last moment, he kept a proprietary hand around her waist. "I'd ask how you two enjoyed your evening, but I don't think I need to," Maggie added.

"I'd say you're right." He gave Anne a lascivious wink, which earned him an elbow in the ribs.

Anne welcomed Maggie as well, then raised a brow in James's direction. "James was just leaving."

The maid took that as a cue and opened the door.

"I'll go . . . I'll go . . ." He smiled, kissing her again, hard and fast on the mouth. "But I'll be back!" Fairly bursting with rapture, he leaped out the door and into a waiting hansom.

He looked, Maggie thought, as if he felt just as she did, as though his world was suddenly full with the promise of new and wonderful things. She walked into the parlor and quietly sat on the sofa, while Anne stood in the doorway, watching the cab as it took James away. Once he'd disappeared from sight, the maid closed the door, and Anne walked into the room as though in a trance.

"Whew!" She pulled her hair off her neck and raised it for a moment, letting it fall in a casual drop about her shoulders. "That man is . . . well, he's quite incredible," she offered by way of explanation. She couldn't believe what had happened between them in the night. Her first time with Stephen, who she had always considered the one and only love of her life, had been joyful and fun, but positively boring compared to what had just transpired with James.

Without seeming to realize she was doing it, she rubbed her hand between her breasts, over and over, as though her heart were aching.

Maggie asked, "Are you all right?"

"What?" Anne asked in return, distracted by her thoughts. She looked up to see Maggie's smile of concern. "Oh, yes. I'm more than all right. How about yourself?"

"I'd say I'm more than all right, also. Adam has developed quite a passion for me."

"And how do you feel about him?"

"Well, I'd have to say I've developed quite a passion for him, too. It was everything you and Mother told me it could be and quite a bit more besides."

"How wonderful!"

Anne sat down next to her, then, and Maggie could see she was trembling slightly. She reached out and took her hand. "What is it?" Maggie asked.

"He's going to keep me. He went out just now to start some paperwork to set up a trust for me. It will be mine, so he'll never be able to take it back no matter what happens."

"Oh, Annie, I'm so happy for you." Maggie reached over and hugged her as tightly as she could.

"Yes, but it's more than the money. It's just that he's so . . . so . . ." Unable to find the right words, she swallowed hard past the emotion choking her. "I'm just so glad."

"So am I." Although for the briefest second, Maggie experienced a terrible flash of jealousy that James would care about Anne so much that he'd do this good thing for her. Maggie quashed the thought as quickly as it came. She would be happy for Anne; she would be happy for herself. Whatever Adam chose to give to her in the end, it was more than she'd had in the beginning.

"How was Adam?" Anne asked. "He wasn't overly angry with you, was he?"

"Let's just say he'd have kissed me good-bye like that"—
she pointed toward the foyer, where James had so thoroughly
ravaged Anne for anyone who wanted to watch—"if he had
a little more of James's flair for the dramatic."

Anne leaned back against the hard couch, took a deep breath,
and let it out. "I feel like I'm dreaming. Or that the world has
tipped sideways."

"It doesn't quite seem real, does it?"

"No. I mean, yesterday, I just couldn't imagine what was
to become of us. Now, twenty-four hours later, everything's
arranged."

"Well, I'm certainly not going to wonder about it too much,
for if it's a dream, I don't want to wake up."

"Neither do I," Anne agreed.

A knock at the door sounded just then, and Maggie, unused
to having servants again, stood to answer it, but the maid got
there first. The place was small enough that they could hear
all the words spoken, but the woman left the man at the door
and came into the parlor, imparting the message as though they
lived in a grand mansion and had not heard for themselves.

She handed out an envelope to Maggie. "It's a messenger
from the Duke of Roswell. He says he's to wait for a reply."

The woman must have worked for the Marquis for a long
while, because she obviously found nothing strange about
receiving a message from such a high personage. Maggie
refused to let her see how upsetting the moment was. "This
will only take a minute. Ask him to wait, will you?"

The maid went to the door and stood next to the messenger,
while Maggie scanned the words.

Anne leaned over, trying to see. She whispered, "What does
it say?"

"He wants to see me."

"Does he say why?"

"No, and I can't imagine what he could want." Maggie
thought of the handful of times over the years that dire circumstances had caused Rose to swallow her pride and ask him for

help. Never for much. Money for rent or food. For medicines, once, when Maggie took a terrible influenza. Twice, Rose had written as she lay dying, her mind focused only on worries about Maggie's future. In all the years, she'd never received so much as a response, let alone any assistance.

"What will you tell him? Do you need a minute alone to think?"

"No, this is easy." Maggie stood and walked to the door, looking at the messenger. "I have no response."

"What?" the man gasped, swallowed, composed himself. "Begging your pardon, miss"—the man, clearly unnerved, worked his hat between his fingers—"but I can't return to His Grace without an answer."

"Then, you may tell him that this is my answer: never. I will never meet with him. You may also tell him that I find his invitation extremely offensive and very much too late." Leaving him standing with his hat in his hand, she closed the door. The maid's brows were raised nearly to her hairline. Anne, knowing well Maggie's feelings about her father, showed very little reaction.

Maggie returned to the parlor, smiling to break the tension in the room, as she said to Anne, "I was thinking we should celebrate today. What could we do for fun before James and Adam return for supper?"

Chapter Fifteen

Maggie sat back in the chair and looked around the crowded restaurant. As always, it was a heady experience to be out in public on Adam's arm. The very nature of the man, and his position in High Society, made them a spectacle wherever they went. Men eyed her bosom, her hair, her backside, searching for some clue as to what sorts of favors she provided to Adam to win and keep his attentions. Women whispered behind their fans, jealously imagining what sorts of delightfully horrible things Maggie had done to earn her place by his side.

He'd coached her at first, telling her how it would be, and what she could do to ease the stress and cope more easily. She'd always been a quick learner, and had readily figured out how to hold her head up while keeping the ground steady beneath her feet, but it was still overwhelming at times. Like now, when she felt every eye in the place was on her, and she'd just dribbled wine down her front.

Not wanting to look down, but knowing she must, she glanced at her breasts, just as a long, thin line of the red wine disappeared into her cleavage.

"Would you like me to get that for you?" Adam asked. Intimately attuned to the slightest nuance where she was concerned, he leaned close and traced the tip of his tongue along his upper lip, leaving no doubt about just how he'd like to go about it.

"You're terrible," she said, turning her head slightly and finding him so near. She could see the dilation of his pupils, the soft gold flecks around the irises, the curve of his long lashes. Even after two months, he still took her breath away every time she looked at him.

"I can't help myself," he said.

"Move a little closer, would you?" she whispered.

"With the greatest pleasure." He shifted and she did, too.

"There. That's better." A potted plant shielded them from the direct gaze of many, and she turned so that she could furtively dab at the stain.

"God, that I were your napkin," he groaned.

Immediately, her cheeks flushed bright red. They'd hardly seen each other in the past week, and they were heading to her bed as soon as they finished their meal. "Stop looking at me like that."

"Like what?"

"Like you want to gobble me up."

"I *do* want to gobble you up."

"Adam!" Even her ears felt on fire. "You're making me blush."

"Good. I love it when you blush."

"Well, I don't," she said as his warm breath tickled her ear and brushed her hair, making it hard to think. "It's unseemly. Everyone will think we're . . ."

"We're what?" he asked, trying to sound innocent. "Lovers?" Her color heightened further if that was possible, and he shifted closer still. Even though they were in such a public place, she was stretched out against him, her breasts pushed against his arm. Her eyes, so large and round, her mouth so soft, only an inch away. It took every shred of self-control to keep from touching his lips to hers.

Desire was an interesting thing, he'd discovered. With the right person, it grew constantly. No matter how long they were apart, or what he was doing, he couldn't stop thinking about her, and he counted the minutes and hours until he could once again join her in her bed. It was all he thought about, and he felt like a man possessed. If he hadn't known her better, he'd have sworn she'd cast some sort of spell over him. He was that bewitched.

"Lovers . . . yes," she answered softly.

"I've missed you. Can't we go yet?"

Maggie glanced across the table to where James and Anne sat with their heads bowed together, giggling like a pair of children. While Adam's responsibilities made him an occasional visitor to their home, James had become a permanent fixture. Without the press of Adam's appointments and meetings, James was usually free to spend his time however he wanted. And it was clear that he wanted to spend it with Anne.

Maggie didn't mind a bit. He'd become a good friend, and she couldn't imagine how quiet the house would be without his presence to color it. "No, we can't go," she said sternly. "It would be rude to leave before they're finished."

Adam nervously eyed his brother, then Anne, of whom he'd never grown overly fond. James was altogether too attached to her, but he'd always been that way. He never did anything by halves, and it was typical for him to have jumped completely into the relationship with her. It was all right, Adam supposed, as long as he remembered the boundaries of who *he* was and who *she* was.

"They'll never notice we're gone," he insisted.

"I'll notice," Maggie said soothingly, and patted his arm. "Finish your wine and think about"—she whispered the rest—"what you're going to do with me when we get home."

He instantly grew hard as a rock. Just hearing that husky voice, watching the way she moved, smelling the perfume she wore, made him feel like a lad again. Stretching slightly, he tried to ease the tightness of his loins. "You, girl, are going to be the death of me. I just know it."

"I'll try to go easy on you."

By the time James and Anne announced themselves finished and ready to depart, another half hour had passed. They all stepped outside together, James and Anne announcing their intent to walk a bit and visit a new shop that had recently opened. Adam turned Maggie toward the corner where his coach was waiting, but something caused him to stop. His entire body went rigid, and Maggie looked up, wondering at the cause. All she saw was an elegant-looking older woman coming toward them on the arm of a young man who looked enough like the woman that he had to be her son.

Maggie took a sideways glance at Adam. His face was a cold mask, his body tight, and she was fairly certain he trembled with a bit of rage. She asked quietly, "What is it?"

"Nothing. Let's go." He took her arm to move her forward, but James's voice stopped them.

"Grace? It is you! I thought as much." James rushed past them, took both of the woman's hands in his own, and kissed her cheek.

"Jamie! How good to see you again."

Maggie watched the scene, surreptitiously eyeing the older woman. She was tall and slender, with a friendly smile and pale blue eyes. Her hair looked to have once been white-blond, but had long since faded to a silver. She had probably been quite striking as a younger woman, and she still was.

The woman was speaking again, her voice soothing and smooth as silk. "James, this is my younger son, Henry. I don't believe the two of you have met before. He's just back from Vienna."

"That's right," James offered. "You've been studying music."

"Hello," the younger man said, smiling and reaching out a hand. "It's so good to finally meet you."

Odd, Maggie thought, but with their tall, slender physiques and reddish-brown hair, Henry and James looked enough alike to be brothers.

"And who is this?" Grace asked, turning her attention to Anne.

"This is my very good friend, Anne Porter."

Grace eyed her up and down, those cool eyes seeming to take in every inch. She returned her gaze to James and said with a smile, "Lovely, James. Quite lovely. I'm happy for you."

James shifted to give Anne a quick peck on the cheek, and his movement cleared the walk so that Grace and Adam were suddenly facing each other. Coolly, Grace said, "Lord Belmont."

"Miss Stuart," he said, placing peculiar and particular emphasis on the word *Miss*. Tightly, he squeezed Maggie's arm. "Let's go."

"Adam . . ." Maggie protested as he took a step. She hadn't been prepared to move and nearly tripped. He didn't slow, but merely grabbed harder and pulled her around the quartet of people toward his carriage. Maggie managed an apologetic glance at Grace as she passed. She mouthed, "I'm sorry."

"It's all right, dear," Grace whispered, managing a pat against her shoulder.

What was that look in her eye? Pity? Commiseration? Regret?

There was no time to assess further, as they had reached the door of the carriage. Adam nearly tossed her inside, joining her with a slam of the door that rocked her in her seat. With a bang of his fist on the roof, the team lurched ahead so quickly that Maggie had to reach for a strap to keep from sliding to the floor.

They didn't talk on the short ride home. Maggie huddled in the far corner, watching Adam out of the corner of her eye. He was like a large cat, ready to spring forward and unleash his fury on something—or someone—and Maggie knew better than to let it be her. Best to wait until whatever storm was brewing had passed.

At the house, they alighted silently and headed straight to her room, where Adam instantly set to work removing his clothes, tossing them in an angry pile next to his foot. He glanced up once, noticing she was still standing there fully clothed while he'd stripped to just his breeches. "Undress," he ordered curtly.

"As you wish." Still worried by the feeling that he might pounce on her if she said the wrong thing, she moved cautiously but quickly, her fingers quickly pulling the pins from her hat and then from her hair, letting the soft swirls fall across her shoulders.

A knock sounded, and Gail poked her head in.

"Get out!" Adam shouted before the woman could ask if they needed anything. She shut the door and scurried away.

"Adam, really!" Maggie scolded. "That was uncalled for." He turned his furious gaze back to her, but she refused to flinch away in the face of it. "I don't know why you're so upset, but I won't have you yelling at the servants."

"I'll talk to them any way I please."

She thought he sounded rather like a spoiled child, and his tone set a spark to her own anger. "Not in my home, you won't."

"You're forgetting something, Maggie. This is my home, not yours, and the servants in it work for me." Adam had no idea what made him say such a thing, for he considered the home Maggie's in every sense. Neither was he in the habit of raising his voice to the people who served him. He was just so upset after seeing Grace Stuart.

"What a perfectly dreadful thing to say to me," Maggie said. His words made her feel like nothing more than a servant herself. She gestured toward the door. "I think you'd better leave."

"You will not give me orders."

"Too bad, for I no longer want you here, and you don't seem to have sense enough to take leave on your own. Go!"

"I'll not leave until I've had what I came for."

Maggie sputtered with outrage, her temper suddenly outdistancing his by leaps and bounds. "You think I would lie with you now?"

"I know you will."

"Well, you'd better think again. What in the bloody hell has come over you?"

"You will not use that kind of language in my presence."

"I am not your wife, and I will speak any damned way I choose." She added the second curse just to infuriate him further. It certainly worked.

"That's right. You're not my wife; you're my mistress. Bought and paid for. Now, remove your clothes!"

"I know you've been raised to snap your fingers and see the entire world jump to do your bidding, but I'm afraid I am not one of the minions who will blindly do as you say." As calmly as she could, she turned away from him, sat at her vanity, and began pulling a brush through her hair. Behind her, she could feel his presence like a keg of gunpowder ready to explode.

Adam saw red. He wasn't sure why he was arguing with Maggie; she was simply there and available, and he needed so desperately to vent his anger. Grabbing her wrist and yanking the brush out of her hand, he said, "Come."

She jerked away and stood, toppling the stool behind her. "What is that woman—Grace Stuart—to you?"

He took a deep breath, obviously surprised to hear the woman's name on Maggie's lips. "She is none of your concern."

"That's priceless! We meet her on the street, she politely says hello, and the very sight of her turns you into a raving lunatic. Tell me what she did to you that the very sight of her could leave you in such a state."

"She did nothing to me." He turned away, surprised to find a wave of distress mounting inside him that seemed to have started at the very tip of his toes and was working its way restlessly through his body, and he knew it would settle somewhere near the area of his heart.

Before he turned away, Maggie caught the look of despair in his eyes. In a softer tone, she said, "I'm not stupid, Adam. Please don't treat me as though I am."

"I've never thought you were stupid," he answered, without turning to face her.

"Then talk to me." She took the step that separated them and rested her hand in the center of his back. "Tell me what's going on so I'll understand why you're so angry with me."

"I'm not angry with you."

"You could have fooled me." He took another deep breath, and his shoulders rose and fell with the pain of some deeper struggle. She wanted to wrap him in her arms and offer him comfort, but she wasn't about to. Not until he explained what was going on.

"Seeing her just reminded me . . ." He stopped and raised a hand to his brow, rubbing against the throb that would soon become a full-blown headache. "It made me think of you, and how wrong it is that I'm doing this with you. I'm ashamed of myself, and angry that I have such a weak moral character." He sighed. "I didn't mean to take it out on you."

Nothing he could have said would have surprised her more. She swallowed as he turned to face her, wishing she'd had more time to compose her features. "You're ashamed of me?"

"Not of you. Just of what we're doing. It's wrong for me to be involved with you when I'm so close to marrying, but I've just never been able to help myself where you're concerned. I wanted you, and I had to have you—no matter what the consequences. Well, I know full well what the consequences are—or will be." Seeing her distress, he reached out a hand in supplication, hoping she'd take it. "I'm sorry."

She stared at his outstretched hand but didn't reach for it. Instead, she raised her eyes to his. "And this Grace Stuart, she reminded you of how *shameful* it is for you to be with me?"

"She was my father's mistress." He dropped his hand and walked to the bed, where he sank down wearily on the deep feather mattress.

"So?"

"He kept her through most of the years of my life. She tore our family apart."

"How did she manage that?"

"My father was never home. He hated me, he hated James. Most of all, he hated my mother. For the last few years of his life, we never even saw him. He flaunted her at us at every turn. Even after he died, it didn't end, and every time I run into her, it reminds me of what she did."

"What did she do?"

"She ruined our family."

"She did? I don't suppose your father had anything to do with it?"

"What do you mean?"

"Well, he was the one who kept her. I doubt she forced him into it. There must have been some reason he agreed."

"Of course there was." Adam's face wrinkled in disgust. "He said he loved her! That she was the love of his life! Can you imagine the indignity my mother suffered at being apprised of such a thing?" He stood up, the memories stirring another pot of fury. "He gave her a home, a fortune, children . . ."

"Ah . . . that explains it, then. Henry is your brother. I thought he looked just like James."

"Her child is *not* my brother."

"What would you call him, then?"

"He is my father's bastard. Nothing more. No matter how much of our money Miss Stuart spends on his Vienna education to polish him up a bit, he'll still never be anything else but the by-blow of some nobleman."

"I see." Maggie took a deep breath. Let it out. Took another. Swallowed. Swallowed again. The discussion was getting too close to a line they dared not cross. The topic was too dear to her heart. This time, she was the one to turn away. She walked to her vanity and picked up the brush he had tossed there, absently running her thumb over the handle. "I think you should go, Adam."

"I think that's a good idea."

The silence in the room was suddenly unbearably oppressive. Maggie felt as though the air had become too thick to breathe, and when he opened his mouth to speak again, she nearly ran to him and covered it with her fingers to prevent the words from being spoken aloud. She didn't, though. Instead, she stood rigid and silent, waiting to hear.

"As you know," he said, "on the morrow, I'm going to the country for two weeks. I think perhaps when I get back that we should . . . that is, I think perhaps we should make some arrangements for you."

"Yes, perhaps you're right." The tears she'd held back flooded to the surface. She pressed her fingertips to her closed eyelids to hold them in. Once they were under control, she turned to face him. "You see, I'm just a bastard myself. Just the *by-blow* of some nobleman, and I'll never be anything more than that either." She had the pleasure of seeing Adam flinch at the shock of her revelation.

"Maggie . . . I didn't know . . ."

"Of course you didn't. But you're right. We're such a despicable class of people, and I'm certain it's been horrible for you to be mixing with the likes of me. I didn't know you felt so strongly about my kind. If I had, I'd have informed you sooner and saved you all this trouble." He took a step toward her, but she flinched back. "Don't touch me. Just go!" She turned and sat again, running the brush through her hair as though nothing at all was the matter.

Adam stood in consternation, wondering how things had proceeded to such a deplorable state. He'd never wanted to hurt her, but he wasn't about to apologize. Grace Stuart and her bastard children had torn Adam's family apart. There was always the chance Maggie would do the same if he didn't get a grip on himself and his unruly desire for her.

He was a strong man, had always had to be, and he knew how to act appropriately no matter how his actions went against his better judgment. He sighed. "As you wish. I'll contact you when I return. To make sure everything's ended satisfactorily."

She shrugged, feeling the weight of the world on her shoulders. "Don't trouble yourself on my account. I'm sure you realize I'm not worth it."

Softly behind her, she heard the door closing, then steps retreating down the stairs.

Chapter Sixteen

Adam settled himself on the smooth leather seat of his carriage, absently rubbing his hand along it while taking in the shiny brass fittings. It was the finest example of personal transportation that money could buy. No expense or luxury had been spared by the makers in outfitting it for the Marquis of Belmont. It looked distinctly out of place parked on the narrow street in front of Maggie's small home.

The horses nickered and the coach swayed slightly as one of the drivers shifted about up in the front. The animals and the men were waiting for him to give the signal to depart, but he couldn't do it. Something told him that if he left now, it would be for the last time. Maggie was hurt, her pride badly damaged by his harsh words, and when he returned from the country, either she would be gone or she'd never speak to him again.

It was odd how such a slip of a girl could tie him up in knots. She'd been right during their argument; he *had* been raised to snap his fingers and see people jump at his every word. That was the way his world worked. She seemed to be the only one who didn't understand it and felt completely free to speak to him in any way she chose.

"You deserved it," he muttered aloud, the sounds instantly being swallowed by the thick velvet fabric covering various parts of the interior. If she'd slapped him he'd have deserved that, too.

Nothing they'd shouted at each other changed his feelings about Grace Stuart or her three children, though. He was right to despise the woman and her bastard offspring. He was, damn it, no matter what Maggie might say or feel about it. She didn't know, and could never understand, what the woman's relationship with Aston had put them all through.

Even casual acquaintances had remarked on the unfairness, on the shame Aston St. Clair had heaped on his wife and legitimate sons by claiming Grace's three children as his own, giving them his name, providing for them with loving bequests in his will. He had left Grace with enough money that she could go about in Polite Society. Adam saw her all kinds of places. At the theater, at the races, at balls and parties.

Yes, mistresses were part of his life and times, but the blasted women always knew and accepted their station. They didn't horn in on the legitimate family, taking the love, affection, and money that didn't belong to them. The Stuart woman had no sense—and no shame.

Adam pushed his head back against the carriage wall and groaned. If he was right about all this and more, why did he feel so wretched?

He didn't have to question himself more than once. Maggie was the only person in the entire world who brought any ray of sunshine into his pathetic life. There was no use pretending it was different. The past few weeks, where he'd been able to come home to her at night, had been the best of his life. Always a busy man, he never had anywhere near the free hours he wanted to spend with her, but the few he managed were pure bliss. Lovely, kind, and gentle-hearted, she made no demands of him, placed no obstacles in his path, created no stress. She was just there. Smiling and happy and giving freely of herself and, in the process, easing the heart and mind of a much older, used and abused man who probably didn't deserve her tender regard.

Now that he'd passed a few contented weeks with her by his side, he couldn't imagine returning to the drudgery of what his life had been like before she burst into it. In spite of all his money, jewels, and properties, she was the only precious thing he possessed.

Was it wrong to deny himself the only thing he'd ever truly wanted?

Was that how Father felt about Grace?

The traitorous thought came unbidden, and for the briefest moment, a buried memory of his father flashed in his mind. Adam had been a young man at the time, only sixteen or so, and he'd been attending one of his first parties as an adult. He'd stumbled upon his father kissing Grace in a dark hallway where no one was supposed to be. Aston had been together with her for over a decade by then, but embraced her as though they were still in the first blush of new love. Adam had never told anyone what he'd seen that night, not even James, and he'd hated his father and Grace Stuart each and every day after.

The incident, viewed in retrospect through wiser, more experienced eyes, seemed different now. More loving. More tragic. Less charged with heartbreak and betrayal. While he would never forgive his father, he was mature enough to realize that there might have been more to their affair than he'd ever let himself believe.

Aston had enjoyed Grace for all the years of his life. Had been lucky enough to die in her arms, while Adam meant to keep Maggie only until he was married. Since he could only have her a few more months as it was, what was the purpose of leaving her? With marriage looming in his face, each day with her was precious. Why send her on her way? The very idea made no sense.

With a sigh, he stepped out of the carriage and onto the street.

Pride was a bitter tonic to swallow, and he rarely apologized to anyone, but he would to Maggie. When he came back from his stressful journey, wife-hunting at the country estate, he needed her here waiting for him with loving arms. It was worth every bit of groveling he had to do to win her forgiveness.

Maggie sat at the vanity, too stunned to move. What had gone wrong? She wasn't entirely certain, but she could never have predicted that this day, which she thought would be so full of love and joy, could end so horribly. Adam was high-born—that was true—but he had no right to judge her or to treat her badly because of what her father had done. Her mother's love for the Duke had been a grand passion, the only one of her life, and he had tossed it back in her face. Maggie refused to be denigrated because of his despicable actions. Not by Adam St. Clair or anybody else.

They had talked briefly about her father, Maggie giving Adam the story she gave everyone. Her father was dead, which in fact he was to her. He'd never existed as a real person, but only as a vague and indistinct figure painted in varying hues by her mother, depending on whether she was feeling charitable in her memories on a given day or not.

Now that Adam knew the truth, if he really felt so strongly about her birth, it was best to end things immediately, for Maggie wouldn't put up with any slight over the issue. Which meant that nothing good could come from a further liaison. Oh, but the thought of ending it hurt. That he could toss her over because of something that was, to her way of thinking, so insignificant was the worst insult of all.

A tap on the door brought her head around. Gail entered, a look of concern on her face. "Are you needing anything, Miss Maggie?"

"No, but would you tell the cook that Lord Belmont had to leave. I'm sorry we've ruined her special dinner plans. Please apologize for me."

"Of course." The girl nodded knowingly. "Can I do anything?"

Maggie hated seeing the look of compassion on her face. The maid couldn't help but to have heard them fighting. "No, I'm fine. I'm sorry the Marquis was short with you."

"Don't worry about it, miss. No harm done. He has a lot on his mind at times."

"I appreciate your understanding." She tried for a smile, but didn't quite accomplish it. "I'll let you know if I need assistance. I'd like to be alone for a while."

"Certainly. Just ring if you need me."

After Gail closed the door, Maggie walked to the hearth and pulled out one of the bricks, revealing her small hiding place. Inside rested a wooden box. She pulled it out, took it over to the bed, and dumped the contents on the mattress, then lay down beside her small hoard of treasure.

Without counting, she knew how much money was there. Forty pounds. She stacked the sovereigns and crowns in piles, loving the heavy feel of the gold and silver, and counted them over and over to reassure herself. It wasn't a great deal, but it was real and solid and hers. So entranced was she with thoughts of her sparse fortune and how many weeks it would last her, that she didn't hear the door open. Adam's voice caused her to freeze.

"What do you have there?" He hadn't meant to frighten her, but she looked ready to bolt through the window.

Not sure what to do or say, she hesitated, then jumped off the bed and quickly scooped the coins into her box and closed the lid. Surely, he wouldn't take it from her!

"It's nothing," she said as she turned to face him.

"Let me see." He held out his hand in that authoritative way he had that prevented a person from refusing to do as he said.

She held out the box, and he accepted it, gave a quick scan of the contents, and handed it back. The silence was unbearable, and although she wasn't sure why, for she'd done nothing wrong, she felt the need to explain herself. "It's just some money I've been saving."

"You can ask me if you need anything."

"I know. I just . . ." Her cheeks flushed, and she stepped around him to place the box out of sight in a drawer. She'd return it to its hiding place after he left. "You've been very generous. I don't want to ask you for money."

"Where did you get it?"

"It's from selling my mother's old clothes and various things." She whirled around. "I didn't steal it if that's what you're thinking."

"It never crossed my mind that you might have." He gestured toward the bed. "Let's sit for a moment, shall we?"

He was very good at making his commands sound like requests. She settled herself on the chair next to the bed while he sat facing her, perched on the edge of the mattress. The silence grew oppressive again. Finally, she said quietly, "It's for when you send me away."

"That amount won't get you far."

"It's better than last time when I had nothing."

Adam had never spent as much time around a commoner as he had Maggie. While his wealthy holdings made him ultimately responsible for the welfare of thousands of people, he had many levels of managers and agents between himself and those who toiled on his behalf, so he had very little understanding of what their lives were like. He couldn't imagine what it would be like to walk out onto the streets of London with forty pounds in your pocket. Especially when you were a female and the options were so limited.

"Do you really think I'd put you out on the streets?"

"I really have no idea if you would or not."

"I'm hurt that you think so little of me." He patted his leg. "Come here."

She took the small step from the chair to the bed and settled her bottom against the hard plane of his thigh. His arms came around her waist to steady her as she asked, "What are you doing here, Adam?"

"I came back to say I'm sorry." He nuzzled a kiss against the side of her neck. "I was a complete ass, and I hope you'll accept my apology."

For which of your numerous insults? she nearly asked, but didn't. He was not a man who was required to explain his words or actions. For him to have swallowed his pride and returned to her room was an incredible gesture on his part. One she could not toss in his face.

"Accepted." She raised her eyes to meet his, and rested a hand against his cheek. He took it in his own and placed a tender kiss in the center.

"Thank you."

She hadn't had much time to think about the horrid words he'd said about his father and Grace Stuart and, therefore, herself, but she knew they had to talk about it and clear the air or they'd never put the conversation behind them. "Adam, why are you keeping me? If it's something you feel so strongly about, how come you decided to do such a thing?"

"I couldn't help myself, Maggie, you know that. From the moment I met you, I wanted you like I've never wanted anything else in my life."

"But if you're so concerned about my background, and about my status, perhaps it's better if I left now. I never want to cause you heartache."

"Oh Maggie," he whispered, pulling her close and placing a kiss on the top of her head. "I wish I could explain to you what my life is like, what my days and nights are like. Knowing you is the only thing that gives me any joy."

"What a perfectly lovely thing to say," she said with a sigh. This was as close as he'd ever come to a declaration of his feelings, and hearing the words made her heart do a little flip-flop.

"It's true, which makes me wonder if I'm completely mad when I consider the way I treat you." He pulled back so he could look her in the eye. "After what I said earlier, I wouldn't blame you a bit if you left and never came back."

"I won't leave you, you silly man. You need me."

"Yes, I do. Very, very much." He brushed a light kiss across her lips, then pulled her into a tight embrace. "Oh, Maggie, I feel the burdens of my life so heavily today."

"Then let me ease your worries. That's what I'm here for." She was ready to help him undress and comfort him the best way she knew how, but he seemed determined to get something off his chest.

"I'd marry you in a second if I could. You know that, don't you?"

"No, I didn't know." Needing to put distance between them, she stood and moved to the window, looking down on the people passing by on the street below. "And I wish you wouldn't tell me such a thing again. It makes all this so much harder."

"I'm sorry. I just need you to understand why I'm so distressed sometimes. I don't mean to take it out on you."

"Then, why do you?" She glanced over her shoulder.

"Because there's no one else who will put up with me when I'm in such a state."

"I'll take that as a compliment."

"You should. I can show my worst side to you, and you still care about me. That matters to me very much." He balanced his elbows on his knees and rested his head in his hands. "I don't want to marry another woman, Maggie . . ."

"But you must," she said, finishing the thought for him.

"Yes, I must, but the women I meet are all so inappropriate for me. I feel nothing for any of them. My heart has been joined to yours since the first time I laid eyes on you. Knowing you like I do makes my choices all the more—"

Much as she knew she was supposed to listen and offer support to whatever he wished to discuss, this had to be beyond the limits. "Adam," she declared, "please, I can't bear to hear about any of this. I understand that you're distraught and wish to unburden yourself, but I can't be the one to listen to you on this topic.''

"But I need you to understand how confused I am. Before I met you, the entire process had been such a trying chore, and now . . . now, I can't contemplate going through with it, and I must.'' He rubbed his hand across his heart as though the very idea was hurting him physically. "It's tearing me apart.''

On seeing his anguish so clearly, she was unable to stay across the room. She went to him and stood before him, sliding her hand under his, gently massaging the center of his chest as he had been doing. "I'm sorry this is hurting you so much. I don't want it to.''

She ran her fingers tenderly through his hair as he buried his face against her stomach and confessed, "I can't keep you, Maggie. After I marry, I simply can't. I know I said it more dreadfully before, so I'll say it more gently now: When I marry I will have to let you go, but how shall I ever do such a thing? I'd rather cut off my right arm than live without you.''

"I don't want to stay after you've wed, anyway.'' He was obviously surprised by this and raised his gaze to hers. "I've developed quite a *tendre* for you, and I can't think how I could bear sharing you with another, be she your lawful wife or no.'' Her feelings went quite beyond tenderness to a deep and abiding love, but she'd never tell him so. What would be the point? He did not need the extra burden. In the long run, it would only make things more difficult than they already were.

He shook his head in consternation. "I never thought this would be so difficult.''

"What could I do to make it easier for you?'' She dared not ask for any ease for herself, for she was already grimly aware that her heart would very likely never recover after he left.

"I haven't the foggiest idea.'' He placed a loving kiss against her stomach. "All I know for now is that, after we fought earlier, I was sitting out in the carriage, and I couldn't drive away. I knew if I left things in such a state between us, that you'd be gone when I returned from the country. The thought of coming back to London and not having you waiting for me was not one I could contemplate.''

"Everything will work out in the end, Adam. I just know it.'' She knelt between his legs and wrapped her arms around his waist. "In the meantime, we need to make each day count.''

"Yes, I agree.'' He inhaled deeply the smell of her hair and skin that he loved so well. "Shall we attempt to start this evening over again?''

"I was just about to suggest the same thing. Let me tell Cook you'll be staying to dinner after all.''

Chapter Seventeen

The sound of male laughter coming from Anne's room brought Maggie up short. With Adam and James away in the country, she couldn't imagine who would be in there. Not James, certainly. She tiptoed down the hall.

Anne was naked, draped across her bed in a pile of pillows with a shawl of lace barely covering her intimate spots. Charles, his easel set, his paints arranged on a nearby table, stood next to her, artfully pulling her hair across her shoulders so it curled just above the swell of her breast.

"How do I look?" Anne laughed when she saw Maggie standing in the doorway.

"Scandalous." She returned her friend's smile.

"I certainly hope so." Anne laughed again. "We didn't wake you, did we?"

"No. I've been up for a while. What are you doing?"

Charles turned to look at her. "We're painting a naughty picture, you silly girl—what's it look like we're doing?"

"Well, I can see that, but why?"

"Why not?" Charles asked, his eyes all innocence and good

humor. Anne shifted to look around, so she could see Maggie while talking to her, but Charles pushed her back. "Don't move. I've got you right where I want you."

"That's what James always tells me," Anne admitted, causing Charles to whoop with laughter. He stepped back to his paints while Anne tried to keep from fidgeting. She looked at Maggie out of the corner of her eye. "This is going to be a present for James. For his birthday." Her eyes widened with an instant of worry. "You don't think it's too much, do you?"

"No," Maggie admitted, never tiring of the fire that had come into Anne's eyes since she'd allied herself with James St. Clair. "I think it will be perfect. James will love it."

Charles looked around the easel. "Would you like me to do one of you for Adam?"

"Wherever would Adam hang such a thing?"

"He's a Marquis, so I'd say that means he could hang it anywhere he wants." Charles shrugged, making Maggie smile. He dipped a brush and stirred two colors together, making a pink hue that matched the flush of Anne's cheeks. "If you don't want people to know it's you, we could tip your face back so you'd appear to be a mystery woman. Others would wonder who you were, but Adam would always know." He wiggled his eyebrows suggestively.

Maggie felt a light blush color her cheeks, which was surprising. In a house full of two mistresses and their gentlemen, sexual discussion was the norm, but sometimes she felt awkward, as though she'd stepped into someone else's life. She wasn't sure she was ready for such confidential posing.

Still, Anne and Charles appeared to be enjoying themselves immensely, and it would be lovely to give Adam something to remember her by. She couldn't have a portrait done; he could never hang such a thing in his home where he might have to explain it to his wife. But perhaps he could hang an artful nude, painted by his cousin, in one of his private rooms. "I'll think about it."

"Let me know," Charles said distractedly, already at work

on the canvas. "I work fast so I'll have this mostly done in a few days, but I have other appointments progressing as well, so I'd have to work you in if you want it accomplished before they return from Sussex."

"I miss James already," Anne said with a sigh from the bed. "Do you really think they'll stay the entire two weeks?"

"Well, Adam has to," Charles answered. "He couldn't possibly insult the twelve special guests they've invited by leaving early. The very idea would give my Aunt Lucretia an apoplexy. But I can't say about James. He doesn't have much stomach for what's going on."

"Why is that?" Maggie asked casually, completely unprepared for Charles's response.

Charles was wrapped up in his work and gave no thought to how his comments might sound to Maggie, so he didn't temper his words. "Because there is nothing more pathetic than sitting in a room and watching all the young ladies vie for Adam's attention. Their mothers are even worse. It's really revolting in many ways. Adam is like a stallion on the auction block, and the girls are all so offensively fawning and disgustingly vapid." He gave a dramatic shudder. "Let's just say that James has always considered himself the luckier of the two to have been born the second son."

Maggie's throat was dry. She'd had no idea why Adam had gone to the country, because she had made it a point not to ask, convincing herself that he'd gone on business. As long as she wasn't directly faced with evidence of his coming marriage, she could pretend it wasn't happening, so she never questioned him about his private life, but with Charles's mention of twelve guests, she couldn't quash her sudden destructive desire to know more. "What's the reason for the party?"

"My aunt is hosting twelve young ladies and their families to spend some time with Adam. She's hoping the event will help him along in his selection process for a wife."

"How did she come up with the twelve women?"

"They're considered the cream of this year's crop of marriageables."

"I see." She really didn't want to know more, but having gone this far, she couldn't stop. "Do you think he'll make a selection from the twelve?"

"There's a good chance, I suppose."

"Why?"

"Well, he wants to make a decision by his thirtieth birthday."

"In February. Yes, I was aware of that."

"And one of the women at the party is considered the favorite by most everyone."

"Penelope Westmoreland?"

"How did you know?" he asked as Maggie sagged slightly against the doorframe. He looked up then at the lovely girl, who appeared as though she'd just been stabbed in the heart by his words. "Maggie . . . ?"

She held out a hand to keep him from rushing to her side. It was one thing to secretly wonder if Adam might marry her sister, but quite another to have the possibility bandied about by someone else. She tried for a smile, but wasn't overly successful. "I think I've discussed as much of this as I can for one day."

Anne realized Maggie's distress, and asked, "Are you all right?"

"Yes, but you know how hard it is for me to hear about this."

Charles wanted to kick himself. "What an incredible oaf I am! Maggie, I'd not given a second of thought to how what I said might offend you. Please forgive me."

"It's all right," Maggie insisted.

"Hardly."

Anne looked over at Charles. "It's just difficult for her, Charles. Adam's told her that he'll send her away once he's wed, so his courtships and marriage are not topics we talk about much."

"He doesn't think it would be fair to his new bride to have

me as his mistress,'' Maggie offered by way of explanation. She agreed, but, oh, how it hurt to say so.

"You don't have to explain Adam to me, Maggie. I know exactly what he's like.'' He dabbed more paint on the easel, Anne's form already taking shape. His hand paused in midstroke. "I feel dreadful about bringing this up. I can't believe he didn't tell you what he was doing.''

"It's not that he didn't tell me, Charles. I've asked him not to share any intimate details with me. I find it's easier that way.''

Charles assessed her with a shrewd look. "You care for him, don't you?''

"A great deal.'' *I love him, love him, love him* . . . The true answer echoed in her head, and she wished she could shout her feelings to the world.

"Then you have a difficult road ahead,'' Charles said.

"I imagine. But no more difficult than Adam. He cares for me, too, so it will be very difficult for both of us.''

"His days must be more horrid than ever,'' he murmured more to himself than to the two women. Wanting to relieve the tension his words had created, he looked toward the sky in mock prayer. "Thank You again, Lord, for not making me my father's heir.''

Maggie made herself smile at that. She could not—would not—be unhappy. She intended to enjoy every minute of their time together without lamenting what might have been. The future was set, Adam had his responsibilities, and they did not include her. Nothing could be changed, so there was no use crying and carrying on over what could never be. The future was coming whether she wanted it to or not.

After watching in curious amazement for a time while Anne's figure took on more shape and color, she left the pair to their task. Downstairs, she ate a light breakfast, then grabbed her cloak. She'd ordered a few new pieces of lingerie as a surprise for Adam when he returned, and she'd received a message the previous afternoon that the seamstress she used for her intimate apparel wanted her to stop by for a final fitting.

The male servant Adam had left at the house, John, took on many roles and chores depending on what was needed, and he served as footman when she or Anne went on an excursion. They didn't have their own carriage, though. Maggie had refused to let Adam suffer the expense of keeping an extra team for her use since she so seldom had need of it. It was much cheaper to hire a hansom cab when she had to go somewhere, and when she stepped out the door, John had her transportation waiting.

He helped her up, then joined her at Adam's insistence that she never go anywhere alone. Even if she'd wanted to, none of the servants would have let her. They were all too afraid of incurring the Marquis's wrath if they let her go off alone and something happened. Knowing from her own experience how difficult it was to find gainful employment, Maggie didn't have the heart to place any of their jobs in jeopardy, so she quietly acquiesced to the numerous demands Adam foisted on them. She'd completed dozens of shopping trips with John, and he was such a quiet, polite young man that she barely noticed his presence, so it was hardly an inconvenience. And she had to admit that there had been the occasional times when she felt safer because he was by her side.

The time spent trying on her new undergarments was fun. The woman who created the shocking swatches of lace and silk was full of bawdy talk and lewd comments about how the various pieces could be used most effectively. Maggie welcomed the woman's suggestions, even though she was blushing slightly when she left the woman's establishment.

Her hands were full of packages when she stepped out onto the crowded street, which made it easy for the strange man to grab her arm and hustle her in the direction away from where John waited for her with the hansom.

"You! There!" she heard John shout. Her parcels scattered

to the ground, which only added to the confusion of the pas-
sersby and allowed the man to make off with her.

Before Maggie could struggle or speak, she was neatly deposited into a waiting carriage. The door slammed with a crack
and the team jolted away, barely giving her time to grab for
purchase. She righted herself, saw male shoes, then raised her
eyes up a pair of male legs, waistcoat, cravat until she was
staring at the face of her father, the Duke of Roswell.

Over the years, the few times she'd seen him in public places,
it had always been quick or at a distance. It was odd to see his
face so closely, for she hadn't realized that she looked so much
like him, the only true difference being caused by the fact that
she was a female and her features more smooth and gentle.

Their bearings were also the same. The Duke gave no doubt
of his position in the world simply by the way he spoke, gestured, and carried himself. Maggie, while never having enjoyed
the fruits of such status in her life, moved with a grace and
style that matched his own. There was no question that they
were father and daughter. They looked and acted too much
alike to be anything else.

At age forty-five, he was an incredibly handsome man, his
blond hair carrying a hint of silver, a few age lines around his
mouth and eyes. And what eyes! A deep blue, intense and
overpowering, and they were fixed on her with a terrible scrutiny. Somehow, she managed to refrain from gasping.

"Oh, good, so you know who I am," he said as he saw
her look of recognition. "I'm glad we may dispense with the
formalities."

"Let me out of here." She leaped for the door, ready to
jump into the street if she had to, but his firm grip on her wrist
stopped her.

"It would be dreadfully foolish to chance injuring yourself
in such a futile endeavor. For if you leap out, one of my men
will simply grab you and bring you back."

"What do you want?"

"I want to talk to you."

"Well, I don't want to talk to you."

"I must admit that I regret that I had to resort to such lowering tactics to bring us together, but you refused my invitation a few weeks ago, and Adam has stuck to your side so completely that I've not had another chance until now to make your acquaintance." The Duke tapped a pensive finger against his lip. "I wonder what he'd think if he knew you were my daughter. It would humor me greatly to know. Perhaps I'll tell him when he returns."

"You'll do no such thing."

"Won't I?" he asked with a malicious smirk on his face. "I'm your father, which entitles me to do whatever I wish where you are concerned."

"You are not my father. My father is dead."

"We both know that's not true, now don't we?" Leaning forward, he grabbed her chin, and she tried to pull away, but he merely tightened his hold. He turned her face back and forth as though looking for flaws. "I do believe you're even more beautiful than your mother."

His words gave her the strength she needed to push his hand away. "Don't you dare speak about her."

"Ah . . . and I see you've inherited her passionate nature as well." He smiled, thinking she really was quite something. "From what I hear, you've inherited much of my nature as well."

"I would certainly hope not. I don't want to be anything like you."

"But you are, my dear. You are. Like it or no."

"What makes you think you know so much about me?"

"It was never difficult to keep track of you. There were always acquaintances who had to be certain to tell me they'd seen your mother. Or you. Plus, there were a few occasions when I sent my own men to learn information I sought. I've really been quite well informed over the years."

"Then you knew when we needed help."

He shrugged. "Usually."

"Why didn't you ever come to our aid?"

"I didn't want to."

"Why? Was it that your pride is so grand, or your dislike of us so intense?"

"No. I was merely teaching your mother a long, hard lesson."

"What lesson?"

"That she would rue the day she refused my offer."

"You made her an offer?" This was a part of their story Maggie had never heard, and one she didn't want to learn about now. Especially from his lips.

"Of course. What kind of man do you take me for?"

Over the years, she'd come up with hundreds of ways to describe what a despicable person she believed him to be, and she had to bite her tongue to keep from replying. Instead, she asked, "You said you were teaching my mother a lesson by ignoring us. What lesson were you teaching me?"

"No lesson. You didn't enter into it."

"I see," she responded bitterly, wanting only to depart his company at the earliest opportunity. "I'm glad my mother never allowed me to harbor any illusions about your true feelings toward your firstborn child."

"Don't take it personally."

"How should I take it?"

He waved a dismissive hand. "I only meant that the fight was between your mother and me. You were not involved."

"How could I not have been involved when I was the cause?" With more emotion than she wanted him to see, she said, "Especially when it affected my entire life?"

"Whatever difficulties you suffered were completely her choice."

She shook her head. "I don't believe you."

"Believe it or no. I care not. But understand this: I offered her a small trust and the ownership of your home. It wasn't a great deal, but then I hadn't taken the title yet, and I had very limited funds."

Unwilling to believe him, she couldn't help wondering if any of it was true. Why would he lie about such a thing after all this time? "What happened?"

"She threw it back in my face. Said she loved me"—he laughed harshly at the word *love* as though it was some filthy epithet—"that she wanted me to stay with her, to recognize you."

"She did love you. She always did."

"So? What she wanted was completely out of the question. I sent her on her way and never looked back. She insisted she could make her own way without my help. I let her."

"She was a girl!" Maggie nearly shouted in her frustration. "Younger than I am now. How could she know what was best when her heart was so involved?"

"It was her worst fault, how she let her emotions run away from her. I had told her from the beginning not to love me. She did anyway."

"Some people can't control that sort of thing."

"In any event, her later lot in life was completely her own doing. She let her pride ruin both your lives. I hope you'll have better sense in your dealings with St. Clair when he lets you go. You're my daughter, so hopefully you've inherited some of my shrewdness and common sense."

"I already told you I'm nothing like you."

The Duke let the slight pass without rearguing the point. "Is he thinking of keeping you after he weds?"

She was silent for a time, wondering where this was going; then she finally said, "My relationship with Adam isn't any of your business."

"That's what you think." He reached into his vest pocket and checked his timepiece, giving Maggie the sense that his first visit with his daughter was keeping him longer than he'd anticipated or wanted. He put her on her guard when he asked, all too casually, "Speaking of Adam, will he propose to one of the twelve when he returns from the country?"

"How would I know?"

He leaned forward and patted her knee. "Let's be frank, shall we? I know everything about your relationship with Adam."

"No, you don't. Not if you think he would confide such a thing to me."

The Duke eyed her speculatively. From the limited accounts he'd managed to generate, Adam doted on the girl. Surely, they talked extensively, in and out of bed. "Why wouldn't he?"

"I have no desire to know his plans, and I've asked him not to share them with me. So, if this is the reason you kidnapped me off the street, I'm delighted to say that it's been a total waste of your precious time." She reached for the door, hoping to bluff her way into getting away from him.

"We're not finished. Sit back." He gripped her wrist and pushed her back against the squab once again. "I've a proposition for you."

"I'll just bet you do."

"I wish Adam to offer for my daughter, Penelope, as soon as possible."

"Poor dear Penny." Maggie oozed sarcasm. "Is she really as desperate as she appears?"

"Hardly. She's the most sought-after debutante this year."

"Really? Then how come she was in a retiring room at a ball, tugging down the bodice of her gown to bare more of her breasts? All the while, she was whining about how Adam never looks at them and how she can't garner his attention no matter how hard she tries. And now you've abducted me to try to help her win his favor. I'd certainly call that behavior *desperate*— on both your parts."

The Duke refused to respond to such ludicrous sentiment, although he did make a mental note to give Penelope a few good lashes when she returned from the country. The foolish girl! Carrying on in public rooms where anyone could hear! He summoned all his control. "She wishes to marry him, but I wish it as well, and you're going to see to it that he does."

Maggie wondered if she was in some kind of horrible night-mare. She actually physically pinched her arm to ensure that she wasn't dreaming. Unfortunately, she was wide awake. "Never in a thousand years."

"We'll see about that."

"Nothing you could say or do would make me betray Adam or help you win him for Penny."

"Are you certain about that?"

"More certain than I've ever been about anything."

"Well, then, consider this, and I'm certain you'll see the benefits of changing your mind."

"Consider what?"

"If you refuse to help, I intend to publicly claim my paternity of you."

"What possible reason could you have for doing such a thing at this late date?"

"I believe that the pleasure he enjoys with you is keeping him from making a decision for which I'm tired of waiting. I want you out of the way, and I want him married to Penelope. If you agree to help, I'll allow you to remain by his side for however long he wishes to keep you. If you won't, I'll claim paternity, have the courts appoint me as your guardian, and I'll have you married off within a fortnight of the ruling." He had the satisfaction of seeing the look of shock on her face, but he misread it. Thinking it was fear, he pressed home his mistaken advantage. "You'll never see your precious Adam St. Clair again."

Amazed, Maggie could do nothing but shake her head. His claim of paternity was what she'd wanted all her life. As a little girl, she'd prayed and dreamed that he would do such a thing. But never in a lifetime of wishing could she have imagined it would come about in such a way. That he would suggest such a thing . . . instigate such a thing . . . think for one moment that she was the type of person who would involve herself in such a contemptible endeavor . . . was unspeakable.

He'd said she had many of his own qualities. Perhaps she did, because the blaze of temper suddenly coursing through her veins was something she'd never known she possessed. "I despise you, and I will deny until my dying breath that you are my father. As to Adam . . ." She had to take a deep breath to control her ragged breathing. "Unlike you, I would never betray the trust of another, particularly when it is a person for whom I care deeply."

The Duke was furious. No one defied him. In fact, it was such an odd, rare occurrence that he couldn't think of exactly the best way to respond. For once, he was at a loss for words. "If you don't do this, I'll . . . I'll . . ."

"The worst thing you could do to me, you've already done. You refused to help my mother when she lay dying. That was the worst. The very worst has already happened at your hands, and I survived. The only other thing you could do that would be worse would be to kill me, but I vow I would rather be dead than betray Adam."

The carriage was suddenly caught in traffic and lurched to a stop. She seized the advantage and rose to leave. He reached for her again, but the imperious look she gave him prevented him from grabbing her this time.

"I'll make you so bloody sorry," he threatened. "You'll rue the day we met."

"I already regret it, but perhaps you're the one who should be worried. I plan to tell Adam everything you said. At the very earliest opportunity." She stepped out onto the street, stumbling at the long drop down with no one there to catch her. "Let's see how your beloved Penelope fares after that!" she called as she slammed the door and huffed off into the crowd before any of his men could stop her.

The Duke sat back, rubbing his temples. It seemed he had seriously underestimated the girl. Not only was she beautiful and smart; she was also loyal, tough, determined, and shrewd. A fighter. A winner. All in all, a magnificent person any father would be proud to call his own.

What a waste that she could never be anything more than his illegitimate child.

Chapter Eighteen

James looked out the window to the lawn and gardens that ran across the back of the lavishly apportioned house they referred to as their country home. Night had fallen so the colors were gone, but torches lighted the way through the maze of paths, and the dots of light looked like beautiful glowing stars that had come down to earth to sit on the ground. He could make out occasional shadows of various people walking in couples or in groups. The entire week had been exceptionally warm and pleasant, and the night air was refreshing and not cool in the least, drawing numerous people outside.

By all accounts, the party was a huge success. His mother, for all her stern, dreadful habits, knew how to host such a large event, and the dozens of guests were all enjoying themselves immensely. Everyone except himself. He'd never been more bored by anything.

He missed Anne.

He missed her bawdy talk, and her fiery passion. He missed her laughter and her funny stories, and her common sense and wit and outrageous behavior. At this very moment, the only place he truly wanted to be was in her bedroom in her bed, lying back against the pillows with her warm, lush body stretched across his chest. With his eyes closed, he could conjure up the feel of her skin, the smell of her hair.

"What am I doing here?" he muttered to the silent room.

Looking down, he stared for a long time at the papers in his hand. They had arrived by special messenger earlier in the day. His great-uncle had finally died, widowed and childless, and James had come into his inheritance. He was now a baron. It was not a particularly old title, nor a wealthy estate, but it was a title and it was an estate.

He'd visited there many times over the years, always knowing that the place would be his one day. It was a beautiful location, if a tad bit isolated in Cornwall, with a nice house, fertile fields, and prosperous tenants. The income was excellent for an estate its size. Those funds, coupled with the money left to him by his father, wouldn't make him a rich man, but certainly one who was well off.

This should have been a great day in his life. The greatest, perhaps. So, why wasn't he excited? He should be down the hall, charming the ladies and amusing the gentlemen, joining in the celebration, but he couldn't force himself to do it. Instead, he'd been hiding in the library for over an hour, hoping no one had noticed he'd disappeared. Everyone was so focused on Adam that he doubted anyone had, and he needed the solitary time to think about the future.

The inheritance wasn't something he'd talked about much, for the simple fact that he'd never wanted it to seem that he was some sort of ghoul, impatiently waiting for the gracious old gentleman to pass on. Few people knew about it, although the information had passed round the party quickly enough. He didn't know who had told everyone. *He* certainly hadn't.

Already, he'd seen the new look of assessment in the eyes of the women. They were apparently wondering if second prize would be acceptable in the St. Clair contest. If they were not selected by the Marquis, there could only be personal benefit to marrying a peer of the realm who also happened to be a Marquis's brother.

The very idea of being assessed in such a light made him slightly ill.

The efficient click of heels coming down the hall told him his respite was nearly at an end. He'd know that walk anywhere. His mother, Lucretia, in a snit from the sound of things, stepped into the room and pulled the doors closed behind her.

"Good evening, Mother." He was always polite to her, but he wasn't sure why. She'd never been anything but rude and overbearing to him all the days of his life.

"James, you must return to the main salon immediately."

"Why?"

"Why?" Her body shook with indignation. "Your absence has been noted. You're being extremely rude."

Not as rude as I intend to be, he almost said aloud. He grinned the grin that had never failed to infuriate her. "Don't tell me one of the lovelies missed me. Which one? I shall rush to her side immediately."

"Don't be insolent," she scolded him in the tone of voice that made him feel as though he were ten years old once again. "I've had three ladies ask where you've gone. Particularly Miss Hawkins."

"Why would anybody be asking about me? Let me guess: They're all wondering if the new baron has disappeared." He could barely manage to keep from rolling his eyes in disgust. "How did they hear about my inheritance? I wonder."

Lucretia pulled herself up to her full height. "I told a few choice guests, and I'll make no apologies for it. Everyone knows. You've become quite a catch, suddenly. This group of women can serve you as well as your brother."

So, it was starting already. "Yes, it would be so appropriate for me to settle for one of Adam's castoffs. By all means, I shall return immediately."

"See that you do," she responded, as usual not noticing his

sarcasm. "I'll give you fifteen minutes." She huffed out, and he collapsed back in the chair behind the large desk.

He'd never gotten along with her, had never felt close to her, had never formed an emotional connection with her. She was a cold, brittle woman who was, and always had been, completely unknowable. They'd never had a family because of it. She had never generated a spark of maternal concern; he'd been raised by governesses and nannies with only a rare visit from her to his rooms while he was growing. Usually, she only deigned to show her face when he'd caused some upset or other.

His mother and father had rarely spoken to one another, Aston seeming to find her as unpleasant as James always had. Because of the irreparable differences between his parents, he rarely saw Aston when he was growing up. When the man occasionally deigned to visit, he was little more than a stranger. As a result, James had never known his father. In many ways, he felt as if he'd been raised as an orphan.

Perhaps that was why he'd sought out Grace Stuart's company in the past year. What he'd found was a gracious woman, a home filled with love, laughter, and a trio of happy, well-adjusted half siblings. They had all loved Aston deeply, and James felt that he was coming to know the mysterious man by learning about him through their eyes. James had been welcomed as though he was part of their family, and he'd embraced them as well. The sense of belonging he'd found was something he'd never realized he was missing, but now he couldn't understand how he'd ever gone without it for a day in his life.

By God, but he wanted what his father had found with Grace Stuart. Love and laughter and a house full of boisterous children. The life being forced on Adam was one for which he refused to settle. Adam and Lucretia could spout about their damnable duty until they choked on it. James would not follow in their footsteps. If it caused a rift with the pair of them, so be it. He had another family now, one that loved and cared about him, and they would support him in whatever decisions he made. And he had already made the most important one of all.

Adam's footsteps were the next to sound in the hall. For the briefest moment, James wished he'd left before facing his brother, but he couldn't have. After he set things in motion in London, there was a very good chance Adam would never speak to him again. He loved him too much to run away without a good-bye.

"Hello, brother. Imagine meeting you in here," James said as Adam stepped into the room.

Adam closed the doors, walked to the desk, and pulled up a chair across from James. "If I hear one more girl sing "Oh, Rose of Winter," I believe I shall go absolutely mad."

"My thoughts exactly."

"In case you're wondering what I'm doing here . . ."

"I wasn't."

Adam chuckled. "Mother sent me to drag you back. She says I'm to tell you that your fifteen minutes are up."

"I'm not going back down to the salon. Wild horses couldn't drag me."

"That bad, is it?"

"Worse, I'd say."

Adam looked James over with a critical eye. Something was up; he knew James too well not to recognize the signs. Walking to the sideboard, he poured himself a glass of bourbon, then refilled the one James had sitting on the desk. He sat down, then lifted his glass in a toast. "To the kingdom's newest lord."

"Hear, hear." James tipped his glass in return.

"For a man who's just become a member of the nobility, you don't sound very pleased."

"It never mattered much to me. You know that."

"You're right. It never did matter much." He leaned forward, resting his elbows on his thighs. "This fit of melancholia isn't like you. What's the matter, James?"

"I've just been thinking about the future." James shrugged

as though it was all inconsequential. "I miss Anne. I don't know what I'm doing here."

Adam nodded. He missed Maggie, too, but the separation couldn't be helped. "You filled an important role, James. You helped me host our guests, and you have an even bigger role to play now."

"What's that?" James asked, although he knew what the answer would be.

"You're in my same predicament now, the one you've always felt lucky to have escaped. You'll need to marry one of these days. You should start circulating among the ladies. Several of them are very sweet."

"Oh, yes, very sweet indeed!" James agreed sarcastically. "I notice you latched on to one of them right away." He rolled his eyes in disgust. "Spare me, Adam. Did Mother send you down here to talk about this?"

"She asked me to mention it, but I was going to anyway. This is a good place for you to start your search."

James shook his head in dismay at how obtuse his brother could be sometimes. "Adam, you know how all these ladies have snubbed me through the past Season and over the years. Being myself wasn't enough. Being the son of a Marquis wasn't enough. Being the brother of a Marquis wasn't enough. Suddenly, I'm a baron, and that's enough. Do you really think I'd be interested in any of them now?"

"They'll be different."

"No, they'll be the same. They'll simply act differently." Suddenly needing to move, he stood and walked to the window, staring out into the darkness until the feel of Adam's eyes burning a hole in his back became so intense that he was forced to turn around. "I want what Father had, Adam. I want what he found with Grace Stuart."

"Don't mention her name to me," Adam said shortly, "not in this house where she caused so much heartache."

James held up a hand, indicating a truce. He didn't have the energy for a fight on the subject tonight. Tonight, there was a much bigger subject to air. "I want to be happy, Adam. That's all I've ever wanted, and I've found it so damned hard to attain. I want to spend my life with someone who loves me."

After a ponderous silence, Adam asked, "What do you mean?"

"I mean I'm going to marry Anne Porter. If she'll have me, that is. I don't know if she'll think I'm much of a catch or not, but I know she'll tell me truthfully how she feels. That's one of the things I like best about her."

"Marry Anne?" Adam asked, as if he hadn't understood. "You can't be serious."

James had the experience of seeing Adam rendered speechless. His mouth literally fell open in surprise. After another thunderous silence, James said softly, "I've never been more serious about anything in my life."

"But she's a whore!" Adam finally sputtered, standing up so abruptly that the chair crashed over behind him.

"Then what does that make Maggie?" he asked bitterly.

"This isn't about Maggie," Adam shouted, pointing an accusing finger. "This is about you. Your name and your lineage. The lineage of your sons. Have you gone completely mad? Don't you care about the scandal you will cause?"

"No, not a bit."

"If not that, then how about the humiliation you'll cause Mother?"

"Why should I worry about her, Adam? She's never given a moment of thought to my welfare."

"She is still our mother!" he hissed. "This will kill her."

"She'll survive it," James said quietly, his determination only growing in the light of Adam's outrage. "If she doesn't, I don't care."

"You always were such a selfish little bastard."

"I'm sorry you see it that way, but I refuse to live the life you are so ready to inflict upon yourself. Do you truly want to risk marrying one of these girls who you care nothing about and take a chance of giving your children the same life we had?''

''It won't be like that,'' Adam insisted with less enthusiasm than he should have used to argue the point.

''It will be exactly like that.'' James finished his drink in a quick gulp and set the glass on the desk. ''I'm returning to London in the morning so I can propose to Anne. If she accepts, I want to start things rolling immediately.''

''Just so I'll know, how will you begin our family's mortification? By sending an announcement to the *Times* or having the vicar begin calling the banns next Sunday?''

''Neither. I want the ceremony held as soon as possible.''

With sudden inspiration, Adam warned, ''I'll block any attempt to obtain a special license.''

''Then we'll *shame* you further by eloping.'' He shrugged in resignation, sorry that the discussion was going this way, but knowing it probably couldn't have gone any differently. ''You'll have a few days to think about this and change your mind. I hope you will.''

''I don't care how much you think you love her. I'll not give my blessing. I won't acknowledge the union, and I'll never receive you in my home. Mother won't either.''

''Ooooh . . . now there's a threat that leaves me trembling.''

''It should. You'll be shunned wherever you go. Your wife will bear the brunt of it. Think about her if you won't think about yourself.''

James's eyes blazed with fury. ''I'm twenty-seven years old, with my own title and my own fortune. I neither need nor require your blessing, and if you choose not to give it in a matter which means so much to me, then I couldn't care less for it.'' He took a step around the desk until they were only inches apart, standing toe-to-toe. ''As to Anne and your opinions of her: I love you, brother, and I always will, but she will be my wife, and I will expect her to receive all the courtesy and respect she deserves because of it. From you and everyone else. If you ever call her *whore* again, I'll call you out. Don't make me."

Adam, frightened and distressed by what was happening, softened his stance and laid a hand on James's shoulder. Quietly, he entreated, "Don't do this, James. Don't do this to Mother and me. Please."

James shook off his hand and stepped away. "I'll leave at dawn so there'll be no need for good-byes or explanations. Make my apologies." He walked out of the room without looking back.

Maggie sat at the vanity in her room and stared at her reflection in the mirror. Tipping her face back and forth, she couldn't see anything about herself that looked different. She appeared to be the same, which seemed impossible to believe. If what she suspected was true, if such a monumental thing had happened, surely there would be some spark of it showing on her skin, in the color of her eyes or the sheen of her hair. But no. Still the same.

She rubbed a hand across her abdomen. In fear. In wonderment. In a complete state of panic. Could it be? Once again, she counted back the weeks. No doubt about it. It must have happened one of the first nights after she'd returned home from working at the brothel. In consternation, she flung herself on the bed and draped a wrist over her eyes.

Damn, but she'd been so careful.

Rose and Anne both had told her the things she could do and use to prevent a babe. And she'd tried them all. Washing herself with vinegars and other concoctions, taking herbal potions, drinking tinctures. Using her mouth and hands as much as she could. She had done everything and tried everything she'd ever heard of, but it had all been for naught, because the most important thing they'd told her—that all the care in the world wouldn't prevent a pregnancy if it was meant to happen—appeared to have come to pass.

"What to do? What to do?" she asked the quiet room as she came back up to a sitting position. First, she had to find out for sure. She didn't know how early a midwife could confirm a babe, but she needed to ask one. Anne would know who to talk with. She would know what to do.

Maggie tiptoed to the door of her room and opened it a crack, hearing no sound and wondering what it meant. James had surprised them both by coming home early, and the pair of lovers had been locked in Anne's room, not coming out for food or drink. Deep into the night, Maggie had heard them talking, arguing occasionally, downright fighting, then whispering in the wee small hours. Something was up. Maggie could feel it in the air, and she hoped with all her heart that James hadn't decided to leave her friend. Maggie didn't know if Anne could take another heartbreaking loss.

All was quiet in the hall. If James had departed, she hadn't heard him go. After they'd been awake all night, it was certainly possible that they were sleeping. Gail came down the hall just then, and Maggie whispered a question as to James's whereabouts, learning that he'd left the house early in the morning. Anne was up, not dressed, sitting in her room.

Maggie walked to Anne's door and knocked, thinking how saddened she'd been originally to see that James had returned and to know that Adam hadn't come with him. In her head, she'd known he couldn't abandon his guests in the country, but in her heart, she'd still wished he had. Now, with this crisis looming, she was glad he wouldn't be home for several more days. It would give her time to learn some facts and formulate a plan.

"Come in," Anne's voice called softly from the other side of the door.

Maggie entered with a great amount of trepidation, wondering what all the commotion had been about and worrying over what condition Anne and the room would be in. She'd heard thumps on occasion, as though Anne had been throwing things at James.

The room looked in perfect order, though. Anne sat in a chair next to a small table, wrapped in a plush robe, drinking her morning chocolate. Her hair was thoroughly brushed, but her dark curls framed a face that looked drawn and pale as though she'd been ill. Her eyes were red from crying, although it had been sometime in the past. She looked pensive, as though the worries of the world lay heavily on her shoulders.

"Good morning." Maggie tried for a smile as she entered.

"Oh, Maggie, it's you. Hello." Anne set her cup down on the tray. By way of explanation, she added, "I thought it was going to be Gail with my dress. Would you like some?" she asked, gesturing toward the tray.

"Yes, thank you. I believe I will." Maggie's stomach was slightly queasy, whether from a babe or simply the nervousness caused by the possibility of a babe, she didn't know, but she sat down and poured a cup of the chocolate, hoping it would quell the unpleasant roll. Taking a small sip of the hot liquid, she looked over the rim of the cup. "I need to talk to you."

"And I need to talk to you. You won't believe what's happened."

The sudden rush of tears to Anne's eyes sounded alarm bells for Maggie. If James had hurt her, Maggie would kill him. "What is it? Is it James? What's he done?"

Anne reached across the table, squeezing Maggie's hand. "He hasn't *done* anything. It's just that . . . that . . . the bastard wants to marry me."

"What?" Maggie was so shocked, she wasn't sure she'd heard correctly.

"He wants to marry me," she said again, shaking her head and laughing slightly at Maggie's stunned look. "I know, I could hardly believe it either."

"I'm sorry. I just . . ." At a loss for words, she closed her mouth, putting some semblance of order to her demeanor before trying again. "What brought this on?"

"He says he missed me. Being away for a few days gave him a chance to think about his life. He inherited some property last week and some money, and he kept thinking about the future and decided he wanted to spend it with me.'' She took a napkin and dabbed at a tear that had managed to escape down her cheek. ''Can you believe it?''

''Of course I can. You're the most wonderful person I know. I guess James is a lot smarter than I gave him credit for.'' She squeezed Anne's hand tightly. ''I hope you had the good sense to say yes.''

''Well, not at first, but he wore me down.'' She moved her left hand out from under the table where she'd discreetly hidden it when Maggie had entered the room. Her finger sported a tasteful engagement ring, an emerald set in a small sea of tiny diamonds. ''We're going to be married on Friday.''

Maggie was already holding Anne's right hand, and now she took her left as well. ''Oh, Annie, I am so very, very happy for you.''

''Will you stand up with me?''

''I would be honored.'' More tears dribbled down Anne's cheeks, and Maggie took the napkin in her own hand and dabbed at them. ''Why are you so sad?''

''I'm not sad. I'm in a state of shock.''

''That's understandable,'' Maggie agreed. She was feeling quite overwhelmed herself by the news. ''What were the two of you arguing about?''

''You heard?''

''I think people probably heard some of it two blocks away.''

Anne ran a distracted hand through her hair and sighed, looking for all the world as though she'd just fought a major battle and lost. ''It's just such a tangle.''

''Why? Don't you want to go through with it?''

''Well, of course I want to, but there are so many problems with him marrying someone like me. I don't think he realizes how hard it will be.''

''In what way?''

''I'm his mistress.''

"Certainly, but he'll not be the first man who broke down and married his paramour."

"No, but there are such horrible things in my background. The stint at the brothel. And the other protectors I've had. People in his society know me, and they might remember me. I couldn't bear it if he was ever slighted or embarrassed because he married me."

"James is a grown man, Annie. I'm sure he's thought about all the consequences."

"I'm not so sure of that. That's why we were arguing so vehemently. I don't want him to go through with it, only to decide in six months or a year that he's made a mistake."

Maggie thought of the way James lit up when Anne entered the room, and laughed at her friend's concern. "I don't think you'll ever have to worry about that."

"I hope not." She leaned forward and rested her elbows on the small table that separated them. "There's more, and it involves you in a way."

"Me?"

"Well, you know that Adam has never cared for me, and he's furious that James wants to do this. They had a huge fight. He won't come to the wedding, and he said he won't ever receive us or acknowledge us."

Maggie suddenly felt as sick as Anne looked. No matter how it all turned out, Maggie would be caught right in the middle between the man she loved and her best friend. "I'm sure he didn't mean it, Anne. I know Adam. He has so many pressures, and he says things when he's angry that he doesn't mean."

"Don't make excuses for him to me," she said sharply. "It's just that . . . suppose Adam never gets over it. Suppose he never forgives James. James insists he doesn't care, and I don't believe he does at the moment, but again, what will he think in six months or a year? Dare I come between him and his brother when they've always been so close?"

Anne stood and walked to the window, looking down on the traffic. "That's what we were arguing about. He had an answer for everything, and I finally gave in." She looked at Maggie over her shoulder. "Do you think I did the right thing?"

"I know you did the right thing." It was easy to answer positively. Anne deserved a great slice of happiness in her life, and she was a survivor. She'd make the best of the situation, no matter what came her way. Maggie rose from the table and went to Anne's side, hugging her tightly. "It will be the very best thing that ever happened to you. I know it will."

"I hope so." Anne pulled from the embrace, but kept her hands on Maggie's waist. "There's something else I need to discuss with you as well."

"What?"

"I'm moving out today. To a hotel until the wedding."

"Why?"

"Because of all the fuss with Adam. I don't want to run into him or fight with him. After the ceremony, we're taking a long holiday. When we return, we're moving to the country. To the property James inherited in Cornwall."

This was the very worst piece of news Maggie could imagine. Having Anne marry was one thing. Having her move to what might as well be India was another. Everything was happening too quickly. She swallowed back the tears that rushed to fill the new void coming in her life. "So, I won't see you many more times."

"No. Not unless you come with us. I'm worried about you, and what might happen with Adam. I don't want to leave you here by yourself."

"You don't need to worry about me." Maggie laughed lightly. "Or about Adam. He'll take good care of me, and I will be all right."

Anne looked her over, with that careful scrutiny she had that seemed to give her the ability to see right to the heart of the matter. "I want you to promise me, though, that you'll come to us anytime, without hesitation, if you need help or a place to live. If you need anything, you have to swear you'll come to me."

"I doubt your new husband would want an intruder such as myself horning in at the start of his marriage."

"We already talked about it. He feels just as I do." She rested a hand on Maggie's cheek. "Swear it to me."

"I will. If I ever need anything, I'll come to you." But even as she said it, she knew it wasn't true. She'd never be able to turn to Anne for help. For no matter how James and Adam were fighting at the moment, Maggie knew Adam would come to terms with James's marriage. Anne would eventually be considered a member of the St. Clair family, which meant there would be no place in her home for Adam's ex-mistress.

Luckily, Anne was so distracted by the weight of her own problems and future that she didn't assess Maggie's promise with her usual acuity. She took Maggie's vow at face value, relieving Maggie greatly when she said, "Good. That's what I needed to hear before I actually went through with this." She hugged Maggie again. "Now, when you came in, you said you needed to talk to me about something. What was it?"

"You know what? It must not have been very important," Maggie lied easily. Her possible pregnancy was the last thing she could mention now. She absolutely refused to dampen Anne's happiness or burden her with unnecessary troubles. "After all your big news, I can't remember what it was."

Chapter Nineteen

The hansom pulled through the gates that shielded the forbidding house from the street, and the driver stopped in the curved courtyard. Maggie's footman, John, raised his hand and helped her maneuver the steps. He gave her an encouraging smile as she took a deep breath and started toward the front door. She hoped Adam was inside and would receive her for a few brief minutes.

He was home from his country estate, and had sent a note and several bouquets of hothouse flowers the previous afternoon. After being gone for nearly three weeks, he had too much to do to stop by right away. The weight of his responsibilities was a heavy one; she understood it and didn't mind when his various tasks detained him. However, James and Anne were to be married in a matter of hours, and unless something happened quickly, Adam would miss the wedding of his only brother.

She assumed that the brothers would reconcile at some point in the future, but what if they didn't? What if his refusal to attend the ceremony created such a schism in their relationship that it could never be mended? Adam and James were both proud men, and there was always the chance that their stubbornness would force them into positions from which they could never recover.

It was wrong for her to have come here, wrong for her to be knocking on his door, but she couldn't help herself. Unless she took this step, she wasn't going to have a chance to speak with him before it was too late. During the fretful hours of the night while she'd tossed and turned, trying to decide what to do, she'd come up with her plan. She'd simply present her card at the front door and see what happened.

If anyone questioned the reason for her presence at the door of such an exalted family, she had prepared an elaborate lie about why she needed to speak with the Marquis, which had to do with her being a widow of one of his friends and needing his immediate assistance with a financial dilemma of great urgency. It seemed as innocent a ruse as any she could come up with on short notice. Whether Adam would receive her was another matter entirely. If he turned her away, she'd go without too many hard feelings, knowing that it was inappropriate for her to have visited in the first place.

If her name meant anything to the man who opened the door, he did a good job of hiding it. He took her card and ushered her into a small salon off the main entrance, taking her hat and cloak and asking her to wait while he inquired as to whether the Marquis would see her.

He was gone a very long time, during which she had plenty of opportunity to assess her surroundings. It was disconcerting to sit in the gloriously appointed room, knowing that Adam lived here but slept occasionally in her small quarters.

What must it have been like to grow up in such a place? It was as quiet as a mausoleum, and everything was perfectly dusted, polished, and arranged, so that it seemed no one could possibly live there. It had the feeling of a museum she'd visited once, where you weren't supposed to touch or even look too closely. Adam said little about the life he'd led here, but James mentioned it occasionally. Theirs had been a lonely, unloving existence.

Maggie might have grown up a bastard child, and they'd had to struggle on occasion to get by, but she'd never been lonely, and she'd never wondered for a second if her mother loved her or not. Their home was small and unassuming, a pitiful abode compared to this, but it had always been full of love and laughter. As she looked around, measuring her childhood against Adam's, she couldn't help thinking that she'd definitely gotten the better deal.

From far away, a lone set of footsteps sounded in the hall, growing gradually closer, until the servant who'd answered the door returned with the surprising announcement that the Marquis was in and available and would see her in the Blue Room. Maggie followed the man up some stairs, through several twisting hallways, until he showed her into a room that was indeed blue. The wallpaper, the drapes, the carpeting, the paintings. Everything was shaded in various hues of blue. The room was small and intimate, facing east so the morning sun was dazzling as it shone through the highly polished windows.

Adam was sitting at a table by the windows. Behind him, she could see the remnants of a flower garden, which probably provided cheery colors in the summer. Dressed casually in breeches and a linen shirt, he looked much as he did when relaxing with her at her home. She hesitated, not sure of what kind of welcome she was going to receive until she saw the smile on his face.

"Miss Brown, what a pleasant surprise." He stood and came across the room with a hand held out to her in greeting.

She gave a quick curtsy. "Good morning, Lord Belmont. I'm sorry to bother you so early."

"It's no bother. Please come in." Tucking her hand under his arm, he escorted her to a small sofa near the fireplace, but she remained standing by his side. "I've just returned from a visit to the country, and I was catching up on some paperwork. Would you care to join me for some morning tea?"

''No, thank you, sir.''

Adam looked over at the servant, dismissing him with a wave. ''See that we're not disturbed.''

The man left, and the need for polite pretense vanished, but Maggie suddenly felt awkward and shy. She looked up into his eyes, but saw only kindness and a hint of laughter there. He raised a brow in question, and she started by apologizing. ''I'm sorry. I know I shouldn't be here.''

''Don't be sorry.'' In fact, he was thinking she looked even prettier than he remembered, and with her beautiful lavender gown and the way she carried herself, she appeared to be precisely where she belonged. Once again, he pushed down the wave of regret that he could not make it so.

''I hope you're not terribly angry with me for coming here.''

''No, but I must say that you're the last person I expected to visit me this morning.''

''I needed to talk with you. I wasn't sure how to go about it.''

''It couldn't wait until tonight?''

She shook her head. ''It's about James . . .''

''I don't want to talk about him.'' Adam dropped back onto the couch, taking Maggie with him in a move so smooth and quick that she had no time to do anything but join him. ''I want to talk about you and how much you missed me.''

She smiled, kissed his lips lightly. ''I missed you every second.''

''I missed you, too, little one. Let me show you how much.''

He fussed with her skirt, pulling it up, arranging her legs until her knees were tucked on either side of his hips and she was splayed wide-open and pressed against him. From the feel of things, he'd missed her very, very much.

Obviously, he was ready to make love in the small parlor, but she wasn't. She felt like an intruder among the wealthy fixtures of the house, and seeing Adam so at ease amid the splendor made her even more uncomfortable. Not for the first time, she realized how much she didn't belong in his life.

Behind his head, she braced her hands on the back of the couch, her elbows straight as she looked down at him in dismay. "We can't do this!"

"Why not?"

"What if someone comes in?"

"No one will." He was taking small nibbles against her neck, working down to nuzzle against her breasts. With a tug of fabric, they fell free, and he began to gently twirl her nipples, which grew instantly hard. He didn't look up at her, but stared at her breasts, working them with his hands and fingers, manipulating the size and shape. "It's my home, Maggie. I can make love to you here if I want. There's no one to tell me I can't."

Still, she hesitated, although it was becoming harder the longer he played with her. "It doesn't seem right."

"Yes, it does. It seems exactly right."

With that, the conversation was finished. Adam went to work on her breasts, sucking and tasting, biting and teasing, until Maggie could only groan and pull him closer. He stayed there until she was ready and wanting to join every bit as much as he did. When he entered her, it was different from the other times. Something about doing it in his home, where she had no right to be, made it seem naughty and erotic so that the pleasure was greater than ever.

When the shudders of passion ebbed, Maggie lay sprawled across his chest, looking the complete wanton. Her pins were scattered everywhere, and her hair hung in complete disarray around her face and shoulders. Her breasts and thighs were bare, her lips swollen from his kisses. He was still partly hard, deep inside her, and he rested silently, letting their breathing slow as he ran his hands up and down her back. She laid her cheek against his shoulder, placing an occasional kiss along his throat.

He seemed unusually quiet. More sad than sated. Terribly melancholy. She snuggled closer, knowing that the time away had not been enjoyable and, she suspected, the altercation with James was weighing heavily on his mind.

Quietly, he said, "I wish you could have come with me to the country. I would like to have seen you in my room there. With the sun shining on your hair, just like it is now."

"I would have liked that," she agreed, although she knew it was something that could never happen, and she closed her eyes to hide her surprise. He never talked like this, never said anything about how he wished she could fit into his real life, and she always took care never to give voice to such thoughts herself, because to speak of them only made her situation that much more heartbreaking.

"And I wish you could be here with me all the time," he said. "This is my favorite room in the morning. I wish I could make love to you here whenever the mood struck me."

Her chest lifted in a soft laugh. "Well, that would certainly give the servants something to talk about."

"Yes, it would, wouldn't it?"

As Adam chuckled, too, a sudden vision came to her, of Adam making love to his wife in this very spot. Usually in her most wicked fantasies, the wife looked very much like Penelope. This occasion was no different; she felt her half sister's presence as though she was watching them from across the room.

The intimate moment was broken for her, and she pulled away, sitting up as much as she could. "I need to be going soon."

He heaved a long sigh, wishing she could stay all day. Forever. But all he could say was, "Yes, I suppose you do."

She framed his face with her hands, kissed him tenderly. "The wedding's in two hours, Adam. Please say you'll come with me."

Closing his eyes as though it hurt to view the world, he tipped his head back and balanced it on the back of the couch. "Oh, Maggie, don't ask this of me."

"Please, Adam. I know it would mean so much to James."

"I can't, little one," he said softly.

She leaned forward to hug him again, but he still wouldn't look at her. "If you can't do it for James, then do it for me."

Her request finally brought his gaze to hers. "You know that I would do anything in the world for you. Anything. But I can't do this."

Maggie wanted to be angry, but she couldn't be. The anguish his decision was causing him was so apparent that it hurt to see it. She shifted away and stood on her feet, adjusting her bodice and skirts. Her hair was a complete disaster, and she knew it would be impossible to pin it back up after Adam had worked his hands through it so thoroughly. She turned to a small mirror hanging on the wall, straightening the locks as much as she could. Adam watched silently until she turned back to face him.

"Do you dislike Anne so much?" she asked.

"Anne has nothing to do with it," he insisted with a shake of his head.

"I'd say she has everything to do with it."

"It's not her. It's—"

"Of course it's her," Maggie declared. "Don't insult my intelligence."

Adam reached out a hand, but she didn't offer hers in return. Refusing to be denied her touch, he took hold of hers and held on, lacing their fingers together. "It's not her personally, Maggie. It's her position. What she represents. She's not an appropriate wife for James, and he knows it."

"I disagree. James thinks she's perfect, and I'd say that's all that matters."

"No, Maggie. That is not all that matters."

For the thousandth time in her life, she felt the cruel sting of the unfairness that ruled their lives. She jerked her hand away from his. "Anne is the best person I know, and I don't care who James's parents are, or how much wealth your family has, or how far back you can trace your bloodlines. I don't care. She's worthy of James in every way. Can't you see that?"

"No. I'm sorry, but I just can't." Adam stood, more weary

than angry, adjusting his breeches and shirt. "Let's don't argue, Maggie. I've just passed the worst few days. I feel badly enough about this as it is without you being mad at me, too."

"I'm sorry. I don't want to fight either." As always, tender words from him worked their magic, for she knew how hard it was for him to speak them. She forced herself to ease her defiant stance, and stepped into the circle of his arms, where she rested her hands on his waist and tipped her face up in an imploring gaze. "Is it so wrong for James to be happy? Even if you don't agree with his choice of bride, couldn't you try to find some joy in the fact that Anne makes him so contented?"

"I can't do what you're asking, Maggie. It's like asking me to believe that the sky is green or that the ocean is red. What James is doing goes against everything I've ever believed in. It goes against everything I've been taught."

"Perhaps you were taught wrong."

"Perhaps," he agreed reluctantly after a long silence, "but I can't change the man I am."

"Everyone can change if it's something they want badly enough."

"Not I. Not over this."

"Then I feel very sorry for you. And for James." *And for me*, she added silently.

Adam ran a frustrated hand through his hair. "I wish I could make you understand."

"I wish you could, too." Maggie glanced up at the clock sitting on the mantel over the fireplace. The time was passing so quickly. As it was, she'd barely have time to hurry home and change before rushing to the small chapel where the ceremony was to be held. "I must go."

"Of course."

"Could you have someone show me the way? I'm not sure I can find my way out."

He smiled at that. "I'll take you downstairs."

His offer surprised her. She couldn't imagine he'd want

anyone to see them passing through the halls together. "There's no need."

"I want to, Maggie."

She took his arm, and they walked through the grand house, their footsteps echoing through the empty halls. As they passed, Maggie tried to take in as much of the color and style as she could absorb so that she could conjure accurate mental images of Adam in the years to come.

At the door, he surprised her again by walking her outside and helping her into the waiting cab. They held hands for the longest time, neither wanting to break the contact.

Finally, Adam stepped away. "You'd best get going. You'll hardly make it as it is."

"I know." She smiled over the upset that had flared between them. He looked so sad and so alone that she couldn't bear leaving him, but she had to. This wasn't her place. Still, she couldn't resist reaching down to rest a loving hand against his cheek. "Do you know where it's being held?"

"Yes," he said, taking her hand from his face and kissing the palm. "I received an invitation."

"If you change your mind at the last minute, you'll be welcome. You know that, don't you?"

"I won't change my mind."

She nodded. Hope was everything. Until the ceremony ended with the happy couple's embrace, she could pray he would appear. "Do you have any message you'd like me to pass on to James?"

Adam stared across the grounds for a long, quiet time, then said, "No. Nothing at all. I'll see you tonight." He stepped back and the hansom lurched forward. Maggie looked over her shoulder, waved once, then refused to let herself look again. The view of Adam standing there, solitary and forlorn, was too upsetting to contemplate on a day that should only be filled with gladness and joy. She faced forward, toward the wedding of her two friends.

* * *

Lucretia St. Clair had hardly noticed the hansom waiting in the front courtyard. When she casually questioned a maid, the servant mentioned that there was a visitor for Adam and that the cab was waiting to escort her away. The fact that the maid said the visitor was female had briefly piqued her interest, but not for long. Adam always had many people stopping during the day, whether for business or social calls. She didn't keep track. It was rare for a woman alone to visit her son, but she paid it no mind.

So it was with incredible interest and undisguised fascination that she watched as he took the unprecedented step of escorting the woman down the hall and outside. It was so unusual for him to do such a thing that she couldn't help peeking out the window to see with whom he walked.

The female on his arm was no woman, hardly more than a girl, slender and petite and incredibly lovely in a lavender gown, with her light brown hair hanging in loose disarray down around her shoulders. Lucretia was not surprised to see Adam with a beautiful woman, for he was always surrounded by them. What surprised her was the emotion passing between the two. Her generally stoic and silent Adam was completely captivated by the young woman. That fact was visible even from where Lucretia stood unnoticed inside the house.

She watched like the worst type of voyeur.

As Adam helped her into the cab. As they talked with their heads close together, their eyes searching intimately. As the girl openly touched his face in a loving, familiar gesture. As Adam kissed her hand in return.

Lucretia gasped.

In all the twenty-nine years of Adam's life, she'd never seen him display any emotion at all in public, and only on the most limited occasions in private. She'd schooled him well in that regard. And now, he was making a common spectacle of himself with a slip of a girl whom Lucretia had never met. From the way they were looking at each other, it appeared that they had deep feelings for one another! Almost as though they might be in love!

The realization sent chills down her spine. The whispers she'd heard among the staff, and the quiet warning from an acquaintance, came back to her. She'd scoffed at all of it. Until now. But surely . . . he wouldn't have the nerve to receive his whore in their home? The very idea was ludicrous. Still . . .

She stood in place for as long as Adam did. He stayed in the drive, watching the street long after the carriage had disappeared. Finally, he turned to come inside, and she took a deep breath and walked toward the front door, assuming the haughty pose and the indifferent demeanor she always used when addressing her servants or her children.

He was so distressed by whatever he had discussed with the girl that he walked right past her in the foyer without even seeing her, completely distracted and intent on the stairs and a return to his private rooms.

"Adam," she said sharply, which brought him to a halt. "Good morning."

"Good morning, Mother."

"We've had a visitor so early? It's not bad news, I trust?"

"No, Mother. Just a friend. Of James."

Her eyes narrowed. The girl was no friend of James, Lucretia was sure of it. Adam was lying. "I don't recall meeting her before. What is her name?"

"Miss Magdalina Brown."

"What did she want?"

He made a keen assessment of her. She knew better than to question him about his affairs, but he was distressed and angry and wanted to lash out at someone for the rift with James, which was now so large that he couldn't imagine how to mend it. For some reason, he wanted to blame Lucretia and her blasted view of the world, which she'd instilled in him from the day he was born. Testily, he asked, "Do you really wish to know?"

"Yes," she said, more hesitantly than she intended. There was an unfamiliar air about him that frightened her.

"She wanted to know if I would come to the wedding."

"The nerve," Lucretia hissed. "I hope you put her in her place." Adam just stared, which worried her even more. "You told her you'll not be attending, of course."

"Don't worry, Mother. I made it clear that I have no intention of doing so. Your younger son will now never forgive me. I hope the knowledge makes you happy, for it pains me greatly. I, at least, always loved him." With that retort, he turned away and continued up the stairs.

She wanted to call after him, to say that James was getting exactly what he deserved and no more. That he'd never been a dutiful son, had never understood the roles that obligation and family played in their lives, and that it was his choice to cut himself off from his only relations by doing such a hideous, shameful thing.

For once, though, she had the foresight to hold her tongue, fearing what reaction Adam might have to her words. Instead, she went to find the housekeeper to discuss the dinner party she was hosting the following evening.

Chapter Twenty

"Shall we begin?" the young minister asked. He was no one James knew, a virtual stranger from a different faith, convinced to preside over the vows for the simple reason that everyone James knew who was affiliated with the Church had refused—at the request of his brother, the Marquis of Belmont.

James glanced at his timepiece. It was eleven on the dot. "Yes, let's do."

Maggie watched from a front pew as he turned to Anne with a glowing smile on his face. Anne's gown was low-cut, cream-colored, with a green trim that matched her eyes. Her hair was down and curled about her shoulder, as James liked it. His wedding gift, emerald earrings and a necklace to match the engagement ring, caught the candlelight, sending green sparks around the chapel whenever she moved. She looked so beautiful that the very sight of her brought tears to Maggie's eyes.

Offering Anne his arm, he asked, "Are you ready?"

"We can wait a few more minutes if you want," she answered gently, squeezing his hand. "I don't mind."

"No." He shook his head. "Everyone is here."

Anne looked over at Maggie. "What do you think?"

Maggie could only shake her head. Obviously, she'd tried and failed. She shrugged in defeat. "I don't think there's any point in waiting."

James looked at Charles. "Looks like you have to be the best man."

"*Have* to be?" Charles responded indignantly, his cocky answer and attitude lightening the moment and causing everyone to chuckle. "I've always been the best man. I've been telling you as much for years. It's about time you listened."

"And you're humble, too," James chided.

"Absolutely." His cousin smiled. "I am the very picture of humility."

At that, James and Anne stepped in front of the minister. Charles walked around the end of the pew and helped Maggie to her feet so they could move to either side of the bride and groom. She took one last look around the chapel. The only people present besides the quartet that made up the wedding party were Grace Stuart and her three children. That was it. There was no sign of Adam, who was the only person who really mattered as far as Maggie was concerned.

She'd expected to be heartsick when he didn't appear, and was surprised to find that she wasn't. Looking at James and Anne as they said their vows, she found it simply impossible not to be happy. They were so ecstatic, so joyful and full of bliss, that she quickly succumbed to the poignancy of the moment. By the time the groom kissed the bride, Maggie had huge tears flooding down her face. She wasn't the only one. The bride and groom, the best man, the groom's stepfamily. Everyone was dabbing at their eyes with handkerchiefs.

In two carriages, they headed for Grace Stuart's house, where she'd insisted on hosting an intimate wedding dinner. The food was delicious, the conversation friendly and loud, the toasts numerous and lewd. The highlight of the afternoon was the presentation of Anne's wedding gift to James: the nude of her painted by Charles. The portrait, after the hooting and hollering over it died down, was much loved and greatly appreciated by her new husband.

Everyone enjoyed themselves immensely, and James seemed to have been completely absorbed into the Stuart family. Maggie was glad for him, glad to see that he had some semblance of family with whom to celebrate the occasion. She seemed to be the only one who noticed the shadow caused by Adam's absence, but she didn't dwell on it. Adam had made a choice, and so had James. Only time would tell what would happen between the two of them.

The meal came to a close, the last bottle of champagne being drunk. James was in the parlor saying good-bye to Grace and Charles. Huddled together in the foyer, Anne and Maggie had a minute alone. After the farewells were completed, the happy couple was leaving for the Carlysle Hotel, where they'd taken a suite. The following morning, they were off to Italy for an extended honeymoon. On returning, they would head directly to James's new estate in Cornwall.

Maggie had no illusions about the future. It might be months, or perhaps years, before she saw Anne again. With the vagaries of life, it was certainly possible that this was the last time they'd see one another at all.

She gripped Anne in a fierce hug, a new burst of tears beginning to fall. She'd shed so many that day that she'd given up trying to hide or stop them. It seemed a day when they would fall at will. No matter. If ever there was an occasion for an outpouring of emotion, this was it. "I love you, Annie."

"I love you, too, Maggie." She took Maggie's face in her hands and kissed her gently on the mouth. "I'll miss you every minute."

"It's going to be so lonely with you gone. I can't imagine how I'll manage."

"It all happened so fast, didn't it?"

"Yes." She hugged her tightly again. "I'm so happy for you."

Anne took Maggie's hands in her own, squeezing tightly. "I want you to promise me that you'll take care of yourself."

"You know I will." Although she couldn't imagine how she'd manage when Anne was going away forever. There were too many changes occurring all at once.

Anne pulled Maggie into another strong embrace. "If you need anything, go to Charles. Or come to Grace. They'll help you."

"I know, but you don't need to worry about me. I'll be fine," Maggie whispered against her ear, although it was a complete lie. How she'd get by, with Anne—her only friend—gone off to a new life, with no family, and the babe on the way, she had no idea.

Just then, James returned with Grace and Charles in tow, precluding further private thought of the future. Maggie was relieved and grateful for the interruption. Her emotions and her nerves were at a fevered pitch, and she couldn't bear another moment of intimate discussion.

"My Lord, but I'm going to miss you, Annie. You, too, James." Maggie smiled at him, winning herself a bear hug, which twirled her around the room in his arms.

More good-byes were spoken, hugs given, good wishes exchanged, and finally, the couple was stepping out the door. Maggie grabbed James one last time, kissing him on the cheek and pulling him close. "Take good care of her for me. Make her so happy."

"You have my word on it."

With a wink and a wave, they were gone. Just like that.

Adam sat in his carriage. It was a foggy, cold, and miserable autumn night, the mist seeming to swallow all of the usual noise of London's streets. Few were out and about in the dreary stuff. The weather perfectly matched his mood, which was somewhere beyond gloomy and disconsolate.

Maggie's door lay just a few feet away. He wanted to go to

her, to learn every detail of the wedding. To hear every word
that was spoken, every vow exchanged, every toast given.

He wanted to hear it all.

He didn't want to hear any of it.

She was probably angry with him over his failure to appear.
Considering what an optimist she was, she would have believed
he'd show up right until the last minute when he'd proved her
wrong. If she was upset, he knew he shouldn't worry about it
or let it concern him, but it did. He valued her opinion, just as
he valued everything about her.

How he wished he could better explain his reasoning about
James's decision to marry Anne. He'd not done a good job of
it when they'd talked at his home earlier in the day. As he
reflected on the statements he'd made in support of his position,
they didn't sound very convincing.

Damn, but he was right. He refused to think otherwise, no
matter how miserable he felt.

The long day was the worst of his life. He'd canceled all
his appointments so he could sit alone and silent in his private
rooms, watching the clock tick toward eleven, imagining the
service, wondering who attended and where everyone had gone
after. What they ate, what they drank, what they said. Try as he
might, he could concentrate on nothing else, and the agonizing
thoughts filled the interminable hours of the never-ending day.

He closed his eyes against the visions. Of James laughing
and smiling. Of pretty Anne, standing by his side in the glow
of love James inspired in those who knew him.

Is it so wrong for James to be happy?

Maggie's question from their morning's argument had
taunted him all day, but he left it alone. If he accepted what
James had done, if he decided James was right in choosing
love and happiness over duty and responsibility, where did that
leave Adam? What purpose did his life serve, all he had done
and all he must do? If he condoned James's selfish behavior,
his own view of the world would begin to crumble as everything
he'd ever believed in and held dear would then have to be held

up to close scrutiny. Were they wrong, his family and peers? In the way they lived, thought, married?

That road was too dangerous to walk, and so he wouldn't.

"Oh, James . . ." he whispered, heartsick at the thought of how his brother must now hate him.

The opening of the front door of the house brought him out of his reverie. Time to face Maggie. He stepped out of the carriage, only to be met by the young footman he'd sent to look after and escort Maggie on her various errands. John . . . something or other. He could never remember the man's name, but Maggie could. Maggie knew and remembered everyone; she was kind and attentive in a way he was not.

"Begging your pardon, milord . . ." the man began cautiously.

"Is something amiss?" he asked, instantly on alert.

"No, sir. If I could just have a word before you go in. I promised Miss Maggie that I wouldn't tell you . . . She said she didn't want to worry you needlessly, do you see?" Adam nodded in commiseration—it sounded exactly like something Maggie would say—as the man continued. "And . . . well . . . I wouldn't want to have her angry with me for going back on my word . . . but I wouldn't want you angry at me for not telling."

"I understand. You're in a bit of a bind either way." He held his hands open in an accepting gesture, hoping to put the man at ease.

"Yes, sir, so it appears."

"What has happened?"

"Well, it wasn't today. But two weeks ago, while you were away."

The man went on to relate how Maggie had been abducted while coming out of the clothing shop, how he had followed in a cab for several minutes until they were all stopped in traffic, and Maggie jumped from the stalled vehicle up ahead.

"Was she hurt?"

"No. Just very angry about whatever occurred while she

was in the other carriage.'' He swallowed, visibly frightened about his immediate future. ''I offer my apologies, milord. It happened so fast, I couldn't stop it, but I thought you should know. Will you be . . .'' His voice broke. ''Will you be discharging me?''

''No, no . . . Maggie's happy with you. I don't blame you for it, and I thank you for telling me.'' As an afterthought, he asked, ''Did you get a good look at whoever was in the carriage?''

''No, but I saw the crest on the door. I asked about. It belonged to the Duke of Roswell.''

Bloody hell and what could this be about?

''Thank you for telling me. Don't trouble yourself over it.'' He gave the worried man a reassuring pat on the shoulder and headed into the house.

It was terribly quiet, and no one seemed to be about. Knowing Maggie as he now did, he believed she'd probably given the other servants the day off to celebrate the wedding. The only illumination in the place was the last embers of the fire that had burned earlier in the parlor. He used the dim glow to make his way up the stairs to her room. No light showed under her door, and there was no noise coming from inside.

''Maggie?'' he called softly, rapping on the wood once as he stepped in. She was huddled in a chair next to the window. For a moment, he thought she was asleep and wondered if he should wake her. Very probably, the day had been as emotionally trying for her as it had been for him. ''Maggie?'' he asked again.

''Hello, Adam,'' she said without turning around. ''I didn't hear you pull up. I wasn't expecting you.''

''I told you I'd stop by this evening.''

''I thought you had probably changed your mind after today.''

He could hear the melancholia in her voice, feel the sadness emanating from her. ''Are you all right?''

Her shoulders lifted in a shrug. "I have to admit I've had better days."

"May I light a candle?" The long hesitation made him think she'd say no, but he wasn't about to chat in the darkness.

"If you wish."

His movements sounded overly loud in the room as he went through the motions and waited while the dim flicker caught and grew to a substantial flame. He set the holder on a dresser and walked to her side. She still hadn't moved, but continued to stare out at the night. He rested his palm on the top of her head, his apprehension growing the longer she refused to look at him.

"How was the wedding?" he asked. "I trust everything went well?"

"It was perfectly lovely."

"Good." He dropped to a knee beside her, but she still didn't look at him. Up close, he could see that she'd been crying, probably for quite a length of time. Her eyes were swollen, the streaks of the tears still visible down her reddened cheeks. "What's amiss, little one?"

"Nothing," she said with a sigh. "Everything."

"Want to tell me about it?"

"Not really."

"A woman I know once told me that it helps to talk it out. I believe her name was Maggie Brown."

"Maggie Brown, huh?" she said bitterly. "What does she know about anything?" This response caused a new flood of tears, and she pressed her fingers into her eyes to try to stop the flow.

"As bad as all that, is it?"

"I'm sorry. I hate to have you see me in such a state."

"You've seen me quite put out any number of times. I think I can handle it." He scooped her up and sat down in the chair himself, settling her on his lap. "Tell me what's happened."

"Nothing really. I just came home from the wedding, and

I'd given the servants the day off. No one was here, and it was so quiet. I sat down and started to think.''

"About what?" he prodded gently when the pause became an extended one.

"Many things, I guess. About Mother and how much I miss her. About Anne leaving with James. With all the excitement about the wedding, I'd not really thought about it.''

"Until today, when you arrived home alone?"

"Yes," she said, looking at him for the first time. "And you'll be leaving soon, and where will I be?" She couldn't add the last and most frightening thought of all: *With our baby coming, what will happen to me?*

Adam had no answers. There were none. A few times, he'd let the future intrude into his thoughts, but he'd always pushed it away. He couldn't keep Maggie, so what was to become of her? Another protector, perhaps one of his friends? Marriage to another? Both options were unthinkable.

She looked out the window again, staring at some unseen vision in the darkness. "I keep seeing James, how happy he looked today with Anne. It hurts that no one has ever loved me like that. That no one ever will.''

I love you like that! The words screamed for release. He wanted to speak them, and she needed to hear them, but he couldn't say them aloud. Having never said such a thing to another, he couldn't find the fortitude to do so now when the words were ones she desperately needed to hear.

What good would a profession of emotion be anyway? Loving her couldn't change anything and would only make their parting more difficult in the end. Best for both of them if she never knew the depth of his feelings.

"I wish I knew what to say to make you feel better, Maggie. I'm not very good at giving comfort. I've not had much experience at it.''

"I don't think there's anything you can say.'' She sighed, wiping her hand against her cheek as a few more tears managed to work their way down. "I just need some time to think and to adjust to all these changes. Everything seems to be happening at once. I don't know how to cope with it.''

This was the moment when she knew she should tell him about her pregnancy, before any more time had passed, but there was a real possibility that he would end their relationship on the spot once he learned the truth. The thought of him walking out, after everything she'd been through the past few weeks, was more than she could contemplate. Talk of a babe would have to wait for another day when her courage wouldn't fail her.

"Let me brush your hair. It will calm you.'' He kept a firm grip around her waist and leaned across to the dresser to grab one of her brushes, then settled her on the floor between his thighs. Silently, he pulled the bristles through, working in long slow strokes, continuing until he could sense her relaxation growing, her tension easing. Eventually, he laid the brush back on the dresser, then massaged his fingers into her shoulders over and over until he could sense her composure being restored.

"Better?'' he asked with a smile, placing a kiss on the top of her head.

"Yes.'' She shifted on the hard floor, came to her knees, and turned to face him, wrapping her arms around his waist as much as she could with him settled in the chair, and resting her cheek against his chest, where she could feel the steady beat of his heart. "I don't know what's come over me this evening.''

"I would say you've endured a number of unsettling events in the past year. Perhaps, tonight, it's just catching up with you a bit.''

"Perhaps.'' She raised her face. "I'm embarrassed to have you see me like this.''

"Don't be. A good part of your distress is my fault. I haven't exactly made your life any easier.''

"No.'' She smiled. "But you, sir, are very much a problem worth enduring. And I decided long ago that I'd have no regrets over my time with you. Knowing you has meant too much to me, and I will always be so very glad we met.''

The sincerity of her words, the emotion in her gaze, was nearly his undoing. He didn't deserve her affection or her adoration. Not after what he'd put her through and what he would do to her in the near future. "Oh, Maggie, I wish I could be a better man for you.''

"Ssh . . .'' she said, placing her fingers against his lips to silence him. "I want to tell you something before I talk myself out of it.''

"What?''

"I love you, Adam. I have since the day I met you, and I will love you till the day I die . . .''

"Maggie, don't say such things to me. I don't deserve your strong emotions. I truly don't.''

"I don't care what you think. I want you to know how I feel so you'll always remember. I love you, and I always will. Please hold on to that in the days and months to come.''

His heart ached at her words, and even though he felt the same way, he couldn't give them back to her. There was simply nothing to be gained by letting her know that his feelings matched hers. Instead, he responded with, "You speak as though we're parting. It hurts me to hear you talk this way.''

"I don't mean to sound so maudlin, but all these changes are weighing so heavily on me tonight. Like a huge wave is about to wash me away, and I'll never find my way back. I don't want to miss this opportunity to tell you how I feel. I love you, and I'm sorry things couldn't have been different.''

"What things?''

She whispered softly, "That I wasn't worthy of you.''

"Worthy of me? Maggie, is that what you think?''

"It's what I know, Adam. All my life it's been that way. If only my father had . . .'' She stopped. No use going down that road.

"If only, what?''

"It doesn't matter.''

"Yes, it does. What about your father? I thought he was dead." A sense of dread suddenly washed over him. Something horrible was lurking in the corner of their relationship, waiting to pounce, something he didn't want to know about, but he couldn't keep himself from asking, "Was he someone I might have known?"

She rose to her feet and moved away from him to lean against the windowframe while she toyed with the knob on the window shutter. "I don't want to talk about him."

"Why?"

"Because he is nothing to me."

"You said *is* instead of *was*. Is he still alive?"

"Not to me," she insisted with a shake of her head.

Just then, she turned her head to look at him as the light from a carriage passing outside caught her profile perfectly. If he hadn't known better, he'd have sworn he was looking at Penelope Westmoreland. He shook his head to chase away the ghastly, impossible image. It couldn't be. It simply couldn't be.

"It's Harold Westmoreland, isn't it?" The sag of her shoulders told him he'd guessed the truth.

"I'll never admit it as long as I live. Not to anyone."

He'd always heard the stories that Westmoreland had sired a bastard child, but he'd thought the child was a boy. Surely, people knew who Maggie was. It seemed incredible that no one had seen fit to whisper that bit of juicy gossip in his ear while she was out and about on his arm. "How come you couldn't tell me?"

"What difference would it have made?"

What difference, indeed? Duke or no for a sire, she was still illegitimate and his paid consort. It changed nothing.

"How come he never claimed you?" A stupid question, he realized the moment he voiced it, so he added, "Or at least helped you?"

"Mother asked a few times when we were desperate, but he

always refused. I wouldn't ask him now. Even if he offered, I'd not accept assistance.''

The full implication of what he'd just learned was only beginning to sink in. The whole thing was shocking and preposterous, but he couldn't give it a rest. ''This makes Penelope your sister . . .''

One corner of her mouth lifted. ''Isn't that the most interesting pickle you've ever heard?''

''What did he want from you the other day, when he accosted you on the street?''

''Heard about that, did you?'' She gave a resigned sigh and left the window to sit in the chair next to him. ''He said I have to convince you to marry her. Or he'll claim paternity of me and marry me off at the first opportunity. If I help him, he'll let me remain as your mistress as long as you want to keep me.'' Flashing a fake smile, she added, ''Isn't that grand?''

''What a bastard,'' he grumbled, leaning forward to rest his chin in his hands.

''He is not a bastard, Adam. He only sires them.''

''That's not funny.''

''It wasn't meant to be.''

''Has he always acted so abominably?''

''I wouldn't know. It was the first and only occasion I've ever had the *pleasure* of talking to him.''

''Your first meeting with him, and that's all he had to say?''

''Yes. He truly is the most despicable man.''

''Have you ever met your half sister?''

''On one occasion. At a ball, I had the misfortune of being stuck with her briefly in a retiring room.''

''After we were already together?''

''Toward the beginning of our affair.'' An unusual stab of bitterness came over her, and she couldn't help adding, ''She was dabbing perfume on her nipples in hopes of enticing you to notice her breasts. Did it work?''

''Don't be crude.''

''I'm sorry, but I can't seem to help being any other way

where she is concerned. Why should she have everything—you included—when I can have nothing at all? And all of it simply because my mother was young and foolish and loved Westmoreland beyond imagining. Why should I have had to suffer so for it every day of my life, especially now when there's finally something I want more than anything?''

''What is that?''

''You, you bloody fool. What did you think?'' She raised a weary hand to her brow and rubbed against the furious headache that was pounding there. ''I know I vowed that I would never discuss your marriage with you, but I must say that it will just kill me if you marry my sister. If you would do such a thing to me, I would prefer you to simply plunge a dagger in my heart and be done with it.''

Adam could see it now, in the tilt of her head, the thrust of her shoulders. He'd always imagined she must have had some aristocratic blood flowing through her veins. There was simply no other way to explain the regal bearing she exuded at a moment like this when her heart was breaking.

He was suddenly as weary as Maggie appeared. Marrying Penelope, an act he'd pondered long and often, had become an absolute impossibility. He would never hurt Maggie in such a despicable way.

He'd repeatedly told Harold that he wouldn't be commanded about. Had warned him regularly not to try anything so foolish as manipulating Adam into a decision. The man was obviously getting desperate and had lost his faith in Penny's ability to lure Adam to a proposal. Well, the Duke had played his trump card a little too soon, and lost all.

He smiled at Maggie, a tender smile meant to show all that he felt but couldn't put into words. Holding out his hand, which she took, he pulled her onto his lap and placed a gentle kiss against each of her eyelids, then vowed, ''I would never do such a thing to you.''

''Thank you.''

''I will speak to your father about your encounter with him.''

"You don't have to . . ."

"I insist. I don't want him to hurt you ever again." He took her lips in a lingering kiss full of promise and passion. "I know your footman is here. Is anyone else?"

"I believe most everyone has returned."

"Let's call for a bath for you, and a late dinner. How does that sound?"

"Very nice."

"Good. We're going to find some peace and contentment to end this dreadful day—if it takes us all night."

Chapter Twenty-One

Adam stood along the wall, sipping a glass of wine and watching the goings-on of his hosts' idea of an intimate party—one that included a lavish sixteen-course feast and dancing for seventy-five guests. James weighed heavily on his mind as a line of dancers swirled past. He recalled many other nights of their lives when they'd stood together at such an affair, laughing and joking as James whispered caustic remarks about the people present. God, how he missed his brother! If ever there'd been a time when he needed his wisdom and advice, this was it.

Lady Mary Roberts, one of the handful of eligible women who hadn't left for the country after the Season ended, stood across the room next to her aunt. She was just far enough away so he could surreptitiously inspect her. For the past two years, she'd been out of the marriage market, never really making her debut, having been thrust into mourning by the death of her mother, then by that of her older brother. Both events had been hard on her, and she was just ready to begin socializing again. For those reasons, he hadn't spent much time considering her, but he was doing so now.

While not as pretty as many of the debutantes he'd escorted through the past Season, she had a pleasant personality and style, never playing any of the coquettish games in which the others had been so well schooled. She was quiet and restrained and nearly twenty years old, giving her two or three years of maturity on the various girls he'd courted. With her dark hair and eyes and her plump figure, she was about as far removed in looks from his thin, fair Maggie as he could get, making her an excellent candidate.

Harold Westmoreland stood at the far end of the room. His wife, who was never known for her beauty or intellect and who was not aging gracefully, was at the other end. It was well known that the Duke rarely spoke to her and didn't want to bother with having her by his side. Penelope stood next to her mother, occasionally casting Adam covetous glances when she thought he wasn't looking. Thankfully, her mother was keeping her on a tight leash, and she hadn't been able to accost him.

For several years, as he'd watched Penny grow into a woman, he'd assumed they'd marry. Both sets of parents wanted it. Penny wanted it. The union of land and fortune that would occur through the joining was nearly unheard of. Adam had never really cared about marrying Penny one way or the other, thinking that one wife could hardly be different from the next. He'd just wanted someone respectful and tolerable who was well trained in how to carry out the duties that would be required of her as Marchioness. Although Penny grated on his nerves, he'd convinced himself it was simply caused by her youth and inexperience, that she'd grow into her role and responsibilities.

Now, looking at her with a more critical eye, he couldn't imagine how he'd ever thought to wed her. She was selfish, rude, insensitive. Her churlish attitude had hardened her features, making her look petty instead of pretty. Six months ago, he hadn't noticed and wouldn't have cared if he had, but he hadn't known Maggie then, either. In many subtle ways, Maggie had changed his outlook on life. His view of the world was different, and he couldn't marry someone who was so obviously self-absorbed. But mostly, he couldn't marry Maggie's sister. He'd told Maggie so, and he'd meant it.

The only problem remaining was what Harold might do to Maggie once Adam proposed to another—an act he intended to carry out shortly. Knowing the man's penchant for temper and revenge, he might very well do something despicable to her, like trying to marry her off as he'd threatened. While Adam liked to tell himself such a thing could never occur, he knew it could. He, himself, had used his name and power to accomplish any number of impossible tasks, and if Harold asked to be named guardian for a penniless, orphaned female, he would be so named.

However, Harold had greatly underestimated Adam's feelings for Maggie and had definitely erred when he tried to use her in his scheming. Adam would never let anything bad happen to her, however removed she eventually was from his life. Harold had to feel sufficiently threatened into nonaction before Adam could move ahead with his plan.

He danced a few times, chatted with the appropriate people, but mostly stood by himself watching the festivities with detached interest. Another hour passed before Harold sought him out. He always did on some pretense or another, making sure each time that they covered the topic of Penelope and a possible marriage.

"Adam," Harold began, tipping his glass in recognition, "will you be joining us at the theater Saturday night?"

"Don't I always?" he asked in return, finding himself relieved that it would be the last time. After he proposed to another, it would be a long while before he would be welcomed at any event by the Westmorelands again. "I also need to discuss something in private with you. What morning next week would be good?"

"Unless you want to discuss a betrothal contract for Penelope, I think I'm probably busy."

"I plan to discuss your *daughter*, but I hardly think this is the place you'd want to do it. Make time for me."

"Why do I get the feeling," Harold snorted, "that the daughter you want to discuss is not Penelope?"

"Because you're right. It's not Penelope." At least the bastard wasn't going to pretend he didn't know who Maggie was. "We need to come to an understanding where she's concerned."

"What's to understand?"

"Let's just say that anyone who was considering harming her might want to think twice before taking any action." Wanting there to be no mistaking of his intent, he let the silence play out.

"Are you threatening me?" Harold finally asked in a low voice.

"Yes, I am," Adam responded without thinking twice about it. He was one of the few men in all of England who could threaten Harold and get away with it. The beauty of it was that Harold knew he could.

Harold took a deep breath, as well as a long swig of his drink. Backing off, he said, "No need to get in a huff. Maggie is a lovely girl. Why would anyone want harm to come to her?"

"Why, indeed?" Adam asked in return.

"By the way"—Harold tried to sound casual and failed miserably—"how did you come to be involved with her?"

"My relationship with her is not any of your business, and I will not discuss her with you. We need to talk further next week, though, about something else that's extremely important. Which morning are you available?"

"Fine," he said tightly, completely exasperated with Adam and his refusal to come to heel. "How about Wednesday? Around ten."

"I'll be there, and I'll be brief. What I need to tell you will only take a minute of your time."

"Will you be proposing?"

"You'll find out what I have to say on Wednesday. Not before."

Adam walked away, loving the chance to keep the bastard in suspense for a few days. Let him wonder. Let him and Penny both wonder. Let everyone in the whole blasted world wonder what he was going to do.

Seemingly unconcerned, he strolled around the room, moving toward the spot where Mary Roberts stood with her aunt. Just as he approached them, the older woman stepped forward, neatly blocking his way.

"Good evening, Lord Belmont. Quite a lovely party, isn't it?"

"Yes, it is, madam," he offered.

"I'm sure you remember my niece . . ."

"How could I forget?" he responded amiably, turning his attention to Mary.

"Hello, Lord Belmont," Mary volunteered. "It's nice to see you again."

The aunt eyed him slyly, then said, "It's quite warm in here. We were just about to take a stroll on the terrace. Would you care to join us?"

A light blush colored Mary's cheeks. "Auntie, please. It's freezing outside and you're embarrassing me. And the Marquis." She smiled up at Adam. "I apologize."

"No apology necessary, Lady Mary. It's terribly stuffy in here, and I was just thinking a breath of the brisk night air might be just the thing. I would be delighted if you and your aunt would accompany me."

The aunt flashed a small look of triumph around the room, then led the way to the doors at the end of the parlor. Adam held out his arm, and as Mary took it, she whispered, "You don't have to do this."

"I want to," he insisted, and he meant it. "In fact, I was just coming over to ask if you'd like to accompany me on a carriage ride round the park tomorrow afternoon. With your aunt's permission, of course . . ."

In one corner across the room, Penelope watched the little scene play out, waited an extra few minutes so that no one would think she'd been affected by Adam's departure with Mary on his arm, then headed for the retiring room where she could pitch a fit in private.

In another corner, the Duke sipped his drink, quietly pondering what Adam was up to. Ever since the morning he'd misjudged Maggie, he'd wondered when the ax would fall over his mishandled meeting with the girl. It looked as if it was about to.

While he wanted to believe that Adam was coming by on the following Wednesday to finally ask for Penelope's hand—surely, he wouldn't be so bold as to go to the theater with them on Saturday if he wasn't!—there was something about the look in the man's eye that made Harold pause. Matters were about to come to a head, and he was almost afraid to hope that the news might be good news.

Still, he intended to be cautiously optimistic, for he could simply not contemplate the fact that Adam might choose another girl over his own. The match was simply too grand for him to do anything else but propose.

"What a nice surprise."

Adam could see the curious, hesitant smile on Maggie's lips as she opened her door to find him standing there in the midafternoon. Since he'd never shown up at such an hour before, she had to know that he'd come about something dreadfully important, and he had.

He'd visited with Mary Roberts several times now, and ever since he'd reached his decision, he'd been trying to find reasons to avoid telling Maggie what was coming. But he couldn't put it off any longer. She deserved to know, and she deserved to hear it from his own lips.

She stepped forward and gave him a light and playful kiss on the lips. "What brings you about in the middle of the day? Or do I need to ask?"

He surprised her by pulling her into a full embrace, hugging her tightly as though he'd never let her go and whispering into her hair, "I missed you. Is that a good enough reason?"

Pulling back, she looked up at him with her sparkling eyes. "That's the very best reason of all."

"Let's go in." He held the door as she moved inside. Then he stood and let her help him with his gloves, his hat. How much he enjoyed the little things she did for him! There was no doubt in his mind that she did them simply because she cared about him. She might very well be the only truly kind person he'd ever met.

What would he ever do without her?

The loveless, emotionless months and years stretched ahead, a grim portrait without any joy or happiness to break the monotony of his barren existence. He found little solace in the thought that Mary would be a passable wife. How had his life come to such a state where he was forcing himself to be happy because he'd been lucky enough to find a *tolerable* mate?

Sensing his anguish, she wrapped her arms about his waist. "Whatever it is, it will be all right. You'll see."

"Oh, Maggie . . ." He pulled her into another embrace, rained kisses across her hair and forehead.

"You seem very distressed. Would you like to go to my room? We could rest a bit."

She took his hand and started him toward the stairs, but he stopped her. "No. I need to talk with you. Let's go sit by the fire in the parlor."

Maggie led the way, and they sat next to each other, their thighs pressed together on the small couch. Slowly and carefully, she straightened her skirts, giving him the time he needed to collect his thoughts. Finally, realizing he might never begin, she patted his hand, then slipped her fingers into his. "Whatever it is, Adam, you can tell me. We'll get through it together."

Adam accepted the small offer of comfort. Who would ever have imagined that such a simple gesture could do so much to ease a man's heart? Looking down at their joined hands, he said quietly, "I've decided whom I shall marry."

She swallowed, forcing herself to remain calm. For months, she'd been preparing herself for this very moment, but she hadn't realized it would be so horribly difficult. "Well ..."

"Well ..."

The clock ticked. The old house squeaked and settled. A servant laughed softly in a back room. Her dress rustled. "You've made your selection, then?"

"Yes. I'm going to propose next week. Probably Wednesday. The announcement will be in the papers after that. I wanted to tell you in person before ..." Adam couldn't believe the tears welling in his eyes. "Before you heard it from someone else."

"Thank you. I appreciate your kindness."

"God, don't thank me," he said bitterly. "Rage at me, or strike me, or weep copiously, but don't *thank* me." He finally garnered the courage to raise his eyes to hers. "Would you like to know why I'm doing what I am?"

"No." Maggie shook her head. "I've no need to know."

"Are you sure? I feel strongly that I should explain my decision to you so you'll understand. It will make it easier for you to bear if you know my thinking."

"No, it won't. I prefer to know as little as possible. Believe me, it will hurt less in the long run."

"I'm sorry," he offered. "So bloody sorry."

"Don't be. We've both known since we met that this moment was coming. It's come sooner than I would have wished, but it's come. Now we have to deal with it."

"We'll need to make some plans for you."

"Yes," she said, her heart breaking at the very idea of going away from him. "How long do I have to decide what I'd like to do?"

"Seven months."

"Why, seven months is an eternity!" she said, trying to sound optimistic. "We've still a great deal of time together."

She swiped the back of her hand across a stray tear that had managed to make its way down her cheek, while she did a quick mental count of the time ahead. Seven months would make it a June wedding, with all of Society in London for the Season. The event would be the talk of the city. With the Good Lord's help, she'd be far away and never have to hear a word about any of it.

Adam tried to talk, couldn't, swallowed, and tried again. "I thought perhaps you could go to Cornwall and stay with James and Anne."

"I doubt the newlyweds would want company." They each flashed a watery half smile at that.

"I suppose you're right."

"It's more than that, though. I wouldn't want to be near them where I would hear about your life. About your family and your . . . your children." Knowing that his firstborn, perhaps his first son, was growing in her belly at that very moment, she could barely speak the word *children*, let alone envision herself living connected to his world through James and having to listen to the glad tidings when Adam's first legitimate child was born. "I know it sounds heartless, but I simply don't think I could bear learning about your children when they come."

"I understand." Adam heard a sound and was convinced that it was his heart breaking. Odd, but he'd not stopped to think about how emotional this moment would be for himself. He'd only considered Maggie's state. Not his own. "Perhaps, I could buy you a place. In the country. Or Paris, maybe."

The words, once spoken aloud, sounded so lame, the offer so disingenuous. Suddenly, he realized that he didn't want to know what type of existence she would manage to carve out for herself. He wanted to always remember her as she had been when she was part of his life. Young and beautiful and so very, very happy.

She seemed to realize it, too, and saved him from himself. "I don't think that would be wise, Adam. Once we part, I think I must go somewhere where you could not find me. If I thought you knew where I'd gone, I'm such a romantic, I'm sure I would dream about you showing up at my door. It will help me immensely if we have a clean break when the time comes."

"Yes, I suppose you're right." Adam released her hands and pulled her into his arms. "Oh, Maggie, when I started this with you, I never imagined that it would be so hard to end it. How will I ever let you go?"

Lying across his torso, she rested her cheek against his chest, where she could hear the strong and steady pounding of his heart. "You'll be able to do it because you know your duty better than anyone." She pulled away and held his face in her hands. "And even though I'm parted from you, you'll always have a piece of me that remains in your heart. No matter where you go, or what happens, you will be able to take comfort in the fact that there is someone out there in the world who loves you with all her heart and soul and will until she draws her last breath."

He swallowed, forcing down tears he'd not shed since he was a lad of six. "I do not know what great and wonderful thing I ever did in my life that made me deserve to be blessed with knowing you."

"I love you, Adam. I always will, no matter what." Maggie brushed a kiss across his cheek. "Can you stay for a time?" She smiled when he nodded. "Then come and let me ease this ache in your heart. Make love to me as though it was the very last time you'll ever have the chance."

Maggie stood in front of the mirror in the fitting room, adjusting the pins in her hat. It was a blustery day, and she didn't want the wind to wreak havoc with her coiffure when she stepped outside.

Madam LeFarge was nearly finished with the handful of dresses Maggie had ordered for the coming Christmas holidays. They were the last ones she intended to buy from the popular dressmaker from whom Adam had insisted she purchase her clothes.

Christmas was her deadline.

She would spend the holidays celebrating with him, and

when they were over, she would tell him about the baby. It was taking the coward's way out, and she should tell him sooner, but she couldn't contemplate spending Christmas alone, which was a very real possibility if Adam reacted as badly to the news as she feared he might. With his proposal occurring, and news of it spreading in the next few days, the last thing he would want or expect would be such an impossible and embarrassing burden placed on him by his mistress.

Luckily, there'd been no change to her waistline yet. If anything, she'd lost a few pounds, so the modiste hadn't noticed anything suspicious in the latest round of fittings. The gowns were all high-waisted so even if she developed a slight paunch, no one would be the wiser and the dresses would still fit comfortably. The added benefit was that, if she began to show, the style would hide what she was not prepared for others to see.

All finished, she reached for her reticule, then the door, ready to step into the hall that led to the front of the shop. Directly across the hall, the door to the adjacent fitting room had been left ajar, and Maggie couldn't help but hear two women talking clearly. Instantly, she cringed as she realized she knew who they were. Penelope was there with the friend who'd accompanied her to the retiring room at the ball.

Her first instinct was to sneak away, but on hearing their words, she couldn't move.

"Weren't you upset when the Marquis went outside with Mary?" the friend asked.

"I thought I was going to die!" Penelope insisted dramatically. "I'd been trying to get across the room to speak with him all night, but Mother is such a stickler for proprieties that we didn't even get to dance. I wish I'd have attended only with Father. He'd have been much more obliging. Perhaps it would all be finished by now, and I wouldn't have to wait until next Wednesday." There was a rustle of fabric. "Father says I shouldn't get too excited, but how could he expect me to remain calm at a time like this?"

"The Marquis is only going to propose to you once."

"My feeling exactly."

"What?!" Maggie couldn't keep herself from gasping aloud.

"I'm so happy for you," the friend gushed to Penelope. "Won't the others simply die of jealousy? You'll have to send a note round to me immediately after he leaves. Remember everything he says so you can tell me word for word."

"As if I'd forget any of it. I just know it will be the most romantic occasion of my life!"

"Do you suppose he'll try to kiss you tonight after the theater?"

"If he does, I'll let him," Penelope said, and both girls giggled. "It's certainly proper once we're betrothed. And Wednesday is only four days away."

Maggie clutched at her chest. This couldn't be! It simply couldn't be! Adam had promised her! He'd sworn to her! It had to be a mistake, but surely, Penny couldn't be wrong about a matter of such grave importance.

She leaned against the doorframe, desperately trying to think, to put the words in perspective. Their two voices faded to a gray din, and a sense of dreadful calm came over her when, eventually, it all became clear.

Everyone had been expecting for years that Adam would marry Penelope when she came of age. In their sphere, it was a perfect match of title, family, and money. Of course, he could make protestations about her, deny his intentions, profess his plans never to hurt Maggie by marrying her sister. But if he did anyway, so what? What could Maggie do or say about it? He would be finished with her soon, and he had no future intentions where she was concerned.

"What a fool I am," she whispered, heartsick at the horrible news.

Her mother and Anne had repeatedly warned her that a man would make all sorts of promises, then turn around and do what he swore he'd never do. It was simply the way of the world: Men could and did act with impunity. How stupid of her to forget. After all, her very own father was a shining example of how easy it was for a gentleman to say one thing, then do another.

Well, Adam deserved whatever happened to him at Penny's hands. Let him make his bed with the heartless girl. If he couldn't see what she was truly like, far be it for Maggie to enlighten him. More likely, he probably didn't care what she was like. Perhaps all that had ever mattered was the money and the property that he'd gain through the union.

A disturbing thought occurred to her concerning his visit the previous afternoon. Was his coming betrothal to Penelope the reason he'd seemed so intent on explaining his choice and reasoning? Maggie was more glad than ever that she'd refused to listen to his justifications. Nothing he said in a thousand years could explain away this hurtful betrayal.

Deep inside, she could feel a new resolve building. London was an impossible place for her now. She had to leave. Without waiting for the holidays to pass. Without telling him about the child. She'd suffer no guilt about her decision, either, although why he would care one way or another she couldn't imagine. If he would do this despicable thing, he obviously had few feelings where Maggie was concerned, and he'd feel even less for her child.

With renewed urgency, she turned to go, but the voices across the hall drew her attention once again.

"Do you think the bodice on this is low enough?" Penny asked her friend. "I want him to have a good view this evening. The more he can see of what he's getting, the happier he'll be that he's reached his decision."

"You're the worst!" The girl laughed.

"Well, men do like breasts above everything. That's what my abigail, Collette, told me. I think I'll ask Madam LeFarge to snip back this lace just a tiny bit more."

Before Maggie could move, the opposite door opened, and she stood face-to-face with her half sister. There was a long tense silence as they stared at one another, and Maggie could almost see the wheels turning in Penny's head as she tried to place her. Before recognition could register, Maggie gave a quick tip of her head.

"Lady Westmoreland." She took a step to escape.

"You, again?" Penny said, her pretty brow furrowing in consternation. Suddenly her eyes widened as the full impact of Maggie's presence registered, and she shrieked loudly. "I know who you are!"

That stopped Maggie's forward progress as she wondered if Penny truly knew. She couldn't resist. "Really? Who am I?"

"What are you doing here?" Penelope hissed.

"Buying dresses, just as you are," Maggie answered.

"As if I should have to be subjected to the likes of you while I am on an innocent shopping excursion." She whirled, shouting down the hall, while she stomped her foot in a petulant display of temper. "How could Adam do such a thing to me? Madam! Madam! Come this instant."

Maggie winced. So she *didn't* know she had a sister, but she *did* know that Adam kept a mistress. What a tangle.

The small Frenchwoman came bustling down the hall. "What is it? What . . ." But she stopped, her intense gaze assessing the two women who were so similar but yet so different. She was obviously distressed at witnessing an altercation between two well-paying clients, and it was apparent that she had no inkling of the intricate web ensnaring Penny and Maggie. If she had, they'd never have been scheduled for fittings on the same day.

Maggie decided to take pity on her by making a graceful exit, but before she could say or do anything, Penny pointed a finger at the disturbed dressmaker and shrieked, "Do you know who this woman is? Have you no respect for me or my family? I'll not be back if I'm to be forced to consort with the likes of her while I'm out in public. It's unseemly."

Maggie gave Madam an apologetic look. "I'm sorry I've upset Lady Westmoreland. I was just leaving."

"*Mais oui,* perhaps that would be best for now," Madam said, gesturing toward the door.

"For now? For now?" Penny wailed. "I'll have your assurance that she'll never be serviced here again!" She tapped her foot, impatiently waiting for the stymied woman's decision. "Well?"

Maggie stepped forward and patted the dressmaker's hand. "It's all right, Madam. Have my things sent to me."

"*Certainement.* Thank you, Miss Brown. My apologies . . ."

"No apology is necessary." She flashed Penelope a deadly look. "I don't seem to care for the clientele here any longer myself. I'll see that you're well compensated for the loss of my business."

Madam scurried away toward the front of the shop, eager to get out of the line of fire and to escort Maggie out the door before anything more horrendous could happen. Maggie tried once again to leave, but Penny stepped in front of her, blocking the way.

"How dare you speak so despicably to me."

Maggie responded, "I'm sure there are many people in your life who have to put up with your displays of temper. I, however, am not one of them. Good day."

"I'm going to tell Father about this."

"Please do." Maggie chuckled. "By all means."

Penny looked shocked that invoking the threat of her father had no effect. She tried for a larger reaction. "When I marry Adam, I'll personally see to it that he puts you out without a penny in compensation."

"I'm sure he'll enjoy discussing the matter with you. Good luck in your efforts." Casually, she pulled on one glove, then the other, making sure that the horrid girl couldn't see her distress. The Devil, himself, seemed to be sitting on her shoulder, though, and she couldn't stop herself from adding, "By the way, Adam simply despises inexperience in his women, so I've been thinking that you and I should meet. I could give you a few pointers on how to keep him from straying."

"Of all the nerve . . ." Penny huffed.

"Perhaps we could have lunch one day, and I could explain

some of what will happen in your marriage bed. He has his preferences, you know. He particularly likes some of the things I do with my mouth.'' With a flick of her wrist, she handed out her card. When Penny didn't reach for it, Maggie stuffed it in the bodice of her gown. "Please call on me if you think I can help.''

With a knowing wink, she turned and walked away, shutting out the squeals of outrage from Penny and her friend.

Up and down the hall, various women were peeking out from all the other fitting room doors as Penelope's peers stared with unrestrained glee at witnessing the juiciest moment to occur in London in years. The story would sizzle through the city within minutes. Maggie ignored each and every one of them, confidently walking through the burning gauntlet of staring noblewomen with her head held high.

How she hated them! How she hated all of them!

Outside, she walked for a time in order to shake off some of her burning rage. Her footman followed along behind, her cab shadowing them from a few feet away. As she trudged through the streets, it gradually dawned on her that her father had insisted they were very much alike, and she'd insisted he was wrong. Perhaps, she thought, disgustedly . . . perhaps, she really was very much like him after all. What a despicable insight! Never before had she displayed such a flash of anger, nor had she ever deliberately set out to hurt another as she'd just done with Penny.

Well, she certainly hoped Penny told their father. She hoped Penny told Adam. She hoped Penny told the whole bloody world.

She just felt so betrayed. So hurt. And so very, very alone.

Not knowing how long she walked or what distance, she continued until her anger finally evaporated. Nothing was left in its place but a wrenching emptiness. Exhausted, hungry, and overwhelmed, she realized the stress of the encounter was making her feel sick to her stomach. Time to head home to her empty house and her empty life. The weight of it was all too much to bear.

Chapter Twenty-Two

With her pregnancy and the stress of the day causing her undue nausea, Maggie tried to force down a light supper. Mostly, she sipped a bit of water while she dressed for her trip to the theater.

She had to see for herself. That was all there was to it.

Adam would be in attendance with the Westmoreland family. Her father and his wife would be there. Many of their friends and acquaintances would be there. Most importantly, Adam would be there with Penny by his side.

Maggie needed to see them together. To watch them talking and touching. To observe them surrounded by all the wealth and privilege they were afforded by their station in life. To be slapped in the face with the evidence of how much she did not belong in Adam's life—for her stubborn heart refused to believe or accept his decision. Only by facing the horrible situation with her eyes fully open could she truly grasp the impact of what Adam was about to do to all of their lives.

Not wanting anyone to know that she was going out, she told Gail she was retiring and didn't wish to be disturbed. After the sounds below-stairs quieted, she took her hooded cloak from the armoire, then let herself out the front door and quickly walked a few blocks until she was able to hail a cab. It was still early enough that there were people about, so the experience wasn't too risky, but the walk needed to be taken alone. For once, she didn't want her footman tagging along.

At the theater, the line of people purchasing tickets was very long. It was raining fiercely, and by the time she was admitted inside, her outer garments were wet and she had to shiver away the chill. The cold quickly dissipated, though, as she joined the throng of people in the pit, huddled elbow to elbow so tightly that she could barely move. The crowd was rude and boisterous, impatient for the play to begin.

Maggie hardly noticed, so intent was she on searching up above. On a previous occasion, Adam had pointed out various boxes and occupants, so she knew which one belonged to her father, and she watched impatiently for it to fill. Eventually, the curtain parted and the Duke stepped through with his wife on his arm. They settled themselves as it opened again and several others Maggie didn't know joined them. At the end came Penny and Adam, Penny's arm slipped through his as though she owned him. They looked like a fairy-tale prince and princess with their exquisite clothing, beautiful physiques, and glittering jewels. Adam helped her to her seat just as the actors took the stage.

Everyone in the theater was caught up in the action of the briskly plotted play. Everyone, that is, except Maggie, who watched a different sort of action taking place above her head. Adam switched his attentions from the stage to Penny. Penny kept up a continual chatter in his ear. Occasionally, she'd say something that caught his interest and they would whisper together for a few moments, their heads pressed close.

Each time, Penny seemed to shift her body imperceptibly closer to his. At one point, she said something that caused him to chuckle and present her with one of his rare smiles. Penny was quick to react, leaning closer and closer until it looked as though her breasts were fully pressed against his arm. If they were, he certainly did nothing to remove them.

Their lips hovered inches apart, and Maggie waited breathlessly for the chaste kiss that she was sure would occur in the back row of the shadowed box. When Adam held back and returned to watching the play, Maggie gulped for air as though she'd been just rescued from drowning.

In the greatest agony, Maggie tried to calm herself, remembering the first night Adam had brought her here. They'd come many times after that first time, but Maggie always fondly remembered the initial visit. Adam had been so handsome; Maggie had been so beautiful. If he'd had any worries before they'd arrived about how she'd carry herself, he'd had none when they left. She'd sparkled by his side that night like a fine diamond, proud to secretly know that she was the dazzling daughter of the Duke of Roswell and Rose Brown, who had been one of the most beautiful women of her day.

Maggie was exceptional that night and each night after when she'd accompanied him to different places and events. But now, as she stood watching from the shadows of the pit, the hurt became too great to bear. Seeing her lover, her friend, with her father and sister! Knowing that she could never join him there! That she would never be accepted into their ranks! No matter how much she loved Adam or cared about his welfare, no matter how much she wished to remain by his side to care for him all the days of his life, no matter how blue the blood that flowed through half of her own veins, she was an outsider and would always remain one.

Once, as a young girl out shopping with her mother, she'd seen a street urchin staring in the window of a candy shop, eyeing all the goodies inside. The wanting on his face had been so great that it had hurt to look at him. Maggie now knew exactly how the boy had felt.

She'd spent her life suffering because she'd been born a bastard and knew well how difficult a life it was. Now her own child, fathered by one of the wealthiest and grandest men in the realm, would be forced into that same life to battle against the same stigmas, while the children Penny would bear him would have everything a child could ever desire.

It was so unfair.

Adam had never said he loved her. He'd never even hinted as much. If anything, he'd treated her as some sort of amusing pet. In her naive, innocent way, she'd mistaken kindness for love and had convinced herself that he couldn't speak words of love simply because they were difficult for him to say.

What a fool she had been all this time! For surely, after what she was witnessing, he couldn't have any true feelings for her at all. Not love, not devotion, not respect. Not even friendship. The hounds at his estate probably enjoyed a greater degree of his affection than she did.

Suddenly, the heat of the crowded room and the stench of too many damp, unwashed bodies overwhelmed her. A huge wave of vomit was building in her stomach, her light repast earlier in the evening feeling like a ball of lead wanting to explode out. If she didn't remove herself immediately, she was going to embarrass herself in the middle of the assembly.

"Excuse me. Excuse me," she whispered as she began hurriedly shoving and elbowing her way to the end of the row. People grumbled but let her pass, seeming to sense her urgency to leave. She had to escape. If only she could make it to the fresh air outside! Ahead, she could see the doors, and she burst through them into the foyer, remembering to tug at her hood before stepping out into the brighter lights. There were several people who might recognize her, and she didn't want to run into any of them.

With her head down, she groped blindly for the front entry, and nearly fell in relief as she made it through. She stumbled, and a man passing on his way into the theater leaped to her aid, steadying her with a hand to her upper arm before she could fall to the walk. Their awkward movements caused her hood to fall back off her forehead.

She tried to politely ease away. "My pardons, sir."

"Are you all right, miss?"

The voice was familiar, and her eyes were drawn for a quick glance at the stranger. She found herself staring into the shocked face of Charles Billington.

"Maggie? Is that you? What's amiss?"

"Nothing, Charles. I'm simply not feeling well." She tried again to move away without success. "I need to be on my way."

"Hold on," he urged as he refused to relinquish her arm. "I believe Adam is inside. Would you like me to fetch him?"

"No!" she insisted, much more forcefully than she intended. On seeing his reaction, she softened her features. "No. I don't require his assistance."

"He doesn't know you're here, does he?"

She shook her head. "And I'd rather he didn't know."

"Your secret is safe with me," he said gallantly. "But I insist on seeing you home myself."

"It's not necessary. I can find my way." Her stomach was still churning furiously, and she was afraid she was about to embarrass herself all over Charles's shoes.

He pushed the hood all the way to her shoulders. "I must say that you're not looking at all well. Let me settle you in my carriage, and I'm sure you'll feel better once you're off your feet."

Because of the heavy traffic, his driver hadn't yet pulled away from the front of the theater. Before she could protest further, they were at the carriage door, and a coachman was helping her up and in.

"Thank you," she managed weakly as Charles sat himself across from her. She closed her eyes and laid her head against the plush velvet squab.

"You're looking a bit green about the gills."

That brought a small smile; Charles had never been one to stand on polite form. "I must admit that I've felt better," she said. Just then, the carriage lurched to a start. As the horses clopped down the busy street, stopping and starting in the evening crush of vehicles, she felt each and every movement. Never before had she realized that a carriage shifted in so many irritating and nauseating ways. She started taking slow, deep breaths.

"Are you going to make it home?" Charles asked.

"I hope so." A particularly violent pitch of the coach changed her mind. "Could we stop?"

"Certainly."

Before the driver could pull the team to a halt, she leaped through the door, the coachman barely catching her arm as she crashed to the street. A black odorous alley lay just beyond to shield her from the curious gaze of any onlookers. She raced into the darkness and found a blessed release by vomiting over and over until there was nothing left in her stomach.

Shaking and feeling wretched, she balanced a hand against a filthy wall, leaning on it for support. After several minutes, her composure returned enough so that she could go back to the carriage. By the lights of the thoroughfare, she saw Charles standing guard, allowing her her privacy and keeping her safe from any stray hooligans who might be lurking.

"Better?" he asked, offering his arm and his handkerchief.

"Much." She grasped both and steadied herself.

"Let's get you home." Not waiting for his coachman, he helped her into the carriage himself.

She leaned against the squab once again, closing her eyes. Through her hooded lids, she could see him watching her with an unreadable expression on his face. Let him wonder. All she wanted was peace and quiet and to be left alone while she figured out what to do, but it was not to be.

"How far along are you?" he asked softly.

For the briefest second, she thought about denying the babe, about insisting that he was wrong. But looking into his friendly, caring eyes, she found she couldn't tell him a lie. It would feel so good to share her dire secret with someone else. Perhaps through the simple act of telling, she could ease some of her burden.

With a sigh and a shrug of her shoulders, she admitted, "Between two and three months is my guess."

"Does Adam know?"

"No," she said, looking down and shaking her head.

"Does he even suspect?"

"I haven't even hinted about it. He wouldn't understand." If she'd been expecting his cousin to disagree, she was mistaken.

"No, I don't imagine he would," Charles said.

She shifted sideways into the seat, pressing her face against the leather and shutting her eyes as tightly as she could, tight enough to close out the entire world.

On arriving home, despite her attempts to send him on his way, Charles was not easily dissuaded. He insisted on escorting her into the house, making her comfortable on the small sofa in the downstairs parlor, having the maid bring a tray of water and dry cakes. Waiting silently until the woman left the room, he then walked to the door and pulled it firmly closed behind her. By the time he found a chair and pulled it up so he was sitting directly in front of her, Maggie's nerves had nearly reached their limit.

Taking her ice-cold hands between his own, he rubbed them briskly. "Have you ever talked with Adam about the possibility of a babe?"

"Yes, when we first became involved. He told me I couldn't let it happen."

Charles snorted. "He always did think he could command people about like he was a god. Perhaps there's another God at work here, trying to show him who's boss, eh?"

"Perhaps." She leaned forward, squeezing the hands that gripped her own. "I haven't told him because I'm so afraid of how he might react. He said he'd put me out immediately if this ever happened. That he wouldn't claim the child. That he wouldn't let me shame his family with it."

"That certainly sounds like Adam." Charles sighed. "What a fool he is about so many things."

"But it was early in our relationship. So much has changed since then. Do you . . . do you think he still means it?"

Charles looked as though he wanted to ease her mind with a lie, but finally decided only the truth would do. "I've known Adam all my life. I'm probably his closest friend—that's assuming, of course, that he really has any friends. And I have to honestly say that I'm sure he meant every word."

"I see." Whatever hope she'd carried in her heart died upon hearing Charles confirm her worst fears. Her face crumbled and tears welled into her eyes.

Charles took the handkerchief she still carried crumpled between their joined hands and dabbed at her eyes. "I'm sorry. I probably shouldn't be so blunt, but I hardly think it would serve you well to encourage false hopes."

"It's all right. I was just so hoping that you'd say something else."

"It was his upbringing, you see? His father was an extremely selfish man who showed little regard for his family, and Adam's mother—well, she is very cold, very hard. It altered Adam's entire view of the world until all he can see is duty and responsibility."

"I feel so sorry for him."

"Don't," he insisted, surprising her. "He's a grown man. He is living the life he chooses to live."

"I tried to be so careful," she muttered, rubbing a hand across her brow. She flopped back against the seat, asking the rhetorical question that had plagued all her thoughts and dreams for weeks, "What am I going to do?"

They talked over every angle of her dilemma, discussing Adam and his stern, set ways. They considered her options, which seemed so few and so inadequate. All of them left her alone and the child a bastard. Since she could discuss her situation, Maggie's nerves and emotions were running at a fevered pitch, so she failed to notice the assessing look that gradually came over Charles as the night passed.

"I have an idea," he said during one of their lengthy silences.

"Good. You've heard all mine. Yours certainly couldn't be any worse."

He walked to the tray left for them by the maid and refilled his glass of wine, taking a bracing gulp before continuing. "It will probably sound quite shocking, but promise you'll hear me out."

"I promise," she agreed, not for a moment able to deduce what shocking thing the man could possibly say.

"How about if you married me?"

Maggie's mouth fell open. "You can't be serious."

"Oh, but I am. Just listen." He moved to the other end of the small room as though needing to put plenty of distance between them before he dared ask, "Do you know very much about me?"

"Not really," she admitted. "I know you're Adam's cousin, that you're very close to him and to James. You were a great friend to James and to Anne when they decided to wed. I respected you for it very much." Carefully, neutrally, she added, "You've always been kind to me, and I've appreciated that as well."

"I want to tell you something about me. Something only a handful of people know." He flushed slightly, embarrassed to admit whatever it was.

She waited, then said, "You can tell me. I'll keep your secrets."

That small assertion seemed to satisfy him. "Did you know I was a soldier for a short while?"

"Yes, I had heard that."

"I fought on the Continent. I was badly wounded."

"Yes, I remember hearing that, too."

"Mostly, I damaged my legs and back. There's quite a bit of scarring and such, so I'm not much to look at unclothed." He turned toward the window and stared out at the dark night while he said the rest. "Unfortunately, part of my wounding was quite personal."

"Personal?" she asked. "I guess I don't understand."

"I can't ever have children. I'm damaged somehow ... inside. I can no longer feel desire, and I don't have much sensation in my lower back and part of one thigh ..."

"I had no idea."

"No, you wouldn't," he said, bowing his head as though shamed. "As I said, not many people know about it."

"Does Adam?"

"Yes, and James. And a few of my doctors who are sworn to secrecy. But that's about it." He returned to the table and poured more wine, sipping slowly. "I don't talk about it. It's not something a gentleman should ever care to admit. It's quite an unmanly thing to have happen to oneself."

"I can only imagine," she said with full sympathy.

"Well, then," he said, finally finding the courage to look her in the eye once again, "since I'll never have children of my own, it's quite obvious that I could never offer marriage to any lady. It wouldn't be fair. But my mother's badgering me about grandchildren, and it has gotten so bad that I can barely stand to go home for a visit." He shrugged as though he'd just found the solution to right all the wrongs in the world. "We could marry. I could claim the child as my own."

"I could never marry you."

"Why do you say that? I'm an excellent catch. I own property. I have a secure income through a trust and through my work, so you and the babe would never want for anything. I've created a substantial reputation for myself with my painting, and the babe would have the benefit of my name and my family's connections. Many women marry for much less."

"But people know you. Surely, some would suspect ..."

He shook his head, cutting her off. "No one will ever know. Besides, the child will probably look enough like me to fool anyone who might be silly enough to wonder."

"Why would you do such a thing for me?" She eyed him quizzically. "It seems like all the benefit would be for me and none for you."

"That's where you're wrong."

"What could possibly be in it for you?"

"The end of speculation about my personal life. Peace of mind. The end of nagging by my mother and my sisters, which, believe me, would be worth a great deal." He moved closer, apparently encouraged by the fact that she hadn't immediately said no. "I must admit that this would be a solution to a problem that's had me vexed for some time now. A man in my position is duty-bound to marry, but I can't. I don't even speak to women anymore, because I don't want to raise anyone's expectations. And"—he nearly whispered the rest—"it's hard for me to enjoy any type of female companionship now that I can't . . . I can't . . ."

"So, if we went through with it, you wouldn't need marital services from me?"

"No. It would simply be a marriage of convenience which would serve us both well."

"You make it sound so calculated."

"All marriages are calculated according to what the gains and losses might be. I only see benefits to both of us."

"I thought your father was an Earl. Aren't you bound by any of the strictures that apply to Adam?"

"I'm the seventh child, Maggie. The fifth son. My brother assumed the title years ago, and his wife's already given him three sons." He settled himself on the chair in front of her again. "Trust me. No one cares who I marry. They only care that I do."

His reasoning and his answers to her questions all seemed to make sense. He made it sound as though it could work very easily, which was frightening. She couldn't believe it when she heard herself ask, "If I agree—and I'm not saying I do, mind you—when would you want to do it?"

"The sooner the better, I'd say, considering . . ." He gestured toward her abdomen.

Maggie nodded. "How would we go about it?"

"I was thinking of a quick trip to Gretna Green."

"Elope to Scotland?" Maggie gasped at the shocking idea.

"I mean no disrespect," he responded hurriedly.

"None taken. It just sounds so drastic. Wouldn't it be easier to do it here in the city?"

"I could get a special license, but I'm afraid word might go round if I asked for one. These things have a way of leaking out. My mother would find out about our plans, and she'd want to delay things to make it a big, grand event . . ."

"And we can't delay the date without telling her why."

"Precisely."

"Or Adam might find out."

"Would that matter?"

"I'm not sure. He might try to stop me just out of sheer stubbornness."

"Too true."

"Although I don't know why he'd care. He's decided to marry Penelope Westmoreland after all . . ."

Charles winced and bit off an oath. "Then marriage to me would be the best solution for both of you. You'd be taken care of, and he'd have you out of his hair before the wedding began to approach." He reached for her hands again and squeezed hard. "Let's do it. What do you say?"

"I don't know, Charles. I just don't know . . ." A savage headache was beginning to pound behind her eyes. "You make it all sound so simple."

"It would be simple."

"What about the two of us? We hardly know each other."

"We're friends. We like each other. That's more than many married couples can say."

"What about the babe? I wouldn't want it raised by a father who didn't care for it." She looked up, beseeching. "Could you truly find any affection for another man's child?"

"It's not as though it's a stranger's child, Maggie. The babe is my cousin's. Some of my own blood flows in its veins."

"I wouldn't want to ever see Adam." Good Lord, but she was sounding as though she was going to do it. "Or Penelope. Or to hear about their life or their children."

"I understand."

"It might cause a horrible situation with the two of you. With your families."

"Let me worry about that."

"How could I avoid being in the circle he inhabits with you? If I became your wife, I don't see how I could."

"I own a small home in the country near my family's estates. You could stay there year-round. I would need to come to London on occasion, though, for my painting appointments, but you would have no need to join me."

Maggie slumped back against the couch. It was a good idea. For herself, for the babe. The child would not be born a bastard, but instead would be part of a large, respected family. Its father would be a well-liked, renowned gentleman. What more could she ask?

What he proposed offered a solution to every problem in her life, but if she took such a drastic step, there'd be no going back. It would be an instant knife in the heart of her relationship with Adam. He'd never forgive her.

After his decision to marry Penelope, did she care?

With a piercing gaze, she looked up. "Let me think about this. You should, too. It's very late, and you might feel differently in the light of day."

He shook his head. "I won't change my mind."

"I'll send a note round by noon tomorrow."

"If your answer is yes, I think we should leave for Scotland immediately."

"I agree."

Chapter Twenty-Three

Maggie's home was usually a flutter of activity in the morning as the servants went about their tasks, but for some reason things were dreadfully quiet, for which she was grateful. If she'd been feeling better, she might have wondered if the servants knew of the morning nausea she suffered because of her condition and were being silent because they were aware that she wasn't feeling well. As it was, she felt too miserable to notice—or to care if she had.

Sitting in front of the vanity, she pressed a cool rag to her lips. The wave of sickness she'd fought for the past hour seemed to have passed as quickly as it had come. Her dress was on and fastened, but she was hardly presentable. There were bags under her eyes; her hair was in tangles. If ever there'd been a time when she needed to use face paints, this was it. Without them, she looked pale and sickly.

The long night with Charles had taken its toll. She was exhausted, both from the stress of her visit to the theater and from the hours of talking after they'd arrived home. On his departure, she'd stumbled to her room, thinking she'd sleep deeply, but for the most part, rest had eluded her. Her mind had raced at a frantic pace as she viewed Charles's proposal from every angle. There weren't any bad aspects that she could see, other than the fact that Adam would be furious.

She didn't know why he would care, really, but he would. In his eyes, she belonged to him, and he was the kind of man who would want to say when their affair ended and what would happen to her when it did. What he envisioned for her after they broke up, she couldn't imagine, for they'd spoken of it only briefly on a few rare occasions. Certainly, his view of her future did not include her marriage to his first cousin and best friend.

Luckily, Adam was out of her hair for a few days. The theater last night, meetings all day, another social engagement this evening. A man of his position, who had just decided to marry, would have many appointments to keep him busy, so she didn't need to worry about him stopping by while she pondered what to do.

Downstairs, a knock sounded at the front door, surprising her, for she couldn't imagine who might be calling so early in the day. A few minutes later, just as she'd finished dabbing a brush of color across her cheeks, she heard Gail's light footsteps hurrying up the stairs.

"Yes?" She bade the servant enter and waited while she firmly closed the door.

"You've a visitor, Miss Maggie."

"So early?" The high flush on Gail's cheeks and her odd, nervous manner set Maggie's senses on alert. "Who is it?"

"Lady St. Clair," Gail said, holding out the woman's card, "the Dowager Marchioness of Belmont."

The name of her guest was so shocking that her mind refused to accept the woman's identity. She stared at the printed card for a long while, running her thumb over and over the name until she finally managed to ask, "Who did you say is calling?"

"Lucretia St. Clair," Gail said. By way of explanation, she added, "The Marquis's mother."

The hand holding the card started to shake. What could the woman want?

Gail, sensing her distress, said calmly, "I've told the maid to bring tea and cakes, and I told the Marchioness that you'd be down shortly." She hesitated. "Unless you're not taking callers?"

Maggie sighed. Nothing good could possibly come from the meeting, but she couldn't refuse to see the woman now that she was ensconced in the parlor downstairs. Taking a deep breath, she turned to look in the mirror once again.

"I'll see her." The light touch of face paints had worked wonders, so she looked casual but elegant, although her hair was still a mess. Looking over her shoulder, she asked, "Could you help me with my hair? Just a quick sweep."

"Certainly, miss." Gail began working at her hair. Once finished, Gail said quietly, "I'm sorry that we admitted her without asking your permission. The maid who answered the door was so flustered that she didn't think to refuse."

"No, she did the right thing." With a final glance at her reflection, Maggie stood and turned in a slow circle for Gail's inspection. "How do I look?"

"Lovely," Gail replied without hesitation as she adjusted a bow at the back. Maggie reached out a hand and Gail grasped it, squeezing hard to offer moral support. "You'll do fine," she insisted. "Just fine."

Maggie descended the stairs, her graceful step preventing anyone from noticing the terrible pounding of her heart. She halted in the doorway to the parlor, taking the older woman's measure as she sat in the large wing chair at the end of the room as though holding court. She didn't rise at Maggie's entrance. Neither did Maggie offer her the courtesy of a curtsy.

"I thought it was time we had a talk," Lucretia began, quickly dispensing with the pretense that there was anything social about the call. "Won't you join me?"

The regal gesture she used in pointing to the opposite chair irritated Maggie no end. The woman had a great deal of nerve to have called in the first place, let alone to act as if the place were her own. What were the social restrictions, Maggie wondered, against talking bluntly with the mother of the man to whom you provided sexual favors?

They can't be much different from fighting in public with his fiancée. The thought came out of nowhere, and she could barely stifle a giggle at the ludicrousness of the situation.

"I prefer to stand. I'm sure you don't intend for this conversation to go on for very long. Neither do I," Maggie added, attempting in her own way to keep some control of the meeting. "Please say what you've come to say and be done with it."

"Very well." Apparently not wanting to feel disadvantaged by the fact that Maggie chose to stand, Lucretia stood as well. "Your relationship with my son has been brought to my attention by numerous parties."

Maggie eyed her dispassionately, neither confirming nor denying what she'd just said, so Lucretia continued. "It appears he's developed quite a *tendre* for you. I witnessed it with my own eyes when you had the audacity to visit my home."

"I'm sorry," Maggie said, trying to sound innocent. "I don't recall ever being in your home. Where exactly do you live?"

"At our family's town house in Mayfair."

"Oh, then I must apologize for my error. I thought the home I visited belonged to Adam. Not to his mother."

"Watch your tongue, girlie. That attitude may help you work your wicked ways on others, but it won't work on me." Lucretia took a deep breath and squared her shoulders, ready to do battle. The effect would have been intimidating on a lesser person than Maggie. Lucretia definitely knew how to use her name and position to put mere mortals in their place. "I know all about you. I know what you're trying to do."

"What exactly is that?" Although she didn't really care what the answer would be, Maggie couldn't help asking. Something had left the woman in a definite snit, and Maggie imagined she'd have no peace until Lucretia had her say.

"Ever since the day James married your whore of a friend . . ."

"That's enough! This is my home, and I don't have to put up with talk like that from anyone. Gail!" she called over her shoulder, and the maid appeared in the doorway. "Lady St. Clair is leaving. Show her out."

With one scathing look, Lucretia halted any action the servant might have taken. "Last I noted, Abigail, you still worked for the St. Clair family. You'd do well at this moment to remember that fact. Be gone this instant."

Maggie nodded at Gail. "You can leave us, Gail. I'll show her the door myself."

Gail vanished like smoke, obviously not wanting to be drawn into any battle of wills that might cause her to suffer Lucretia's wrath later on. Maggie swirled away from the dowager and walked to the foyer, opening the door and gesturing outside with a false smile on her face. Lucretia glared at her from the parlor, but didn't move, so Maggie said, "Good-bye, madam. Your presence is no longer welcome."

Lucretia hesitated for a few moments, wondering how such a slip of a girl could dare throw her out, but she refused to go until her mission was finished. Reaching into her bag, she extracted an envelope and advanced on Maggie. Maggie stood her ground.

"Your presence in my son's life is creating hardship for others, and I won't have it."

"What hardship could I possibly be causing others?"

"He informs me that he has selected a wife."

Lucretia eyed her meticulously, hoping for a reaction, and Maggie was so glad she already knew the planned course of events. The information was not news, and she could handle it dispassionately. "I am aware of that."

"Then you realize that you will only bring heartache to the girl and her family if you remain."

Maggie had no intention of telling the woman that she'd never planned to remain, nor had she been asked to. "I'd say whatever occurs between Adam and myself is our business, certainly not yours or anyone else's."

"That's where you are wrong." Lucretia handed out the envelope, which Maggie took from her. "It is time for you to end your relationship with my son, but I'm sure you will need funding to accomplish the separation. Present this draft to my banker by Wednesday, and he will see to it that you are remunerated for your troubles."

The woman had an incredible amount of gall, and Maggie shook her head in wonderment. "If I accept your money, what are the terms?"

"You will be required to sign papers agreeing to separate yourself from Adam immediately. You will leave London and never return. You will neither see nor contact Adam ever again for any reason."

Flicking open the lip of the envelope, Maggie raised a brow as she glanced at the amount Lucretia had written there. "You must want to see me gone very badly."

"I do." Trying to assume a more generous air, but failing greatly, she added, "You are young and possibly think yourself in love with Adam. I assure you he doesn't return the emotion . . ."

After the scene she'd witnessed in the Duke's box at the theater, Maggie could hardly argue the point, so she remained silent, as Lucretia continued. "Or perhaps you're doing this for the excitement of being allied with such a great man. Perhaps it is simply the trinkets his wealth can provide. I don't know what motivates one such as yourself, and my contacts were not certain, either. However, it matters not to me."

"What does matter to you?"

"Only to see you gone before you can disrupt our lives any further. Don't fool yourself. You are nothing more than a well-paid whore. You'll never be anything else, no matter how desperately you try to attach yourself to the fringes of my son's world. You don't belong in his life. You could never hope to fit in."

"You're certain about that, are you?"

"More certain than I've ever been of anything. Adam is

marrying into the Westmoreland family. The only daughter of
the Duke of Roswell . . . '' Maggie could barely keep from
wincing at the statement, but she'd never let the heartless
woman know how close she'd struck to Maggie's weakest
point. "A lovely, lovely girl of impeccable breeding and social
position about which you can only fantasize. Both families
have been awaiting this union for years, and I'll not have it
disrupted by the likes of you." Lucretia looked her up and
down, searching for flaws and obviously finding her lacking.
"Use the money wisely to make a new life for yourself which
is more appropriate to your station."

"You really need to work on your insults," Maggie said,
shaking her head. "You're not very good at delivering them.
And I've endured about enough of them for one day. Now, if
you'll excuse me . . ."

"I'll not be dismissed!"

"Too late. You already have been."

Maggie moved out into the street, refusing to stay inside
with the woman one moment longer, but short of physically
carrying her away, she didn't know how to make her depart.
The action proved a judicious one. Lucretia followed her out,
and Maggie slipped behind her to stand in the doorway,
blocking any attempt she might make to reenter.

"Don't forget," Lucretia warned, "the draft is only good
until noon on Wednesday. You must be gone by then."

"And if I don't choose to leave?"

"Then you will tangle with me, and believe me, I don't think
you'd want to risk it."

Maggie stepped back inside and slammed the door in the
woman's face, turning the key in the lock with a determined
motion that Lucretia couldn't help but hear. She stood silent
and still, barely breathing until she heard Lucretia's footsteps
moving away. Noises made by her climbing into the carriage
came next, followed by the jingle and clop as the driver urged
the team down the lane. Only then did Maggie move, collapsing
against the door.

"Why can't everyone just leave me alone?" she asked bitterly. Why couldn't they all just let Adam be happy? Why couldn't they just leave her in peace? Maggie had never done anything to any of them except try to give Adam a few months of joy. What was so wrong with that?

She was so close to being gone on her own that they might as well say she'd already departed. Everyone—her father, her half sister, Adam's mother, Adam himself—absolutely everyone was going to get what they wanted without any need to continue interfering with Maggie's life.

Taking the stairs slowly and carefully, she headed to her room. After her fights with the likes of Penelope and Lucretia, her energy had vanished. She no longer possessed the will or the determination to continue the charade that she was to have an ongoing relationship with Adam. In fact, considering his decision to marry Penny, she no longer wished to have any kind of relationship with him at all.

Oh, how the thought hurt. To never see Adam again. To never touch him, or lie down with him. To never talk with him or soothe his weary heart after a long, trying day. As the wayward thoughts careened through her mind, she shook her head in disbelief at her own stupidity. Her scattered emotions, which seemed to be working overtime these days, were preventing her from thinking clearly. She kept ignoring one essential, overriding fact: Adam didn't want her; he never had, and he'd made it clear from the beginning.

What was left for her now?

If she stayed on, the answer was clear. More heartache. More pressure. More agony. And once her pregnancy began to show, only more shame and humiliation. All this screaming and yelling was coming before they had any idea that she was pregnant. Think how great the pressures would be once they knew!

Looking down, she noticed that Lucretia's bank draft was still clutched in her fist. Perhaps Lucretia was right. She should just take the money and leave, get out of the lives of these horrible, powerful people. Find a quiet place where she could lick her wounds, give birth to her child, and build a new life. But if she took the money and ran away, she would have to do it alone. All alone. She couldn't bear the thought of the solitary existence facing her if she struggled to raise the child by herself. The task seemed too daunting.

Gradually, as if a lamp had been lit after a long period of darkness, she began to realize that there was only one thing to do.

She walked back down to the parlor to the small writing desk she kept near the front window. Looking at the clock, she could see that it was just before eleven. Plenty of time. She penned the note to Charles first, and the moment she finished blowing on the ink, called to her footman to deliver it to his home. It would arrive by noon with plenty of minutes to spare.

The other, she penned to Adam without much thought as to what she wanted to say. After all, if she pondered long hours, she could never find the words to convey how much he'd meant to her and how great her heartache was over his betrayal. No reason to mention any of it really. He just needed to know that she'd be gone so he wouldn't wonder if something had happened to her. Although she was hurt and angry, she was gracious enough not to want to cause him undue worry.

"What a silly goose you are," she muttered to herself. He probably wouldn't even miss her. In fact, he'd very likely be glad she'd left on her own, keeping him from the messy emotional task of sending her away.

Adam,

With the announcement of your engagement only days away, I think it's best if I depart. I know we talked about my staying till summer, but I can't do it. Leaving is best for everyone concerned, as I'm sure you'll agree after you've had time to reflect. I would never want to cause any undue heartache to you or Penelope. Best wishes in whatever comes your way. I hope my sister makes you happy.

She didn't hope so at all. She hoped he'd be miserable and regretful all the days of his life for doing such an idiotic thing, but she didn't want him to think she was petty and bitter at the hour of their separation.

For a long moment, she paused and thought about Lucretia and her offer of blood money. Even though she knew it was best to let it go and keep the woman's act a secret, she couldn't do it. Lucretia's behavior had been too outrageous, and her words had cut too deeply.

She dipped her pen again.

> *Please tell your mother that I've made my own arrangements. She can keep her money. I neither want it nor need it, and I was gravely offended that it was offered.*

Once the ink was dry, she placed the note in the same envelope as Lucretia's bank draft, wrote his name on the front, then waxed the flap, hoping to keep the prying eyes of servants away from it as long as possible. If luck played a part, she'd be most of the way to Scotland before someone found it in her room.

With a sigh and a last, longing look around her childhood home, she went upstairs to pack a bag so she'd be ready to leave the moment Charles's carriage pulled up outside.

Adam sat in a quiet corner at his club, sipping a drink. He enjoyed it most at this time of the afternoon. There were a few gentlemen present, but none of the crowd that would be there later for gambling or a quick drink in between social engagements, although the various soirees this time of year were not numerous. Most people were at their country estates, preparing to celebrate the Christmas holidays.

That was where Adam should have been, but he couldn't abide the thought of going. James was still on his honeymoon, and the halls of the huge estate house would only have echoed with his absence. Maggie couldn't have come with him, and with such a short time left in their relationship, he wasn't about to spend it away from her. Plus, it would be their only Christmas together. Surprisingly, he wanted to make it memorable, not only for her but for himself as well.

He knew he was throwing the lives of numerous people into chaos by his decision to remain in London. His own mother, who'd refused to go to the country without him, was most put out, having to reach to the very bottom of the social barrel to find enough guests for her holiday dinner parties. Several families had also chosen to remain in the city with him—those such as the Westmorelands who had marriageable daughters. Everyone wanted their little darlings close by in case the Marquis needed company at the theater or on a cozy winter carriage ride through the park.

Well, Mary Roberts would take care of all that nonsense in quick order. He'd passed several afternoons and evenings with her, and she'd do. A pitiful approbation to be sure, but accurate. She'd do. Of course, everyone would be agog once he proposed, for she was an unlikely choice, being not overly pretty or exceedingly wealthy like some of the others. But she had excellent bloodlines and her dowry was fair. She didn't irritate him, could converse pleasantly, and was always extremely deferential to his wishes.

If the fact that his choice would thoroughly outrage certain people—namely his own mother as well as Penelope and Harold—was also a major deciding factor, he chose not to look at his motives too carefully. It was hardly a valid reason for choosing a bride, but it was definitely a major determinant. Ten separate acquaintances had made sure he heard about Penny's little altercation with Maggie at the dressmaker's. Penny would never be able to mention it, but would Maggie? The hateful words thrust by her vicious half sister had to have cut deeply, but Maggie had given as good as she got, and he was proud of her.

A wistful look came into his eyes. He wished they'd all just disappear so he could have a peaceful, solitary month of celebration with Maggie. That was all he really wanted. To be with her. He patted the small box in his coat pocket, smiling as he imagined the look on her face when she saw the ring he'd purchased for her Christmas present. It wasn't grand or extravagant like the jewelry the women in his circle would expect from a man like himself. But Maggie wasn't an ordinary woman. She'd want something tasteful but elegant, so he'd purchased it specifically with that fact in mind. The small amethyst stone circled by tiny diamonds had garnered his attention instantly. When the purple stone caught the light just right, it was the exact color of her eyes.

Staring blindly across the room, he pictured a fantasy moment from some undetermined number of years in the future. He'd see her across a city street, just stepping out of a carriage. Older but lovelier. Their eyes would meet in silent recognition. She'd give a small wave and a smile and . . . the ring would be there on her finger, the last bit of himself she would always carry.

He jerked upright. The dream was supposed to have been a flight of fancy, destined to bring a smile and a laugh, but it didn't. There was an aching hollow in his chest, and he rubbed his hand across the center. Was that what he really wanted? To have a chance encounter with her in a few years? To know her simply as an old lover, perhaps married, perhaps used badly by another?

The ache became steadily worse.

Needing a different vision, he closed his eyes and fantasized again. Ah . . . there she was, lying back on a pile of pillows, in his bed at the family home in Sussex, the summer sun shining in the window. She was naked, except for the violet-colored ring, her stomach swollen with his child. He ran his hand over her bulging abdomen, bent his lips, and kissed the warm flesh. They both laughed as the baby gave a kick . . .

With a start, he wrenched his eyes open. The ache around the area of his heart had become unbearable. Suddenly, he felt so terrible that he thought he might become sick to his stomach. His forehead was perspiring, and he dabbed at it with his handkerchief. Cautiously, he took a slow, measured sip of his drink, needing to quell the rising panic that seemed about to sweep him away. So distressed was he that he didn't notice the approach of the waiter until the man was directly in front of him.

"I'm sorry to bother you, Lord Belmont, but one of your servants is downstairs, and he needs to speak with you. He says it's a matter of the utmost urgency."

"Thank you," Adam said, standing on shaky legs.

James! was his first thought. Something had happened to James on his honeymoon adventure. His heart was pounding. In all his years as an adult, he'd never had a servant show up looking for him. Something dreadful must have happened. Trying to hide his agitation from anyone who might be watching, he walked to the front of the building.

The sight of the footman from Maggie's house increased his perplexity and alarm. He took a deep breath. "What's happened?"

The young man looked him straight in the eye and said without hesitation, "Miss Brown seems to have disappeared, milord."

"When?"

"Yesterday afternoon," he said, and he actually shifted back as though he thought Adam might strike him for the admission. "Although we didn't really realize it until this morning."

"Why do you think she's disappeared?" he asked, even as he said it knowing she must be gone. A servant wouldn't have chased him down otherwise.

"Well, she told Miss Gail—that's her maid, milord—that she was going out for the evening with your cousin, Master Billington."

Adam nodded. He had no problem with that. He knew they

were friends, and Charles was a good escort for nights when Adam, himself, couldn't provide one. "Yes?"

"She said she'd be late and told us not to wait up. So we didn't." He swallowed nervously. "When Miss Gail went to her room this morning, she hadn't returned."

"Did you try Charles's house?"

"Yes, sir. First thing."

"And?"

"His man said he'd gone out of town. Didn't know where. Didn't know when he'd be back."

There was a long hesitation as Adam pondered the answer. Finally, he asked, "Why didn't you come to me at once?"

"Beg pardon, milord, but I've been looking for you one place and another all day. I finally caught up with you here." He held out an envelope. "Miss Gail found this in Miss Brown's room."

Adam looked at it as though it were a venomous snake about to bite his hand. Whatever it contained was the answer to this riddle, but with great clarity, he knew he didn't want to know its contents.

"Thank you," he said, finally accepting it with one hand and tapping it against the other. His ears rang, and his entire world went black except for the ivory rectangle of parchment from which he could not tear his eyes. How well he remembered the last time she'd penned him such a note. She'd written to say she was leaving, gone off on her foolish adventure with Anne. What kind of idiotic thing had she done now and why?

A noise from far away caught his attention. He had to force himself to stare. To decide at whom he was looking. Ah, yes, the footman. "What did you say?"

"Your mother stopped by the house yesterday morning."

"My mother?"

"Yes, to see Miss Maggie. Miss Gail says they argued quite vehemently."

"About what?"

"Gail couldn't hear, milord, for your mother had ordered

her away, but Miss Maggie was terribly upset after, and she left with Master Billington a short time later.''

His mother? His blasted mother had learned of Maggie, had sought her out? Had fought with her? After Maggie's public battle with Penelope, he couldn't imagine what worse thing could occur.

The footman was speaking again, the club's servants watching all, and Adam merely stood like a deaf and dumb imbecile. Rubbing his brow, he forced himself to get a grip on the situation.

''What?'' he asked again.

''What would you like me to do, milord?''

''Go back to her home. Wait for me there. I'll stop by later to talk with Gail and the other maid.''

''Yes, sir.''

The doorman, sensing trouble at the appearance of the Marquis's servant, had already had his carriage brought round. It waited outside. Adam hurried into his hat and cloak and settled himself safely inside before tearing the wax seal on the letter. He had to scan the words numerous times before they made sense.

''By God, what have you done?'' he cried aloud, but he wasn't sure if he was speaking about Maggie or his mother. He'd deal with Lucretia first. ''Take me home,'' he ordered the driver, ''fast as you can get me there.''

Many minutes later, he walked into his home at a much more subdued pace than he would have thought possible. He'd calmed himself as much as he could, trying to extinguish that initial surge of apprehension that had overcome him at the club.

Once inside, he went to the library and had two stiff shots of whiskey, a drink he usually avoided, but he needed the hard, steady burn it would provide. Gradually, his hands stopped shaking, and he called for the butler, who appeared shortly.

''Where is my mother?''

"Above-stairs, sir. In her rooms, I believe, dressing for tonight's soiree."

"We're having guests?" Gad, he'd forgotten.

"Yes, milord. They should begin arriving in an hour."

He couldn't deal with guests. Not tonight. Not after this. "I need to speak to my mother. Fetch her."

"Lady St. Clair asked not to be disturbed."

"Fetch her anyway. Impress upon her that I require her attendance immediately. I don't care what she's doing."

The butler bowed carefully and left. Adam slowly sipped a third whiskey, trying to calm himself further while he waited. His summons had been rude and unusual enough that he knew he'd not have to wait long, and indeed, he didn't. Lucretia, wrapped in a thick dressing gown, her grayed hair braided loosely, her face bare of decoration, showed every bit of her fifty years as she huffed into the library like a swan on the attack.

"I have no idea what makes you think you can summon me like a commoner. What has come over you? I've guests arriving in a few minutes."

"I needed to tell you that I won't be attending."

"This couldn't have waited until I was dressed?"

"No."

For the first time, she seemed to take note of his countenance, which wisely caused her to hesitate. "But . . . Penelope and her parents will be here. I invited them especially for you."

"Is there some reason I should care that Penelope will be here?" he asked tightly.

"Well, I simply thought . . ."

"Thought what?" The silence began, lengthened, became dreadfully uncomfortable. He waited until his mother actually began to squirm. "When I mentioned that I had made up my mind as to a bride, did you perhaps think I had settled on Penny?"

She licked her lip nervously. "Well, of course. Who else

would you marry? It is the best and only match for you both. I will accept no other decision.''

"Did you tell others that I had selected Penny?''

"I would never usurp such a grand moment from the girl's family. Naturally, the announcement will come from the Westmorelands.''

"Naturally.'' Adam eyed her skeptically. What a horrid liar she was. She'd probably told half of London by now. He tossed the envelope on the desk between them. "I believe this is yours.''

Lucretia's eyes widened in recognition. He saw overt trepidation at first, but she instantly covered it. With her usual haughty disdain, she reached for it and glanced inside. "So, the girl is not only a whore,'' she said maliciously, "but a stupid one at that. If she had any sense, she'd have cashed it.''

Adam's eyes narrowed, taking her measure. He felt as though he was truly looking at her for the first time. What a bitter, hard woman she was. Every harsh word James had ever uttered about her came back to him with a biting clarity. "Did you tell her that I was marrying Penny?''

"What if I did?''

"Did you?'' he shouted, which made her jump.

"I was doing her a favor. She deserved to know that Penelope was the standard by which she was being judged, and that she would be found lacking by all. I merely pointed out the realities of life to her.''

"How kind of you,'' he said sarcastically as he rose to his feet. "I've half a mind to marry her just to spite you for this.''

"That trollop?'' Lucretia gasped.

"I must warn you that you're treading on very thin ice, Mother. You might wish to watch your tongue for a change.''

"You are not your father or your brother. You would never do such a dastardly thing to the family name.''

"Wouldn't I?''

Lucretia harrumphed, refusing to be cowed. "You may have completely lost your senses, but I am still in full possession of mine. The girl was a dalliance for you, and it was long past time the association ended. The rest of your life is just beginning, and it would be an insult to your fiancée to begin your relationship with her while consorting in your private hours with a paid whore.''

''You don't seem to be listening to me. Whether I see Maggie—or any other woman—is none of your affair.''

''It is and will remain so as long as you insist on acting like a spoiled child. You have to do your duty. I'll settle for nothing less.''

''My blasted duty,'' he spat out tersely. ''That will certainly warm my bed at night, won't it, Mother?'' His rage, at her words, at her assuredness, at her contempt for Maggie, was so great that he could barely contain himself. In a soft voice, full of venom, he vowed, ''If you ever involve yourself in my personal affairs again, I will banish you to the country for the remainder of your days.''

''You wouldn't dare.''

''Would you like to test me?'' He took a last, long swallow of his whiskey, watching her over the rim of the glass.

''What has come over you that you think you have the right to speak to me so despicably? I'll not stand for it, I tell you.''

''And I tell you, for the last time, that I will not put up with interference in my personal life from you or anyone else. I am weary of your presence, Mother. Get out of my sight.''

''I will not be dismissed like a servant.''

''Go,'' he shouted, sending her fleeing in a flurry of velvet.

The moment he was alone, he felt better. Liberated. Yes, that was it! Imagine doing just what James had done. Marrying for . . . love. Yes, marrying for love and friendship and affection. His mother and their friends be damned. What if he did it? Could he? Would Maggie have him after the way he'd treated her? Long after Lucretia's footsteps quit echoing in the halls, he remained standing, unable to move because of all the dangerous thoughts cascading through his head.

He loved Maggie and did not want to spend one moment of

his life with anyone else. The very idea made him free, excited, happy. The world was suddenly full of possibilities.

What if he did what he bloody well pleased for a change? What if he married Maggie and to hell with everyone else? It went against everything he'd ever been taught or believed. Could he do it?

Yes.

He had to find her. Nothing mattered but that. He had to find her, to apologize for Penny and his mother, and every stupid, hurtful thing he'd ever said. Then he had to marry her as quickly as possible.

Chapter Twenty-Four

MY ONLY LOVE

Maggie opened her eyes, blinking several times against the brief bit of late afternoon sun pouring through the window. She had to take a moment to get her bearings. In the past two weeks, she'd spent the night in so many different beds, in so many different rooms, that it was difficult to remember where she was.

Slowly, it came to her. Lavinia Billington's. That was it. Charles's mother's home in London. They'd stopped as soon as they arrived back in the city, just in time for the noon meal. Two of Charles's sisters had been visiting. Charles, with his flair for the dramatic, had wasted no time stirring things up by making a grand announcement of what they'd done. This caused a multitude of tears and exclamations, causing his mother to stir herself into a frenzy of activity. She refused to listen to their politely made objections, and Charles merely shrugged as they watched her begin planning announcements and parties, which they stridently insisted they didn't want.

The trip to Gretna Green had been quick and uneventful. The weather had cooperated. Although it had been frightfully cold the entire journey, the skies remained blue, the roads dry and hard-packed. They made good time. Charles was an interesting and polite traveling companion, taking charge of the arrangements and seeing to her comfort.

There was a great deal about the trip and her new marriage that seemed like a dream happening to someone else, but she was well and truly married. By all accounts, to a kind and good man who would provide for her and her child. Most women were not so lucky, and she felt the usual stirrings of guilt because she wasn't happier—for surely she should be. The fact was that she felt wretched, both physically and emotionally. She missed Adam and her home and Anne and her old life. The new one, which had been foisted on her by her pregnancy and swift marriage, had arrived too quickly, without warning, and was not yet one she chose to welcome or embrace.

She sighed heavily.

Things would work out. That was what Charles kept insisting, and undoubtedly, he was right. They both needed more time. Time to get to know one another better. Time to make plans. Time to come to terms with what they'd done. Time to settle into a routine like two normal, married people.

That was the thought that brought her sitting up on the edge of the bed. Lavinia had welcomed her with open arms, as Charles had said she would, in spite of the fact that, shortly after their arrival, she'd learned she was to be a grandmother again. They'd sat down to lunch; Maggie had been famished as she was much of the time these days, but after eating a huge meal, a wave of nausea had quickly overwhelmed her, and she'd had to rush for a retiring room.

Lavinia was no fool, having birthed eight children herself, and by the time Maggie had come back to take her place at the table, Charles had already told her about the babe. Even the news of Maggie's impending motherhood hadn't dimmed Lavinia's excitement over Charles's nuptials. She was downstairs at this very moment planning a myriad of dinner parties and soirees to introduce her new daughter-in-law to friends and family.

Maggie had no desire to meet any of them. She wanted only to be left alone. In order to avoid the festivities Lavinia was hastily throwing together, they needed to head for Charles's country house as soon as possible. Maggie was hoping she could persuade Charles to whisk her away before Lavinia was able to put them on display. The very idea caused her the greatest unease, something that she didn't think was good for her or the babe.

Looking in the mirror, she grimaced over how pale and wan she looked. Somewhere, she'd heard that most pregnant women glowed with health and well-being. She was not one of them, and in fact, seemed to look and feel worse with each passing day. Wanting only quiet and privacy while she struggled to regain some of her energy and peace of mind, she needed to get out of London right away.

With a quick brush through her hair, she headed downstairs to find Charles.

Adam stepped from his carriage and looked up at the front of his Aunt Lavinia's home. It was fairly bursting with activity. Best of all, Charles's carriage was parked in the drive. He hurried up the steps and knocked on the door, impatiently waiting for someone to answer.

The past fortnight had been the worst time of his life as he'd waited for some word of Maggie. There were no hints as to where she was except for the fact that she'd gone out with Charles on the afternoon of her disappearance and had never returned. With glaring certainty, Adam knew that Charles was aware of her location. The bastard had probably been involved in some misguided attempt to help her secrete herself away.

Lavinia was one of the few people who'd not gone to the country for the holidays, and her home was just one of the places he'd stopped every day in his attempts to locate Maggie.

At the first visit, Lavinia had insisted she didn't even know Charles was gone, let alone to where, and at each subsequent visit, she'd had to provide the disappointing news that she'd not heard a word from her son.

Well, he was back today. The carriage was proof.

Adam knocked again, and Hodson, Lavinia's longtime butler, opened the door, then stepped back to allow him entrance. He'd never had to stand on formality with his aunt and was always welcome.

"Is Master Charles about?" he asked the man casually as he removed his gloves.

"Yes, just returned this morning," the usually stoic retainer answered with a dreadfully unusual smile.

Before Adam could ponder what it might mean, Lavinia started down the stairs. Short and round, her gray hair pulled back in a workable bun, she was nearly the double of his mother, except that she'd always managed to look different, due, he supposed, to the complete differences in their personalities. As she descended, Adam noticed that her usually happy face was red and tear-streaked. She dabbed a handkerchief at her eyes, but the move couldn't shield the crinkling of the smile lines around her eyes. These were obviously happy tears.

"Adam . . . oh Adam, I'm so glad you've come," she gushed as she saw him from the bottom of the stairs. "Charles is back."

"Yes, I saw."

"Such news . . ." she said more to herself than to him. "Such good, good news . . ."

He stepped to her and took her hand. "Aunt Vinnie, what has you in such a state?"

"You scalawag! As if you didn't know!" This caused more tears. "Keeping such a wonderful thing from me. I'll bet you knew all the time, didn't you? That's why you've been stopping by, waiting for their return. You knew all the time."

"Knew what?" he asked, but she didn't appear to hear and the feeling of dread began to spiral out of control.

"And she's so lovely. Oh, I just couldn't be happier . . ." Somehow they'd moved to the front drawing room where Lavinia received callers. "I'll find Charles." She smiled, patting his hand as though he was still a child. "You must stay for dinner. We're just having family tonight, but I'll host a full-blown reception as soon as it can be arranged . . ." With that, she disappeared down the hall, completely distracted by whatever great news Charles had apparently brought home.

Several trays of food and drink were already arranged around the room, as though Lavinia planned on receiving many guests throughout the remainder of the day. Adam, having skipped his midday fare, absentmindedly helped himself to various tidbits, so distracted that he couldn't have said what he was putting in his mouth.

Momentarily, he heard steps coming down the hall, but they were light and quick. Female ones, he could tell. The figure stopped in the doorway, and he glanced up expecting to see one of his cousins. He looked. Looked again. Blinked twice, wondering if his eyes were playing tricks.

"Maggie?"

"Adam?" She had to focus her eyes in order to convince herself his presence was real and not an illusion. Why had he come here so shortly after they'd arrived?

Oh, God, I can't face him alone! She took a fearful step back. "What are you doing here?"

"I was looking for you. Actually, I was looking for Charles." He smiled, taking a step toward her, and she took another back, which took her out into the hall. "Where have you been?" he asked. "I've been looking everywhere."

"I need to find Charles . . ." Panic struck as she glanced down the hall, looking for Charles, a servant, Lavinia, anyone who might serve as a barrier between them.

"Aunt Vinnie just went to fetch him. Come here." He took another step, and when she glanced down the hall again, he grabbed her arm and pulled her into the room, ushering her to one of the small settees, where they were forced to sit so closely their thighs touched. He slipped his hand into hers and kept it with a firm grip, wondering why he was certain she'd run off if he let go. She was trembling and looked pale and drawn as though she'd been ill. When she turned those lovely violet eyes on him, they glistened with tears.

"What's the matter, little one? Are you feeling all right?"

"Oh, Adam . . ." Up close, she could see that the past two weeks had been as hard on him as they had been on her. He looked as miserable as she felt.

"Tell me what's amiss," he said. Her hands felt like ice, and he tried to warm them between his own. Since she seemed to have been rendered speechless, he tried to fill the uncomfortable gap. "I know what happened with Mother. And with Penelope. I know they both hurt you, and I'm so sorry. I swear it won't ever happen again." No response. "Are you angry with me?"

"With you? My goodness, no."

She tried to pull her hands away from his, but he held tight. "I know you're upset with the way I've treated you, and you have every right to be. I've been thinking so much . . . ever since I found out what Mother did." She glanced down at their joined hands, and he raised one to lift her chin so she'd be looking at him when he told her. "I love you, Maggie. I don't know why I couldn't say it to you before. I love you more than anything."

This time, she succeeded in pulling her hands away. Jumping to her feet, she rubbed at her ears as though hearing his words made them hurt. "Don't say such a thing to me."

"Why not? It's true."

"But it doesn't mean anything."

"It means everything. It means I want you with me always. I can't live without you."

"What?!" she gasped.

"You heard me. I want you with me. I don't care what anyone says. I don't care what anyone thinks. I had plenty of time to think while you were away, and I realized what I truly wanted. I want you. Whatever I said or did, whatever others said or did, that made you run away, let's put it behind us and start again.''

"You're serious." She covered her mouth with a look of horror and turned her back on him. "Oh, God, you're serious . . .''

"Of course, I am. You know me well enough to know I'd never joke about such a thing as this. Will you marry me?"

Marriage? He wanted to marry her? Now? After she'd made it impossible for them to ever be together? She started to shake violently and had to put distance between them, so she crossed to the other side of the room. He wouldn't stop talking, and his words, meant to be those of love and adoration, felt like sharp spikes jabbing and poking in her most vulnerable spots.

"Stop it, Adam. Stop it, please. You're hurting me."

"How?" He stood and went to her side, resting her hands on her shoulders and turning her to face him. "How am I hurting you?"

"Don't do this. Please," she begged, looking at his chest, unable to look him in the eye. He wasn't supposed to care about what happened to her! He'd said he wouldn't! That he'd never change his ways. That he'd never marry the likes of her. After all that had happened in the past few weeks, this was simply too much to bear.

Charles's voice came from the doorway. "Maggie, are you all right?"

"Oh, Charles . . ." Rescue! Safety! It seemed so absurd that she would seek it from Charles rather than Adam. The whole world had tipped out of alignment, even the floor seemed to have tilted, and she could barely walk over to him. His hand beckoned to her like a lifeline, and she grasped it as tightly as she could. He pulled her close, and they huddled with their heads close together.

Charles whispered, "I just found out he was here from Mother. Did you tell him?"

"No, I couldn't. Oh, Charles, it's just the worst thing. I need to get out of here . . ."

He squeezed her hand. "You go on. I'll take care of this. We'll talk after he leaves."

"All right. Thank you." She looked over her shoulder, her heart breaking at the forlorn look in Adam's eyes. So much needed to be said, but she couldn't voice any of the words. "I'm sorry, Adam. I'm so sorry."

Adam stood stock-still. Her voice was so charged with emotion, the regret coursing so loudly about the room, that Adam felt tears come to his eyes. As she made a rapid exit, his heart was pounding so loudly that he wondered if Charles could hear it in the deafening silence. He looked at his cousin. Waiting. Refusing to start the conversation that would explain whatever was coming.

"I'm glad you're here," Charles said softly as he went to the door and closed it firmly. "I was going to come find you today after everything settled down with Mother and my sisters."

"Why?"

"Well, mostly I didn't want you to hear the news from anyone else."

He didn't want to know the answer but knew he had to ask. "What news?"

"I guess there's no gentle way to say this, so here goes." He fiddled with a napkin on the table. "Maggie and I were married last week."

Adam's knees buckled, and he had to reach for the back of a chair to steady himself. "What did you say?"

"We were married."

"You can't mean it," he said desperately.

"It's true, Adam. I'd say I'm sorry, but I'm not. I simply thought we should talk, so we could work out a few sticky problems."

"You're my cousin and my best friend. You've married the only woman I care about in the entire world, and you think we might have a few *problems* to work out?'' He struggled to control his breathing, his outrage and shock so great that he could barely speak. ''How observant of you. By all means, let's discuss the first item on your list.''

''Certainly,'' Charles murmured agreeably, trying to inject some calm into the situation. ''For starters, Maggie doesn't want her path to cross with yours in the months and years to come, and I agree it's a good idea. You and I need to work out a way to make it easier on her.''

''She never wants to see me again?'' The finality of her rash act was only beginning to register, and he heard the childlike tone in his voice, but he was simply incredulous that she'd wish for such a thing.

''Adam, she doesn't want to hurt you, but you know a clean break is the only way. It's for the best.''

''The best for whom? I love her. I wanted to marry her myself. I can't believe she'd do something this wretched.''

Charles gave him an encompassing, unemotional stare. ''Frankly, she didn't think you'd care what she did one way or another. What with your marriage looming, I didn't think you would either.''

''Not care? About her? About this?'' He made a futile gesture in the air, indicating the marriage and all it entailed. Suddenly, there wasn't enough air in the room. ''I have always been your friend. How could you do such a thing to me?''

''I had my reasons.''

''There couldn't be a reason good enough in the entire world for what you've done. I could kill you.''

''Why? Why are you even angry?'' When Adam made no response, he continued. ''The way I see it, I'm merely cleaning up the mess you've made of that girl's life. You should be thanking me instead of threatening me.''

''I offered her everything,'' Adam tried to insist, even as he knew he voiced a lie. In the great scheme of things, he'd offered her hardly anything at all.

''No. You offered her a few tumbles. In *her* bed, may I

remind you, not your own. I guess she wasn't worthy enough to share the bed of the great Marquis of Belmont.''

"What a despicable thing to say to me.''

"Why? Isn't that exactly how you feel? Exactly how you've always felt?''

"Maybe in the past. But I don't feel that way any longer.''

"How bloody convenient.'' Charles laughed, but it was a mean sound. "It's incredibly interesting to me that you've had this great change of heart when she's no longer available to you. Well, for once in your life, you'll just have to accept the fact that you can't always have everything you want.''

Adam ignored the slight, wanting only for Charles to see how inappropriate he was to be Maggie's partner. "She should have a real husband. Someone who can give her children.''

"I'll give her children if she wants them,'' he lied, thinking about Adam's babe already growing in Maggie's stomach.

"You?'' Adam gave a derisive snort. "With your injury?''

"I've been feeling better lately,'' he lied again. "She's pretty and very sweet.'' Overly sensitive at the insult to his manhood, he goaded Adam in return. "If she needs bedding, I'm sure I'll be *up* to the challenge.''

With the rude taunt, Adam's temper exploded. "You're nothing but an impotent swindler. How dare you think to touch her with your filthy hands!''

Seeing red, Charles answered, "If I decide to touch her, it will be with more than my filthy hands.''

"You bastard!'' Adam's anger flared to a fevered pitch. The thought of Charles lying down with Maggie was the ultimate betrayal, the ultimate insult. Before he realized what he was about, he clenched a fist and let fly with a hard right. Charles hadn't been expecting such a thing, and caught the blow full on his left cheek. His head snapped back, and he stumbled across a small table, scattering china and cups into tiny pieces. Quick as a cat, he was on his feet ready to give as good as he got, which was exactly what he was doing when they heard the indignant shout from the doorway.

"Boys! Boys! What on earth ... ?" Lavinia ran into the room with Hodson and several footmen on her heels, the male servants jumping in immediately to pull the two combatants apart. Both puffing hard, they were bloody and bruised, various bits of clothing torn and hanging. With arms pinned behind their backs, they both continued to struggle.

Lavinia stepped between them, a flat hand to each chest. "I swear, the two of you haven't matured a minute since you were ten years old. Fighting in my parlor like a pair of street urchins!" She turned an assessing eye on her son. "You stay in here." Then to Hodson, who continued to tightly grip Adam. "Show Lord Belmont to the door, please."

The look she gave Adam let him know she'd brook no argument. He wrenched his arm away from Hodson and walked out of the room to the foyer, wiping at his bloody lip with his forearm. On his heels, he could hear Lavinia stomping angrily. She was a tiny woman but formidable when vexed.

A female servant was holding the door, all the men in the place having been summoned to help end the altercation in the sitting room. She held out his things, and he draped his cloak over his arm. Lavinia looked very much as if she might pick him up and bodily toss him out.

Though he knew she was waiting for him to go, and that he had to depart, he couldn't force his feet to move. His heart felt as though it had been shattered into a million pieces. His lifelong bond with Charles was completely severed. His relationship with Maggie was finished in the most horrible way possible. With glaring certainty, he knew that if he left now, he'd never have another chance to speak with her, but there was no way he could ask to see her.

Feeling very much as though he might burst into tears, he looked imploringly at his aunt. "Aunt Vinnie, I'm sorry."

"I'm sure you are, Adam, but I'm so furious with you at the moment that I want you to leave. You may come and make your apologies another day when we're all more calm."

"I didn't mean for any of this to happen."

"I'm sure Charles didn't, either. His emotions have to be very strong. There's so much that's happened to him all at once, what with his marriage to Maggie and their new babe on the way ..."

Birds were silenced. Clocks stopped ticking. Carriage wheels out on the street quit turning. Mouths went still. People froze in place. Time, itself, seemed to stop.

Deathly quiet, Adam asked, "What did you say?"

Just then, footsteps in the hall brought his head swinging up and around. Maggie stood there, haloed from behind by sunlight shining in a window. He wanted to lash out at her, to strike her with words and hands. A great storm of fury, more than he'd ever known could exist inside a man, was building, and for the first time, he understood how a person could be enraged enough to commit murder.

He hissed, "Is it true?"

"Adam ..." She held out a beseeching hand.

"Is it true?" he shouted.

Maggie flinched. She had never wanted him to find out this way. Wishing more than anything that she could lie, but knowing she couldn't, not about this, she nodded. "Yes."

"I will never forgive you for this as long as I live."

Chapter Twenty-Five

Adam vanished so quickly that it was as if he'd disappeared in a cloud of smoke. Lavinia closed the door and leaned against it wearily.

"I'm sorry, dear," she said to Maggie, "but that was my nephew, Adam . . ." She paused, confused. "Well, you obviously know who he is. I don't know what's come over him. Or Charles."

"I can't imagine, either," Maggie lied, feeling shaken and sick at heart.

Charles stepped out of the drawing room just then, with several bewildered servants on his heels. Lavinia scattered the servants back to their duties with a look and a gesture of her hands.

"Oh . . . my . . ." Maggie winced at Charles's condition. His nose was bleeding, his clothing was in tatters, and an eye was turning black and blue.

"I'm sorry, Mother," he said. "I'm sorry about everything."

"As well you should be."

Maggie stepped to Charles's side and squeezed his hand. "Are you all right?"

"Nothing a few glasses of brandy and a soak in a hot tub won't take care of. Adam never could fight worth a—"

"Charles!" Lavinia glared at him. "I won't have you talking this way."

Charles sighed, and Maggie could see what the effort at levity was costing him.

"You're right, Mother. It was uncalled for." He ran a bruised hand through his hair. "I know you had plans for us for supper, but I don't think I'm up to it just now. Maggie and I are exhausted. I just want to see her home."

Thank you, Maggie mouthed, facing away from Lavinia so she wouldn't see.

"You won't mind, will you?" He tried to flash his mother one of the smiles that had never failed to charm her, but with his bottom lip split and oozing blood, it was painful. "We'll come another time."

"I suppose it's not the best of nights for it," Lavinia reluctantly agreed.

Within minutes, they were in his carriage, huddled under heavy quilts and headed for the house where he both lived and painted. Maggie fussed over him. "Are you really all right?"

"Yes. It only hurts when I breathe."

"That's not funny."

He took a sharp breath, then let it out slowly. "Lord, what a mess I've made of things."

"What happened between the two of you?"

"Adam said some things . . ." He rubbed an injured hand over his eyes, closing them against whatever visions he was seeing. "I don't know . . . He just made me so bloody angry, so I said some things back."

"What things?"

"Let's just say that I don't think we'll have to worry about his path crossing with either of ours. I can't imagine it happening ever again."

With that admission, Maggie leaned forward, her elbows on her knees, and started to cry. They were quiet tears, and it felt good to shed them, as though they'd been waiting forever for the opportunity to wet her cheeks. Not even bothering to try to stop them, she rested her chin in her hands and let the tears slide where they willed themselves to go. Before long they were dripping down her wrists and onto her lap. Charles let her have her silent moments, giving comfort by stroking his hand up and down her back.

"It's been a hell of a day, eh?" he asked as the carriage rattled to a halt.

"Yes. A horrible, horrible day." They sat in silence for a very long time before Maggie noticed they weren't moving. She looked around. "Are we here?"

"Yes." He gave a weary nod.

"Why didn't you say something? The way I'm feeling, we might have been sitting out here all night."

"I imagined you'd notice the cold sooner or later." He opened the door, then held out a hand to her. "Let's go in, shall we?"

"I'm a mess," she insisted, swiping at her eyes with her sleeve. "What will your servants think?"

"There's just my manservant. And the cook. They won't notice."

"At the moment, I'm so fatigued that I don't care if they do."

Charles stepped down slowly, his ribs and other places obviously giving him quite a bit of discomfort. It was already dark, the winter day being a short one, so it was hard to see much, but the street was a busy one with many people coming and going. Charles had said he lived in an area frequented by musicians, actors, and the like. His own house was a small one, in a line of town houses, and from his descriptions, she imagined that it would be very much like her own.

He gave her a minute to take in the street and the surroundings, then gallantly offered his arm. "Shall we?"

"Thank you, kind sir. I would be delighted."

They hadn't taken more than two steps away from the carriage when a young, dark-haired man appeared out of the shadows blocking their path. His sudden arrival frightened her, and she instinctively took a step back. Charles held tight to her arm.

"Hello, Robert," he said calmly, obviously addressing someone he knew. "What are you doing here?"

"I've been waiting for you to return!" the man said, sounding thoroughly put out. "Where have you been?"

"Robert," Charles began slowly, as though addressing a stubborn child, "I've explained to you time and again that my whereabouts are not your concern."

Appearing not to hear, Robert said, "It's been over two weeks!"

"You've been watching the house all this time?"

"Of course. I had to know the minute you returned."

"So you've been standing out in the street in the middle of the night?"

"Your man wouldn't let me wait in the house," he said, petulantly.

More gently, Charles said, "You'll make yourself ill acting like this. What are you thinking?"

"If I catch pneumonia, my death will be on your hands."

Charles sighed, then squeezed Maggie's hand as though needing reassurance. "Robert, this is Mrs. Billington. My wife."

Robert gave a quick intake of breath at the introduction. "What? You can't be serious!"

"Yes, I am. Very serious. That's why I've been away. We've only just returned home, and we're exhausted. I'll speak with you later."

He made a move to step around the young man, but Robert blocked their way. "My father has been asking about what happened to the money. I've been frantic about how to answer him, and now I learn that you've been off frolicking on your wedding trip. How much did it cost? I wonder. How were you able to afford such a thing?"

The door to the town house opened, and a man stepped out

with a lantern in hand. "Master Charles, I thought I heard your carriage." He hesitated the briefest second. "Is there a problem, sir?"

"No. Robert was just leaving."

"Very good, sir."

"Charles . . ." Robert was nearly begging.

"Just go, Robert. Go away." Charles brushed him aside this time, and the manservant hustled Charles and Maggie into the house, closing the door on Robert and the cold winter night. As the door swung shut, Maggie happened to catch a glimpse of Robert. He looked angry, so angry he was trembling.

Charles handed his cloak and hat to his manservant, amid welcomes and secret signals passed with raised brows, which Maggie knew would lead to private discussions between the two men later. No doubt Robert's antics on the doorstep for the past two weeks would be the main topic.

She couldn't help wondering what was going on with the young man. He and Charles were obviously having a disagreement about money. Why? And what kind of dealings would Charles have been involved in that would have forced one of his business partners to huddle on his stoop in the middle of a winter night? That question made her ask herself an even more important one: What did she really know about Charles?

What had she gotten herself into? He'd told her that he had a sufficient income, that he could provide her a stable home, but was it true? She had only his word to go on, and it was too late now if he'd been less than honest about his life and finances. She had made her choice and would have to live with it. Behind her eyes, she could feel a fierce headache forming.

She reached for the clasp of her cloak, but found that her fingers were too chilled from the night air to manage. Charles reached to help her. His cheeks were red, and she was fairly sure it wasn't all from the cold.

Softly, he said, "I'm sorry about that. It will be taken care of."

"Is he a friend of yours?"

"Never a friend. Merely an acquaintance." With an agonizing sigh pushing at his injured ribs, he added, "What a day!
Tomorrow will be better. I promise."

Adam sat in the Blue Room in the east wing of his home,
staring out the window as he'd done all night ever since
returning from Lavinia's the previous evening. Day was just
breaking. He was still covered with blood; his clothing was
ripped and torn, but he didn't care. All he could think about
was Maggie and what she'd done.

He'd headed for the small room immediately on returning
home. His valet, the only one brave enough to knock, had tried
to convince him to come out a few times, but had eventually
given up, the entire staff seeming to come to the conclusion
that he was best left alone until whatever crisis he was suffering
through had passed. So he'd sat here in the cold and the dark,
and couldn't seem to move away from the small room where
he felt her presence so strongly. After all, this was the only
place in his enormous, unwelcoming palace where she had ever
set foot.

It was the same room where he'd made such sweet, desperate
love to her on the morning of James's wedding. How brave
she'd been that day, to breach the fortress of his home, to
insinuate herself into the part of his life where he'd never made
her welcome. How wise she'd been in her counsel about James,
about the unmendable split that would be created if he didn't
attend the marriage ceremony.

How stupidly proud he'd been in return. Refusing to attend.
Refusing to acknowledge the marriage. Refusing to accept Anne
as his sister-in-law. James had been gone for months now
without so much as a note sent in the interim, while in all the
past years of their lives, they'd hardly passed a day without
speaking. Maggie had been so bloody right about how his
arrogant pride would hurt James, but then, she usually was

right about such things. She understood people as he did not and never would.

What a joke to be Adam St. Clair, Lord Belmont, one of the richest, most powerful aristocrats in the kingdom. None of it mattered. Not really. Not the titles or bloodlines or the wealth and authority they vested. Not the duties or the responsibilities, because none of it could give him what he really desired. Not James's forgiveness. And certainly not Maggie's love.

In all his life, he'd never considered himself a greedy man, simply because whatever he'd wanted had been his. The finest homes, the best clothing, the tastiest foods, the rarest wines, the brightest jewels. Everything had been his for the asking. So he'd rarely asked for anything, because everything was simply there. His.

In all of his twenty-nine years, he could only think of one thing he'd truly wanted. But it wasn't a thing; it was a person. Maggie. She was the only thing. For the longest time, he'd lied to himself and convinced himself that it wasn't possible, he simply couldn't have her. She was not one of the things he could ever possess.

When he'd finally come to the realization that he couldn't live without her, what had happened? His vows of love, his proposal of marriage, were tossed back in his face. While secretly carrying their child, she'd run off to wed another without a single thought to how Adam might feel about it.

A small voice called out from deep inside: *But you told her you would never want a child with her. You told her you would abandon her if it happened. What was she supposed to do?* Unquestionably, he'd said those things, and he'd meant them at the time, but no longer. He was a changed man. Changed because of her.

Prepared to throw caution to the wind, he'd been ready to toss aside every tenet he'd ever learned, every role he'd ever assumed. To suffer the ridicule and torment of his peers. To be ostracized, scandalized. And for what?

For nothing.

What was left now?

Only one thing. Hatred.

He hated her with a strong, livid passion. It was a torrential thing that seemed to have taken on a life of its own over the course of the night. His heart seemed not to have been merely broken, but to have been dragged from his chest and ripped into a thousand pieces while it was still beating. In retribution, he wanted to hurt her, and to continue hurting her every day for the rest of her life. He never wanted her agony to end, just as, he firmly believed, his own never would.

If that small, insistent voice kept chirping that one of the reasons he was so enraged was that she'd chosen so well, he paid it no heed. At heart, Charles was a good and honorable man. He would take care of her and Adam's child. Adam's first. Very likely his first son. In the long run, Maggie would end up happy with the decision she'd made, but Adam never would be, for no matter how many legitimate children he sired, no matter how many sons his lawful wife birthed, he would always know that his firstborn, the child conceived by his one true love, was being raised by someone else just down the street.

He didn't want Maggie to be happy. Not ever. For her choice of marrying Charles, this good resolution in the face of pending calamity, he could never forgive her.

As dawn slowly crept over the winter sky, and the gray, dreary day came into focus, he realized the one thing he could do that would effectively torment her all her days. He could think of nothing else. Nothing better. She believed it was his intent, anyway. Let it become reality.

His decision made, he returned to his suite of rooms. The bath was a long one, much needed to wash away the blood and soreness from the day before. The shave was tricky, considering his black eye and swollen cheek and lip. His bruised knuckles ached so badly that he'd finally had his valet finish the job, something he usually did himself. Dressed in his finest morning clothes, he ate a light breakfast, then headed off in his carriage.

At the Westmorelands', he wasn't surprised to find that the Duke was still abed. His refusal to leave, and his insistence on seeing Harold at once, had the desired effect. The butler deposited him in a sitting room, then hurried off to find the appropriate people to see if anyone dared awaken the exalted gentleman.

Adam waited patiently, taking little time to wonder what Harold would think. He'd never kept their appointment two weeks earlier when he'd intended to end any speculation regarding an engagement with Penny. What they'd thought of his rude lapse, he didn't care. He'd done little the past fortnight but search for Maggie. Well, his days of worrying over her were at an end.

Fifteen minutes later, a footman appeared with the news that the Duke would be down shortly and had asked if they could talk over breakfast. No, Adam said. Take him to the Duke's study. This wasn't a social call.

The perplexed footman hustled off, returned shortly, and led Adam to the room he'd requested. Harold arrived shortly. Not shaved, but dressed.

"This better be good," he grumbled as he huffed into the room. Not until he was seated behind his desk did he look up and notice Adam's injuries. "Bloody hell, what happened?"

"Nothing that concerns you." With no emotion whatsoever, he continued. "I've been busy the past two weeks. During that time, have you accepted a marriage proposal on Penelope's behalf?"

"No."

"Good." He opened the folder he'd brought along and laid a stack of papers on the desk. "I accept your offer."

"Just like that?"

"Just like that." Harold suddenly appeared much more awake, and Adam shoved the papers across to him. "I assume my proposal is accepted as well?"

"Of course," he croaked, whether from sleep or surprise it was hard to tell. Clearing his throat, he added more forcefully, "Certainly."

"These documents contain a list of the items I need considered in the contracts. Pass them on to your solicitor and tell him to work out the details with mine. I'd like to sign the final copies by next Monday."

Harold's brows shot up at this. "I'm sure we can work it out by then."

"Very well. I'll see you when they're ready." Adam stood to leave.

"Wait!" Harold stood, too, waving a hand to try to get Adam to sit back down, but he remained on his feet. "Would you like to see Penelope?"

"What for?"

"To ... I don't know. Perhaps you'd like to ask her in person?"

"Not really."

"How about discussion of the details?"

"Like what?"

"Well ... ah ... sending out the announcements to the papers. Choosing the date of the wedding. Things like that."

"I don't care about any of those things. Whatever she chooses to arrange will be acceptable to me."

Harold's eyes narrowed. "Are you sure you're feeling all right?"

"What makes you ask?"

"It's just that ..." He took a deep breath, blew it out. "After all this time, this just seems so sudden. You're obviously extremely upset. Has something happened?"

"Nothing has happened. Send a message round when the contracts are ready for signing." With that, he showed himself out.

Harold stood in shocked silence for several minutes, then dropped back in his chair. If he wasn't so grumpy about being awakened by his valet, he'd swear he was dreaming. The papers Adam had left were still there in the center of the desk, living proof that he'd really been present. He was almost afraid to touch them, as though they were some living, dangerous thing.

Nothing about this felt right. If he knew anything in the world, he knew Adam St. Clair and how he made decisions. He didn't make them hastily. He didn't rush into anything, and he most certainly didn't leave important, crucial details about his life to others. Whatever had happened to him in the past few days had been overwhelming and brutal, and Harold was nearly tempted to hold off on the contracts until he could figure out what was going on.

He liked Adam; he always had—which was the main reason he wanted him as Penelope's husband. If a man had to have a son-in-law, there could be none better than Adam. He would be a welcome addition to the family, which was why Harold didn't want to see him rushing into some half-baked, crazy scheme from which he'd be unable to extricate himself later on.

When that idiotic thought finished spiraling its way to conclusion, Harold physically shook himself back to reality. The match between Penny and Adam was something he'd been working toward and planning on for over a decade. It wasn't crazy or half-baked, and if Adam was having a hard time about something in his personal life, he'd get over it eventually and be glad he'd finally selected Penny.

"What the hell? It will all work out for the best," he muttered to himself as he picked up the papers and began leafing through them.

Shortly, he heard Penny rushing down the hall. He should have known her maid would drag her out of bed once Adam's presence was noted by the staff. She hurried in, barely dressed, her hair not even combed.

"Father," she started, breathless from her run down all the stairs, "I heard Adam was here."

"Yes."

"It's about time he showed his face. What did he want?"

Harold held up the papers, for some reason feeling no victory in the announcement. "He's finally decided to offer for you."

Penny didn't even smile. "Did you talk to him about that awful woman with whom he keeps company?"

Harold had heard more than he wanted to about Penny's untimely encounter with Maggie. From Penny and from others. No one knew Penny better than he did, and he actually felt sorry for Maggie at having to put up with her during such a public spectacle. "Don't be stupid," he said.

"Well, I'll show him. If he thinks he can treat me so shabbily, I won't accept," she insisted with her cute, upturned nose stuck up in the air.

Harold sighed. He'd sheltered her too much in her upbringing, so perhaps some of this was his fault, but by God, she was going to have a hell of a surprise when the realties of life started slapping her in the face. "I've already accepted. We'll sign the contracts on Monday."

"You might have asked my opinion," she pouted.

He silenced the whine with a raised brow.

She asked, "When will the wedding be?"

"He said you can set it for whenever you want."

"Doesn't he care?"

"He said any date would be fine."

"What about all the planning?"

He shrugged. "Up to you."

"When is he coming by to ask for my hand?"

"He's not."

"What do you mean? He has to! I've picked out the dress I'll wear and everything!"

He really, really could not abide these silly romantic notions she seemed to harbor about all this. "Adam considers the matter handled by speaking to me. I suggest you don't make too big an issue of it."

"Oh, how could he do this to me?" she wailed, stomping her foot. "I hate him. I hate him already."

Chapter Twenty-Six

Maggie heard the knock on the front door, but she simply couldn't rouse herself to answer it. With the birth only a month away, she was huge as a house, and rising to her feet by herself was a matter of great accomplishment.

"Appleby!" she called to Charles's valet, hoping he could get the door, until she remembered that he had gone out, escorting her personal maid on a few errands. The cook was busy in the kitchen, and wouldn't think of answering the door anyway. Charles was out interviewing with a new client. There was no one else. The rapping sounded again, and she struggled to her feet.

"I'm coming, I'm coming. Hold your horses!" she muttered ungraciously, fiddling with the lock, which had to remain in place at all times, lest "Mad Robert"—as they'd taken to calling him—decided to make himself at home in the downstairs parlor. It had been known to happen on more than one occasion.

He had followed them to Charles's country home where they'd spent three months, then back to London again when they'd come to the city for a showing of some of Charles's paintings. Once they'd arrived, one thing and another had caused them to stay on, and now it was June and an unpleasant one at that. No one could remember when it had been more unbearably hot.

Through it all, Robert kept a vigil. Outside their home, outside Lavinia's, riding behind their carriage when they went somewhere. Maggie suspected that he followed Charles other places, but, if he did, Charles never mentioned it. He had tried everything to rid himself of their shadow. Incessant talks, harsh words, kind words, small amounts of money. Nothing worked. The poor young man was simply obsessed with Charles, and whatever the reason, Charles had been kind enough not to share it with her. She didn't want to know; she only wanted Robert gone from their lives.

As she swung the door open, fully expecting to see the pathetic creature on the doorstep, and thinking about all the nasty names she'd call him for causing her to rise on such a hot, sticky afternoon, she blinked, then blinked again, then asked in wonder, "Annie? Is it really you?"

Looking lovelier than ever, Anne threw her arms open wide, and Maggie fell into them. "Maggie! Oh, Maggie!"

"What are you doing here?" Maggie managed to ask between hugs and kisses.

"We arrived last night. Too late to call. And now I've spent all day trying to locate you." Anne stepped back, taking in Maggie's bulging physique, then rubbing a hand across her swollen stomach. She flashed a huge, watery smile, and said sarcastically, "I leave you alone for a few months, and look what happens!"

"I'm so glad you're here."

"So am I." She gave Maggie another tight hug. "You look so beautiful."

"I feel like a cow," Maggie insisted, which caused Anne to chuckle as they held hands and walked into the parlor. Once they were seated, Maggie said, "Tell me everything . . ."

Anne did, beginning with her wedding night and moving on to their sea voyage and the small villa they'd rented on the coast of southern Italy. The food, the flowers, the heat, the water. It sounded like a fairy tale, a magical time filled with only romance and love.

The longer Anne talked, the more Maggie realized that her friend was glowing. That was the only word adequate enough to describe how she looked.

"And look at you," Maggie couldn't help commenting during a pause in Anne's narrative. "You look well loved and so happy."

"I am. Oh, Maggie, I am. I wake up every morning afraid to open my eyes for fear that I'm dreaming."

"How is James?"

"He's so good. He'll be along shortly, I imagine. He wanted to come with me, but he had some things to attend to, and I couldn't wait to see you."

"I'd say marriage definitely agrees with you."

"It does, very much." With her usual critical eye, she gave Maggie an assessing look. "How about you? Does marriage agree with you?"

"Of course, it does."

"You don't look very happy."

"It's hard to be anything but miserable when you're as pregnant as I am." She tried for a smile to make it sound like a joke, but it didn't work. She wasn't happy, and Anne was too shrewd to be lied to about it.

Softly, she asked, "Is it Adam's child?"

"Yes," Maggie admitted without hesitation. A few tears slipped down her cheeks, and she wiped them away.

"I thought so," she nodded. "What happened?"

Maggie shrugged. "I found out I was with child, and I was so scared. I didn't know what to do."

"Damn, I wish I had been here. Did you tell him?"

"No. Charles learned of it, though, and he convinced me that marrying him would be the best solution."

"Well, that's a relief. I thought perhaps Adam had tossed you out once he learned you were in the family way. If that was the case, I was seriously thinking about killing him." Anne took her hand. "And was Charles right? Did it turn out to be the best solution?"

"It was the very best solution." She paused and swallowed back a wave of tears. With her pregnancy so advanced, her emotional state was running at a fevered pitch, and everything made her weep. "But I am so desperately unhappy."

"It's not because of Charles, is it?"

"No, oh, no. I've grown to love Charles very much. He is a wonderful man. He's kind and considerate and cheerful. It's just that . . ." She broke off, unable to finish the thought that was so traitorous to her generous husband.

"You wish you were sharing this time with Adam?"

Maggie sighed with relief that Anne understood. All these months, there'd been no one she could talk to about her appalling attitude. She felt ungrateful—which made her only more wretched. How could she not be happy after all the wonderful things Charles had done for her? What was the matter with her that she couldn't see any of the good but only the bad? Having her first child should be the greatest moment of her life, but she didn't look forward to it at all. Everything seemed wrong without Adam by her side to share in the building memories.

"Yes," she said, "I wish every day that he was here, which only goes to show how stupid I am."

"What makes you say that?"

"Because he is such a despicable swine. He doesn't deserve one second of grieving from me." With great difficulty, she pushed herself up from the couch, and Anne steadied her on her feet. "Did you know he's marrying next month?"

"We just learned of it this morning. Is it true what I heard?"

"That it's Penelope? Yes."

Anne looked mortified. "Did you ever tell him how you're related to her?"

Maggie nodded. "In all the time I knew him, I only asked him to do two things. The first was to attend your wedding."

"Well, we all saw how that went."

"Yes. The second was to please not marry my sister."

"You're right," Anne said with a sigh. "He's a despicable swine."

"He's worse than despicable. Not only is he marrying her, but he's doing it after he swore to me that he would never hurt me by doing such a thing. He went behind my back, and I had to learn the truth from Penelope while we were standing in a dressing room at Madame LeFarge's. Then his mother accosted me in my home because she wanted to be sure I'd heard. Lucretia even offered me money to go away."

"Gad." Anne shook her head in disgust. "No wonder you ran off with Charles. I would have, too."

"Exactly. Except, then, when we returned from Scotland, Adam showed up all sorry for how he'd treated me, professing this great love for me and saying that he'd had a change of heart and wanted to marry me. That he didn't care what anyone thought or said about it." Maggie rubbed a hand between her breasts, trying to massage her broken heart. "It was the most horrible moment of my entire life."

"He must have loved you very much, Maggie, to offer to do such a thing," Anne said, hoping the realization would ease some of the ache. "James has always insisted that Adam loved you, but that he couldn't admit it to himself or to you. What did you say to him?"

"What could I say? Charles and I were already married."

"How utterly dreadful," Anne commiserated. "I wish I'd stayed here. Maybe I could have helped prevent all this somehow."

"You couldn't have changed anything." Maggie waved a distracted hand. "He got engaged to Penny the day after he learned I was married. And here. Look at these." While they'd been talking, she'd rifled through her writing desk, looking for the folder hidden in the bottom of the drawer. She pulled it out and handed it to Anne. No one had seen the contents, not even Charles.

"What are they?" Anne asked, scanning the various items, but Maggie could see from the troubled look in her eye that she knew.

"Someone's sending them to me. It starts with the first bit of printed gossip about his betrothal. It goes on to the official announcement of his engagement and then all the news about them both that came after that."

"Where did these come from? Who's doing this?"

"It has to be Adam. Who else? Every time he and Penelope are together and it's mentioned in the papers, or they host an event or attend one or some such nonsense, he cuts out the article or saves the invitation and sends it to me. It's as though he wants to keep hurting me with the news over and over again."

"Why, that is simply the most ghastly thing I've ever heard. Have you showed these to Charles?"

"What could he do?"

Anne closed the file and handed it back to Maggie. "You know? This morning, I stopped by our old house, expecting to find you. Your maid, Gail, is still working there, and she was dying to gossip. She said Adam spends most of his time there now."

"You're joking! He hated that place. He always insisted it was beneath his status."

"I know, but it's like he's made it into a sort of private haven where he can be by himself for long periods of time. She said he's never been the same since the day you left."

"What does she think is the matter with him? Did she say?"

Whatever answer Anne might have given would have to wait till another time, for just at that moment, James and Charles arrived outside simultaneously. The two men burst into the house together, amid hugs and welcomes. Maggie huddled herself in the corner while her three favorite people in the world laughed and talked. It was simply impossible to be in the same

room with the trio and not have a smile on her face. For the
first time in a very long time, some of the sadness weighing
so heavily in her heart began to lift.

Penelope stood on the back terrace of the mansion looking
out toward the gardens. Moonlight combined with burning
torches, and she could make out large numbers of people strolling
along the walkways. It was absolutely too hot to remain
inside, and out here, there was a slight breeze off the river to
help cool heated skin. She fanned her face to aid in the process.
No one noticed her where she stood off to the side, hiding in
the shadows.

With her wedding only weeks away, her life was much freer
now, which was one benefit of pending marriage. One of the
few that she could see. If she wanted to stroll outside by herself,
she could. If she wanted to walk through the gardens, no one
would detain her. If she wanted to huddle on a bench, stealing
kisses in the dark with her fiancé, no one would chastise her.

A bitter laugh escaped her throat. As if that would ever
happen! In the six months of their engagement, Adam had
kissed her exactly twice. Both times it was a brief peck on the
cheek as though he were a brother or cousin. While she knew
such a chaste embrace was the only appropriate one she should
have before she married, she couldn't help wishing that Adam
would take her in his arms and sweep her off her feet in a
moment of unbridled passion.

It could happen that way, she knew. She'd hidden more than
a few romantic novels under her bed over the years. He should
be fevered for her by now, waiting with unveiled impatience
for their marital joining, but he continued to treat her with the
same cool detachment he'd always shown. Why, he treated
her very much the way her father treated her mother! With
unwavering respect and courtesy, but never any show of genuine
emotion.

At times, although she'd never admit it to anyone, it seemed as though Adam didn't even like her, let alone love her. While she understood all the reasons that led to a union such as theirs, in her eighteen-year-old heart, she couldn't help wishing for a grand *amour* with her betrothed.

How could he not love her? she'd asked herself a thousand times. She was the most beautiful, charming, refined of all the young ladies who had come out that year—or any year in recent memory. Her dowry brought wealth beyond imagining, her rank as the daughter of a Duke was the highest of any girl in the land, and yet . . .

Adam treated her as though she were just one choice among many. As though there'd been nothing special at all that had led him to select her over another. The cad hadn't even proposed. Once long ago, she'd hinted that she wished he would, and he'd glared at her as though she'd lost her mind. She would never forgive him for depriving her of that one sought-after romantic moment.

Lights flickered behind her as more people moved from the crowded ballroom and down the steps, searching for fresh air, and she couldn't help turning to look back inside. Her father's ball, to be hosted in another week, would put this one to shame. No one could throw an elaborate party like the Westmorelands. The engagement ball would merely be the first of many, a prelude to two weeks of festivities leading up to the wedding. She had a new gown for each night, the most fabulous, exquisite, fashionable ones anywhere. Mother had brought in a special coiffeur from Paris to do her hair for each occasion. The family's most priceless jewels had been unlocked for her to wear.

She was so miserable!

On the path below, two women strolled by, whispering and snickering. It was too dark to see who they were and the voices weren't familiar. They had stopped directly below her, so she couldn't help listening when one said, "I just heard this afternoon. His brother, James, is back in London." Penelope's ears pricked up; she'd heard the same thing.

The other woman said, "I wonder what they'll do now. If

they invite him to the wedding, they'll have to ask his wife, and I can't imagine Penelope allowing her to attend.''

Penny had been secretly wondering the same thing. She'd heard that James's wife was some kind of loose woman. Only once had she dared to broach the subject with Adam, and he'd told her that James was not a topic for discussion. His tone had been so threatening that she hadn't tried to glean any further information again.

The first woman responded, ''Yes, but I hear the Marquis is strapped for a best man. If his brother refuses, it's not like he could ask his cousin, Charles, to take James's place.''

This brought great guffaws as the other said, ''Wouldn't you have loved to stop by Lavinia's that day last winter? Imagine the two of them brawling in the parlor over who would get to marry a common whore!''

What?! Penelope's brow rose nearly to her hairline. Adam fighting with Charles? Over a woman? Adam had said that he didn't want Charles or any of his family at the wedding, and she hadn't questioned why, for she didn't like Charles. In his company, she always felt that he was making fun of her for some reason she could never fathom. Now, hearing this, she found it all too much.

''I'd say Charles got the best of the bargain, though,'' one of the women was saying. ''The Marquis's castoff mistress is very beautiful. And gracious, too, or so I've heard.''

Penelope winced. So the woman of whom they spoke was that hideous Maggie person. Penelope knew she was gone from their lives, but she thought her father had forced Adam to get rid of her at Penelope's insistence. What a fool she was!

''Yes, I've seen her several times. Just the other day, in fact. With her pregnancy so advanced, she's absolutely radiant.''

Pregnant? A deep feeling of dread started to settle.

''Just think: After losing his great love to his cousin, St. Clair is left with Penelope, the poor man.''

''He's consoling himself well enough, though. He was at dinner last night with one of those actresses with whom he consorts. Wait till Penelope hears about what St. Clair has been doing with some of them!'' They both chuckled maliciously, and Penelope's distress was so great she felt as though her heart might burst from her chest.

''Did I tell you what I heard about the babe Cousin Charles supposedly fathered with St. Clair's old mistress?''

''No. What?''

There were whispers then that were obviously too scandalous for the pair to talk about aloud. Penny strained against the balustrade, trying to hear or see. The whispering ended abruptly, and a woman said, ''That is absolutely too delicious to be true! He's the father, is he? Well, I'll be. Do you suppose he intentionally married her off to Charles?''

Who? Who is the father? Penelope had to prevent herself from shouting the question.

''Could be. Of course, you've heard how Charles's wife is related to everyone?'' The women began moving away now, their voices fading with each step. ''She's Penelope's . . .''

The rest was lost to the night.

''She's my what?'' Penny asked the dark sky. Oh, this was so absolutely horrible! Was everyone talking about her behind her back? Were they all relishing these hateful tidbits? Was her pending wedding, the romantic moment she had dreamed about all her life, simply the fodder for wicked gossip stirred up by Adam?

Whatever he'd done, she'd put a stop to it right now! She was not about to be mocked so malevolently right before her glorious day. With a firm resolve, and a flaring temper that only one who had always gotten her own way could possibly understand, she huffed back into the ballroom, determined to confront her wayward betrothed. She would not be a laughing-stock! She would not!

It took an hour to locate him. He'd stuffed himself away in a small reading room, at the end of a deserted hallway, where he'd managed to find a breeze blowing in. The only window was wide open and he sat in the casement, letting the air flow over his back. He was sipping something dark-colored, and if she could have seen the look in his eye, perhaps she'd have been more wary, but the light from the single lamp was too dim for close assessment.

"Where have you been?" she asked testily. "I've been looking everywhere."

"Hello, Penelope." He took a sip of the contents of his glass and studied her over the rim. "I didn't know I was required to gain your permission before leaving the ballroom."

She ignored the taunt and bravely forged ahead. "I need to speak with you. About several matters of the utmost importance."

"Go right ahead. Nothing's ever stopped you before." He gestured openly, then crossed his arms over his chest, waiting.

"James is back from his honeymoon."

"Yes, I heard."

"I'll not have him and that . . . that . . . woman he married at my wedding."

"Don't worry." He chuckled. "They wouldn't come if we asked them."

This stopped her cold. The very idea that someone would choose not to attend her wedding was ludicrous. Why, it was the social event of the Season! People were fighting for invitations. A frown creased her brow. "Whatever do you mean?"

"I mean, dear heart, that they don't like either one of us."

"Well!" His statement threw her off balance, for she simply couldn't imagine someone not liking her.

"Was there anything else?"

"Yes, as a matter of fact." Realizing she was losing some of the fortitude she needed for the fight, she mentally pulled herself together and forged ahead. "You didn't want Charles at the wedding, and I was just wondering . . . That is, I heard something . . ." This was harder than she'd ever imagined. She had absolutely no background for discussing such intimate, scandalous things with a man. "It's just that people are talking, and ... well ... I want my wedding to be special, and if he and his wife were to show up ..."

"Don't worry," Adam snapped. "They won't show up. They don't like us either."

"Why is that? Did something happen between you and Charles?" There! She'd said it!

"We had a disagreement."

"Over what?"

For the first time, his attitude toward her seemed to soften just a bit. He relaxed his angry stance. "It's late, and I stopped having fun several hours ago. I think, perhaps, it's time we left."

"Who is Charles's wife?" Adam merely stood stoically silent, and she forced herself to pose the question that had frightened her so when she'd heard the women talking outside. "Who is she to you?" His continued silence infuriated her, so she asked, "Who is she to me?"

"Enough!" He swallowed back the contents of his glass. "Let's go home, Penny."

"I will not! Not until you answer my questions. People are talking about me. About us. I won't have it!"

"They've always talked about us. You just weren't paying attention."

"Not like this," she hissed. "Who are the actresses with whom you're consorting?"

He raised a brow. "This is not an appropriate topic for discussion between us, and you will not speak of it further."

Dear Lord, but he sounded just like her father. The very idea enraged her. "I won't have it, do you hear me? I won't have you keeping time with whores and actresses while people are laughing at me behind my back!"

Adam moved away from the window and towered over her. "I know your father has been incredibly lenient with you in your upbringing, but you should know something about me: I will not be so tolerant. My private life is just that. Private. You will not question me about it, nor will you try to order me about in my affairs. Do I make myself clear?''

"Do you still love that odious Maggie person? Is that why you don't care for me?''

"I'm going to find your mother,'' Adam said with a sigh, "and we'll leave.''

Having come this far, she couldn't seem to stop herself. She whispered, "Is she having your child?''

Even though Adam didn't answer, the silent, damning truth reverberated around the room, and she suddenly saw so many things with a glaring clarity.

He didn't love her. Never had and never would. All her lifelong dreams about love and passion were just girlish fantasies. This cold, hard man would be her husband, and she would live the lonely, barren existence her mother had endured all the years of her life as her father lusted away after one woman and another.

"I'm not going through with this.'' She took a step back. "I won't marry you. I'm going to talk with Father. Now.''

Enraging her further, Adam merely shrugged. "Do whatever you have to do. It matters not to me in the least.''

Long after he should have been able to hear her, he could still imagine her angry footsteps disappearing down the hall. He eased back against the casement, once again letting the night breeze cool what it could, while he counted the days until they were married. Twenty-one. Twenty-one days.

So, people were talking, were they? And Penelope had finally heard some of the stories. Well, it could only do her a world of good. Perhaps she'd grow up a bit. With a little luck, she'd come to understand something about life and the miseries of the people who surrounded her. Perhaps she'd learn that sometimes you should be careful what you wish for, because you just might get it. Like her marriage to a bastard such as himself.

A year earlier, although Harold had been hinting at it for

years, she'd set her cap to catch him, and now she had him whether she wanted him or not. He had no doubts that the wedding would go forward. Penelope could pout and whine to her father until she was blue in the face, but Harold was dead set on the union, and there would be nothing she could do to change what was about to happen. They would be wed in three weeks.

For a moment, he thought about refilling his glass, but decided against it. He was already far past his limit. If he'd been a little more sober, he wouldn't have been so hard on her, but everything about her grated on his nerves, and while he could handle her sober, half-foxed was another matter entirely.

For the past two months, all she'd talked about when they were together was what she'd wear to which party during the grand fêtes before the wedding. How anyone could be so completely self-absorbed and so utterly boring was something he'd spent long hours contemplating while he'd ignored her completely. He'd also spent a great deal of time calculating the increased wealth and property he was about to receive once they were wed. It was the only consolation now.

He was long past the time when revenge against Maggie had mattered. The anger that had flared over her marriage to Charles had fled quickly, leaving in its place only a hollow feeling of betrayal. In the end, only loneliness remained, a deep, burning sense of loss for her and the way things had once been in his life. For not only had he lost her, but his first child, and James and Charles as well. He was left with his mother, and Penny and Harold, and the shallow, silly existence in which they all passed their lives. He'd tried to fill the gaping hole with various women, but it was a waste of time. Nothing helped.

The breeze stirred his hair, and he closed his eyes, inhaling deep the smell of summer roses blooming just outside. He imagined his brother and his cousin, with their two lovely, spirited wives. Sitting together somewhere, perhaps in Charles's home, laughing and talking over a good meal. Maggie would be smiling and happy.

God, how it hurt to think of it, so he shifted his image of her, reliving his favorite fantasy, bringing her from Charles's home to his own. To his country estate and his bedroom, where he'd always imagined her lying naked on his bed in the morning sun. The amethyst ring, which he'd purchased as her Christmas present and always carried in his pocket, would glisten on her finger. She'd be swollen with his child, and he would lean over and place a gentle kiss on her bulging abdomen just as the babe kicked against her stomach . . .

Quietly, he let the dream play out.

Then, alone and unseen, he left the ball and returned to his private sanctuary in Maggie's small house.

Robert huddled in the shadows across the street from Charles's home. The June night was excessively warm, and everyone had their windows open, trying to find a hint of comfort after the scorching day. Candlelight flickered in one of the upstairs rooms, and he could hear chatter and laughter, although he couldn't make out any of the words.

Charles was in there. Along with his cousin James and their two wives. They had dined together each night for the past week, ever since James had arrived back from his honeymoon. With her pregnancy so advanced, Charles's wife rarely went anywhere, so they stayed at home and welcomed various guests in the evenings. There was always a cluster of friends surrounding Charles. He was just one of those people to whom others were instantly drawn.

Once upon a time, Robert had been one of those people. *He* had been invited to the dinners and the parties. *He* had shared the laughter and the camaraderie. *He* had been liked and respected by Charles and all of his friends. Moving in Charles's circle had made him feel smart, witty, and refined, and he longed for a return to those heady days when he'd felt so much a part of it all.

When Charles had offered him the chance to invest money

in some of their ventures, he'd jumped at the opportunity, wanting to seem worldly and knowledgeable in Charles's eyes. He'd made a few pounds on the first verture, and a few more on the second, and even more than that on the third. It had seemed so easy, and when the possibility for greater gains came his way, he'd quickly and eagerly said yes. The only problem was that he didn't have access to the kinds of funds Charles requested for the undertaking, so he'd used money that wasn't his to risk.

Robert absolutely had to have it back! His father's last and most gripping threats had finally been made, and Robert was at his wit's end trying to come up with a solution. Through it all, he'd looked to suave, charming Charles Billington to rescue him from his own folly, but Charles had refused to make things right again.

When he looked at the world through his troubled grip on reality, it seemed to Robert that all of his problems began when Charles had met his wife. Everything had been fine up until then. Charles had been working on finding money to repay what Robert had lost, but the woman seemed to have cast a spell over Charles, with their quick friendship and even quicker marriage.

Her beautiful gowns, her jewels, their home in the country, their parties with friends—Robert was certain that all of it was being financed, most lavishly, with funds that should have been returned to him long ago.

Now, the babe was coming, and Charles would have many more reasons to spend money on his family. Robert saw, with a disturbed sense of crystal clarity, that whatever chance he had for a resolution of his situation would end once the child was born. Each day, he became more convinced that if Charles's wife was gone from their lives, everything would return to normal.

Something had to be done. Very soon.

Chapter Twenty-Seven

Maggie looked at her hands, then lifted the hem of her skirt to catch a glimpse of her feet. The swelling was down considerably, but then, she'd hardly stood up in the past month. The end result was that she seemed to be better physically, but emotionally, she was feeling completely housebound. After a string of unusually hot days, followed by an equal number of uncomfortable nights, the house was too miserable for words. She simply couldn't get enough air if she remained inside one more second, and she knew she had to get out or go mad.

For the first time in two weeks, James and Anne were dining elsewhere, taking in a new restaurant before heading for their home in the country the next day. While Maggie wished they could stay for the birth, she understood their need to flee the city before Adam's wedding drew any closer. Luckily for them, they could go. She was stuck until the babe came and was old enough to travel. Thanks to Charles and their reserved style of life, she was able to live as though nothing important was happening in the outside world, and most times, she could block the quickly approaching date from her mind.

"Charles, I'm going to wait outside," she called up the stairs.

"I'll be right down," he answered.

There was a neighborhood pub just a few blocks down. They had decided to walk to it, take the cool evening air, let Maggie rest for a bit on one of the benches, then head back. The exercise would do her good, she was sure, and she needed the fresh air so desperately. She opened the door, pleased to see all the commotion on their small street after being shut inside for so long.

Many people were out, trying to find some relief from the heated rooms indoors. The evening shadows of the summer day were exquisite, and she looked up above the buildings surrounding her. Somewhere far off, where she couldn't see, there had to be an incredible sunset occurring. Everything around her was cast in shades of purple and orange.

Wanting to see if she could get any kind of look at the dazzling sky, she shuffled her ungainly physique toward the corner, hoping for a broader view past the row of houses. It never occurred to her to wonder if she was safe. Theirs was a quiet, pleasant neighborhood, and Charles was right behind her.

Not twenty feet away, Robert stepped out from a doorway. Maggie rolled her eyes in frustration. They had come face-to-face on numerous occasions. With the way the man followed them about, it was impossible not to. Maggie had tried to be polite, and had always come away with the overwhelming impression that the young man was lonely and confused. Nothing could be gained by a display of anger. Charles had displayed plenty, and it never worked.

"Hello, Robert," she said. "Isn't it lovely this evening?" No response. Where in the past he'd always been civil, tonight he was glowering at her with such a display of open dislike that it made her uneasy. With a resigned shrug, she tried to circle around him. He stepped in front of her so that she couldn't pass. She moved the other way with the same result. A third attempt was equally unsuccessful. She blew out a long, frustrated sigh. Walking was hard enough these days without something like this.

"Oh, for pity's sake. Let me by!" she ordered him.

"I hate you," he said vehemently in response.

Her head swung up, and she stared into his pretty face. He was breathing hard, his cheeks were bright red, and his eyes shone with a fierce, disturbing glow. She was suddenly afraid, and took a hesitant step back, thinking to head for the house. Just then, Charles called to her from behind, and she could hear his footsteps approaching.

"Maggie? I brought you a shawl, in case it's cooler when we walk home."

Her eyes wide with apprehension, she turned to look at him over her shoulder. Until Charles moved next to her, Robert had been mostly shielded from his view. There was a long awkward silence.

Softly, Charles asked her, "Are you all right?"

"Yes," she whispered in return. "He seems terribly upset about something. Perhaps we should go back in."

"Let's do. Then I'll come back out and deal with him by myself." He took her arm. "My apologies . . ."

They started toward their residence, but Robert's sharp command stopped them. "No. Don't move."

As she swung back around, Maggie's eyes widened with horror. Robert was holding a pistol. It looked very heavy, for his hand was shaking and the long barrel wobbled greatly, but for the most part, the end was pointed directly at her abdomen. Instinctively, she protectively covered the babe with her hands.

"Robert!" Charles said sharply. "What are you doing? Have you gone completely mad?"

Robert kept his gaze fixed on Maggie. "I hate you. This is all your fault."

Later, much later, in the times Maggie could bear to recall it, the next few moments would replay in her mind in agonizing slowness. All activity on the street went still. People stopped talking, children quit playing, horses quit snickering. One distant voice penetrated the silence.

"My Lord, look! That man's got a gun!" Everyone turned toward the odd trio, frozen in place. The pistol came up. Robert's finger flexed against the trigger as he steadied the barrel.

"No!" Charles roared.

It was the last word he ever uttered. Robert fired just as Charles jumped in front of her to push her aside so that Robert could not hurt her or the babe. He was struck in the center of his chest and collapsed to the ground in a jumbled heap.

Many times throughout her life, she would relive the horrifying sight in her dreams, crying out in her sleep at hearing Charles's final shout, which always caused the slowness of her dream to end, everything speeding back to regular time.

There was pandemonium in the street. Bedlam, and outcries, and running from the onlookers. Someone was screaming. A woman. Screaming long and loud. The piercing wail never ending. Who was that woman screaming?

In her recollections, she was always surprised to realize that it had been herself. Screaming in shock and horror while kneeling beside her husband as blood poured from his chest, soaking across his shirt until it seeped down onto the cobbles in a huge pool.

Robert's gun, holding only the one shot, was empty. He didn't even try to run, but tossed the offending weapon on the street, where it skidded under a wagon. Several men grabbed him, while others ran to get a surgeon and a constable. The surgeon arrived much too late and was unnecessary. The constable, along with several others, took Robert away in a cart.

Maggie stayed in the street, cradling her dead husband in her arms. The neighbors whispered among themselves, wondering what to do, but none dared disrupt the heart-wrenching scene to ask her to move away from the man who had done such a brave, heroic thing, so she remained by his side, stroking his hair and crying soft words as the day ended and night began.

Finally, Anne arrived and took her inside.

* * *

Adam stood at the front of the ballroom, near the base of the stairs. The guests of honor formed a receiving line to welcome newcomers to the lavish party that would continue till dawn. It was the first of many that would lead up to the day of the wedding in two weeks.

Harold Westmoreland stood with his family. Wife, son, and daughter—the unhappy bride-to-be, Penelope. Adam was placed next to her, with his grim-looking mother, Lucretia, standing on the other side. If they hadn't all been so pathetic, he'd have laughed aloud at the ludicrousness of the situation. Since his fight with Penny the week before, he'd seen her twice. She hadn't spoken to him either time, and he hadn't tried to make any apologies.

Harold had pulled him aside at their club to inform him that Penny had been ranting and raving all week that she would not marry Adam St. Clair. He had mentioned it, not because he wanted to know what Adam had done to cause such a debacle, but to ensure Adam that the wedding would go forward as planned. Tired of listening to Penny's tirade of complaints, the Duke had taken to keeping her locked in her rooms during the hours he was home so he would not have to be accosted by further tantrums.

Penny was miserable, but she was too well bred to show it. She looked ravishing in her gown and jewels, like some kind of fairy-tale princess. When others were in hearing distance, she chatted, laughed, flirted with Adam. Once they stepped away, she fell silent, her venom leaching into the family members standing nearby, none of whom had any illusions about the supposedly happy couple.

Adam wished he could find some bit of tenderness in his heart for her, but it seemed impossible. Every time he looked at her, he saw Maggie. Especially from his current angle. In profile, they looked like, well . . . sisters. What a foolish, foolish thing he had done. Whatever happened to him now was certainly only what he deserved for the mess he'd made of all their lives.

The music was about to start up, and the engaged couple would be required to lead off the set. The dance would undoubtedly be excruciatingly painful. Penny would keep a smile on her face, her eyes on his cravat, and no one watching would ever have to know how greatly angered she was. If he was any kind of gentleman, he would do something to ease her distress, but sadly, he didn't care enough about her feelings or his own to rectify the situation.

He glanced at his watch. Gad, but it was still early. The painful night was never going to end, and the next two weeks of hot, stuffy parties stretched ahead like the road to Hades. He tugged at his collar, then turned slightly. Harold had several servants standing behind the receiving line, constantly waving large fans to try to cool them down. The bit of moving air felt good on his face.

As he turned, he saw Harold's butler had entered the ballroom and was whispering in the Duke's ear.

Harold's brows shot up. "You're certain?" The look in his eye when he glanced over at Adam sent a shot of fear up Adam's spine. The butler whispered something else, and Harold responded, "Yes, yes. All right. I'll take care of it."

The servant departed, and Harold turned to those standing around him. "Adam, Lucretia. I need to talk to both of you. Come where we can find some privacy."

"What is it, Harold?" Adam asked, but Harold waved away the question. With Penny and the rest of his family following also, he moved them through the pulsing throng up the stairs of the ballroom, and as they went, Adam was certain he could hear a whisper of dangerous news spreading behind them through the crowd. At the top, Harold led them across the hall to a small sitting room, and closed the door once everyone was inside.

Looking a bit shaken as he turned to face them, he said, "I

just received the most distressing information. I thought you should know right away.''

Adam's heart was pounding. ''What is it?''

''It seems your cousin, Charles Billington, was killed earlier this evening.''

''What?'' Everyone gasped collectively.

''How?'' Adam managed to stammer.

''He was murdered. On the street in front of his home by some man with a gun. Shot in the chest.'' This revelation brought silence. Murder was so very, very rare. And for it to happen right in front of a man's home! To one of their own kind! What was the world coming to?

Harold stared at Adam, demanding his attention. ''He was taking the night air. With his *wife*. She was standing by his side when it happened.'' The murmurs of the others who didn't know all the nuances of the situation covered the silent, visual messages flashing between Adam and Harold.

''Maggie?'' Adam asked, horrified. ''Is she . . . is she all right?''

''Yes. She was unharmed. But greatly distressed. It seems he died in her arms.'' This brought another wave of protest from those in the room. Even though they didn't know the young widow, this was too terrible for imagining. Harold continued softly. ''They've taken Charles to your Aunt Vinnie's. James and his wife are there as well. Along with Charles's widow.''

Adam was too stunned for speech. Charles dead? Murdered? Maggie alone and suffering? Their baby! What of their baby? Was the child all right? He had to know, but he couldn't ask Harold. Not in front of the assembled company. ''I've got to go to them,'' he said weakly.

''I thought you might want to,'' Harold agreed. ''I've already ordered your carriage brought round.''

''What?'' Penny stammered, turning to Adam. ''You can't leave. The ball won't end for several hours. I won't have it, I tell you! I won't!''

"Penny, for the love of God!" her father chastised her. "Shut up!"

"I most certainly will not," she hissed. "After all I've put up with! Now, to have him think he can just run off in the middle of my ball. What will people say? What will they think?"

This last brought Adam out of his shocked state. "Who the hell cares what they say or think?"

"I do."

"Well, I don't, and I can't believe that you think we should stay here chatting and drinking punch after something like this just happened to my best friend."

"He's not your best friend anymore! He doesn't like us, remember?" Her angry eyes narrowed. "It's because of her, isn't it? You're just using this as an excuse to go see her."

"Don't you understand anything?" Adam threw up his arms in exasperation. "About life? About people?"

"I understand that you'd rather spend the night coddling the grieving young widow than staying here by my side where you belong. How could you ruin my party in such a despicable manner!"

"I've got to get out of here," Adam groaned as he turned toward the door.

"Don't you dare leave!" Penelope ordered. "I forbid it!"

Shaking his head in disgust, Adam looked to Harold. "Take care of this for me."

"Go. Go." Harold waved him away. "I will make your apologies to whoever feels they're necessary. *Most* everyone will understand why you had to leave." His tone and his emphasis made it clear that Penelope was not among that group and that she was lacking because of it.

Adam quickly stepped to the door, but before he could open it, his mother laid a hand on his arm. "Mother," he said, his aggravation growing by the moment, "I don't have time for this."

She leaned closer and whispered, "Don't you dare leave this

party. How could you think to embarrass Penelope like this? How could you do this to her or to me?"

"Stop it."

"Someone has to talk some sense into you."

"Mother." He took a deep breath, struggling to remain calm. "Charles was your nephew. Vinnie is your sister. He was her best-loved child. Doesn't that mean anything to you?"

"Not at the moment. We currently have other, more pressing responsibilities."

"No. We have nothing more important to do than offer Vinnie the support she needs right now."

"Isn't it enough that one member of our family is already there, embroiled in the scandalous mess?" She squeezed his arm as tightly as she could. "Must you go enmesh yourself as well?"

"Yes, I must. Charles was my friend."

"*Was* your friend. I'll never forgive you if you do this to us."

"Fine," he said calmly, which caused her to gasp. "Good night." Without looking back, he stepped out of the room and pushed his way to the front door. The crowd parted as he hurried out, the gossip having already made the rounds.

By the time the carriage rumbled to a stop in front of Lavinia's house, Adam was shaking with emotion. What a waste the last few months had been. To have spent them angry with James, with Maggie, with Charles. To have harbored such animosity toward Anne. Now this. The tragedy of it made everything else seem so trivial. All the fighting and jealousies. The silences and separations. For what? So that the last words he ever uttered to Charles were those of hatred and spite?

Faced with the magnitude of what had happened, he could barely recall why he had been fighting with any of them. It all seemed so petty.

Tears flooded his eyes as he recalled all the friendship and joy Charles had routinely brought to his life where there had always been so little of both. The very thought that they'd never see each other again, that he'd never be able to apologize for that last meeting, that he could never thank Charles for taking care of Maggie and the babe . . .

Oh, the regrets were piling up so fast he could hardly make note of them. All he wanted now was to see James and Anne, to make peace. Then, to see Maggie. To talk to her and hold her. To see with his own eyes that she was fine. To find out what she needed, how he could help.

He stepped out of the carriage. A few lights glowed inside, and there were several other vehicles in the circular drive. He bustled up the steps, knocking briskly. The door was opened shortly by Hodson, who was dressed as impeccably as usual, which might have been funny considering it was the middle of the night, but it was obvious the man had been crying.

"Good evening, Lord Belmont," he said with a shaky voice.

"Hello, Hodson. I just heard the horrible news. I had to come by." He took a step to enter, then realized Hodson stood in the center of the doorway, blocking his way. For the first time in Adam's life, he was shocked to understand that he wasn't being welcomed in his aunt's house. Any other time he'd visited, the man had merely opened the door and ushered him inside without hesitation. On this occasion, there was no welcome in his eyes or his demeanor.

Adam finally asked, "May I come in?"

"I'm sorry, milord, but your aunt has given me a list of who is to be allowed to visit at this dreadful time." There was a long pause as Hodson waited for the rest of the message to sink in. There was a list, and Adam's name wasn't on it.

"Perhaps it was an oversight, Hodson. Please, I'd like to pay my condolences to the members of my family."

"I'm sorry, sir. Please try again tomorrow. Perhaps Lady Billington will be up to receiving you then."

The door started to close in his face, and Adam stuck out his hand and braced it against the wood. "Hodson! Please."

"Who's there, Hodson?" The male voice came from behind

the retainer, and Hodson visibly relaxed as he turned to look over his shoulder. "It's your brother, sir."

James stepped into the doorway, taking the butler's place. "Thank you, Hodson. I'll handle this." Hodson tiptoed off and left the two brothers facing each other in an awkward silence.

"Hello, James," Adam finally began.

"What do you want?"

"I just heard. I came to see what I could do."

James snorted. "I'd say you've done plenty already."

"Please, James. This isn't the time for bickering."

James softened a bit at that. "No, I guess it's not."

"I wanted to see Aunt Vinnie. And Maggie, if I may."

James shook his head. "They're not receiving callers. Perhaps you should try again in a few days."

"May I see Charles?"

"The undertaker is still here," he said by way of denying the request.

Adam wondered how inappropriate it was to say the next bit, but he had to know. "I heard Maggie witnessed the entire episode." James merely shrugged in acknowledgment. "How is she holding up?"

"She's doing as well as can be expected."

"And the baby? Is the babe all right?"

"The baby is fine as far as I know."

Adam nodded with relief. "I have to see her, James. Please."

"No, Adam. Not now."

"When?"

James ran a frustrated hand through his hair. "Just go back to your party." He started to shut the door.

"James, please . . ." Adam didn't even try to stop the handful of tears that worked their way down his cheeks. "Will you at least tell her I was here? Tell her"—he swallowed past the lump in his throat—"tell her that if she needs anything, anything at all, that she should get in touch with me immediately. Will you tell her?"

"I'll tell her, but I can't see how it will make any difference."

His shoulders slumped, the emotional toll of the long night weighing heavily on his shoulders. He stepped back, unable to further bear the anguish on his brother's face. "Go, Adam. Go back to where you belong."

James shut the door with a soft, resounding click, and Adam stood alone on the lighted stoop, shaking his head as he realized he wanted to go to where he belonged, but felt as though he no longer belonged anywhere. He needed to spend the next few hours with friends and family who would offer understanding and comfort, but there was no one in his life who would give solace at such a ghastly time. In a daze of pain and emotion, he stumbled to his carriage.

Maggie sat in the chair she'd placed next to the coffin. All her tears had been cried out early on and now she felt nothing. She was numb, dry-eyed, and devoid of emotion. There was such a sense of unreality about what had happened that she felt as though she was a spectator, watching horrific events as they happened to someone else.

Rubbing at the small of her back, she shifted in her chair. In the past few hours, she had started feeling a great deal of pain there, and she kept telling herself it was merely caused by the stress of all that had happened. A severe twinge gripped her just then, as though her body was trying to prove her a fool or a liar. She took a deep breath, then let it out slowly as sweat pooled on her brow. What a day to be feeling so poorly.

A clock chimed somewhere, and she realized Charles had been dead for nearly thirty-six hours. Maggie had hardly left his side in all that time. She couldn't bear the thought of him lying alone in the small curtained parlor. She hadn't eaten or slept, but had sat silently with him. Keeping watch. Keeping company. A handful of people had stopped by to pay respects, and she couldn't have said who they were or what remarks they'd made. Lavinia's competent staff had kept a tight rein on who was admitted into her home, wanting only for all of them to have a quiet few days to come to grips with Charles's death.

Soon, men would come to take him away forever. She should go upstairs to change for the funeral, but she couldn't leave him for one second. This good man, who had saved her life, not just on the night he was murdered, but long before that, deserved to have her stay with him every minute until they had to part forever.

"Oh, Charlie," she whispered, laying her hand on the smooth wood, "whatever will I do without you?"

It was the only thing she had managed to think about during her vigil. People had tried to get her to leave, to rest, to eat, but she couldn't. All she could do was sit here with her husband, hoping he would be able to send some message to her about what she should do now.

He had said that he would arrange things so that she and the baby would always be cared for, but she had no idea if he had. They had been together such a short time, and Charles had always been so busy with his painting, and other business endeavors, that she couldn't imagine when he would have dealt with any paperwork of that sort. Even if he'd arranged things for their future, she felt a huge wave of guilt when she wondered about accepting any aid.

She was an impostor. As his wife, as his friend. Completely undeserving of any lasting signs of affection on his part.

Her thoughts turned to Adam, who would be married to another in a matter of days. How she wished he could be here with her now, to hold her hand and talk with her in that stable, patient way he had. He would be calm and in control, and he would have so many answers to her questions about what would happen to her next.

More than anything in the world, she wished he would take her home to the small house where she'd been so patiently raised by Rose Brown. They could sit on her old bed, and Maggie would be able to tell him what she could tell no one else. That she was the cause of Charles's death. That if she hadn't married Charles, he might still be alive today. That she was the one who was supposed to be killed. That she was the one who Robert had wanted out of the way. And if she had died as she was supposed to, who would have missed her?

Instead, it was Charles, with his close family and loving friends, who was dead. Poor Charles, whose only grand mistake in his life had been to marry her. He had died without ever finding love or happiness because she was too forlorn herself to give them to him. Guilt and remorse were her bitter companions, and if Adam were present, she could pull them out and show them to him and let him shoo them away.

Another pain shot across her back as a door opened behind her and soft footsteps sounded. Unwilling to let anyone see that she was feeling so indisposed, she took a deep breath and held it until the pain began to subside.

Anne pulled up a chair and sat down. She was already dressed in her funeral black, her face pale and strained. "Maggie? It's time, honey. We need you to go upstairs."

"I don't want to leave him," she responded, gesturing to her husband.

"I know, but we need to get you ready. And you need to eat a bit, and rest if you can. It's going to be a long, hot, stressful day, and you need to keep your strength up."

"Who will sit with Charles? I don't want to leave him here with no one to watch over him."

"James is dressed. He said he'll come down for a while."

"As long as you promise Charles won't be alone."

"I promise."

Maggie finally agreed. She could trust James to continue her vigil. As she stood on shaky feet, and Anne stood with her, Maggie noticed the envelope Anne held in her hand. "What's that?"

"It's for you."

"For me? From who?"

Annie sighed. "From Adam."

"He was here?"

"Yes, he's stopped by several times."

"I can't imagine why."

"He wanted to see you, but we didn't know if you'd feel up to it. James told him to contact you in a few days." She handed out the paper. "He left you this."

"I'll read it later," she said, seeing the curious look on Anne's face. She stuffed it into her pocket with the seal still firmly in place. Another pain gripped her then, and she only wanted to get away from her friend so she wouldn't see the mounting discomfort. Holding Anne's hand tightly in her own, she headed for the stairs to dress for the funeral.

Chapter Twenty-Eight

Adam sat in the last row of the small chapel. It was nestled off to the side of the large church where the Billington family had arranged to hold the funeral. Not knowing if he'd be welcomed after being rebuffed at Vinnie's door, he'd waited until everyone had entered before doing so himself and taking a seat in a shadowed corner. Vinnie, with her oldest son and his family, took up the first row on one side. Maggie, flanked by James and Anne, took up the other. The remaining handful of pews were filled with his cousins and their families, plus several longtime friends and servants.

The air inside the church was warm, and it was already hot outside. They were all going to have a miserable ride to the burial at the family plot just outside the city.

The minister was making quick work of the spiritual readings, and the ceremony was different from others he'd attended where death was viewed as a type of excessive social event. Aunt Vinnie had elected to have a quiet, private affair. With Robert scheduled to hang in a few days, anything more would have been unseemly.

The young man's family, many of whom were well known to various members of the Billington clan, was in a complete and utter state of shock and embarrassment. No one knew for certain why Robert had killed Charles, although the rumors were rampant and vile, and Adam suspected that Vinnie had refused to provide fodder for the gossipmongers by allowing casual acquaintances to attend the funeral or the burial. The family wanted only to grieve and to do so in private.

Since he hadn't been able to speak with his aunt, he was only guessing, of course, but that seemed the most logical explanation for the simple service and the handful of people in attendance.

Without so much as the singing of a hymn, the service concluded. James, along with Charles's brothers and brothers-in-law, stood to carry Charles outside. Adam felt a rush of sadness and shame that he had not been asked to help. He remained in the back pew, head bowed, taking covert glances at the people passing by.

Maggie looked terrible. Her face was deathly white, and her black dress appeared heavy and uncomfortable. She was stooped forward slightly, breathing hard, and sweating profusely. Anne's hand was clutched in her own as they passed, both of them so wrapped up in the moment that they didn't notice him. For that, he was grateful.

He waited till the end, and was the last person to exit the church. The family was gathered at the bottom of the steps, a sea of black clothing and hats, stoically waiting for the coffin to be loaded into the hearse. Vinnie stood next to it, overseeing this one final moment for her son. Maggie was by her side. Adam made his way through the crowd, whispering condolences. Aunt Vinnie eased much of his heartache by hugging him tightly and thanking him for coming. As he turned to face Maggie, he didn't feel nearly so out of place.

Maggie had not noticed Adam in the church, but she couldn't help but see him now as he made his way through the groupings of Billington relatives. They were shorter and fair-complected, and he towered over most of them. She waited quietly while he hugged Charles's oldest brother, while he kissed Vinnie. This was the first time she'd seen him in six months, and he looked as handsome as she remembered, but thinner and sadder—if that was possible.

"Hello, Maggie," he said, bowing slightly and taking her hand in his own. She looked worse up close, and he wished he could scoop her off her feet and remove her to a cool, shady spot.

"Hello, Lord Belmont." She felt him wince at the formal address, but she couldn't speak familiarly. It was no longer proper. "Thank you for coming."

"I'm so sorry," he said softly, wishing he could keep the emotion out of his voice. He continued holding her hand, knowing he should drop it, but he couldn't, not now after it had been so long since he'd touched her. The question was an inappropriate one, but he felt compelled to ask it anyway. "You look tired. Are you feeling all right?"

"I've had a few bad days." She was unbearably hot, the dress so tight and cumbersome that she couldn't catch her breath. It seemed as if there was no air around her, and her discomfort was mounting by the moment. All these people watching the small exchange with Adam made it worse. Adam appeared to sense the increased attention from those surrounding them, because he gave her hand a tight squeeze and finally let it drop.

"I can imagine it has been horrible." He felt inane. Words were so inadequate to express what he was feeling. "Take care of yourself."

"I will."

They were talking like strangers who had never meant anything to one another. He couldn't stand it! Filled with overflowing emotion, his voice breaking, he said, "I loved Charles like a brother . . ."

"I know you did," she responded to the heartfelt declaration. "He loved you, too."

Her admission made him feel Charles's loss all the more. What a waste all the past months had been! Struggling for control, needing to prolong this one moment with her, he said, "If there's ever anything I can do for you, please let me know."

"That's very kind. Thank you again."

Adam felt dismissed, as though he was just another face in the crowd, but what had he expected? That she would fall into his arms? That she would express her grief aloud so he could give voice to his own? That she would declare her undying love?

Feeling like a fool, he took a step back so he was directly behind Maggie as the pallbearers finished with their loading. People started talking and milling about, discussing who would ride with whom to the burial. Maggie stood, rubbing her back, as Anne whispered in her ear, "Are you sure you're all right?"

"I'm so hot . . . If I could just sit down for a moment . . ." She swayed to one side, then the other. Several people reached out a hand to steady her. Anne gripped her arm and helped her into a carriage. James and Anne followed her in, and as quick as that, they were gone.

Others took it as their cue to depart as well, and in a matter of minutes, the funeral procession started down the busy street. Adam stood in front of the church, watching them all leave, and when they were nearly out of sight, he moved to his own carriage, and his driver followed along at a slow pace, just keeping the line of black carriages in view.

It took nearly two hours to arrive at the cemetery. Adam wished more than anything that he could join with those who stood at the graveside, but he didn't. He had his own private good-byes to make to Charles, so he sat in the overheated carriage, waiting for the short service to end. Afterward, people hugged and chatted briefly before heading once again to Vinnie's house for a funeral supper, and soon, the only people left were Anne and James—and Maggie.

Anne and James lingered a distance away, giving Maggie her privacy while she remained by the grave. She was a lonely, tragic sight, dressed in black with her swollen stomach so visible, her face so pale. In her hand, she held a single red rose. It looked as though she was speaking to Charles, making a final good-bye of her own, and Adam tried to imagine what she was saying. What final thoughts would be foremost in her mind?

Suddenly, her eyes closed, her head fell back, and she fainted, falling like a stone onto the grass. In an instant, Adam leaped from his carriage, rushed to her, and knelt by her side. Anne and James came rushing up as well, and Anne knelt across from him. With Maggie's welfare foremost in all their minds, the animosity that had flared between them instantly vanished.

"Maggie?" Adam said, leaning forward, his face hovering over hers, his hand holding one of her own. Pulling a kerchief from his pocket, he dabbed at the sweat pooled on her brow, then used it to fan her face. "Maggie? Can you hear me?" There was no response, and he looked at Anne, who was patting Maggie's other hand, trying to rouse her. "Has she been ill?"

"No, but she's hardly eaten or slept since Saturday night." They were silent for a moment, pondering how long it had been since she'd had adequate sustenance. "I think she's just very distressed this morning."

"And it's so hot. This black isn't helping. We need to get her out of the sun."

Just then, Maggie's eyes fluttered open, and she didn't look at all surprised to find him there, watching over her. "Adam? What happened?"

"You fainted, little one."

"I'm so warm . . ." Pain swept across her stomach, and she moaned in spite of her desperate attempts to keep her discomfort to herself.

"What is it?" he asked frantically, his eyes running down her form, looking for the cause. "Are you injured?"

"No," she groaned, squeezing his hand tightly. "I think it's the babe. It might be coming."

He looked over at Anne, both their eyes wide. "Isn't it early?"

"Her time is still a few weeks away. All the stress of the past few days must have moved things up a bit."

"We've got to get her someplace cooler and off her feet." He scanned the grounds, looking for a shady spot, and saw a small stand of trees several yards away. It wasn't much, but at least they could get her out of the sun for the moment. He scooped her up, thinking how frail she seemed even with the babe grown so large.

"What are you doing?" Maggie managed to ask between labored breaths.

"First, we're going to cool you down a bit, and then we need to get you out of here."

"No, I have to stay with Charles," she said. "I have to stay with him . . ."

"You're not feeling well enough to stay any longer," he said with a smile, thinking what a loyal, devoted person she always had been and loving her all the more for it. "I'm sure Charles would understand."

He settled her in the shade against the base of one of the trees. One of his footmen had been watching the events from a discreet distance, and he brought over a small jug of water that had been stashed under the driver's seat. Adam wetted his kerchief with it and dabbed at Maggie's face while looking at Anne. "Do you know her birthing plans?"

"Yes, she has retained a midwife from Charles's neighborhood. She was to birth the child in her room at Charles's house."

"We need to get her home, then."

This decision caused Maggie to panic. "No, I can't go back there. Don't make me. I can't bear to . . ."

Her eyes were round with alarm, and Adam looked up at his brother, who was standing behind Anne. James leaned down and whispered, "It happened right in front of Charles's house. Practically in his doorway."

"All right," Adam said, turning once again to Maggie and saying softly, "You don't have to go back there ever again if you don't want to."

"Thank you," she murmured, closing her eyes in relief while breathing heavily as another pain gripped her stomach.

"How about Aunt Vinnie's?" he asked James.

"Her house is packed to the rafters with guests, and they're having a family gathering this evening which may last for hours."

"Well, that's no good." He looked at James and Anne, as the three of them silently considered the available options. Finally, he stood to face them. "It's settled, then."

"What is?" James asked.

"I'll take her to our town house. Help me get her to her feet."

Neither James nor Anne moved a muscle. James was the first one to speak. "You can't do that, Adam."

"Why?"

"Well, there's already some talk. Taking her home would only exacerbate it. Plus, Mother is there."

"I'll send her away."

"You're not thinking clearly," James said, resting a comforting hand on his shoulder. "Think of the scandal such an event would cause. And think of Charles's memory."

"You're right. You're right, of course," Adam said, rubbing a hand over his hot brow. "But what would you have me do? We can't leave her here to give birth in the grass." He knelt beside her again, wetting the linen once more and cooling her face as the best idea of all suddenly dawned on him.

He asked her, "Are you feeling better?"

"Yes. I've cooled down considerably."

"Good. We're leaving here."

"Where are you taking me?"

"I'm going to take you home. To your old house on Mulberry Street. Would you like that?"

Maggie couldn't believe the flutter of excitement his suggestion caused. "Do you mean it?"

"Yes, I do."

"I should like that very much, indeed."

He stood and faced James and Anne again, saying, "She can have the baby there, where everything's familiar and she's surrounded by her things. The staff is small and discreet . . ."

James added, "We could spread word that she's retired to the country and isn't receiving any callers . . ."

"Yes," Adam agreed, "and she can stay at the house as long as she likes. What do you think?"

With tears in her eyes, Anne answered, "I think it's a wonderful idea. She was born in that house. Her mother would have liked to know that Maggie would give birth there as well."

"I'll take her in my carriage," he said, relieved to have found a solution. "Anne," he said to his sister-in-law, "you'll accompany us, won't you?" The request for forgiveness was clear in his eyes as he added quietly, "Please?"

"Of course I will," Anne said, readily welcoming his overture. She and James both smiled in acknowledgment and acceptance of Adam's offer of peace.

To his brother, Adam said, "You'll come as well, won't you?"

"Certainly, although I think I should probably run and fetch the midwife first."

"Yes . . . yes . . ."

James looked as though he was going to say something else. Instead, he pulled Adam into a quick, tight hug. "I've missed you," he said, a suspicious wetness suddenly clouding his vision. He turned and ran to his carriage before Adam could respond.

Adam swallowed past the lump in his throat; then he and Anne helped Maggie into his carriage. They had all just settled in when a shooting pain gripped her, and Adam squeezed her hand while she struggled for breath.

"How long has this been going on?" he asked.

"Several hours, I guess," she said weakly.

"You silly girl," he muttered, pulling her closer to his side.

"I don't think you should come with us, Adam," she managed to spit out once the pain had subsided. "Think of the scandal it could cause if anyone found out."

"I have, and I don't care. I want nothing more than to be nearby when our child is born."

"But what about your wedding? And your mother and Penny? What about my father and . . ."

"Ssh . . ." Adam rested his finger against her lips to silence her protest. "We'll worry about all of that later. Right now, you've more important things on which to concentrate."

"I think the sun has addled your wits."

"On the contrary. For the first time in a long time, I'm finally thinking clearly."

The temperature inside the coach was ghastly, and hoping to find a breeze, Adam rapped on the roof so the driver would begin moving. It seemed to take forever before they rattled to a halt on her old street. As Adam had suspected, it was a great relief for her to look out and see her own front stoop welcoming her as it had most all of the years of her life.

A coachman opened the door to the carriage. Adam jumped out, then helped Maggie and Anne descend. Once Maggie's feet touched the ground, a fierce contraction gripped her and they stood in place, with Adam holding her hand and Anne rubbing her back. After it passed, Adam lifted her and carried her to the door.

Just as he reached it, it was opened by Gail. "Lord Belmont, is everything . . ." She stopped, amazed by the sight in his arms. "Miss Maggie!"

"She collapsed at the funeral," Adam explained as the woman gasped in dismay. "We think her baby is coming."

"Oh . . . oh . . . how terrible. How wonderful," Gail said as she turned and led the way up the stairs.

At the top, Adam said, "Gail, do you remember my sister-in-law, Anne St. Clair?"

"Yes. Hello, ma'am," Gail said. "It's grand to see you again."

"Hello, Gail." Anne smiled in return.

Gail held the door, and Adam led the way into Maggie's old room. Carefully mindful of his precious cargo, he laid her on the center of the bed. "You just rest now, and see to the babe. Let the rest of us take care of everything else."

Maggie took his hand and squeezed hard. "Stay close by. Please? It would ease me greatly to know you are downstairs."

"I will remain. It you need anything, just send someone down to fetch me."

He placed a kiss on her forehead, then stepped aside as Gail and another female servant, both of whom looked excessively competent, entered behind him, ready to take over. Although he wanted to stay, the women shooed him into the hall, telling him this was no place for a man and assuring him that they'd have things well in hand until the midwife arrived.

Anne came downstairs many minutes later, and she laughed heartily at Adam, already pacing feverishly. "At this rate, you will wear out the floor before it's over."

"This is the most horrible thing I've ever experienced," he said, thinking of the pain Maggie had endured in his carriage on the way across the city.

"Well, she's barely begun, and it will be hours—or more likely days—before there's any news." He shuddered at the thought, and she laughed again. "I don't want you down here glowering at all of us through the evening, so I'm throwing you out."

"I can't leave. Maggie needs me. She asked me to stay."

"She doesn't know what she wants at the moment."

"But . . . but . . ." he stammered as Anne moved him to the door and held it open.

"Make yourself useful. First, go to Vinnie's and tell her what's happened."

"I forgot about Vinnie," Adam said, slapping his forehead.

"Yes, she'll be worried that we haven't returned. Tell her

that Maggie is with me, and that I will keep her posted as to how things are progressing. Then, go to Charles's house. Maggie's maid is still there. Have her pack a bag of Maggie's personal items. She'll know what Maggie needs.''

"Yes, of course. Ah . . . some of her things are still upstairs. Until I return, you might find something useful in some of the drawers . . . '' His cheeks flushed with the embarrassment of having to admit that he'd never packed Maggie's clothes away, having received a small comfort over the passing months from being surrounded by her belongings.

"I'll look,'' Anne said, happy to realize how much Adam had truly loved her friend all this time. "After you drop off the bag, go to your club for supper and drinks. I'll have James join you there. If there's any news, I'll send a message.''

"Are you sure I should leave?''

"Trust me. You do not want to be here. This is a small house, and birthing can be . . . well . . . unpleasant. Now, go!''

"Watch over her for me,'' he insisted.

"I will.'' She pushed him through the door, meaning to close it, but he looked so forlorn that she couldn't resist pausing to give him a tight hug, which he returned in full measure. "She'll be fine.''

"She has to be.''

"Go!''

Adam's carriage pulled to a stop in front of his town house. He'd run his errands for Anne, then stopped by the house on Mulberry to drop off Maggie's bag, with every intention of remaining, but had quickly changed his mind. There were women bustling up the stairs, moans and groans drifting down, and he couldn't bear the activity or the sounds. Anne had come down to assure him that everything was progressing nicely, although they were still at the beginning stages. If that was the beginning, Adam dreaded to imagine what it would be like later on.

Unusually squeamish, he'd left in a hurry, easily convincing himself that there were other pressing matters he might as well address during the hours when he desperately needed to fill his idle time.

One of the Westmoreland carriages was in the drive in front of his town house, and he was glad of it. He'd be able to finish his business with them without having to track them down. His mother had to be about as well, so he could deal with her, too, but he couldn't face any of them right away.

Once inside, he headed directly to the Blue Room, where he locked the door, then downed two stiff shots of whiskey. After his breathing steadied, he said a few prayers. For Charles and the repose of his soul. For a safe delivery for Maggie and the babe. He gave thanks for the return of Anne and James to his life. Then, fortified, he headed downstairs, ready to do battle.

As he reached the foyer, his mother stepped out of one of the salons down the hall, pulling the doors shut behind her with a determined click. She looked up, saw him, then started toward him in a grand huff. "Where have you been?" she sputtered in outrage. "The Westmorelands have been waiting an eternity."

"They'll get over it. Or not. I don't care."

"What has come over you that you would behave so atrociously?"

"I've merely spent the day fixing my life."

"Whatever do you mean? There's nothing wrong with your life."

"Not anymore," he said. "I was lucky enough to pass part of the afternoon with James."

"I heard he was home again," she said bitterly, "along with his whore of a wife."

"Her name is Anne," he said as calmly as he could, wondering how he'd ever put up with her cruel, caustic ways for so long. "She's married to James, which makes her your daughter-in-law."

"Never! I will never acknowledge her as such."

"Your loss, I'd say."

"Have you gone completely mad?" she hissed.

"Perhaps," he admitted, grinning like a fool. "But if this is madness, I welcome it. I haven't felt this content in a very, very long time. You must prepare yourself, because they will be coming to stay with me."

"You can't mean it!" Lucretia said, two bright red spots of fury coloring her cheeks, a fist clutched across her large bosom. "How could you welcome them here! How could you do such a thing to me! To the family name!" His composure seemed only to outrage her further. "Harold and Penelope might see them."

"Harold and Penny will be gone long before they arrive. Which reminds me. I need to speak with the Westmorelands immediately. Would you care to join me?"

"What is so urgent?" she asked, suddenly looking worried.

"I'm calling off the wedding, Mother."

"No!" she said, greatly distressed. "I won't let you ruin your life like this."

"It's not up to you."

"I can't believe this. I can't believe it!"

"While we're on the subject of changes, I've decided that this is a good time for you to retire to the country. You need to begin making plans to return to Sussex."

"Me?!" She struggled to speak through her indignity. "I'll go nowhere."

"You're leaving, Mother. The sooner the better."

"I won't go, I tell you."

"You will, if I have to bodily carry you from the house." A maid passed by, and he didn't even stop speaking. His words and actions would be shooting about the halls before long anyway. No use hiding anything. "I don't want James's wife upset by you."

"Upset by me? This is my home. That whore will not set foot inside it." She glanced toward the door as though she needed to rush over and personally block the entrance.

"Anne will be welcomed here!" he said tersely. "This is not *your* home. It is mine, and Anne and James will stay with me whenever they are in London."

Tired of the argument, he stepped past her. "Now, I need to speak with Harold, so I suggest you start packing while I do. You've been whining all month about having to remain in London for the wedding with this heat. Now's your chance to escape. The dower house should accommodate you nicely, and it's long past time you moved in there anyway. I will expect you to leave tomorrow morning, and I would appreciate it if you stayed in your rooms until your departure."

Without waiting to hear if she had further comment, he walked to the parlor and stepped inside. Harold was pacing back and forth. Penny was on the settee, sipping punch, fanning herself, and as usual, looking thoroughly put out. When he entered, she jumped to her feet.

"Where have you been?"

"Don't start with me today, Penny. I'm not in the mood for it."

Ignoring his request, she counted out his sins against the tips of her fingers. "You ran out on me Saturday night, you missed each and every party that was hosted for us yesterday, and you completely absented yourself from last night's ball."

Adam didn't respond, looking instead at her father. "Hello, Harold. I'm glad you're here. I need to speak with you."

"Your mother just left us. She was in quite a state of agitation. What's happened?"

"Something occurred today at Charles's funeral. I need to discuss it with you, but first I have something to say to your daughter." He turned to Penelope. "I'm very glad you mentioned all of the parties I missed in the past two days. As you might recall, my first cousin and best friend was murdered Saturday night. The fact that you cannot bring yourself to understand my feelings in this situation shows me exactly how much we do not suit."

His statement stopped her in her tracks, frightening her into calming herself. "I'm not saying that we don't suit," she said.

"I am." He paused, letting the weight of his words sink in; then he said more gently, "You know it's true, Penny. You loathe me. Just last week, you were begging your father to get you out of this. Here's your chance."

"Why, you worthless cad! After all I've been through! You don't know how I've suffered being engaged to you. And now, to think that you want to cast me aside, to embarrass me in front of all Society. I won't have it! We're getting married in eleven days. I suggest you prepare yourself."

"No, I suggest you prepare *yourself*. We're not marrying."

"I know something has you distressed, Adam," Harold intervened, "but let's not act hastily."

"I'm not acting in haste. I never should have gotten us into this mess in the first place, and I take full responsibility for the failure." He turned to Penny again. "You may play it anyway you want. Tell everyone I broke it off, that I'm the cad you believe me to be. Say anything about me you wish to justify our parting. I care not what it is."

She studied him for a long, painful moment, then turned to the Duke, wailing, "Father, he can't do this to me, can he? My life will be over. I'll be the laughingstock of the entire world." She crossed the room and gripped Harold's arm. "Say you'll make him go through with it. Swear it."

Harold forcibly pulled her hand away and stood between the two of them, glaring back and forth. From the stern, uncompromising look in Adam's eye, Harold knew the man was not going to marry Penelope. Not next week. Not ever.

He turned to look at his daughter. "I think it's safe to say that the wedding's off."

"What? You can't mean it! You'll not let him get away with this. Tell me you won't!"

"What would you have me do, Penny? Call him out?"

"Yes, yes," she agreed heartily. "Kill this scoundrel. Shoot him through his black heart. He deserves nothing less."

Harold sighed. He was a realist. There was nothing to be done. If Adam refused to go through with it, he couldn't be forced. Oh, certainly, they could threaten and posture and eventually sue for breach of promise and other nonsense, which would only drag out the mess, leaving nothing but bones for the scavengers to pick over once the scandal cleared. Penny's reputation would never recover from such a public bloodletting. Best to cut their losses and start charting the public reasons and the private excuses that would be circulated to explain the couple's estrangement.

An idea was already forming that would create little speculation. After Charles's untimely demise, no one would be surprised if the wedding was called off. In fact, people would expect it to be postponed. A period of mourning by Adam would be required, during which affection would wane and wither.

Yes, he thought, *that would work*. He could see it all now. No muss, no dirty gossip.

"Go wait in the carriage, Penny."

"I will not. It's too hot outside."

"Go!" he shouted, his patience with the girl completely gone. "I need to speak with Adam." When it looked as if she would continue to refuse, he took her arm and escorted her out.

"I hate you," she spat over her shoulder at Adam as Harold gave her a hearty shove and closed the door on her backside.

Once her footsteps retreated down the hall, Harold said, "Well . . . let me have it."

Adam shrugged. "I've decided to marry someone else."

"What?" All Harold's quickly formulated plans vanished in an instant. A severe pain began pounding at the center of his chest, and he truly wondered if he might be about to suffer a heart seizure.

"I haven't asked her yet," Adam explained, "but I expect she'll say yes, eventually. I don't intend to give up easily."

"You're joking, right? Tell me you're joking." He studied Adam, and saw he was serious. "Who?"

"You know who." Adam stood silently, letting the weight of the monumental announcement sink in.

"Maggie?" Harold gasped. "You're going to marry Maggie?"

"If she'll have me. She's at her old house on Mulberry at this very moment."

"What's she doing there?"

"She's birthing my first child. Perhaps your first grandson."

"I won't claim him."

"I'm not asking you to. I have no intention of disputing Charles's paternity of the child. I would never hurt my Aunt Vinnie, or tarnish Charles's reputation, in such a way. The child will remain his, but I shall raise it as my own. I only share the truth with you, because I feel that you should know it."

"What if it's a boy? What about the succession? Have you thought of that?"

"I'm not going to worry about it."

"This is a bloody disaster."

"Well, you can't hide from it. Besides, everyone knows anyway. Not about the paternity of Maggie's child, but about the fact that you are Maggie's father. Over the past few months, I've learned that there are numerous people who know about you and her mother, Rose Brown. You have no secrets worth keeping."

"People can talk all they want. They'll get no confirmation from me."

"If you think that revealing yourself to be Maggie's father would be an embarrassment, then I'm sorry for you. For if that's how you truly feel, I can guarantee that you'll never see your grandchild." Adam took a step toward the door. He wanted to get back to Maggie's house, to see if James had returned, to see how Maggie was faring. "It matters not to me what you decide to do. I only warn you so you have some time to figure out how you'll explain all this to your wife and to Penny. Word is bound to get back to them. I'm surprised they haven't heard the truth already."

"I've got to get out of here," Harold mumbled. "I think I'm going to be ill."

Adam held open the parlor door as Harold stepped into the hall. "And please, Harold, have pity on Penelope. Make her next match with someone who shares her view of things. Find someone who will care for her."

"A debacle—that's what it is. A bloody debacle . . ." Harold tottered off, muttering like an old man.

Chapter Twenty-Nine

Adam woke to the sound of footsteps whispering down the stairs. While he slowly opened his eyes, it took him a moment to get his bearings and remember that he was in the front parlor of Maggie's house. A hint of early-morning light was just beginning to filter in through the windows. He was crunched onto the small sofa, his large form hanging over the edges in several uncomfortable ways, and someone had thoughtfully covered him with a blanket. His head had fallen sideways, and there was a crick in his neck. Groaning, he rubbed the painful spot as he straightened himself.

The footsteps were coming his way. Blessedly, he realized that all was quiet upstairs. Was it finally finished?

After all the fighting and haranguing at his town house the previous afternoon, he'd enjoyed a long, private dinner with James in his hotel room. Just thinking of how wonderful it had been to sit and talk with his brother again brought a smile to his face. James, with his usual wit and good humor, had waved away any lingering guilt he'd had over his treatment of their mother and of Penny Westmoreland.

As James had caustically pointed out, Lucretia had always been unhappy and always would be—no matter how Adam lived his life, no matter whom he married. As for Penny, she'd hardly be lacking for suitors. Hopefully, after enough time had passed, she'd realize how lucky she was to have escaped marriage into the St. Clair family. And if Harold had any sense, he'd find her someone more suitable in age and temperament.

Adam had keenly felt every day of James's eight-month absence from his life, and he was determined to make amends in every possible way for whatever hurts his behavior had caused. He'd already informed his staff to ready James's old rooms so he and Anne could stay there before they left for Cornwall—although James had decided to wait a day before occupying them, giving Lucretia a chance to vacate the premises.

Knowing how much James had come to cherish Grace Stuart, Adam had vowed to be civil to the woman, and had even offered to meet her children—his half brothers and half sister. James had insisted that Adam would never regret befriending them. While Adam had his doubts, he kept them to himself, intending to have an open mind about the coming encounters. He was determined to be a better man.

Adam had left James at the hotel and returned to Maggie's house. Even though the women kept trying to shoo him away, insisting he shouldn't be present, the idea of going home to his loveless, empty town house was abhorrent. He couldn't stay away from Maggie any longer, and he wanted to be close by in case she needed him.

Someone opened the parlor door, and he experienced a moment of panic as he realized that he'd heard no baby's cries during the night. Had it gone well? Were Maggie and the babe all right?

Just then, Anne tiptoed into the room, peeking to see if he was awake. His eyes were wide with alarm, and he jumped to his feet. "Is it over?"

"Yes," Anne said, smiling. She looked rumpled and tired, but ecstatic in spite of it.

"Maggie? The baby? I didn't hear anything . . ."

"They're both fine," she said. "They're resting."

His knees suddenly weak, he collapsed back against the settee. "I'm so glad . . ."

"She'd like to see you," Anne said, laughing softly, "if you think you're up to it."

He shook his head as though coming out of a long, deep hibernation. The past few days had been so emotionally trying that he wasn't sure he had the energy left for any further fervent upheavals. "I'm so drained of strength that I feel as though I've given birth myself."

"Look at it as a rehearsal," she said. "I imagine the two of you will go through this many more times in the future, and the next time you'll be much better prepared."

There was a question in her statement, and Adam looked into her emerald eyes, thinking what a beautiful woman she was, how lucky James was to have chosen so well for himself. Wanting to calm any of Anne's fears about his intentions, he vowed, "Yes, I imagine Maggie and I will be going through this many more times."

A look of relief passed across her lovely face, and she asked, "You'll be staying, then?"

"I'll be marrying her—if she'll have me."

"Oh, I imagine she'll have you. If you play your cards right."

"I hope so. I want to finally do the right thing."

"Good," she said, then added more softly, "You know, she never stopped loving you. All this time . . . she never did."

"Thank you for telling me," he said. "I'll keep that in mind while I'm wearing her down."

A moment of awkward silence occurred; then Anne broke it. "Where is my wayward husband?"

"Back at your hotel, but I've asked him to move the two of

you over to our house in Mayfair. Later today, if that's all right with you.''

"Are you certain?''

"More certain than I've ever been of anything.'' He stood and held out a hand. "Anne . . . I . . .'' The words were hard to say, but he refused to swallow them back down. This was a new day in his life, one of changes and new beginnings. "I'm sorry for everything. The things I said and did . . .''

"Pah,'' Anne said, waving away his discomfort and his apology. "Don't worry about it now. It's all behind us.''

He reached across the space separating them and took her hand in his own. "I'm so glad James found you.''

"And I'm so glad I found him.'' Tears welled into her eyes, the emotional day and night taking their toll. "Now, you take yourself upstairs. Your family is waiting for you.''

"I like the sound of that,'' he said, dropping her hand and letting the ardent moment roll away. "What are your plans for the morning?''

"I'm going to catch a few hours' sleep at the hotel, and then, I told Maggie I'd be back to sit with her. Could you keep her company in the meantime?''

"It would be my pleasure.'' He took her arm and escorted her to the door, where a maid had her cloak waiting. As he helped her into the cab next to the stoop, he was delighted when she leaned down at the last second and gave him a kiss on the cheek.

"There's hope for you yet, St. Clair,'' she said, her saucy attitude once again to the fore.

"Yes, there is, isn't there?'' He smiled, feeling light, happy, and carefree. The carriage started to rumble away, and he remembered to ask, "By the way . . . is it a girl or a boy?''

"Maggie's waiting to tell you . . . '' she called, and he watched and waved until she disappeared round the corner.

* * *

Maggie shifted restlessly against the pillows. She was exhausted, tired, and sore, but energized at the same time. Sleep was impossible. There were so many things to think about and decide, so many major changes to deal with all at once. First and foremost was knowing where she would live in the coming months. Rest would not be found until the issue was resolved.

She couldn't go back to the house she'd shared with Charles. Passing the spot where he'd died, whenever she entered or exited the house, was out of the question. Living with Lavinia wasn't an option, either. While she liked the older woman very much, the thought of accepting her charity, when Maggie had been nothing but an impostor in Charles's life, was unthinkable. And wrong.

What to do?

She hoped that Adam would let her stay here, in her old house—at least until she could have Charles's estate settled. Then, when she and the baby moved on, she'd have funds to secure another location.

During the unending hours of the night, when she'd labored so fiercely, Anne had told her numerous times that Adam was downstairs. Knowing that he was close by had given her comfort during her struggles. Surely, he must still care for her—perhaps a tiny bit since he'd gone to all the trouble of bringing her home and then waiting with her to the end.

Despite what she'd done to him, she hoped he could still summon a fond memory of the connection they'd once shared. Perhaps the remembering would encourage him to grant her small request for assistance.

Anne had promised to send Adam up directly, but it seemed as if she'd been gone for ages. The waiting had frayed Maggie's already fragile nerves. "What's taking him so long?" she asked Gail, who was peeking out the window down to the street.

"He's saying good-bye to Mistress Anne."

"They're not arguing, are they?"

"No. In fact, she just kissed him on the cheek."

"Thank heavens," Maggie said. The last thing she needed

was for him to have words with Anne and be in a temper. He and Anne needed to find some civil ground on which to stand while they dealt with each other. They all needed it so badly.

"Ah . . ." said Gail. "She's gone. He's coming."

Straightaway, they heard his footsteps on the stairs. Maggie's heart was pounding. He couldn't refuse! He absolutely couldn't!

With a quick glance around the room, she decided everything was ready. All traces of the birthing were gone. She'd bathed and dressed in a clean cotton nightgown. Gazing down, she smiled in wonder at the sleeping baby in her arms and whispered, "How could he not love you?"

"Are you ready?" Gail murmured as Adam reached the top stair.

"Yes," Maggie answered, nodding, and Gail moved to the door, opening it just as he knocked softly.

"May I come in?" he asked.

Gail gave him a quick curtsy. "Mistress Maggie is expecting you." Tactfully, she stepped behind him and closed the door on their private moment.

Over the past months, Maggie had rehearsed this scene a thousand times. What she'd say. How she'd say it. The explanations she'd give. The apologies she'd make. The forgiveness for which she'd ask. But as she sat staring at him, from the center of the bed where they had shared so many wonderful intimacies, all her prepared words vanished from her head. All she could do was look at him and smile in wonder at how the very sight of him healed something in her broken heart.

"Hello," she finally managed to say.

"Hello, yourself," he said in return. He stood there, speechless, trying to recall the statement he'd carefully drafted, the apologies he'd intended to make, the vows of love and protection he wanted to give, but he couldn't think of a single one. All he could do was stare in wonder at the sight of Maggie holding his child in her arms.

Her beautiful hair had been washed and brushed, and it curled in beautiful display around her shoulders and down her back. Her cheeks glowed a healthy pink, and her face was still rounded and full with the extra birth weight she'd carried, her breasts large and abundant. Her magnificent violet eyes glowed up at him with love and affection, and the last brick in his wall of reserve vanished as though it had never existed.

She looked, he thought, like an angelic, heavenly Madonna, so superb it hurt his heart to gaze upon her. He gestured toward the edge of the bed. "May I?"

"Yes," she said, smiling and patting the spot next to her with her free hand.

He approached cautiously and eased himself down, peeking at the tiny face hidden in the soft blanket. "Is it a boy or a girl?"

"A girl," Maggie said proudly.

"How wonderful." He reached out a finger and lightly touched the rim of cloth circling the babe's face, too scared to do more. "Have you decided what you'll call her?"

"Charles and I had thought to name her after our mothers. Rose Lavinia."

"Lovely," he murmured, "a perfectly lovely name." He leaned closer for a better look. "Hello, beautiful Rose."

"Would you like to hold her?" Maggie asked, chuckling at the look of terror that crossed his face. "You can't hurt her."

"Are you sure?"

"Yes. She's much tougher than she looks."

"Just like her mother," Adam said. He had never held a baby before. Had certainly never thought he'd have the chance to hold this special child.

His hands trembled as he reached out, and Maggie placed the soft bundle in his care. Rose immediately snuggled against his chest as though she knew she belonged just there and nowhere else, and he was unprepared for the wave of startling emotion that blasted through him.

Their child. His child. His first and only. Tears flooded into his eyes, and he forced them down.

"May I look at her?" he asked, indicating the tightly swaddled blanket, and Maggie opened the folds so that he could see how pretty she was in her pristine white gown. "She's so tiny," he said, inspecting her feet and hands, her little legs, "and so perfect."

"Yes, she is, isn't she?" Maggie agreed. She'd been thinking the same thing for the past two hours whenever she stole a peek of her own.

Adam ran his hand across the silky blond down covering little Rose's head, and the touch caused the babe to open her sleepy eyes. "Oh, you little vixen," he whispered in awe, pulling her closer and hugging her tenderly against his chest. "Look how beautiful you are!" He could already picture the suitors who would be lined up, waiting to call.

He looked up at Maggie, his gaze full of wonder and joy, only to find her weeping copiously, huge, silent tears streaming down her face. "What is it, little one?"

"I thought you'd never see her," she said, hardly able to speak over the well of emotion she'd experienced at the sight of Adam holding their child. "I'm just so happy it's come to pass . . ."

"So am I." He pulled her close as her tears fell with abandon.

As he sat on the edge of the bed, cradling her and their daughter, he had a good length of time to ponder how strange life was. That he could have met this darling girl, loved her so fiercely, but lost her because of his stern, set ways. That the two of them had made this precious child. That it had taken the death of kindhearted Charles to bring them back together, to make him see how silly he'd been in the way he'd lived his life.

"Oh, Adam," she eventually said, once she regained enough control to speak. "I'm sorry to carry on so . . ."

"Don't apologize," he said, kissing her on the forehead.

"These have been trying times, and Rose's birth is a miraculous occasion. You are certainly entitled to a show of emotion."

"Do you truly care for her?" Maggie asked, hope blooming in her heart.

"How could I not?" he answered, glancing down at the exquisite child sleeping so peacefully in his arms.

"Then, may I ask a favor of you? Not for myself, but for Rose?"

"You may ask anything you like, my darling Maggie, and it is yours."

"May we stay here? Not for long," she hurried to add, worried that he wouldn't like the idea. "Just until I've discovered the state of Charles's finances and can decide where we might go next. I promise we won't be a bother to you. You'll hardly know we're here."

"Of course you can stay here. For as long as you like."

"Thank you. You've greatly eased my mind," she said, lowering her eyes as she admitted, "I've been so worried the past few days about what would happen to us. I hate being afraid about the future."

"I know you do, and I swear to you that you will never have to worry again. I plan to take good care of both of you from now on."

"Oh . . . I didn't mean for you to think . . . that is . . ." She flushed with embarrassment. "I would never expect you to take care of us. It would be a great help, though, if you could help me learn about Charles's affairs. I really have no idea what's left for us to live on, and I don't know how to go about finding out."

Adam suspected that there was probably very little remaining. Charles had been a master at juggling funds, and what he owed and what was left to pay the final bills was anyone's guess. Obviously, Maggie had no idea of Charles's shortcomings, and he wasn't about to disillusion her, especially when the answer hardly mattered.

He smiled, knowing how stubborn she could be. He'd never

considered himself an eloquent man, and he wanted to say the right things in order to convince her of their future. Taking her hand in his own, he asked, "May I tell you something?"

"Certainly," she said hesitantly, a tad frightened by the serious look in his eye. If it was bad news about Charles's estate, she didn't think she could stand to hear it.

"When I first met you, I was a different man. Stuffy, and proud, set in my ways and so sure of myself."

She smiled at the memories of how overbearing he could be. "I remember."

"One day, when we were arguing—I don't even remember what it was about, now—you told me that I could change if I wanted to, but I didn't believe you."

"I remember that, too." She smiled again, wondering where this was leading.

"Well, I've discovered that you were right. I can change, and I have." He shifted closer. "I want to be happy. It's all I want, and it's all that matters to me. And I have finally discovered what it will take to make me contented all my days."

"What is that?" she asked.

She obviously hadn't any idea what he meant, and he chuckled at her look of consternation. "It's you, Maggie."

"Me?" she gasped, completely taken by surprise.

"Yes. You and Baby Rose. If the two of you would share your lives with me, you would make me the happiest man in the kingdom."

"What are you saying?" she asked, shaking, afraid to be optimistic.

"I'm saying that I love you. I've always loved you, from that very first time I set eyes on you while you were dancing on the beach sand and cut your foot. All these months, I never stopped. Not for a moment." His eyes searched hers, looking for some hint of returned emotion. "I love you, Maggie. Will me marry me?"

"Oh, Adam . . ." she said, hardly able to breathe. This was the answer to all her prayers, but she couldn't agree. Adam had said it himself: These had been a string of emotionally trying days; he wasn't thinking clearly or he would never have proposed such a thing. "I couldn't," she said, sick at the thought of having to refuse him. "I simply couldn't."

"Why?"

"For one thing, it's too soon . . . With Charles only passed on a few days . . ."

"I agree. We will both be in mourning, so we would have to meet secretly. I could spend time here with you and Rose— and no one would know. I'd be very discreet. In six months or so, when the mourning begins to ease, we could be seen together occasionally. After the full year has passed, we could wed in a quiet ceremony." Sensing another protest on its way, he added, "A year is a long time to wait, but in the end the prize will definitely be worth it. I will have you and Rose by my side."

"But what about your mother?"

"I don't care what she thinks. I've already sent her to the country. She'll no longer be living with me."

"And Penelope?"

"I've spoken with her and your father. I broke off the engagement yesterday."

"So, it's over," she said quietly, relieved to know that this great heartbreak was never going to occur.

"I never should have gotten myself into it in the first place. It wasn't fair to Penny. When I found out about you and Charles, I was just so . . ." He paused, ran a hand over his tired eyes. There was no point in rehashing all the old hurts they'd caused each other. "Penny and I were a horrible match, straight from the beginning, and I broke it off as much for her as for myself. I told your father to find someone who will care for her."

"Do you think he will?"

"I don't know what he'll do. In the meantime, I am free to

spend the rest of my life living it as I choose. And I choose to live it with you. What is your answer?''

"I don't know, Adam,'' she said, feeling terribly disconcerted. This was all so sudden. She'd been hoping for some aid, perhaps a place to stay, perhaps a bit of financial assistance. Nothing this monumental had crossed her mind. "If we married, what would people say?''

"What do you care about what people would say?'' He grabbed her by the shoulders, giving her a soft shake. "Buck up, girl. You are the daughter of the Duke of Roswell and the great beauty Rose Brown. Show some backbone!''

"You're making this so hard!''

"How? How am I making this hard?''

"You're asking for such enormous decisions without my having the opportunity to think them through. I'm so tired . . . so confused . . .''

"I know, I know . . .'' he said, backing down. He was swept away with a desperate need for her to say yes, and his fervor was overwhelming them both. "I'm sorry to pressure you so fiercely. For now, I only need you to answer one question.''

"What?''

"You told me once that you loved me. Do you still?''

How could he even imagine she didn't? "Yes,'' she said, "with each and every breath I take, I love you, and I will love you until my dying day.''

He smiled and patted her hand. "That's all the answer I need for now. Don't worry about any of the rest. We have plenty of time to make our plans.'' He kissed her on her forehead again, and leaning down, he kissed Rose as well. "Now, I think it's time for the two of you to rest. Anne will have my hide if she returns to find you fatigued.''

Just the mention of *rest* had her yawning. She wanted to talk further, but she was suddenly too tired to continue. The knowledge that he loved her, that he always had, had lifted a great weight from her shoulders. All the guilt, worry, and fear that had engulfed her the past few days floated away as though on a receding tide. For the first time in a long time, she felt contented, and as Adam tucked her in with Rose snuggled by her side, she couldn't help smiling as her eyes gradually closed.

Barely awake, she asked, "Will you sit with us for a while?"

Quietly, he answered, "I wouldn't want to be anywhere else."

Epilogue

MY ONLY LOVER

Adam sat behind his desk. Outside, it was a beautiful July day, and the roses in the flower gardens behind his study in the Belmont estate house filled the room with their delicious scent. There was much work to be done, but he couldn't seem to complete any of it. He'd managed to get through only two of the letters—one from James and one from Harold Westmoreland—but he couldn't concentrate long enough to look at any of the others.

It was a day for remembering, not working. Two years earlier, Charles had been shot and killed while protecting Maggie from an assassin's bullet. The following summer, he and Maggie had been wed in a small ceremony attended by a handful of people. James and Anne, his Aunt Vinnie, Grace Stuart, and her children.

As always, he marveled at how quickly things could change for the better. He and Maggie were blissfully happy. Rose was growing like a weed, and would have a new baby brother or sister any day. His relationship with James was stronger than ever, and his friendship with Anne was powerful and unbreakable. Grace Stuart had finally won him over with her elegance and quiet refinement, and he had been unable to prevent the growing attachment he felt toward her children, who were bright, boisterous, and loving—and so much like James in every way.

Although he'd not made any peace with Penelope, and hadn't ever expected to, he and Harold had managed to find common ground, coming to terms with what had happened. Harold even visited on occasion as he grudgingly worked at establishing a relationship with Maggie. It was funny to watch the two of them as they circled warily, trying to find ways to deal with each other.

Adam wanted to think that he had had something to do with bringing them together, but he knew he hadn't. It had all been because of Baby Rose. Harold had met the child once and instantly fallen in love with the little charmer. No one was immune, not even the exalted Duke of Roswell.

Just then, tiny footsteps came thumping down the hall, and Rosie entered, a two-year-old bundle of energy. Every time he looked at her, he felt such a rush of love that his eyes watered with tears, and his heart ached from knowing she was so precious and that she was his.

"Papa, Papa," the girl squealed with delight as she set eyes on him. She ran to him with her arms raised, and he couldn't help thinking that she had to be the prettiest girl in all of England. With her white-blond hair, bouncing in ringlets around her cherubic face, her rosy cheeks, her violet eyes, she looked like a lovely painted china doll.

"Hello, sweetcakes," he said, scooping her up to hold against his chest. "How is my beautiful Rosie this morning?"

"Pony . . . " she said, looking over his shoulder and pointing outside.

"We're on our way to the stables," the governess explained, and Adam nodded. The small girl was in love with the horses, and as she had all the grooms wrapped around her finger, she went out every morning and the men took turns sitting her on the backs of the gentlest mares.

"Where is your mama, little miss? Is that sleepyhead still in bed?" Adam asked, which resulted in Rose patting his cheeks with both her tiny hands.

"Bed . . . bed . . ." chattered the girl. Then she continued on in the gibberish that only Maggie seemed to understand, until she'd finished with whatever story she'd been telling and wiggled to the floor, impatient to run outside. As quickly as she'd come, she disappeared through the doors and ran out into the backyard, trouncing along so fast that the poor governess could barely keep up. Adam followed Rose out and leaned against the balustrade, watching her go and smiling so hard his face hurt.

Once she was out of sight, he retrieved the two letters off the desk and went upstairs to see if Maggie was awake yet. She was at the end of her pregnancy and hugely swollen because of it. While she felt like a beached whale and thought she looked like one, he found her magnificent, and the joy he'd taken from watching her as she'd increased over the months never dwindled. To him, she grew more beautiful with each passing day.

Knowing how tired she was, he peeked into their room, ready to tiptoe inside, but she was sitting up, relaxed against the pillows and having her morning chocolate. She was naked under the single sheet, and it draped across her enlarged breasts and bulky stomach.

"Good morning, lazybones," he said when he saw her welcoming smile.

"You'd feign laziness, too, if you couldn't even roll over on your side without assistance." Looking thoroughly put out with her predicament, she said, "I'd like to get up, but I can't maneuver myself to the edge of the bed, so I've decided to remain here all day."

He chuckled and came to sit next to her, kissing her tenderly.

"I could probably think of a few ways to help you pass the time."

With a definite twinkle in her eye, she asked, "Where is Rose?"

"Gone to visit the horses."

"Ooh, we have at least an hour to ourselves. We'd best make the most of it, don't you think?" She made an attempt to shift over to make room for him on the bed, but even as she tried, he could see her rubbing the small of her back.

He leaned closer and started massaging where her hand had been. "Right there?" he asked.

"Yes."

"Are you having some pains?"

"Just a few small ones."

"Do you think today could be the day?"

"Perhaps," she said, relaxing gradually as he rubbed deeper.

"Then, no bedplay for you, you insatiable devil," he said, managing a swat on her bottom before she rolled once more to her back. He kissed her again, cherishing the closeness, the feel and smell of her. "Are you scared?"

"Not if I know you'll be close by."

"I'll never leave your side. You know that."

"Yes, I do," she agreed, thinking he looked more handsome than he had the day she'd first met him. Love and the care of his family had softened his features until the lines on his face were now caused by smiles instead of worry. She'd given him that—that sense of peace and belonging he'd always lacked in his life.

And he had given her many things in return. Trust, children, friendship, security, and she never tired of seeing the love he felt for her shining through his magnificent dark eyes. There was something wonderful about having all that bald emotion focused on herself.

"What do you have there?" she asked, for the first time noticing the letters he'd tossed on the bed when he first entered.

"News," he said enigmatically.

"If any of it's bad, don't tell me."

He laughed at that. "It's all good. Well, I think it is, anyway. Anne can't come right away . . . "

"Well, that doesn't sound like good news . . ."

"Because," he said, ignoring her interruption and drawing out the moment, "she and James are going to have a baby."

Maggie gasped with joy and surprise. "Say it again! Tell me it's true!"

"It is, and she's having a terrible time just now with her stomach. James doesn't want her to travel for a few weeks until the worst of it has passed."

"How wonderful!" she said, swiping away a few happy tears that had managed to work their way down her cheeks. "I'm so delighted for both of them."

"So am I."

"And the other?"

"Is from your father."

"Now, I know you're not telling me the truth. Anything he has to say couldn't possibly be good news."

"Well, let's call it *interesting* news, then." He paused, waiting to raise her curiosity, and it piqued immediately, for as much as she insisted she didn't care about Harold, she couldn't seem to help herself where he was concerned.

"What?" she asked impatiently.

"Penelope's eloped. With an American."

"Oh, my . . . Good for her!" Maggie said, starting to laugh, her big belly shaking with the effort. The poor girl had been on her third engagement. Her first fiancé, Adam, had cried off. Her second had died in an accident before he could return from Jamaica to meet her. The third . . . well . . . "That Earl Father picked for her was sixty years old if he was a day."

"Sixty-three," Adam concurred.

"Father must be beside himself."

"That would be putting it mildly. He's coming here for an extended visit. He says he wants to spend some time around his *sane* daughter."

"Well, it's nice to know I've grown in his esteem," she said sarcastically, "even if I could only accomplish it by his deciding Penny is mad." Another pain moved across her back, and she rubbed at it distractedly, thinking instead of all the changes, all the glad tidings. "Could you fetch my robe for me?" she asked. "I think I'll ring for a bath. If this is going to keep up, I should get it out of the way in case I'm feeling worse later."

"Certainly," Adam said, walking to the chair across the room and retrieving the robe off the back. "I'll ring for Gail."

As he turned back around, a morning breeze eased its way through the drapes, bathing the room in an odd yellow light. On the bed, Maggie was haloed in it. She had pulled the sheet back, revealing the swells and curves of her pregnant form. Her hair was curled around her shoulders, and her hand rested on her mounded abdomen. The amethyst ring he'd given her when they became engaged—the ring he'd carried in his pocket for months—sparkled its purple hues around the room. It was the only thing she was wearing.

Maggie looked up to where Adam stood quiet and still, and couldn't help being a bit frightened by the extraordinary look on his face. "What is it?"

"It's the strangest thing, but I used to dream about this very moment," he said, coming closer, resting against the mattress once again. "When we were apart . . . I used to dream about you. I would close my eyes and see you like this, here in my bedchamber at Belmont, looking so swollen and full, with the morning sun coloring your skin, wearing only this ring." He pulled her hand to his lips and kissed it.

Gazing down at her stomach, he continued. "I'd lean down, and kiss you here"—he patted her stomach and touched his lips to her warm skin—"and the babe would give a kick against my mouth."

They both laughed as the child, waiting impatiently inside to burst out, did exactly that.

His hand still rested on her stomach, and she covered it with her own, asking, "How did your dream end?"

"Just like this," he said, glancing around the room and noticing that the peculiar yellow light had vanished and everything seemed real again, "with the two of us here together. But I was always sad when it was finished."

"Why?" she prodded gently.

"Because somehow I knew that if I could just get to this moment in my life, that I would be happy all my days, but I didn't know how to make it happen."

"Yet, it has come to pass in every way," she said, smiling at the fire in his eyes. "It's not a dream."

"But it is," he insisted. "It's a dream come true."